Life and Other Inconveniences

"Deeply touching, real and raw, but infused with the love and hope that make life possible, despite everything."
—Abbi Waxman, author of *The Bookish Life of Nina Hill*

"Master storyteller Kristan Higgins deftly balances humor and heart in this latest tale of a young woman navigating her relationship with a dying grandmother who long ago abandoned her when she needed her most . . . another must-read from Higgins, who has long been an auto-buy for me."
—Colleen Oakley, author of *Before I Go* and *Close Enough to Touch*

"Higgins is a mastermind of family dynamics in this poignant novel about two different generations of women struggling to find common ground. I couldn't put it down!"
—Emily Liebert, author of *Some Women*

"Readers will be riveted as the well-drawn characters uncover one another's hidden depths and heal old wounds. This rich and memorable story will instantly win readers over."
—*Publishers Weekly* (starred review)

"Higgins explores another set of deeply affecting topics using engaging characters and a full spectrum of realistic emotions: humor, anger, anguish, and pride, among others, but above all, hope. Funny, heart-wrenching, insightful, and lovely."
—*Kirkus Reviews* (starred review)

"Kristan Higgins's new book *Life and Other Inconveniences* already has us hooked."
—PopSugar

"Wholly original and heartfelt, written with grace and sensitivity, *Good Luck with That* is an irresistible tale of love, friendship, and self-acceptance—and the way body image can sabotage all three."

—Lori Nelson Spielman, *New York Times* bestselling author of *The Life List*

PRAISE FOR
THE NOVELS OF KRISTAN HIGGINS

"[Higgins] only gets better with each book."

—*The New York Times Book Review*

"A special writer at the top of her game."   —NPR

"Oh, what a satisfying and delicious read! I admired the writing, the wit, the keen eye at work here. Thank you, Kristan Higgins."   —Elinor Lipman on *If You Only Knew*

"Hilarious. . . . Kristan Higgins is spot-on with her dialogue and characters. A fantastic story."

—Fresh Fiction on *If You Only Knew*

"Well-placed flashbacks; snarky, snappy dialogue; and conflict both tender and traumatic will shove you into love with a perfectly irresistible array of imperfect characters. You'll adore every bit of this story. . . . Higgins's latest is sexy, screwy, funny, and fulfilling—a simply radiant read."

—*USA Today* on *The Best Man*

life
and
other
inconveniences

KRISTAN HIGGINS

BERKLEY
New York

BERKLEY
An imprint of Penguin Random House LLC
penguinrandomhouse.com

ISBN: 9780451489449

Berkley trade paperback edition / August 2019
Berkley mass-market edition / April 2020

Printed in the United States of America
1   3   5   7   9   10   8   6   4   2

Cover art: cherry blossom tree by Minamoto Images / Stocksy United;
couple by Bill Varie / Getty Images
Cover design by Eileen Carey
Book design by Laura K. Corless

This book is dedicated to Heidi Gulbronson,
my wonderful, warm, wicked-fun friend of so many years.
I forgive you for the Stick Girl jokes.

ACKNOWLEDGMENTS

In researching this book, the following people and organizations were incredibly helpful. I thank them for their generosity and time. Any mistakes are mine.

Jeff Pinco, MD
Annette Willis, JD
Stacia Bjarnason, PhD
National Suicide Prevention Hotline
The Mayo Clinic
The Tuberous Sclerosis Alliance
The Amniotic Fluid Embolism Foundation

Thanks to my agent and friend, Maria Carvainis, and her able team for absolutely everything.

At Berkley, it is such a joy to work with my brilliant editor, Claire Zion. Thanks to the wonderful Craig Burke and the fabulous team in publicity—Erin Galloway, Diana Franco, Roxanne Jones, Bridget O'Toole and Jin Yu. Marketing, art and sales, where would we authors be without you? Sitting by ourselves in our pajamas with only the dogs as companions, that's where. Thank you for the humbling and overwhelming support and enthusiasm.

Mel Jolly has been my virtual assistant for a few years now, and I look back and wonder how life worked without her. Thank you, Mel. You are wonderful.

Thanks to Madison Terrill, my intern, for her enthusiasm, creativity and work ethic, and for making last summer's work such a pleasure.

To author and singer Xio Axelrod for her talent, her writing and her friendship.

To the Plotmonkeys—Stacia, Huntley, Anne, Joss and Jennifer—thank you for your help, encouragement and laughs. I love you guys.

To my sister for being the best person there is.

To my husband, daughter and son, who are never surprised by the good reviews and think it's cute that I still am, thank you for your faith in me. You are, quite simply, the loves of my life.

And to you, readers. Thank you for picking up this book and giving it a few hours of your time. I am so grateful.

life

and

other

inconveniences

CHAPTER 1

Emma

Y ou don't have a brain tumor," said my best friend, who, conveniently, was also a neurologist.

"Are you sure?" I asked.

"Yes, Emma. Don't look so disappointed."

"I'm not! I just . . . you know, my vision was wonky last night. Then I spaced out driving into the city today." Granted, last night I'd accidentally turned on the superbright flashlight while it was aimed right at my face, but still . . . the retinal afterimage had taken some time to subside. As for spacing out, I drove into Chicago a few times a week, so it was normal that I didn't take note of every detail on the forty-five-minute drive. Still, I couldn't help asking, "Are you sure it's not parahypnagogia?"

"Stop looking up medical terms," Calista said. "You're healthy. You're not dying. Riley will not grow up motherless, and besides, she's sixteen, and if you did die, I would adopt her and raise her as my own. Screw her baby daddy."

"I did screw him. Hence our child. But I'll make sure you get custody. She does like you better."

Calista smiled. "Of course she does. Are we still on for drinks Thursday?"

"We are. Thanks for checking me out."

"Stop staring into flashlights."

"You put it that way, it sounds so stupid," I said.

"It *is* stupid, hon. Now go. I have actual sick patients."

I kissed her on the cheek and walked out of her office. Yes, I was a hypochondriac. But I was also a single mother, so my death did figure prominently into my daily musings. As a therapist, I knew that was a normal fear—leaving my daughter, the upheaval it would cause her. She'd have to live with her father back in Connecticut, and he had two other kids (and a wife). And what would happen to my grandfather, who'd taken me in when I was a knocked-up teenager? We still lived with him, and I didn't want him to be alone. I'd lost my own mom at a young age . . . Would Riley be as screwed up as I'd been?

Calista was right. I had to get over this. I knew I was healthy, but diagnosing myself with all sorts of horrible diseases was kind of a hobby. After all, the Internet was invented for a reason.

But I trusted Calista, who was brilliant *and* my friend. Feeling considerably cheered, I walked out onto Michigan Avenue, blinking in the spring sunshine. The Magnificent Mile glittered, washed clean by two days of bone-chilling rain earlier this week, but in typical midwestern fashion, we suddenly seemed to be in the middle of summer, even if it was only May.

No brain tumor. Hooray. Also, drinks with Calista, which still sounded cool and adult, despite our being thirty-five. Unlike me, Calista was single with no kids and had her act completely together, whereas I still felt like I was faking the adult thing.

Except where Riley was concerned. I was a good mother,

that I knew. Even if she was struggling a bit these days, I was on it. I was there. I stalked her social media accounts and read her texts (don't judge me . . . she was still a minor child, after all). Tonight was Nacho Night at our house, and even if Riley had been a little sullen these days, nachos would surely cheer her up.

The twisting skyline of the City of Big Shoulders glittered in the fresh air. I loved being in Chicago proper. Today, before my brain tumor check, I'd seen a client in the shared office suite I leased with a group of therapists. I was still new to the profession and grateful to have access to the posh space. Most of the time, I worked from home, doing online counseling for people who didn't want to be seen walking into a therapist's office. TheraTalk, the secure Skype-like software that let me see patients online, was less than ideal, but that was okay. I found I counseled the really troubled people better with a little distance.

Pain was always hard to see up close. If I teared up online, or wanted to smack a client, it was easier to hide.

But the office made me feel like a proper therapist, and my client today, Blaine, was an easy case. She had adjustment disorder, which was the general diagnosis that allowed me to get paid by her insurance. Blaine had never *adjusted* to her in-laws and liked venting about them. I'd suggest ways to answer that didn't involve curse words or the throwing of wine bottles, which was Blaine's fantasy, and she'd nod and agree and come back next month with a new story. Easy-peasy and actually kind of fun to hear the tales. Her real issue was feeling confident enough to contradict her mother-in-law, and not backing down, but we were getting there.

Maybe I'd swing by the Ghirardelli shop and get some ice cream. Then again, we had ice cream at home, if Pop hadn't eaten it all, and I couldn't justify spending six bucks on a cone.

I walked past an empty storefront, then jerked to a halt.

Turned around and looked. My hands and feet tingled before my brain caught up.

Yep. That was a harbinger of doom, all right.

To the untrained eye, it looked like a pink leather handbag, adorably retro but with a sassy blue tassel sexing it up a bit. Nevertheless, I knew what it was. A pink purse of doom.

Shit, shit, shit.

For a second, I forgot where I was, transported instantly to my childhood, when I always felt like an outcast, like a stupid, unwanted kid, like I'd done something wrong just by breathing.

GENEVIEVE LONDON DESIGNS, *Coming Soon*

ACCESSORIES, FASHION & HOME GOODS
FOR THE DISCERNING CONSUMER

My reflection in the glass showed me for what I was—not a discerning consumer, not a fashionable woman, just an ordinary-looking person with her dark blond hair pinned up in a graceless bun, wearing dark pants and a dark shirt, both polyester. This morning, I thought I looked nice. Crisp. Professional.

Right now, I looked droopy, hot and . . . scared.

This was not how Genevieve would've crafted me.

For years, I'd done a bang-up job of forgetting that Genevieve London was my grandmother and had raised me from the age of eight to eighteen. It was easy, considering we hadn't spoken for seventeen years.

Riley would see this, of course. She knew her great-grandmother was *that* Genevieve London, though they'd never met. Some of her friends had Genevieve London purses and shoes. The arrival of one of her shops in Chicago would not be good news. Riley, being sixteen, was bound to have strong feelings about this one way or another. Bad feelings, probably, given the black rain cloud she'd been living under for the past few months.

Coming soon.

At least I'd had this warning. God! Imagine walking past this store's grand opening and seeing the Gorgon after all these years. I could use the drive home today to figure out what to say to Riley and how to head off any expectations she might have . . . like the idea that Genevieve might want to see us.

Riley's friends hung out on Michigan Avenue all the time, now that they were sixteen, and someone was bound to see the store and tell her . . . and Riley was sure to tell them she was Genevieve's great-granddaughter. Would her friends even believe her? Genevieve London was an international brand. Riley and Pop and I . . . we were just regular folks.

I hurried up, walking briskly to my car, sweat streaming down my back. I'd dressed up today to look the part, but I regretted it now. My left heel was rubbing in the unfamiliar pump.

All these years without a Genevieve London boutique in Chicago. Sure, Genevieve's stuff was in all the high-end department stores, but a dedicated store . . . ugh. I'd been naive enough to imagine she'd stayed out of Chicago because she knew we were here. But no. Her empire was expanding still.

I didn't want to assume this would bother Riley . . . and I didn't want to assume that it wouldn't. I didn't want her to think I was upset. I didn't want her to feel rejected, and I didn't want her to get her hopes up, and I didn't want her to sublimate any of those feelings if she had them, and I didn't want her to feel she couldn't tell me about them if she had them, and I didn't want her to feel that she *had* to tell me about them if she didn't want to.

Being a single mother *and* a therapist was very complicated.

A few years ago, I'd told Riley the facts: Genevieve London of the adorable purses was my grandmother, and I'd lived with her for ten years after my mother died because my father couldn't take care of me. I explained that Genevieve wasn't the nicest person, so we didn't talk anymore. Since my father never came to visit, it was easy not to say anything more about the London side of the family.

I only told Riley because my grandfather (on my mother's side, clearly) had recommended it, and Pop was seldom wrong. Can't hide the truth forever, he said. I'd answered that I didn't want to hide it as much as ignore it, which he said was the same thing.

To the best of my knowledge, Riley didn't tell her friends about her link to Genevieve; the girls never mentioned it or asked me questions when they came over, the same three girls Riley had been friends with for ages.

But sixteen was the age when you tried to impress your friends, after all, and how many girls had great-grandmothers who designed handbags owned by Adele, the First Lady and Oprah, or had a two-page ad spread in the spring edition of *Vogue*? I pictured Riley and her friends going into the store, a snooty manager giving my precious daughter a cool once-over before cutting her down with a razor-sharp comment. Because if I knew my grandmother, she'd have instructed her manager to do just that. She would've written it herself and told her staff to practice it. "Ms. London doesn't *have* a great-granddaughter," the manager might say. "Is there something I can show you?"

My grandmother had eviscerated me; I didn't want her near my child.

Traffic on 290 West made the trip home longer, and the midwestern heat pulsed down through the windshield, daring my Honda's AC to keep up. By the time I pulled up to Pop's humble house in Downers Grove, my skin felt hot and tight, and the rearview mirror showed my blond hair flattened by heat, a clenched jaw, red cheeks, and worry making my brown eyes look too wide. Overall, a little on the crazy side.

I took a deep breath. "Hi, honey," I said, practicing. Smiled. "Hey, baby. No, not baby. Hey, sweetheart, how are you? Did you have a good day?"

My grandfather wasn't home; though he'd retired last year from his job as an elevator mechanic, he still did electrical work on the side. My other grandmother—the nice one— had died when I was seventeen, just a year and change before I came out to live with Pop.

Riley's shoes, the kelly-green Converse high-tops, were in the middle of the living room, and there was a glass next to the sink that hadn't been there this morning when I left for the city. "Hi, honey!" I called. "I'm home!"

No answer. I listened and heard nothing but quiet.

I went upstairs, trying hard not to run, wondering if I *should* run, and if I had run that day so long ago, if everything would have been different.

I knocked once, harder than I meant to, and threw open Riley's door.

My daughter lay on her bed, earbuds in, looking at her laptop, and the relief made my knees wobble. You never realize it until you're pregnant, or holding your baby in your arms, but your heart, soul and peace of mind will never be yours again. The tiny hijackers take over before they draw their first breaths, and you would do anything to keep them safe. Anything.

"What?" she said, taking out one earbud.

"Hi! How was your day?" My voice was too loud, too bright.

"Fine." Her tone indicated otherwise.

It was okay. She was here, and she was safe and alive, even if it was one of *those* days, then. The dark days. Normal teenage behavior, hormones, etc. She was due to get her period in about three days (yes, I kept track), so it was probably just that.

She was so beautiful, my girl—blazing red hair down to her shoulders, thick and curly, milk-white skin with freckles, and her eyes. Her blue, blue eyes, clear as a September sky.

Telling her about the Genevieve London store right now didn't seem like a good idea (or I was a coward, or both). I sat on the edge of Riley's bed and put my hand on her shin, unable to resist touching her. "How was lunch today?" I asked.

"Gross." She flicked her gaze at me, then resumed watching whatever was on her screen. "Hamburgers, not French toast sticks like they said. The meat was gray."

"That *is* gross. How about if I make French toast for supper?"

"You don't have to."

"Do you want me to?"

She shrugged.

"Are you going to Mikayla's tonight?"

Another shrug. That wasn't good.

"Okay. Well, French toast for supper, extra syrup for my girl." I kissed her head, and she gave me a half smile, and I felt the painful rush of love I always did for my only child. *Thank you. Thank you for that smile, for still talking to me, for being my favorite person, my greatest love.*

Feeling fairly stupid, completely reactionary and tentatively happy, I went back downstairs.

My daughter was safe. She almost smiled. She wanted my French toast. I thought she was okay.

This uncertainty was new for me. Until this past year, Riley had been a sweet, happy person. As a tot, she'd played for hours in cardboard boxes, or pretended to be a waitress or a hairdresser. It wasn't so long ago she'd still been playing with Josefina, her American Girl doll. She loved books and babysitting. While the statistics said most of her peers were having sex and trying out drugs and alcohol, Riley still read the warrior cats series and slept with Blue Bunny, her first stuffed animal. I was grateful . . . no tweeny fuming, not for my girl. Jason, her father, had been a happy teenager. Me, not so much, but I liked to think my daughter's sunniness was at least in part due to my good parenting.

Physically, she'd been a late bloomer—athletic like her dad, thin, getting her period just before she turned fifteen, only recently needing a bra. At first, it had been okay; a little weepiness every twenty-nine days, cured by a girls' night with just the two of us watching obscure shows on the National Geographic channel, eating brie and apricot jam on crackers.

When I myself was sixteen, I'd been so aware of my odd status in Stoningham—the ward of an important, wealthy woman but abandoned by my parents, desperate to be normal, whatever that was. Riley had always seemed better, more confident, happier than I'd ever been, thank God. She'd been content to avoid romantic drama, had the same friends since she was eight, wanted to put off learning to drive till she was older. Her social life, such as it was, consisted of sleepovers with her longtime friends. She was a happy, happy kid.

And then came winter, and everything seemed to change.

The brie and shows about life in Alaska weren't enough. The long-suppressed terror buried deep in my gut showed its teeth, even as I used every tool and resource I had to convince myself over and over that Riley was . . . well . . . normal. *Not* clinically depressed. That the gods of genetics had *not* cursed her with the same thing that had haunted my mother.

Somehow, the things that had always seemed so good and wholesome took on a darker cast after this past winter. Why *didn't* she want to go to a dance? All her friends were going, weren't they? Was she clinging to her childhood in an unhealthy way, and if so, why? Was she afraid of growing up? Had something happened to her . . . rape, or bullying, or drugs? Was I missing something? Was it boy troubles? Girl troubles? Both? Was she gender fluid, or gay, or trans? None of those would change my love for her, but maybe she wanted to tell me. Should I just ask? Or would that be intrusive?

I analyzed her moods, trying to slip her some therapist questions without making her suspicious. Her pediatrician had pronounced her "completely normal with a side of awesome" at her annual physical, but still. When you know depression can be genetic, and when your own mother committed suicide, you watch like a hawk.

Genevieve London's overpriced, elitist store might throw my daughter in any number of unpredictable ways. And after seventeen years of feeling free from my grandmother, seeing the new store was just too much Genevieve London for one day.

A tremor of danger hummed in my gut, warning me there was more to come.

I ate one of the oatmeal cookies I'd baked the day before. I had an online appointment—this client liked messaging rather than video conference, and that was fine with me. His problems were chunky—PTSD from a wretched childhood—and it was easier to be wise if I had time to think.

Then the landline blared, and I jumped, because who ever used landlines? The harsh ring of Pop's 1970s phone was horribly loud, and I snatched it up immediately. Probably a telemarketer. Since it was a phone from the days of yore, we had no caller ID or even an answering machine.

"Hello?"

There was a pause, and just as I was about to hang up, someone spoke.

"Is that you, Emma?"

Her voice punched me in the stomach, the unmistakable, blue-blooded tone of the Gorgon Genevieve herself, immediately recognizable even after seventeen years.

I hung up.

Almost immediately, the phone rang again. I let it, and the sound brayed through the quiet house. Two times. Three. Four.

"Mom? You gonna answer that?" Riley called from upstairs.

"Sure thing, honey!" I said, snatching it up again.

"Don't be childish, Emma," Genevieve said. That voice, so elegant and frosty, always with that tinge of disappointment.

The store. She was probably calling to tell me about the store. "What do you want?"

"I see we've lost all social graces," she said.

"Why would I waste them on you?"

She sighed. "Very well, I'll get right to it. I have cancer. I'm dying, so you have to come home and do your familial duty. Bring your child."

My mouth opened and closed noiselessly. A) Cancer wouldn't kill her, because she was just too mean. B) I wouldn't go "home" if I had a gun to the back of my head. And C) she'd kicked me out seventeen years ago. Her final words hadn't exactly been a blessing.

"Funny," I said, "you talking now about family and duty. Oh, gosh, look at the time. I have to run. Have a nice death!"

"Don't hang up, Emma, for heaven's sake. It's so like you to fly into hysterics."

I clenched my teeth. "I'm not hysterical, and I'm not coming home. I *am* home, as a matter of fact."

"Fine. Come back to Connecticut, Emma, and say goodbye to me as I live out the last of my days."

"You haven't called me since I left, Genevieve. Why would I care about the last of your days?"

There was a pause. "We've had our differences, it's true."

"You kicked me out when I needed you most. Why should I care if you need me now?"

The frost of her voice turned to sleet. "You were irresponsible."

"And pregnant, and eighteen."

"As I said, irresponsible. At any rate, it's just for a couple of months."

I snorted.

"Must you make that unladylike noise?"

"Genevieve, I'm sorry. I don't care enough about you to uproot my child—it's a girl, by the way—so I can change your diapers in your dotage."

"Nor am I asking you to, Emma. I'm simply asking you to come home so I can see my granddaughter and great-granddaughter before I die."

"You blew your chance on us a long time ago. Besides, don't you have a son? Ask him." Not that my father had ever taken care of *anyone* very well.

"This is not work for a man," Genevieve said.

"It's not work for me, either."

"Emma, it's not my fault that you were a floozy who couldn't keep her legs crossed and threw away her future."

"Sweet talk will get you nowhere, Gigi," I said, using the only nickname she'd allowed back then. God forbid I'd just called her *Gram*. "Besides, do you really want a floozy taking care of you?"

"I'll pay for your travel expenses and give you some money in the meantime."

"No, thanks. Hanging up now."

"Jason is separated from his wife, you know. Oh, but I forgot, you and he are still so close. Of course he's already told you."

My stomach dropped. The Gorgon had me there. Jason had *not* told me. And given that he was the father of my child, my one experience with being in love and my closest male friend, that stung.

Then again, Genevieve was the master of stinging. She was a wasp in every sense of the word.

I curled the cord around my finger. "The answer is still no. Please don't call again."

"Very well," she said. "Would you accept a bribe? Come home, and I'll make your child my heir." There was a pause. "My only heir. Even if she doesn't have a real name."

Riley was my grandfather's last name, my mother's maiden name. Another sting from the queen of wasps. "What about Hope?" I asked. "You're cutting her out of the will?" Hope was my much younger half sister, the child of my father's brief second marriage, and she lived not too far from Genevieve at a home for children whose medical needs were too complex for their families to handle alone.

"Hope has a trust fund for her care that will last all her life."

"Good. Make me her guardian. Otherwise, we have nothing to talk about. Bye, Genevieve," I said.

"Think about it. We'll speak soon."

"No, we won't." But she had already hung up.

I went to the kitchen table and sat down, my mind both racing and empty at the same moment.

Genevieve was dying. I waited for some emotion—rage, satisfaction, grief—to hit me. Nothing did. My stomach growled, so I ate another cookie.

Once, I had loved my grandmother and wanted desperately for her to love me. That hadn't happened. Try getting someone to love you for ten years and failing . . . It leaves a mark.

So she was dying. I told myself I didn't care. What about Hope? Would my sister care? Would she miss Genevieve, who, from what the staff at her facility told me, visited at least several times a month? It was hard to tell; my sister was nonverbal. She was a sweet girl, full of smiles and snuggles when her seizures weren't stealing away her days, or her rages weren't taking over. She had a severe case of tuberous sclerosis, and every complication that went with it.

At least Genevieve had done right by my sister.

An image of my grandmother and her housekeeper/ companion Donelle on the terrace in the summer flashed through my head. Cocktail hour observed religiously, their laughter, the breeze coming off Long Island Sound. My room, painted the faintest blush pink, my giant bed and fluffy white comforter, the tasteful throw pillows, the window seat that overlooked the wide expanse of grass, the rock walls that bordered the yard, the giant maple tree. The bathtub I could fill so deep I could float in it.

I also remembered how I wasn't allowed to have posters in my room, or funny signs, or the tie-dyed pillow I made with Beth, my best friend in high school, or the goldfish I won at the Ledyard Fair. I wasn't allowed anything Genevieve deemed "tacky." I wasn't allowed a bulletin board on which to pin mementos or souvenirs. I had to make my bed and replace the pillows exactly as Genevieve wanted, and the second I took off my shoes, they had to go into the closet. It wasn't a prison by any means, but it wasn't really my room, either . . . it was a catalog page from Genevieve London Home Designs, and my personality was not welcome.

I remembered Genevieve's rage when I told her I was pregnant. How she'd told me to abort my baby or give her up for adoption. Five minutes ago, she'd offered to leave that same child millions.

Like that could undo everything. I'd made a life with my baby, got through college an inch at a time, working nights at a grocery store, leaving Riley with Pop, fighting to stay awake in class.

Money wouldn't undo the past.

And yet . . . Riley was almost done with her junior year, since she'd started kindergarten a year early, being a smarty-pants. We'd already looked at some colleges online and visited the University of Chicago in April. I didn't have a lot saved for her college, but I had some. A little bit of every single paycheck had gone into a savings account since before she was even born . . . but when I said little, I meant it. A drop in the bucket. I was hoping Jason would help—counting on it, really—though, legally, he wasn't obliged to pay anything. He had another family back east, and while he'd never missed a child support payment, he'd never given any extra, either. He worked in construction; his wife did tech part-time.

Genevieve, however, was frickin' loaded. Her company was traded on the New York Stock Exchange. Sheerwater, her house in Stoningham, Connecticut, had to be worth at least $15 million alone.

It didn't matter. Riley would be fine; I'd take out more loans even though my own were still choking me and would be for a long time; she'd take out loans, too. Maybe she'd get one of those full scholarships at the Ivy League colleges for incredibly bright kids. Maybe do a couple of years at a community college. Maybe Jason would take care of everything.

I wasn't going to sell my soul, not even for my daughter.

It wasn't worth it. We couldn't go. We *shouldn't* go.

We weren't going to go.

CHAPTER 2

Genevieve

ere are some facts about getting older.

You hate young people because their manners, clothes and speech, as well as their taste in books, music, film and television, are all inferior.

You leak when you laugh, cough, hiccup, sneeze.

Putting on a bra becomes nearly impossible. Your arms don't bend that way anymore. Nylons are even worse, because you can lose your balance and fall.

You go through a second puberty, sprouting hair from your ears and nose while your eyebrows and lashes thin and your upper lip grows hairs as thick and sharp as wire.

You wait all day to have a drink.

You nap when you don't want to and can't sleep when you do.

You have regrets. Once you dismissed them as a waste of time, but as you get older, they creep back.

* * *

was always an attractive woman. A great beauty, to tell the truth. Grace Kelly and I could've been sisters, people used to say. It was true. My parents had been quite attractive . . . I always thought like marries like in most cases. Of course, you see the aberrant couple—Beyoncé and her rather homely husband (yes, of course I know who Beyoncé is, I do live on this planet). But more or less, beautiful people marry beautiful people. And if one is extremely wealthy but also homely or plain . . . Prince William, for example . . . one can marry a great beauty like Kate Middleton and create attractive children.

I was beautiful *and* wealthy *and* went to a fine school. I took care with my appearance and wardrobe, watched how I spoke and was well aware that I projected an image. Garrison said he knew the first moment he saw me that I would be his wife, and that was exactly what I'd hoped for—that the best-looking young man from the best family with the best prospects and, of course, the best heart would see me and know in an instant I was the one.

I didn't let him down.

After he died, I most certainly did not fall apart and start leaving the house in a bathrobe or letting my hair get long and stringy. Did Jacqueline Kennedy? Did Coretta Scott King? Joan Didion? I think not.

Not only did I keep up appearances, I exceeded them. I became a style icon and an industry leader. Well into my forties, heads still turned when I walked down Madison Avenue. I was sleek, chic, tall and slender, and I wore three-inch heels every day. Though I didn't date publicly, I eventually had a few gentlemen friends . . . lovers, if you must know. My financial adviser. An art appraiser from Christie's. I would never marry again, nor did I want to, but I enjoyed the occasional dinner in the city, a night in a suite at the Mandarin Oriental or the Baccarat (never the Plaza . . . their rooms were so tacky).

And then, abruptly, I became invisible.

That was the first inkling I had that I was aging out.

Oh, I was still fashionable and attractive, but suddenly, I was an older woman. Heads no longer turned, despite my excellent bone structure and thick hair. Doors were no longer held. Young men looked right through me, often bumping into me as if I were made of fog.

I wasn't just invisible to men. Females, too—the twittering teens who'd swarm past me on the street, giggling too loudly, exclaiming about themselves in utter self-absorption. Young women were too busy checking their phones or fondling their own hair or adjusting their breasts in their push-up bras.

Men my own age who once had given me an appreciative glance stopped seeing me, their gazes trained on those hair-fondlers. I found myself hating the young. They were so loud, so self-obsessed, so needy, always wanting all the attention on themselves.

It seemed to happen overnight. Once, a bartender would flirt with me, admire my taste in alcohol, since I always specified Chopin vodka or Hendrick's gin. He might say, "I love a woman who appreciates the finer things," or, "I bet you could teach me a thing or two," with a crooked smile or a lifted eyebrow. Now it was simply "Coming right up." Or, far worse, "Yes, ma'am."

For decades, I was a regular at the same hotel restaurant and bar in the city. It had been Garrison's favorite place to take his clients. I stayed loyal after he died, bringing my contacts there, the buyers, the fashion journalists and editors. The manager always greeted me by name—as was appropriate. It was simply good business to recognize a returning customer, especially as I became a tastemaker. I would hold interviews at this hotel, not wanting to let people see my apartment, which would've been entirely too

personal. Often, I'd book a hotel suite for my corporate
guests or recommend it to friends. The hotel was appropriately grateful for the free publicity and stream of business.
*Seated in the rooftop bar at the Lyon Hotel, Genevieve
London sips a classic gin martini and gazes over the city.*

Until the day when I went in and the maître d' said,
"Can I help you?"

Not "Mrs. London! How wonderful to see you again!
James, please escort Mrs. London to her table."

When I told her my name, she didn't give a flicker of
recognition. "Enjoy your lunch," she said, passing a menu
to a minion.

I didn't move. "One can have one's teeth straightened,
you know," I said. "Ask your dentist. You could be quite
pretty. And please get your superior. Tell him Genevieve
London is here and unhappy with the service."

Of course it was cruel. But, really, did Helen Mirren get
treated this way? She did not.

No longer did young women look at my shoes with
envy . . . they were wearing bedroom slippers, or aptly
named UGGs. At home in Stoningham, of course I was still
recognized, but sometimes in the summertime, I'd have to
wait in line at the wine shop or farmers' market, and it was
as if I were simply invisible. Waitresses would walk past
me without even taking a drink order. At Rose Hill, where
Hope lived, new staff no longer mistook me for her mother.
My gentlemen friends invited me out less frequently, which
was fine, as they were now talking about things like sciatic
pain and little blue pills. On what would be my final inter-
lude with the man from Christie's, I caught a glimpse of his
dangling scrotum, so reminiscent of a turkey wattle, and
decided my sex life was over.

I had read the articles on hating one's neck and the lack
of male attention, but I hadn't quite expected it to happen
to *me*.

I was aging well, mind you. I'd always had perfect skin,

and I took care of it, never falling prey to the tanning fad, always wearing a hat when outside, as well as excellent makeup and sunscreen. My neck was crepey, but a little laser treatment from a dermatologist kept that to a minimum. I didn't mind the wrinkles, as they were slight—a few crow's-feet à la Audrey Hepburn, a slight softening of the cheeks.

I did mind the hairs. Every morning when I flossed and brushed and put on makeup, I peered into the mirror—the magnifying mirror that showed every eyelash at ten times its natural size—and looked for hair, tweezing each whisker away before it had a chance to grow. Every night when I washed with gentle cleansers and moisturized with serums and lotions infused with hyaluronic acid and vitamin C, I did the same. And yet there was the day when, in a restaurant restroom, I found an eyebrow hair at least an inch long. An inch! I swore it hadn't been there the night before.

The upper lip hairs. The chin hairs, as if I were a nanny goat. The nostril hair! I had no recollection of my mother having to trim her nostril hair, yet there it was, a cluster of *fur*, as if a small animal had taken up residence in my nasal cavity. I had to check moles, since they seemed to be fertile soil for hair follicles. Every day, it took longer and longer for me to get ready.

I had to look my best. It was a matter of discipline. If I let one thing go, what would be next? Me wandering down to the post office in a bathrobe covered in dog hair?

Another indignity: the noises. The grunts and *oomph*s as I got into or out of a chair, coming out of me of their own volition. The crackle of my knees as I went up the stairs, the pop of a joint if I knelt down. When I rolled my neck to loosen the muscles, the cartilage whispered and creaked like an old windmill. Despite my daily yoga classes, my body was loosening, sagging, drifting ever downward.

I learned not to wait to go to the bathroom, as the second

I saw the toilet, my bladder wanted to empty immediately. I had to file down my toenails because they became thick and yellow and difficult to trim. Though I had strong suspicions about the hygiene of the local nail salon, I finally started making regular appointments there, simply because I couldn't bend in the shower to spend the necessary time. Donelle didn't even try, and her feet looked more like malformed hooves than anything found on a human.

Friends call you less as you age. Or, if they do call, they simply recite a litany of their pains and diagnoses. "My polyps! My bunion! My irritable bowel!" I did not degrade to that level—Mother would spin in her grave—but those calls were much more frequent than the invitations I used to receive. That was one reason I kept up with Friday night cocktails. It was my link to sanity some weeks. I'd invite Miller Finlay, who had done some renovations on Sheerwater a few years earlier, and the Smiths, my neighbors from down the street. In July and August, I'd include some of the more pleasant summer people—the Drs. Talwar: Vikram, a cardiologist, and Saanvi, a thoracic surgeon; the lesbian couple, Alesia and Anne, both of them veterinarians.

It made me feel . . . relevant. Vital. I was not invisible, not in Sheerwater, not when I had all but sold my soul to ensure that, yes, I would live well, with dignity and grace and style. I would *not* be remembered as a shriveled little lump under coarse sheets in a nursing home with frightened eyes and filthy diapers. No. I would go out on my own terms, definitively and decisively and with grace, as I had lived my life.

And I would make sure my nostril hairs were trimmed back, thank you very much.

CHAPTER 3

Emma

The night of the fateful phone call, I told Pop about Genevieve's offer when Riley was safely in her room, music playing.

"Don't trust that ancient windbag further than you can throw her," he said, his impressively bushy eyebrows lowering in a scowl.

"I know."

"Did she try to bribe you?"

"Yep. She said she'd put Riley in the will."

"Don't trust her." He paused. "How much is she worth?"

"I have no idea. The house, though . . . a lot."

He grunted. "She'll probably sell it for your sister."

"Hope has a trust that takes care of her. She's set for life."

"At least there's that. Well, listen. Riley doesn't need that old cow's money. You made it work all by yourself." He tugged at his flannel shirt and nodded at me.

"It took me eleven years to get my degrees, Pop."

"Well, you had a baby! Riley won't. She's smarter than you. No offense."

"None taken. I also had you, Pop. We'd have been homeless without you."

His craggy face hardened. "You would've been homeless because of that woman, who's now trying to bribe you two back to that pit of vipers."

"To be fair, there's only one viper." Donelle might have been a somewhat inept housekeeper, but she had always been pretty nice. I wondered abruptly if she was still alive. Genevieve would've told me if she died, wouldn't she?

Pop harrumphed. "That woman has enough venom for an entire pit, then."

He had me there. "I'm gonna take a walk," I said. It was a lovely night, and walking through our homey little neighborhood always soothed me. Peeking into the neighbors' windows, waving to the folks coming home from work or sitting on their porches, smelling the good smells of dinner cooking.

It was so normal here. Pop was the typical midwesterner, stoic and kind, understated in all things but generous to a fault, hardworking and decent. The houses were small and tidy, the yards neat, the trees sturdy and unremarkable. It was so safe.

Stoningham was not normal. It wasn't safe. The little borough twisted and turned along the rocky shoreline of Long Island Sound, every house prettier than the last, every yard landscaped and designed, crews of Spanish-speaking laborers uprooting every weed, deadheading every blossom. Live-in housekeepers and nannies were the norm. The people of Stoningham were the überpreppy set, driving their Mercedes and Audis, all the kids going to the best colleges. If anyone worried about money, they hid it well. There was competition in the very air, and Genevieve had been the undisputed queen.

I wondered if it was still the same. After all, I hadn't

been back in seventeen years. Jason still lived there, but we didn't talk about the town, and he rarely saw Genevieve, certainly never to speak to. They ran in different circles. And she hated him.

Money. It was so fraught. Money ruined people, both the lack and excess of it. Here, we had food and a good strong roof over our heads, and I knew how damn lucky we were. While my grandfather had been steadily employed since he was seventeen, Grammy's health insurance hit its limit three years before she died of ALS, and their life savings was sucked into that particular black hole. When I came to stay, Pop opened his doors, but he hadn't been able to help me with college or grad school. Even though I'd worked, the mountain of my student debt resembled Kilimanjaro.

The dream of having my own house was secondary to helping Riley pay for college. My career was just getting started, and it was only last year that I'd been able to quit my longtime job at the grocery store. Half of my clients talked about their debt, their financial fears, their inability to get on top of things, the anxiety it caused, how they were putting off marriage, children, home ownership, moving. A lot of them lacked faith that they'd ever get caught up.

So Genevieve dangling this carrot, though I recognized it as the bribe it was, was hard to ignore. Once, she had been all set to send me to college. I wondered if she'd do the same for Riley. If Riley could walk into adulthood, into a career or grad school without debt, it would be a game-changer. Right now, she wanted to be a doctor, and I'd already done the math. With interest on student loans, it was more than likely she'd be half a million dollars in debt before she even joined the workforce.

And then there was Hope. Genevieve *had* to make me her guardian. My father, Clark, was useless, as thin and translucent as wax paper in my life. He had money, but it was all Genevieve's—an allowance from his mommy. When Hope's diagnosis was made and her mother abandoned her, Genevieve took guardianship and paid her superexpensive bills. I doubted very much my father would suddenly decide he wanted to take care of his daughter.

Since Clark dumped me at Genevieve's a month after my mother committed suicide, I would only see him at Christmas, when some financial exchange always took place between him and Gigi. In those first few heartbroken years, I'd asked over and over to come live with him again. His answer was that I was better off with Genevieve, and if I wanted a pony, she would probably buy me one. Of *course* I felt unloved and abandoned. I still did, although now that I could recognize he had his own problems, I could even concede it was probably the kindest thing he could've done for me. To the best of my knowledge, he never visited Hope. I asked the staff about her visitors; it seemed like it was just Genevieve and me.

Hope was born a year after Riley. I hadn't learned of her till she was three years old, hadn't been informed that I even had a sister until then. I'd called my father, still hoping that he'd fall in love with the idea of having a granddaughter. After all, I myself was in love with Riley and couldn't understand how anyone couldn't feel the same. It was then I learned I was a big sister.

She'd been born with tuberous sclerosis, a rare condition that caused noncancerous growths to occur. For some people, TS meant having a slight skin condition. Sometimes, people with TS would have seizures because of benign tumors in their brain. Autism wasn't uncommon. If TS was caught early, there were some good treatments out there. But Hope's case was extreme; she had tumors in her brain, heart, kidneys. She had severe seizures, some motor difficulties and cognitive difficulties. Sometimes she'd have terrible rages and could trash a room in seconds or hurt herself by banging her head. By the time I learned about her, she was already living at Rose Hill.

I flew out to meet her, this sister of mine, younger than

my daughter. She was beautiful, small for her age, not talking yet, and walked with a listing gait. "Hi," I said, bending down to look in her eyes. Brown, like mine. "I'm Emma. I'm your sister."

It was love at first sight. If I could have afforded it, if my father or Genevieve would have let me, I would've adopted her or had her come live with us. But Rose Hill was a beautiful place, and the staff was all so kind, well educated and lovely. From then on, Pop gave me a plane ticket back east for Christmas so I could visit Hope. Most years, I managed to make it again in the summer, too.

She never did learn to talk, but I liked to think Hope recognized me. She cuddled right up against me and let me brush her hair and sing to her. When Riley was ten, I started taking her with me. Her aunt, a year younger than she was.

I never saw Genevieve on those trips. Sometimes, Jason would drive up for dinner; Rose Hill was about a half hour from Stoningham. He never managed to bring his sons up to meet us, though.

If I did go to Connecticut this summer—not that I would, but if I did—I could make sure I'd be appointed Hope's guardian. Her mother was a party girl I'd never met, but I knew she had signed away parental rights upon Hope's diagnosis. And Clark was way out of his league with Hope. Genevieve wasn't a monster; she'd realize I was the only one who could be Hope's guardian. Whether or not I had to go to Connecticut to make it happen was another issue.

"Hey, Emma," someone called, and I jumped, so lost in my thoughts was I. It was Marjorie Pierce, one of our neighbors, just getting out of her car. Marjorie was a sweet, middle-aged lady who'd brought casseroles the first year of Riley's life.

"Hey, Marjorie!"

"How's that beautiful Riley doing?"

"She's great!" I smiled.

"Thinking about colleges yet?"

Couldn't think about much else. "Getting started."

"It'll be hard for you, won't it?" She made a sympathetic face.

My stomach curled in on itself. "Well, you know how it is. You want them to grow up, even if it means leaving you." I sounded as fake as I felt.

"It's agony," she said. "Don't kid yourself. Have a good night, sweetheart."

I turned and headed back home.

We weren't going to Connecticut. I wasn't going to present Genevieve with her great-granddaughter so the old hag could feel better about herself. I wasn't going to sell my soul for the chance of money for my child. Even if it would make her future easier. Even if part of me wanted to rub Riley's wonderfulness in Genevieve's face and say, "See what you missed out on? See this amazing person you abandoned? I did it without you or your help, you old bat."

"We're not going," I reminded myself.

But the night air sat uneasily on my shoulders just the same.

Three days later, I was in my office, the tiny den downstairs, counseling Jim, who was telling me how his life would be complete if only he could find a woman tall enough to satisfy him. He had a fixation on women over six feet tall. "If only the Giantess of Nova Scotia was still alive," he said.

I had been well educated on Anna Swan. The things they don't tell you in grad school . . .

"You said in the last session that tall women were kinder, Jim. Do you really think height has anything to do with character?" He himself was five foot six.

"I do," he said dreamily. "There's this website . . ."

"How many hours did you spend there?" By his own admission, most of Jim's free time was spent on porn and chat sites featuring tall women.

"Seven," he said. "Seven today, that is."

"And did you see any people this week?"

"Other than Natasha?"

"Natasha from the porn site?"

"Yes. So sweet. And tall! Six four."

"Or so she said. Jim, all this time on the web hurts your chances of meeting people in real life. Natasha is paid to be sweet to you. She's paid to tell you she's tall."

"Her feet hang off the bed."

He had me there. "Okay, sure. But it's interesting that you choose to interact with people you can't really know. Maybe stipulating that a girlfriend has to be taller than six feet is a way for you to have an excuse for why you don't have someone." Jim had social anxiety. His love of tall women wasn't a bad thing . . . but it did give him a perfect reason to avoid not-tall women.

"Anna Swan," he said dreamily. "Even her name was beautiful."

"When was the last time you went outside, Jim?"

"Oh, a week or so ago, I think."

"Last time, we talked about taking care of yourself, showering, eating good foods, getting some fresh air." His hair looked pretty greasy, and he hadn't shaved in a few days. "Our time is up, so here's your homework. Take a shower, go to the grocery store and buy yourself some green veggies, okay? You could use a little sunshine and fresh air."

He started to stand, and I caught a glimpse of flesh.

"Jim! Do you have pants on?" I barked, covering my eyes. He sat right back down. "Sorry."

"You can't keep flashing me. It's inappropriate."

"I know. Sorry again."

I gave him my therapist smile—kind, wise, not horrified that he'd been pantsless this whole time. "Listen. You're a nice guy, Jim. You have a good heart. People will like you. Not just women on the Internet. Trust me on this."

"Thanks, Doc."

"Talk to you next week." He smiled and started to stand again, and I clicked off before I could see his parts.

I should take more clients in person, I knew. It would pay more. But I still felt like an imposter, sitting in that swanky office, nodding wisely. Also, I wanted to be home when Riley got out of school. Once she went to college (gah! next year!), I could do more, earn more, but for now, it was important to be around. Especially when she was going through this dark phase.

I checked my e-mail. Jason.

> Hey! How are you? How's our beautiful girl? Was won-
> dering if you'd be out to visit Hope this summer and if
> we could see each other. Would also love to have Riley
> visit the boys.

> Also, just to let you know, Jamilah and I are separated
> right now. The boys are doing okay with it. Lots of
> love, J.

Time to call Beth, the one person from Stoningham other than Jason that I kept in touch with, the only one of our old group who'd even *tried* to stay in touch. Then again, we'd all been eighteen, all about to go to college and be fabulous, so I didn't really blame them (much).

"You calling about Jason?" she said by way of answering the phone.

"I am indeed."

"It's true. He's staying with his parents. Everyone seems to be on Jamilah's side. Because . . . you know. She's awesome. Sorry. I wish I didn't worship her and want to be her, but I do."

I sighed. "That's fine. I can say that because I'm a thera-pist and don't have petty emotions."

Beth snorted.

"Did he cheat on her?" I asked, wincing. I hated infidelity. My father had cheated on my mother, though it took me years to figure that out. All those "business trips" . . .

"I don't *think* so," Beth said. "More likely she cheated on him, because she could bag Derek Jeter if she wanted to. She's that beautiful, Emma."

"I know. I get the Christmas cards." I heard a rattle of glassware in the background. Beth worked part-time at Noah's, which was both the townie bar and also a place that served locally sourced kale and goat cheese. In other words, Beth knew everyone and everything. And while we saw each other only once in a while, she was still one of my closest friends. Every few years, she'd come to Chicago, and she and Calista and I would go out together, sleep at Calista's fabulous apartment, get silly. When I visited Hope, I usually saw Beth, too. Just never in Stoningham. I was always too afraid that I'd run across Genevieve, and somehow, she'd reach through the seventeen years that had passed, like the evil queen in a Disney movie, and shatter everything.

Sort of like she was doing now . . .

I was just about to tell her about my grandmother's call when the front door banged open and Riley stormed up the stairs, eyes red, face blotchy, shoulders tight. "Gotta run," I said to Beth.

"Talk to you soon, babe."

I followed Riley up the stairs. "Hey, honey," I said.

"Not now," she said, slamming her door.

Being able to express anger meant a child felt safe and loved, said the therapist part of my brain. The mother part didn't care. I opened her door. "For one, that is no way to greet your mother. Don't slam doors, especially in my face."

"Sorry," she muttered.

"For two, what happened, honey?"

She burst into tears. "I hate everyone!" she said, and my heart cracked. I put my arms around her and smoothed her thick red hair, panic kicking up in my chest. For a minute, I just let her cry, selfishly savoring the fact that my daughter was seeking comfort from her mommy, and I could breathe her in and hold her close.

Then she pulled back and dashed her arm across her eyes.

"What happened?" I asked again.

"They're just . . . bitches, Mom. That's it in a nutshell."

"Who?"

"Annabeth and Jenna and Mikayla," she said, her eyes welling again.

Those were her three best friends since they were teeny. Her *only* three friends, so far as I knew. Group friend dynamics were so hard; it was heady stuff to belong, and hell when you didn't.

"What did they do?" I asked.

She shook her head and used Blue Bunny to wipe away her tears. "Apparently, they all went to a party this weekend. A party I wasn't invited to. And they all . . ." She gave me a look. "They all hooked up with boys from a fraternity at Northwestern! *And* got drunk. Now it's like I don't even know them anymore. They sat there at lunch today, practically high-fiving each other because they're not virgins anymore."

"Are you kidding me?" Like Riley, Mikayla had started school a year early. She wasn't even sixteen yet, and in Illinois, the age of consent was seventeen. If she'd slept with a college boy, he'd be criminally liable for statutory rape . . . and if Mikayla's parents knew what she was up to, they could be charged with child neglect or abuse.

"They *said* they did it. Or they almost did it. I don't know. That's not the point. The point is, they're sluts all of a sudden!"

"What did you say?"

"I said, 'Why would you *do* that?' and they just looked at me like I was a stupid little kid."

I would have to call the girls' mothers, of course. Which wouldn't help Riley, but my God, if my child was being given alcohol and being taken advantage of at frat parties—raped, let's call it what it was—I'd have the boys arrested, drawn and quartered and dragged through the streets. Then hanged, then disemboweled, then burned.

"I don't understand why they're doing this," Riley said.

I took a slow breath. "Sex, you mean?"

"Everything! I didn't know they wanted to have boy-friends or hookups or whatever! It's like all of a sudden, no one's talking to me, and I'm totally left behind." She burst into fresh tears. "They're having sex! I mean, they're just too young! And drinking? At a frat party? They were so *proud* of themselves. Are they idiots?"

"Yes," I murmured. "Most teenagers are at one point or another."

"Last week we were friends. We had so much fun at the coffee shop the manager asked us to quiet down, we were laughing so hard! Today, they just froze me out. Talked about what they were doing this weekend and no one even looked at me, and when I reminded them that they were sleeping over here and we were going to the movies, they just kept talking like I didn't say anything, and I wanted to get up and walk away, but I didn't. I just sat there like an idiot."

"Oh, sweetheart," I said, putting my arm around her again. "I'm sorry. That must have felt horrible." Was she not included because they knew I wouldn't let her go? Because she wasn't into boys yet, or maybe ever? Was this somehow my fault?

Her shoulders shook. "I thought we were the same, you know? Like we weren't in a rush to get into all that boy stuff and drinking and drugs. Annabeth was talking about trying E! We belonged to the Clean Edge Club! We founded it! But I guess they all quit and didn't even talk to me about it, and, Mom, I feel like such a loser."

Damn it! Why did girls have to do that to each other? The primal, maternal part of me wished I had those girls in front of me so I could slap their smug little faces. It seemed like no one's adolescence was complete until a friend turned on them or, in this case, the whole group.

"You're not a loser, Riley," I said, hugging her tight. "You're the best kid I know."

"Said my mother. Sorry, I know you mean it, but that means next to nothing right now."

Ouch.

When your child is little, you are their everything, able to solve just about any problem, make everything okay with a little talk or kiss or snuggle. Now I was impotent.

She sat up and wiped her eyes again. "So now everyone's talking about summer, and guess what? Mikayla's not working at the ice cream shop this year. Guess where she got a job? Genevieve London Designs, right there on Michigan Avenue. And when I said, 'That's my great-grandmother,' Jenna gave me this look, then the three of them looked at each other, and I could *tell* they'd talked about this and they didn't believe me."

Clearly my fears had come to pass more quickly than I had expected. "I can say something to them if you want."

"No! That would make it ten times worse! So now my summer will be spent totally alone. The three of them are planning a college visit to Purdue and Notre Dame, and guess who's not invited? *I'm* the one who always wanted to go to Notre Dame!" She grabbed a wad of tissues and blew her nose. "Why do they have to be so mean, Mommy? What did I do wrong?"

The *Mommy* got me right in the heart. With her puffy eyes and red nose, she looked like she was about four years old.

"You didn't do anything wrong, sweetheart. They did. They're treating you like crap because . . ." *Yes, why?* asked my therapist brain. "Because sometimes people can only feel good about themselves if they make someone else feel bad."

"Well, it worked. I feel horrible. I wish I could just . . . go away. Go to sleep and never wake up." Riley put her head in my lap, and I stroked her coppery hair, but my heart froze in terror. I read into everything, but an indirect statement like that could be a hint of suicidal ideation. Add to that a sense of isolation, stressful events and impulsivity, plus the rise of teenage suicide . . .

. . . and my family history.

Riley heaved herself up. "I have to study for finals. We were all going to get pizza at Jenna's house and study there, but I guess I'm uninvited to that, too."

"Well, their loss. You're great in chemistry, and they aren't."

She gave me a damp, grateful look.

"Honey, I'm really sorry. I have to call their mothers."

The grateful look fell to the floor with a nearly audible thud, replaced by more tears. "Thanks, Mom. In case I wasn't enough of a pariah today. Can't wait for tomorrow."

"You know I have to, sweetie. They're underage."

"I *know*. Go. Ruin my life even more." She yanked a thick book out of her backpack. "I have to study."

I was dismissed.

Yes. Once upon a time, watching Animal Planet and eating late-night snacks with my arm around her could cure any blues my daughter might have. I ached for the days when I had the power to make her happy.

With a deep sigh, I went downstairs and called the girls' parents. Got the expected response of "not *my* daughter!" followed by shock and fear. Each thanked me—we'd known each other for years now, but because of my oddball situation of living with my grandfather, being in college all through my twenties, working at the same grocery store where they shopped and, let's not forget, being single, I'd never really become one of the group.

Like mother, like daughter.

I texted Jason that Riley was going through a bit of a rough patch with her friends, and he texted back immediately, soothing my heart a little.

I'll call tonight. Or now. You tell me when.

Tonight is good, **I wrote back.** Thanks.

Of course! I love my girl! TTYS.

At least there was that. Riley adored Jason, though maybe that, too, had been waning in the past year. He came out twice a year for father-daughter time, and they did all the fun things I could rarely afford—saw *The Lion King*, went shopping, had dinner at swanky restaurants. Sometimes I was included, though less and less as Riley got older. But he never forgot her birthday and Skyped with her at least a few times a month.

When Riley had been conceived, Jason and I loved each other. She was not the result of a one-night stand or an unhappy relationship. But he wasn't here, and he had two other children. And a wife, even if he was separated.

For the next two days, I waited to see how the friend drama would play out. Stalked Mikayla, Jenna and Annabeth's social media. Just as Riley thought, they'd frozen her out. Snapchat showed pictures of the three of them with captions like Besties 4evah!!! and 3 musketiers. (They couldn't even spell.)

Then came the redhead comments. Emma Watson looks SO MUCH better without that stupid red hair.

Riley's hair was glorious, even though she wore it in a ponytail most of the time. The kind of hair science couldn't replicate.

LOL I know! I would kill myself if I was a ginger!!!

Right??? Plus what if you had albino skin and those freaky eyes!!!

My daughter, like me, was very fair. Her eyes were far from freaky . . . they were pure sky blue. They were exquisitely beautiful.

And freckles! Dude, you can laser those off. Just sayin.

My daughter had freckles.

Or use acid LOL.

And so I made more calls, to the parents, to the principal. This time, the parents weren't quite so nice. "You know how girls are," said Mikayla's father.

"They weren't specifically talking about Riley," said Jenna's mother.

"We'll keep an eye on it," said the principal.

Every day for the rest of the week, Riley came home with her eyes red, shoulders tight, and went to her room.

As a therapist, I knew she couldn't run away from her problems. She'd have to tough it out, make different friends, develop coping mechanisms. Most teenagers went through this kind of thing.

As a mother, I was furious and terrified.

Then, on Friday, I got a call from the school. Riley was in the nurse's office; Mikayla had shoved her in the girls' room and held her down, then stuck a wad of gum in her hair.

My heart went ice-cold. I canceled my appointments from the car, raced to the school and took her in my arms.

She pulled away instantly. "Not here, Mom," she hissed. "It's bad enough."

The principal stood by, his professionally sympathetic face on. "I'm so sorry this happened, Ri—" he began.

"Save it," I spat. "If anyone touches my child again, I will sue this school and see you fired. Do you understand me?"

"There are four days left in the school year. Things will settle down over the summer."

"That's your answer? You'll hear from an attorney by the end of the week. Shame on you for not shutting down this situation, you limp dick."

"I know you're upset," he began.

"Fuck you, George," I said. "You screwed up. Fix this."

As we walked to the car, Riley's shoulders were slumped. "You okay?" I asked.

"Fine."

I drove her straight to the most expensive salon in town,

where they teased out the gum and gave her a shampoo and blowout. I told them to bill Jane Freeman, Mikayla's mother, who was a frequent client there. Then I dropped my daughter home. "Be back in ten," I said, then went to Mikayla's house. Tore into the driveway with a screech.

Jane answered the door. "I hear there was an altercation at school," she said.

"I'm filing a restraining order against your child," I said. "Keep her away from Riley, or she'll end up in juvie. You think I don't know how the system works? Watch me, Jane. And take a look at yourself while you're at it. A nasty, bullying little shit doesn't appear in a vacuum."

I got back in my car and reversed onto their lawn, leaving ruts in the perfect green.

Pop was waiting at the kitchen table when I got home. "How is she?" I asked.

"She's okay. Are you?"

"Nope."

We looked at each other. He ran a hand through his white hair and sighed. "Guess we're going to Connecticut," he said. "I'll start packing."

Of course he'd come with us. "Thanks, Pop." My throat tightened.

"Get that look out of your eye," he grumbled, clearing his plate. "I got the dishes. Go talk to your kid."

Riley was already in her pajamas, her face pale, circles under her eyes. Only her hair gleamed with its fiery color, smoother and shinier than it had been this morning.

"How you doing, honey?" I asked.

Her eyes welled with tears. "Okay," she whispered, her hand going to her hair. "You were kind of awesome, Mom. Telling the principal to fuck off."

I smiled. Fake smiled, because rage still pulsed through me.

"So, honey, I had an unexpected phone call last week," I began. She didn't answer. "From Genevieve," I added.

Her big blue eyes widened even more. "Really?"

"Yes."

"Did you call her? Because of me? Because Mikayla's working at the store?" Accusation was heavy in her voice.

"Actually, no. She says she has cancer and she wants us to come to Connecticut and spend the summer. See her before she dies." I was too wrung out to be tactful.

Riley's eyes widened. "Wow. She's got balls, asking you that."

"Yes, she does." I paused. "Do you want to go?"

Her look of surprise was almost comical. "Are you serious?"

"Mm-hm."

"You really want to take care of that old hag? She booted you when you were *pregnant*, Mom."

"I don't want to take care of her. But . . . I do want her to meet you. See what she missed out on." I took a slow breath. "It's your choice, though. Totally up to you."

"Then, *yes*." For the first time in days, my daughter smiled. "Let's get outta here, Mom!"

"Okay, but forewarned is forearmed. She's not the nicest person."

"So you've said before."

"I just don't want you to get your hopes up. That she'll . . . approve of you."

"Because I'm your bastard child?"

"Exactly."

"So we're not in the will, then?"

"We're not," I lied. Better to have Riley surprised than disappointed. Pop was right. I didn't trust Genevieve one bit.

"Will I get to see my dad, too?"

I hadn't talked to Jason about this yet, but it was more than time that Riley meet her half brothers. Four times, a trip had been scheduled, and four times, it had been canceled; three because his boys were sick, once because a snowstorm had locked Chicago down. "Sure," I said.

"This is kind of fabulous," she said.

"You think?"

"Yeah! I mean, sure, she's a nasty dinosaur, but does she still live in that house with the name?"

"Sheerwater, and yes, as far as I know." I sat down on her bed.

She grabbed her laptop and Googled it. "Holy crap, it's beautiful! There's a pool, and the ocean is right there! Dude. It's amazing."

"Yes."

"Sheerwater. Do we get to live at Sheerwater? I could get used to living in a house with a name."

"It would just be for the summer, honey. And I don't know, but I think so."

My daughter looked at me, her extraordinary blue eyes so expressive. "I'm sorry she's sick," she said gently. "Are you sad?"

She took my hand, and a lump formed in my throat. In fifteen months, my daughter wouldn't be living here anymore, and everything would change. These little moments, these small but huge gestures of love, would be rarities.

"No, not really," I said. "She wasn't . . . we weren't close, you know? She did her duty and made sure I knew I was a burden."

"Will your father be around?"

"I doubt it." Riley had met my father—once, when she was three. He'd been in Chicago for a Bruce Springsteen concert and decided to come see us. He'd been shocked when I answered the door with a toddler in my arms. I honestly think he forgot I had a baby.

Riley lay back on the bed. "So she wants us to come. That's kind of cool. I'll finally see the famous Genevieve London up close and stay in a house with a zillion rooms that overlooks the ocean."

"You sure you want to?"

"Heck, yeah, Mom! It'll be fun!"

I pretended to ponder that one. "Fun. I'm not seeing the fun here."

"Oh, come on. You can rub my wonderfulness in her face." She grinned.

I smiled back, the knot in my heart loosening a bit. "That's the only reason I want to go."

CHAPTER 4

Genevieve

I t always infuriated me when people said Garrison died of a broken heart. As if, had I also loved our son Sheppard, I, too, would've done the right thing and died when we lost him.

I did not.

I wanted to, however.

But someone had to raise Clark—the other son, as I started to think of him. Clark, whom, truth be told, I had never loved quite as much. A mother isn't supposed to admit that, but in my case, it was true.

Clark, never as charming or intelligent or handsome, remained alive, growing pudgy, pale and sullen after Sheppard . . . went away. We couldn't say he had died, because no body was ever found. We couldn't say kidnapped, because there had been no evidence of that. He just vanished.

Clark remained. He became an adolescent with all its sticky horrors, then a college student who would only serve to disappoint . . . first in his education (one must work *ex-*

ceptionally hard to be expelled from Dartmouth), then in his marriage to that tragic woman. I worried for my granddaughter after she died. Emma—such a common name—was too much like April, her mother, always wanting approval, too moody, too reliant. Not enough like a true London. Not her fault, really, with Clark as her father, but still. One hoped the superior genes would win out.

Sheppard, on the other hand, would stay forever perfect. My true son. As much as I wanted to love Clark the way I loved my older son, it never happened. The Missing—it was a dark, powerful creature and thus deserved its capital letter, let me assure you—the Missing wouldn't let me.

It's been fifty-five years since I've seen my beautiful boy, but I can picture his face so clearly—his clear, shining eyes with their long blond lashes, the dimple in his right cheek, his hair so lightened by the summer sun that it was nearly white. Seven had been a magical age, though the same was true for each year of Sheppard's brief time with us. At seven, he still curled against my side at night as I read to him, while Clark, two years younger, played on the floor, making all sorts of irritating mechanical noises as he pushed his trucks around. The week before Sheppard went away, the teacher took me aside to tell me how polite he was, how kind and bright.

She was right. He was. He was the loveliest boy in the world.

He had the makings of a fine athlete even then, and clumsy Clark would try to keep up. Sheppard would wait for his little brother, reaching out a hand, boosting him into a tree, steadying the bike. So kind. One of the things I loved most about Sheppard was his generosity. Clark worshipped him, and everyone agreed Clark was a very lucky little boy to have such a fine big brother.

The day Sheppard went away, he'd had a loose tooth—his first, the bottom right. Central incisor (I'd looked it up later, to help the police identify him). I'd never see that tooth gone, never see the sweet gap in his smile, or the bigger tooth that would grow in its place. Sheppard would never need orthodontic work. He would never have acne, never become a sullen teen who sat in front of the television and grunted out replies.

Or maybe he had. I *hope* he had, God yes. What was the term again? Forced adoption, yes. Of all the scenarios, that was the only one that was even remotely acceptable. These days, when I'm feeling weakest and most afraid, I'm tempted to do what I swore I never would . . . picture our reunion.

I can't do that now. Therein lies despair, as the saying goes.

At any rate, some thought I betrayed my older son by not doing the romantic thing and dying of a broken heart. My husband took the easy route and simply died—just stopped—while sitting in the Adirondack chair by the stone wall, our favorite place. He left me just three years after Sheppard went away. I'd found my husband there at the edge of the yard, his feet propped up on the stone wall that divided Sheerwater from the stone-hewn beach. He'd been smiling.

That had been our spot, before, where we used to sit together, the boys tucked in bed, sleeping. Garrison and I would sip our drinks, holding hands, knowing how lucky we were, feeling rather smug, really. We were successful and happy. Wealthy and grateful. Blessed by two fine sons, one better than the other, but perhaps Clark would change and become more like his brother. Garrison would kiss my hand, and we'd watch the sunset, our voices rich with love and satisfaction.

So the fact that my husband would die in our special place, abandoning me, leaving me alone with this mountain of grief and giving me another that would be impossible to climb . . . it was so brutally unfair. Even as the pain ripped me in half, the anger surged harder. *How dare you, Garrison? How can you do this to me?*

But he had, and Clark and I were left alone.

I knew I wasn't a good mother to my other son, but I was all he had. And he was all I had, too; my parents were long gone, and my sister and brother were unable to understand my grief. I hated them, anyway, with their living children whom they gathered closer to them, because thank *God* it hadn't been them. Thank *God* tragedy struck me instead.

A year after I buried my husband, I started my company, and people were stunned. *How does she DO it? How can she even get out of bed in the morning? First her son, then her husband . . .* Or worse—*She must have ice in her veins, leaving that poor little boy with a nanny all day.*

Frankly, it made me want to kill them. Violently. I'd smile and murmur graciously while they exclaimed their surprise that I was *working*, that I could manage to *go on*, that they thought of me and *dear* Sheppard so often, and I was in their *thoughts*, their *prayers*. Yes, I imagined myself stabbing them repeatedly. Driving a stick through their eyes and into their brains as they clucked and cooed at my ironlady resolve. *Die*, I imagined saying as I twisted the stick in their eye socket, their blood spattering my Chanel suit.

Because what was I supposed to do? I'd tried to curl up and die the day the police told me they could no longer allocate resources to search for my son. I wanted to die the day my husband's heart stopped beating as he listened to the waves lapping at the shore, thinking, no doubt, of our firstborn. I'd tried to die the day the most promising lead—a small boy matching Sheppard's description found in Boston—had turned out to be someone else's child. The day I got that news, I left the police station without a word, went back to my car and clutched the steering wheel and screamed like an animal. Oh, yes, I would have loved to die that day, when the Missing gnawed at my heart and lungs, taking all the breath from me, laughing as it did.

But I lived. It came almost as a shock, living. Should I have committed suicide? I might not have loved my second son as much, but I wasn't about to saddle him with *that* legacy. Should I have become a drug addict, swallowing pills to numb the pain? An alcoholic? Should I have moved away from the town my family had helped found, the home where Sheppard had lived? *Really, tell me*, I wanted to say to the well-meaning, wonderstruck idiots. *What else should I have done?*

"Thank you," I'd say. "Clark and I must keep going, after all." A reminder to them that I had another son . . . and to pinch my own soul, because at times I forgot about Clark, frankly. I just didn't care as much. Let him get Cs. Let him skip practice. Let him stay out late. It didn't matter. The Missing and I would wait for him, me dry-eyed and irritable, the Missing waiting for that chink in my armor so it could devour me.

To make up for it, I gave Clark a car on his seventeenth birthday. College was a given; Dartmouth had a building with his grandfather's name on it. I was not concerned about his future. I wanted to be, but Sheppard had taken my mother's heart with him that day.

So . . . I lived. As one does when one is not given a choice, when one's heart refuses to stop beating, when God doesn't listen as you beg him to bring back your son who is probably dead, to bring back your husband who definitely is, to end all the pain of your barren, useless heart. Very few people understood. Miller Finlay, whose family owned a construction business and who'd overseen the repairs and renovations on Sheerwater, did. He'd lost his wife. He knew the Missing, though we never spoke of it, except at his wife's wake. The first time he'd come to Sheerwater after her death, our eyes locked, and the bond formed. His cousin was Jason, who had ruined Emma's future, but Miller was a different sort. Decent. Ruined, like me.

I had no choice but to stay alive. All those years, I worked. I ate. I dressed. I spoke. I waited for old age or accident to take me.

CHAPTER 5

Miller

M iller Finlay hated being a single father.

He hated being a father, period. He was fairly sure he hated his daughter 95 percent of the time. She was three, but it wasn't her age. He'd pretty much hated her since the moment of her birth. Six minutes before, to be precise.

Tess was not adorably naughty or energetic or challenging. She was horrible. Malevolent. Not the usual word used to describe a toddler, but Miller could think of nothing else to describe her screaming in the supermarket, a grating edge in her voice as she announced she was *hungry* (because she'd thrown her breakfast plate to the floor and demanded sugar in place of the eggs). Or when she screamed, "Daddy, no *hurt* me!" when he insisted she stay buckled in the cart. "Daddy, please, I *hungry*!"

The other parents would side-eye him and give him a wide berth. Sometimes they'd offer to buy her a muffin, not noticing she'd shredded and discarded the muffin Miller had already given her. Still, she'd take the stranger up on their offer, making him look like a monster who didn't feed his child. Once, after Tess had announced to a shoe store that he gave her boo-boos, someone had called the police, and he'd had to explain to his former classmate, now chief of Stoningham police, that Tess's black eye was from her banging herself while jumping on his iron-framed bed after she had locked him out of the room.

She was exhausting and never ran out of energy. She was always angry, always crying, often lying on the floor kicking her legs and contorting her body. When she cried and he tried to hug and comfort her, she only screamed louder and arched her back as if in pain until she literally broke free of his arms.

He wanted to love her and just . . . didn't.

The pediatrician said she was normal and had above-average intelligence. A therapist had said the same thing, mentioning that when she could truly verbalize her feelings, things would improve.

Which did nothing for the here and now.

Every night he lay awake, sweating as he tried to "sleep train" Tess, steeling himself to her screams of rage, the hours upon hours during which she never seemed to "cry herself out" as Dr. Spock had promised. Instead, she shook the bars of her crib—which had one of those protective tents secured over it. Or, he'd lay awake waiting for those things to start happening, because Tess had never slept more than three consecutive hours in her short life. Every night since her birth had been punctuated by her screams. Colic. Teething. Rage. He didn't blame her. He'd scream, too, in her place.

When she finally did fall asleep in a sweaty heap, Miller would listen to the quiet. Even though he knew he should fall asleep instantly, though he really *needed* to be asleep, Miller would remember life before Tess. The day the damn two lines had finally appeared, and Ashley sobbed with joy, and they hugged and cried and laughed. After thirteen years of marriage and seven of actively trying, after four years of being screened for adoption and filling out paperwork, and one heartbreaking "almost" adoption, they would finally, finally have a baby.

He remembered the day of the ultrasound, and when the tech told them it was a girl, he realized how much he'd hoped it would be a girl (though he probably would've felt the same way if it had been a boy). He put his face against Ashley's beautiful, taut belly and thanked God for being so generous. He was not a praying man, but he had thought those words. *Thank you, God, for my daughter.*

He remembered going into the hospital when, four days after her due date, Ashley went into labor. He'd been proud, concerned, excited—his beautiful wife, so ripe, so brave. Oh, the fucking *hubris*, such excitement, such complete and utter stupidity. In a day and a half, his life would be over, his wife would be dead, and he'd be the father of a screaming, rage-filled baby.

That was three years ago. Three years, one month, one week and four days.

He glanced at the clock. Four fifty-one a.m. Maybe he could get a little sleep. Closing his eyes, he felt his thoughts skip and slide, and for a moment, he was sleeping, floating, resting.

The wail came, ripping the quiet of the gray morning.

It might be time to call an exorcist, if only the problem were as simple as demonic possession.

The night, such as it was, was over, not that he'd slept for more than ten consecutive minutes.

With a sigh, his eyes gritty from lack of sleep, his legs heavy, neck stiff, he got out of bed, pulled on a T-shirt and entered the chamber of doom. Tess stood there, blondish hair snarled, her lower lip out in a pout and her face wet with tears and crusted with snot. He unfastened the safety net (a straitjacket was probably the next option) and lifted her out, bracing for another day of fatherhood.

"Good morning, sunshine," he said.

"No!"

At least she hadn't taken off her diaper and smeared shit on the wall, as she had yesterday. Last night, he'd dressed her in pajamas that zipped up the back, and so far, Tess hadn't figured it out. But she would. He knew his daughter, and she would.

"How are you today, Tess?"

"No!" she yelled, arching her back away from him.

"Easy, honey," he said as she writhed in his arms and pierced his eardrums with her cries. "Daddy's got you. Let's change that diaper, okay?"

"I hate you," she said. Unfortunately, she was quite advanced with language.

"Well, I love you," he lied. A hundred and eighty-four minutes till he could drop her off at Ashley's mom's and go to work.

Dressing her was like wrestling a Tasmanian devil.

As Tess kicked, wriggled and flailed, he held her down as firmly as he could without breaking her. No changing table, as she could writhe off it, even with him right there. Live and learn. Now there was just a mat on the floor. As he pulled off her pajamas and pulled the tabs of her diaper, she reached down, grabbed the sodden diaper, and swung it, hitting him in the face. It exploded, little pee-soaked beads going everywhere—his hair, his nose, his mouth, the wall, the carpet, Tess's hair and face.

"That's not nice." He gagged, wiping off her face with her shirt, then mopping his own. Jesus.

Tess saw his moment of weakness and, moving at the speed of sound, twisted away and ran.

"Tess! Come back! Get back here, honey!"

She answered in a war cry that made his blood run cold.

Miller knelt there a minute, feeling a hundred years old. Even the air was heavy, pressing him down. Then, wearily, the sharp smell of urine thick in the air, he got up to follow.

The house was ominously silent. "Tess? Sweetie? Want some breakfast?"

She hadn't gone outside (the house had a coded alarm system, thanks to past experience).

"Tess? Daddy's going to have some waffles. Do you want a waffle?"

Nothing.

He looked in the kitchen cabinets, the pantry, the broom closet. No Tess. Living room, den, under the couch, behind the chair, behind the curtains.

Aha. A sound. A small sound, unlike Tess.

Where was the cat? Shit. Where was the cat?

It was insanity, having a pet when your child might be a sociopath. But Luigi predated Tess. Miller and Ashley had gone to the shelter after the adoption fell through—the seventeen-year-old birth mother changed her mind and wanted to keep the baby. Another memory, the two of them sitting in the car at the pet shelter, holding hands, Ashley crying, so beautiful even in her grief, Miller helpless. As if a cat would help.

But Ashley had chosen Luigi, who was essentially a limp bag of organs covered in long, silky fur. He was the mellowest cat in the world. He used to drape himself over Ashley's legs and purr for hours. Even though she more than deserved it, Luigi had never scratched Tess. A study in self-control, old Luigi.

If the adoption had gone through, they wouldn't have gotten a cat. Maybe a puppy for their son, that other baby.

If the adoption had gone through, maybe Miller and Ashley wouldn't have had Tess. They would've devoted themselves completely to their son, their long-awaited child. They'd talked about names, hopefully, almost in a whisper, presciently afraid to believe their luck. Evan. Morgan. James would be the middle name, after Miller's father, who had died the year before.

If that teenage twit hadn't changed her mind an hour after giving birth, Tess wouldn't have been born, and Ashley would be alive.

That son would be five now, about to start kindergarten.

Instead, Miller had a baby he really couldn't take care of but had to keep just the same. It was shameful to admit how many times he'd wanted to put his child up for adoption.

"Tess? Honey? Daddy misses you."

There was the sound again. Yep. Definitely a mew of despair. "Remember how we talked about being gentle with Luigi, honey?"

Still no answer. She wasn't in the hall closet.

He opened the door to the half bath, and there was his naked daughter, smearing the cat with Desitin.

"Shit."

"Shit," Tess echoed. Then she smiled up at him, and there it was, that tiny flicker of hope that he could love her. Those little teeth, her pink cheeks and brown eyes, her snarl of curly hair that he could never brush out. "Kitty pretty now. You go away. I no want you, Daddy."

The flicker was doused.

You're so lucky, people said at the funeral. *You'll always have a piece of Ashley. At least the baby's healthy. Her mother's an angel now, watching over from heaven. She'd have wanted it this way.*

Fuck that. Seriously.

A hundred and seventy-eight minutes till he could drop her at Judith's.

Miller swooped down and took the cat away from Tess, getting a wail of rebellion from his daughter, a twist of fury in which she flung herself against the floor, clunking her head. Her rage cry changed to a pain cry, and grew in intensity.

"Sorry, pal," Miller said to Luigi, tossing him in the cellar and locking the door. The cat's misery would have to wait. At least he was safe. Miller kind of wanted to lock himself in the cellar, too.

He picked up Tess, who fought to get away, and felt her head. A lump was rising there. Back to the kitchen for a bag of peas, rendered useless when she tore the bag and they clicked and bounced on the floor. Since she was already furious, he carried her back to her room, dressed her against her will, hating that she was so strong and he had to grip her so hard. He tried to mop up her face, which was streaked with Desitin, tears, diaper bits and mucus, both dried and fresh. Then he put her in her car seat, which he always brought in the house, since he could buckle her in it. Brought her in the bathroom and wedged the seat in the linen closet so she couldn't flip herself over.

Miller got undressed and took a shower. Tess cried the entire time. When he buckled her in the sturdy high chair and attempted to give her breakfast, she smeared the honey-eyed pieces of waffle in her hair, then threw them at him. When he offered her milk in her blue cup, she said, "No blue!" so he got her the green cup, which she then threw. He turned on the TV, hoping Big Bird could work his magic, and packed her lunch, as well as a bag of Cheerios and a banana. Judith would hate that she hadn't eaten, would hate that she had to supervise breakfast on top of all she already did.

He heard a noise and glanced over his shoulder. Tess was heaving herself in the high chair, scootching it to the counter. Before he could get to her, she grabbed his cell phone and threw it down.

"Tess, no throwing," he said, dragging her chair back. He picked up his phone. The photo that served as the phone's wallpaper was a picture of Ashley and him on their tenth anniversary, and now a jagged crack ran right through the middle of Ashley's face.

I hate our daughter, he told his wife silently. *I hate her. Your fault for dying.*

Tess was digging her spork into the padding of her high chair. Good. Let her. She didn't deserve a nice high chair. Let her have one that was stained and tattered and ripped. Like her father's soul.

A hundred and thirteen minutes left.

He went into the dining room, where Tess couldn't see him, and pushed the heels of his hands against his eyes until the impotent rage faded.

His daughter was only three. She hadn't meant to kill her mother.

She was Ashley's child, too, and some days that was the only thought that kept Miller from walking out forever.

He took her out of the high chair.

"Time to brush those pretty teeth," he said.

Of course, Tess hated having her teeth brushed. She clamped down on the toothbrush, which was rough with bite marks.

"Your teeth will hurt if we don't brush," he said. "Come on. I'll sing the ABCs and you brush, honey. Let go of the brush. Stop biting it, honey."

He twisted it until he was afraid he'd break her tooth. Well. If her teeth were busy clenching that brush . . . he took his own toothbrush and managed a few swipes of her tiny little teeth before she caught on and screamed, which made it easier to get the molars.

"Shit!" he said as she bit him. "Okay, we're done."

Back in the car seat. More crying. When he and Ashley had bought this house, they'd had to gut it, and, being in construction, Miller had known that really good insulation was a must. Good thing, because otherwise the nice Oliveras family next door might move.

Once again, Miller wedged Tess's seat in the linen closet and went to get Luigi, who was sticky and miserable.

"I'm so sorry, pal," he said, filling up the sink with warm water.

Unlike Tess, Luigi didn't mind baths. Miller lathered him with baby shampoo a few times, then combed out his fur. Tess was silent, having fallen asleep, so at least there was that.

He tried not to feel so guilty that he liked the cat so much better than his kid. Giving the cat a bath made him feel paternal and gentle.

God had a twisted sense of humor.

By the time Luigi was Desitin-free and purring, Tess was awake. "I hungry, Daddy!"

"Should've eaten your waffles, then," he said. No way was he caving into her tyrannical demands.

"Shit. Shit! Shit!" she yelled.

He knew she learned the word from him, and felt guilty. She was hungry, so he couldn't blame her. He made her another waffle. She took one bite, then winged it, Frisbee-like, into the living room, where, unerringly, it hit the TV screen and stuck there, then slid down, the honey leaving a sticky trail.

An eternity later, Miller grabbed the backpack of clothes and diapers, wrestled Tess back into the car seat and carried it out to the Jeep, getting his hair yanked in the process, and finally, finally headed over to his mother-in-law's.

Tess was quiet as he drove. Miller glanced in the rear-view mirror. She had what he thought of as her serial killer face on—oddly pleased and . . . well . . . plotting.

"Daddy loves you," he said, thinking of his dead wife.

She ignored him.

When he lifted his daughter out of the car seat, she was stiff and resistant. At least she didn't head-butt him, which she did often, and which hurt them both.

"Hey, Judith," he said as his mother-in-law answered the door.

She sighed. "Hi, Tess." He put his daughter down and she ran inside, yelling a greeting to her grandfather. Something crashed. His father-in-law's sharp voice reproached her.

Ashley had been an only child. Judith was only sixty-two, but she looked fifteen years older these days. Miller had hoped, after Tess's first few months, that his in-laws would beg him to let them raise Tess.

No such luck. She'd been colicky and fitful. After colic came teething. Now that she had her molars, it was something else. Growing pains. Inability to verbalize emotions. Demonic possession.

"Listen, Miller," Judith said now. "I can't do this much longer. I'm sorry. We're exhausted. You need to put her in day care or get a nanny."

Five day care centers had kicked Tess out. Three nannies had quit.

"I understand. Uh . . . I'll look around."

"We'll give you a couple of weeks, but we're just too tired." Her eyes held all the accusations he felt himself . . . Why hadn't he saved Ashley somehow? Why hadn't he sensed something was wrong?—*your fault, why didn't you, you should have*—and Miller felt his soul die a little more.

"It's fine. I appreciate all your help, I do. I'll pick her up at five."

"Try to come earlier."

"Will do."

He got back in the car and sat there for a few seconds. He'd have to go home at lunch and clean up the disaster that was his house. Maybe take a nap. But since Ashley died, Miller felt as if he hadn't slept more than a few minutes at a time. It wasn't just Tess. It was reliving the last moments of his wife's life. It was the helpless terror that one day he would hurt Tess in a moment of weakness or exhaustion, shake her or slap her, and if that happened, he *would* have to give her up, and he would've failed his wife and become a man who hurt a child, hurt *his* child, which was something he knew would ruin him more than he was already ruined.

It was guilt, because he suspected Tess knew exactly what he was thinking. It was the bone-deep belief that if Tess had a father who loved her, she would be a different child.

CHAPTER 6

Genevieve

The first time I realized something was off was this
past January.

It was Friday, and Friday meant cocktails with the
Jamesons and Smiths, my neighbors, and Miller. Donelle
was once again complaining of a swollen toe, so it was I
who made the drinks. I suppose I didn't mind. No one
could make a better martini than I could, either, so really,
the "swelling" served us all well.

My precious little Pomeranian, Minuet, lay on her red
pillow on the window seat, watching the snow fall in the
most adorable way, head cocked, her black-and-tan fur
shining and clean, a perfect example of what a dog should
be. The other dogs—Mac, Allegra, Carmen and Valkyrie—
were all bigger and sloppier, and for cocktail hour, I banished them to their playroom in the basement. It was hardly
prison—a carpeted room with seven dog beds, several
dozen dog toys, a view of the lawn and, tonight, the full
moon rising over the Sound.

Just the week before Donelle had taken down the Christmas decorations—well, she watched as the people Miller had sent over took down the decorations. Miller himself was staring into a scotch, since the poor man didn't appreciate a good martini.

I was feeling rather festive; ironically, the taking down of the holiday decorations always made me feel happy. Four Christmas trees, the garlanded mantels and doorways, wreaths on every door and window, candles galore, the trees along the drive all wrapped with white lights . . . simply overseeing that was a great deal of work. Christmastime was just one more thing I had to do. The expectations of my holiday décor were high, of course; just last year, Sheerwater had been featured in *Martha Stewart Living*. (Martha was such a dear, though I did not understand her affection for the man with the long hair and silly name. Sloopy? Snoopy?)

Sheerwater was also the pièce de résistance on the Stoningham Wassail Walk, in which dozens of local residents held candles and walked through town, caroling at certain stops, my home being the last. Donelle served spiced apple cider and donuts, and we let people in to gape at my house, which was, admittedly, impressive.

Then had come the dreaded Christmas dinner with Clark and what's-her-name, his latest floozy. What *was* her name? He introduced her as his "girlfriend," to which I'd said, "Really, Clark, you're not fifteen, and she's hardly a girl." Amber. No, Topaz, that was it. Some cheap gemstone. At least they hadn't stayed over, though dinner lasted an eternity. New Year's Eve was a holiday I loathed, as it marked another year without Sheppard and Garrison, and yet I attended the historical society's annual party as usual, making small talk, sipping champagne as if surviving the passage of time was something to be celebrated.

But now, the house was put back to order, and Minuet was entertaining us by simply being herself. The Smiths, an attractive younger couple who had the grace not to ask too many questions or be too familiar, which was why they were regulars on my guest list, had made themselves comfortable. They hadn't known me when Sheppard was alive, so there was no demeaning sympathy in their eyes.

My boy had loved Christmas.

I was indescribably relieved not to have to listen to holiday music anymore. One can only stand Handel's *Messiah* so many times, and certainly not by caterwauling pop stars who have no gift for phrasing. At the moment, Debussy's piano trios were playing over the sound system (another favor from Miller), and the house felt clean and welcoming.

Donelle was regaling Kim and Mark with local gossip—new money buying the Josiah Green house and planning to tear off the back to make an all-glass wing. As if I'd allow that. I was president of the Stoningham Historical Society, and we'd never approve such a tacky addition. Anne and Alesia, the veterinarians, were coming a bit later, and the Talwars, who summered and spent the holidays in Stoningham, had returned to their home in New Haven, so it was a smaller group than usual.

"How are those martinis coming, Genevieve?" Mark asked. "Need any help?"

"Of course not, but thank you, dear," I said. Mixing a good cocktail was an art form, and while Mark was a nice enough person, he did things like add fruit juices and, once, a maraschino cherry. I shuddered at the memory.

I looked down at the bar cart. The gin—Hendrick's (far superior to any gin, really), the vermouth (Noilly Prat, of course), and a bowl of lemons.

Then something happened. I was holding an ice cube in one hand, a long-handled silver spoon in the other. There was a small pitcher half-filled with ice already. Suddenly, I wasn't sure what I'd been doing. Who'd put all the ice in the pitcher? Had I? Why?

The evidence was there . . . gin, vermouth, lemons. We

were having martinis. And I was making them, but though I'd done this hundreds, thousands of times before, I was suddenly . . . blank.

The ice was starting to hurt my hand. Why was I holding an ice cube? And the lemons . . . should I squeeze them? Make lemonade? Should I start cutting them up? Those didn't sound like the right things to do, but I wasn't sure what was.

"Allow me," said a voice, and I startled. Miller, that nice Miller. He took the ice cube from my hand, smacked it with the bar spoon (bar spoon, yes, that was it!) and added the chunks to the pitcher. Repeated the action a few times, then poured some vermouth into the . . . the . . . the little oddly shaped cup. Jug? Trigger? No, *jigger*. Jigger.

"Four-to-one ratio, if I remember?" he asked.

"That sounds about right," I answered, though I honestly had no idea what he was talking about. My heart was hammering, and as I smoothed back my hair, I noticed my hand was shaking. "I go by instinct." My voice, at least, sounded the same.

He smiled a little, and I remembered that he was sad, though I couldn't remember why. "I'm sure you do," he said, pouring the gin into the pitcher. Was that how to do it? I couldn't remember anything. Anything! The skin on my throat began to burn with humiliation.

"Lovely to see a man who knows how to make a good martini," I said, faking some chatter. "Manners being what they are today. Make sure you teach your child the art of a perfect cocktail." Did he *have* a child? Dear God! What if he didn't? Why couldn't I remember?

"Well, she's not quite three, but I'll add it to the curriculum."

"One can never start too soon." My voice shook a little.

He smiled again, stirring the mixture.

Then, suddenly, my hand was reaching for the lemon and the knife, and I sliced off a thick section of peel—a twist, that was it, a generous length, because I liked my martinis with a good spritz of lemon oil.

My brain was back in full control. It was January 10, a Friday, and this was what Donelle and I always did. Cocktails with the neighbors and Miller. In the summertime, the Talwars would be here each weekend, and sometimes I invited the Batemans, but they preferred to winter in their apartment on Park and Eighty-Third. Yes, it was 970 Park Avenue, New York, NY 10028.

If I could recall that address, what had just happened?

Miller poured the drinks from the pitcher, and with a little flourish to cover for my lapse, I twisted the peel over the first glass, rimmed the glass and dropped the lemon peel in, repeating the gesture for each drink.

"Thank you, dear boy," I said.

"Now I know your secret to the perfect martini." He took two glasses over to the Smiths. He said the right words, but he was still sad, and I couldn't remember why.

As the Smiths told us about their lovely children—two at boarding school, two still home, all of them well-spoken and not overly loud—it eventually slid into my head that Miller's wife had died. Perhaps I'd known that all along. I mean, really. How does one forget such a detail? Of course I hadn't forgotten.

Lapses happened, of course. Here and there, especially when I was thinking about Sheppard. Entire hours could slide past me like rain down a window when I was thinking of my son. Occasionally, I forgot a name, which was completely normal, given that I'd met thousands of people— Genevieve London employees, people in the fashion industry, townspeople, board members, school friends and all the rest.

But I'd never forgotten quite like that before.

"Gen, could you get me another?" Donelle said, pushing her glass at me.

"Remember the days when *you* worked for *me*?" I asked fondly.

"Not really," she said, and we all laughed, especially Donelle. After all, she was my best friend. Possibly my only true friend, ironically. I'd wanted to fire her a thousand times those first few years—all her questions, her lack of boundaries, the way she took to Clark, magnifying my own neglect.

But Clark needed someone who cared, and at some point over the years, I stopped resisting Donelle's friendship. If my mother could have seen it—her daughter, having drinks with the help, especially Donelle's type (white trash, to put it indelicately, a high school dropout with poor grammar)—she would've heartily disapproved.

But I'd stopped caring. Donelle hadn't been the best housekeeper, but she'd been here, and she never quit—well, except that one time—and she never asked for more than the generous compensation package I still gave her, even though we now had a cleaning service and such. Donelle wasn't a spring chicken anymore, after all. She still lived in the servants' wing with Helga, our cook, and occasionally did something around the house when she wasn't busy reading or watching her lurid television shows.

Clark had given her a hideous pink-and-gold crocheted blanket for Christmas. It draped over one's legs and looked like a mermaid's tail, and she adored it, exclaiming over the too-bright color, hugging him and kissing him soundly on the cheek.

Clark had given *me* a box of Crane's notecards embossed with a tiny pineapple, which made me roll my eyes. After all, my company *made* stationery. I'd had my own personalized stationery with my trademark lily of the valley sprig against a pale green background for *decades*. One would think one's son would know these things, but every year since he'd been a sophomore at Dartmouth, Clark had given me the same gift, indicating a total lack of thought.

If I could remember those details, certainly my confusion at the bar meant nothing. That's what I told myself, anyway.

But then in March, I was coming home from visiting Hope and stopped at Franklin's General Store—Donelle, who went to Stop & Shop, had failed to pick up any decent cheese. While I was choosing a creamy brie, the owner greeted me by name, and a few minutes later, a sweet young girl with a Franklin's name badge came up and asked, "Excuse me, but are you really Genevieve London?"

"I am indeed," I said.

"I just love your bags!" she said. "My parents gave me a wallet for my sixteenth birthday, and I'm going to ask for a purse for graduation."

"You have wonderful taste," I said.

"Would it be too much to ask for a picture?" she said, already fumbling in her pocket.

"Of course not, dear," I said, knowing she'd Snapchat and Instagram the photo immediately. The younger demographic was quite taken with me these days. The girl clicked, thanked me again and scurried off to text her friends, no doubt.

I bought Donelle the insipid Lady Grey tea she loved, added some Carr's whole wheat crackers and blackberry chutney to go with the brie, and paid. I asked the owner, sotto voce, to send me the name of his enthusiastic employee so I could send her a purse from the new spring line. She'd be thrilled with the bag, and it would create a wave of consumer envy among her peers.

Then the fog descended, just like that. Suddenly, I didn't know why I was holding a piece of paper with a stranger's name on it. If I had paid for my items. Apparently I had, because no one stopped me as I left the store. I recognized my car, because the license plate said LONDON. Starting it was no problem; it was where to go that remained a mystery.

Where had I been earlier today? To New York? No, that wasn't right. Or was it? What did I usually do on weekdays?

What time of year was it? Was it fall? No, but it was raw and the trees were bare. I'd been visiting someone, but I couldn't remember who. My mother? It couldn't have been!

When I saw someone looking at me, I smiled, waved and backed out carefully. Took a left and hoped it was the right way home.

It wasn't. It took me ages to find my way back to Stoningham, and by then it was dark and I was nearly weeping with relief and terror. I didn't tell Donelle. I simply made a quick martini (with absolutely no problem) and downed it, and after that, I felt much improved.

A few weeks later, I lost my balance as I walked down the upstairs hall from my bedroom to the front staircase, so much so that my shoulder hit the wall, and the Felrath Hines sketch nearly crashed to the floor, but I grabbed it instinctively and held it hard. My vision blurred, and dizziness washed over me. For a moment, I couldn't push off the wall and stand up straight.

Not uncommon for an eighty-five-year-old woman, but uncommon for this one. After all, I had a yoga teacher come to Sheerwater four times a week, long before yoga had become so common. I could stand in tree pose for five minutes and not so much as waver. My posture was perfection. Mother had insisted on ballet for just that reason. "You can always tell breeding by a lady's posture," she'd said, and it was true.

Still rattled, I went to my office, which was in the turreted section of Sheerwater, and had absolutely no difficulty on the stairs. As ever, my office made me feel safe, with its deep blue walls, walnut bookshelves and custom-made desk, and the oil painting of the storm-tossed sea Garrison had given to me as a wedding gift. The cream-colored couch was modern and rounded to suit the turret's shape, with throw pillows of my own design in shades and patterns of blue. The bright blue-and-red Persian Heriz rug was an antique, and quite valuable.

The office reminded me of who I was . . . or who I had been, at any rate.

Without further ado, I sat at my desk and went to the Mayo Clinic website. I typed in some symptoms—dizziness, blurred vision, weakness. After a pause, I added forgetfulness and a sense of being lost. I would erase my browser history later, in case Donelle was feeling nosy.

I waited, then perused the list of suggested diseases. Concussive syndrome fit, but I hadn't had a concussion. Ménière's disease, which sounded attractive because of the French name, but didn't quite match. Meningitis . . . surely I'd be feeling worse.

Brain tumor.

I pondered that a moment, then clicked on it. In addition to loss of balance, dizziness and forgetfulness, there were a few more symptoms listed.

Unexplained nausea and vomiting. No, thank goodness.

Change in the pattern of headaches. I had that, didn't I? I'd had a ferocious headache the week before, rather worse than most. Then again, I'd had to have Charles drive me into New York for a meeting that day . . . such nonsense, more of a photo op at the company headquarters than anything else. Also, Beverly, my successor as CEO, had been terribly busy and let me know it, which I resented. I didn't like feeling insignificant. I'd thought that was the cause of the headache, but perhaps it was a brain tumor.

Personality or behavioral changes. That one gave me pause. Lately, I had been feeling rather . . . strange. More nostalgic, not just for my lost boy and husband, but for other people, too. Pondering chances I may have . . . sidestepped.

I clicked back and referred again to the list of possible ailments. Dementia. Please. I did *not* have dementia. Parkinson's . . . no.

Brain tumor it was, then.

I sat back in my leather chair and looked at the picture

of Garrison on my desk. I didn't keep one of Sheppard here, as it was too painful to see his face every day. Nor one of Clark, since a photo of my other son would fail to bring a smile to my face or a happy memory to my heart. I had a picture of Hope on the bookcase, of course, her sweet smile brightening my day, but I didn't keep it on my desk.

But my husband . . .

On most days, I'd forgiven him for dying so young. In the past ten or fifteen or seventeen years, I'd felt his loss more acutely. Sometimes, though I would never admit it to anyone, I talked to him.

"It seems I'll be with you soon, my darling," I said now.

And Sheppard! Suddenly, it was as if my heart lunged in my chest. If Sheppard *had* died, I would see him again, at last, at last. My true son. My perfect boy. Tears slipped down my cheeks at the thought of holding him again. Would he still be seven? Would he fit so perfectly in my arms, against my side? Would I still smell the sunshine in his hair, the sweet, grassy scent of my darling son?

For once, the Missing subsided at the thought of my reunion with my baby. My boy.

I looked away, out at the bright blue sky, the shimmering Sound. The flag stood out stiffly, and the rope clanged against the pole as the wind scraped across the rooftops of Sheerwater.

I knew what I had to do. I wasn't going to end my days in diapers, not recognizing Donelle or the Talwars or Minuet. Or Clark.

Suicide was for the weak, Mother had always told me. Granted, that was before depression was recognized as a serious medical illness, but I had to agree with her, at least partially. How else would I have stayed alive all these years? Because I was strong.

I'd see Dr. Pinco, that lovely man, and get an idea of my prognosis and how much time I could expect to be myself.

Though I'd been waiting much of my life to die, I hoped I had a few months left. To prepare. To do it right.

One more spring, one more summer here. A little time, perhaps, to look back. A few more months to do the things I most enjoyed . . . and perhaps see a few people from my past.

And then, I'd kill myself. Gracefully, of course. I wasn't going to make a mess.

CHAPTER 7

Emma

"Are you nervous? You don't have to be," I said, clutching my daughter's hand as the airplane began its descent into the Hartford area.

"Maybe she'd be less nervous if you stopped asking if she was nervous," Pop said from the window seat.

"I'm not nervous. I'm psyched," Riley said.

"Good! Great! Of course you're not nervous. Why be nervous?"

"Mom. Chill." My daughter gave me a look and withdrew her hand from mine.

We were seated in first class—Genevieve's initial shot across the bow, showing off with her wallet—in addition to the limo she'd sent to Pop's little house. For a second, I'd thought Pop wouldn't get in, but he loved Riley, and he was coming with us. He paid for his own ticket, though.

My throat was tight—strep, I thought, absentmindedly feeling my glands. Nothing there. Yet. Oh, wait. Maybe there was a small nodule? Lymphoma? I sighed. Calista would slap me right about now; I knew damn well my throat was tight from nerves, not from cancer.

My daughter cut me a look. She was the only one of us who was thrilled, even though our amenities in first class had been a glass of water pre-takeoff and a snack box. Still, she watched a movie on the tiny screen and had a cup of coffee just because she could. She hadn't been on her phone. I wasn't sure if she was in touch with any of her friends—I imagine Mikayla would be keeping a good distance, but what about the other two? Or anyone in her class? Was it healthy that she was avoiding social media, or unhealthy? Either case worried me. And reassured me. And worried me. God, it was hard being a parent!

My stomach was in knots. (Small bowel obstruction? My mind flashed through the scenario—me in a hospital bed, all-liquid diet, Riley's face white with worry, Genevieve looking smug. Fine. I didn't have an SBO and mentally cursed WebMD.)

No matter what, I had a sinking feeling this visit was a mistake.

Bradley airport was tiny compared with O'Hare, but bigger than I remembered it from seventeen years ago. We went to baggage claim, and there he was—Charles, Genevieve's chauffeur, holding an iPad that said LONDON.

"This is so cool," Riley said.

"Hey, Charles," I said, giving him a hug. He was a bear-shaped man, employed by Genevieve since before I came to live with her. He'd always been so nice.

"Oh, my goodness," he said. "Look at you, all grown up! It's good to see you, Miss London. I mean, Dr. London."

"Don't you dare. It's Emma to you. This is my grandfather, Paul Riley, and my daughter, Riley London."

Charles shook hands with Pop, then turned to Riley. "It's a real pleasure to meet you, Miss London."

"Whoa. You can call me Riley."

"I'm afraid I can't, Miss London. Protocol." He winked

and, when our bags came, put them on the cart and walked us out to the sedan. The plates said LONDON3.

My grandfather cut me a look. "I guess the dragon lady couldn't be here to meet you in person," he muttered.

Charles held the doors for us and then got in himself.

It was about an hour's drive to Stoningham, and the Connecticut highway was about as bland as could be until we got past Middletown. Then Connecticut began to show its rural side—the rolling hills and tiny towns with sweet names . . . Middle Haddam, Chester, Deep River, Old Lyme. Riley peppered Charles with questions about where we were, what there was to do in Stoningham, if he'd worked for Genevieve for a long time.

The trip had already improved her mood. For one, there was no doubt now that she was indeed related to Genevieve London, much to her friends' surprise. Jenna had even invited Riley over, but Riley told her she had other plans (meaning we stayed home and watched *Odd Mom Out*). That made me proud, the fact that Riley hadn't been fooled by her friend's sudden re-interest. But going to Connecticut for the summer, staying at Sheerwater (yes, I was allowed in its sacred halls once again) . . . that had given my daughter some swagger. And however it had come, she needed it.

When I called Genevieve back and told her we were coming—including Pop, who would be staying elsewhere—there'd been a long pause. "Thank you," she finally said.

"On one condition, Genevieve," I said. "You do not mention money or inheritance to Riley. Not a whisper, not a hint. I don't want you dangling your bank accounts in front of my daughter and snatching them away if she uses the wrong fork."

"By which I assume you're referring to the fact that I didn't fund your teenage folly."

"Teenage folly? You mean your great-granddaughter? Yes. This summer isn't about the money. It's us giving you a chance to make amends, and you making me Hope's guardian."

"How very gracious you are, my dear," she said, and I heard a slurp. Five o'clock somewhere.

But she agreed, and here we were.

My clients, the ones I saw in person, were fine with me leaving for two months. I'd TheraTalk with most of them; two were about done anyway, and said they'd call me if they needed me. I'd had to give up my office space, though; luckily, a classmate from my PhD program had sublet it. Once I got back, I'd have to find another space, but I'd deal with that later.

Pop had found himself a little apartment over an antiques shop on Water Street. I was unspeakably grateful that he'd be nearby. He'd always hated Genevieve, who had viewed my mother as insufficient wife material for her wretched son.

Then again, she had a point. My mother had taken her own life. Maybe Genevieve had sensed something, even back then. She was many things, but she wasn't stupid.

We crossed the Connecticut River, then the Thames. "There's the Coast Guard Academy, Pop," I said, pointing. He was an Air Force man himself, but he nodded. We went through Mystic, and I remembered going to the aquarium with Jason on a date. Or a field trip, maybe, but we'd held hands. Kissed in the dim light of the myriad fish tanks, and it had felt like the most romantic thing in the world.

He knew we were coming, of course. He was excited, he'd said on the phone. Talked about being separated, wasn't sure where things were headed there. The boys couldn't wait to meet Riley in person, though they knew her from Skype and phone calls.

My heart leaped into overdrive when, just before we hit Rhode Island, Charles exited the highway and entered the land of stone walls and gracious houses, tall oaks and two-hundred-year-old farms. The woods and fields gave way to narrower streets, and we went over the bridge that led to the borough.

Welcome to Stoningham, the sign said.

I found that I was holding my grandfather's thumb, same as I had when I was little, back before my mother died, when seeing my grandparents was the happiest thing ever. He gave my hand a squeeze.

"Oh, my gosh, this town is so cute!" Riley said.

And it was. The sky was Maxfield Parrish blue, the lights of the Colonials that lined the streets glowing in what seemed to be a welcome. People were out, walking their dogs. At the library green, some kids tossed a football. As we came onto Water Street, Riley exclaimed over the little shops and restaurants. "There's a café, Mom! Hooray! Oh, and an ice cream place! Even better!"

I smiled, but my stomach cramped again. It felt like I had never left.

The town hadn't changed much. Still adorable with its colorful buildings and crooked streets. I caught glimpses of Long Island Sound as we drove, smelled garlic and seafood. Would Genevieve have dinner for us? Would she hug me? I swore if she made Riley feel one iota of shame, we'd be out of Connecticut forever.

Charles turned onto Bleak Point Road, where the most expensive houses in town sat like grand old ladies, weathered and gracious. All had names, which Riley read aloud as we passed.

"Thrush Hill. Summerly. Wisteria Cottage. Cliff View. Pop, we have to name our house when we get back!"

"Name it what? Crabgrass?" Pop asked.

"That's kind of perfect, actually," I murmured, having gone to war many times with weeds in our small yard.

"Oh, Sheerwater! We're here!"

The iron gates (yes, gates) opened, and we turned onto the crushed-shell drive. Sheerwater had ten acres of land, the very tip of Bleak Point, and it looked like a park, with beautifully gnarled dogwood trees on either side of the driveway, their intertwined branches making a tunnel of white blossoms. Spring was late this year.

We rounded the gentle curve, and my hands were sweating now.

"Holy guacamole," my daughter breathed. "It's even prettier than the pictures!" In the rearview mirror, I saw Charles smile. Beside me, Pop stiffened. He'd never been here, of course.

There it was—my grandmother's twenty-room cottage, pristine and gracious and lit up like the fires of hell.

CHAPTER 8

Genevieve

'd been waiting for them to arrive all day, and had busied myself pretending I wasn't. I reframed this summer as me doing *them* a favor, welcoming all three of them to Sheerwater, the most beautiful home in Connecticut, or at least in the top ten.

And yes, the three of them. That supercilious Paul was coming, since he didn't consider me trustworthy, despite the fact that *I* was the one who'd taken in Emma, thank you very much.

All day long, I'd prepared, dressing carefully, plucking hairs from my chin, taking even more time than usual with my hair and makeup. We'd readied the house; the dogs were impossible to keep up with, their fur everywhere, the occasional clump of vomited grass that had gone undetected, and so we'd requested a bigger cleaning crew than usual. I'd given Donelle the list of things to be done, and she, once a moderately competent domestic, had relayed the information to the various crews. She forgot so many details when giving orders . . . but I'd had another episode the other day, and the idea of my blanking while talking to the help was . . . intolerable.

Oh, it was a small thing. We'd been watching a movie last week, Donelle and I. Unlike Donelle, I didn't also tap-tap-tap at a computer while watching. Why watch a movie if one really wanted to shop for magnetic eyelashes, her latest and most bizarre online purchase?

At any rate, we were in the den, an oak-paneled room with leather couches and an enormous TV on the wall. Once, Garrison and I read in here in the evenings, back when reading was a given, not something destined to make my eyes strained and tired. Even so, this was usually my favorite time of day—my work, such as it was, finished, dinner over, no one in the house except Helga, Donelle and me. Charles had his own apartment over the garage, and Helga never joined us in the main house, preferring her own living room in the servants' wing.

Minuet lay in my lap, enjoying the worship I was lavishing upon her. Valkyrie sprawled next to Donelle on the other couch, shedding on the leather. Maximilian, who was a touch senile, was woofing softly at his reflection, confused as to who that other Great Pyrenees–golden retriever mutt was, also afflicted with patchy fur. Allegra, the pug, had found her spot next to the couch and was snoring softly through her poor, tormented airway—her pinched nostrils and elongated palate making her sneeze and gasp like a Channel swimmer. Carmen, the miniature poodle, was sulking in the corner, as I had just raised my voice at her for expressing her anal glands on the carpet.

I wasn't sure when I'd broken down and acquired so many dogs. One day I'd been asked to speak at a benefit for the Stoningham Animal Shelter, and the next day, I had three dogs—Carmen, Valkyrie and Allegra, none of whom I adored. Maximilian came next. (At the time, he'd been quite beautiful and regal, though regrettably, that didn't last. His breed aged quickly.)

Minuet was my most recent acquisition, and favorite, I'll admit. She was flawlessly behaved, unlike the other dogs, and her coat was heaven. Though my wrist was stiff and achy these days, I loved stroking her, her fur impossibly soft against my palm. I paused for just a second, and Minuet raised her tiny head and looked at me with those adorable brown eyes. "Yes, yes," I murmured, resuming. "Forgive me." Then I glanced back at the television.

Suddenly, I had no idea what the movie was about. None. Granted, Allegra had just sneezed and coughed again, but it was as if the previous moments were gone, eaten by the brain tumor. There were men on the screen, and they weren't modern men, it seemed. The African American man and the white man were special friends. They were in one of those . . . My mind reached for the word and kept groping. What *was* it called? A house? A cellar? A locking house? That was almost right, but not quite.

"Why are they in the lock house?" I asked Donelle. She knew about my diagnosis, of course.

"In jail, you mean? Because they're murderers. Well, Andy's innocent, Red isn't. Still, I like him best."

Jail. Andy. Red. Red was a famous actor. God. He'd played God in something. His face was very kind. I *hoped* God looked like him, in fact. I supposed I'd find out soon.

"You having one of your spells?" Donelle asked. Valkyrie let out a long hiss of noxious gas.

"What have you fed that dog?" I snapped. "And yes." I looked down at Minuet. What if the brain tumor made me forget how to care for my little dog? What if I hurt her somehow?

Donelle came over and sat next to me on the couch, dressed in ridiculous pajamas with monkeys on them. "Don't worry, Gen. It'll pass."

The sting of tears surprised me. Mac woofed at his reflection and pawed the glass, reminding me of what was to come if I let this . . . this *tumor* get out of control.

"I'd like to practice tomorrow," I said.

"Sure thing, hon."

Because Emma was coming soon, and I had to be ready.

The Shawshank Redemption, that's what this was. Morgan Freeman and what's-his-name. The one who'd been Susan Sarandon's common-law husband. Not knowing his name didn't concern me, since, to be honest, he had peaked early in his career. Not like Paul Newman.

Garrison had had a little Paul Newman about him. Beautiful bone structure.

At any rate, the episode was several days ago. This morning, I'd been a bit dizzy; I hadn't slept well, and who could blame me, with Emma coming back after all these years? Otherwise, I was fine. Just fine. Now dinner was in the oven, and a local girl was staying to serve and clear, though I had no idea if she knew how. We may have used her at Christmas, but I couldn't remember.

The cleaning service had scrubbed the carpet where Carmen had relieved herself, and washed all the hardwood floors, scoured the kitchen and put fresh sheets on the beds. New towels in the bathrooms. Floral arrangements everywhere—Emma would have her father's old room; I'd redecorated it in the palest, most feminine yellow to spite him when he didn't come home for four years running. Also, I was rather known for my home décor. One had to refresh the look every few years.

Only Sheppard's room remained the same.

And Emma's, more or less.

I thought the child might like staying in her mother's old room.

Riley. Not a real name, for heaven's sake . . . Was there something wrong with Catherine or Elizabeth? I knew Emma's mother's maiden name was Riley, of course, but did one really want to saddle a child with the name of a woman who committed suicide? Apparently so.

I'd had my travel agent book their flights so they'd land after dark. The thought of an entire day with Emma and the anticipated accusatory glare was simply too much. It was nearly dark now, the sky that particular shade of heartache blue.

Garrison had died in early June, on an evening such as this.

The Missing gnashed its sharp teeth, ever hungry. Life would have been so different if Garrison were here, a distinguished grandfather in a tweed coat, eager to meet his progeny, smelling of pipe smoke and scotch. I would've been a better grandmother, had I not had to do everything alone. Alone, and emotionally hardened all these years.

Garrison had been so much more than my spouse. He was the only other person who had loved Sheppard nearly as much as I did. The only other person who felt the Missing the way I did.

The crunch of a car on the driveway announced their arrival. Unexpectedly, I felt a twinge of nervousness run through me. "Get the door, Donelle, won't you?" I said. She rolled her eyes and got up. "Not yet!" I snapped. "When they ring the bell."

"Yes, Your Majesty," Donelle said.

"I'm sorry, have I overtaxed you today? Shall I rub your feet and spoon-feed you soup?"

"It's not that. It's you being all fake, like you're not dying to see them."

"I'm not dying to see them. I'm simply dying."

Another eye roll. The urge to fire her was strong.

The bell rang, and I picked Minuet up from her cushion and stood in front of the fireplace, suddenly self-conscious. I was wearing a dress by Vivienne Westwood—summer white wool with black checks—and a vintage Tiffany carved jade-ite cabochon necklace that had been my mother's. The Cartier watch with a green leather band. The Stuart Weitzman black pumps. One did have to keep up appearances, and quality items aged well.

It was a pity that Emma hadn't cared about those things when she was a girl here. Perhaps we could've been closer if she'd shown even a little interest in my work. My empire. My solace.

Instead, she'd been only interested in feeling sorry for herself and, later, obsessed with that boy.

They were inside now. The dogs were barking, all except perfect Minuet. Mac ran outside, but Charles would catch him. Besides, Sheerwater was a fenced-in property. The dog would be safe.

They were all in the foyer now. That wretched Paul, Emma, her bastard child. Donelle hugged them, the traitor, rather spoiling the moment, which I'd wanted to be a bit of a power play, to be honest. I set Minuet down on her red velvet pillow, where she curled up in a tiny circle, then looked at the tableau in the foyer.

For a second, my breath stopped, and I felt dizzy, as if I were floating. It must've been that brain tumor again, no matter what Dr. Pinco had said in his gentle, too-kind way.

Emma had grown up. She was a woman now, not a girl, and she'd turned out rather . . . well, pretty, if in a common way. She certainly hadn't dressed to impress and wore jeans and a white oxford shirt. Valkyrie nosed her hand, and she petted her head idly, not looking away from me.

The child standing next to her was tall and lanky, with hair the color of fire. She looked over at me, and raised an eyebrow.

"You must be the famous Genevieve London," she said, taking a few steps toward me.

"And you must be my great-granddaughter," I answered. I looked her up and down. Leggings, for heaven's sake, and a sweatshirt that said *DePaul University*. Hair in that maddening half ponytail, where the girl seems too lazy to pull her hair all the way through the elastic.

She offered her hand, and I shook it. At least she had a strong grip, and I felt an unexpected . . . connection. She smiled, and then I noticed her eyes.

They were gloriously blue.

Like Sheppard's. The shape, the color, that pure, perfect blue, proof of God's mighty hand, eyes into which one could stare for hours, marveling at the beauty and depth of that breathtaking color.

I pulled my hand back and drew in a shaking breath. To cover, I said, "Clearly, we must go shopping. You're a young woman from an important family. There's no need to look homeless."

The child cut a look to Emma. "I'm a young woman from an important family, Mom," she said.

"Of course you are," that wretched old man said. "You're a Riley."

"And a London," I said.

"Her important family didn't care much for her when she was born," Emma said.

"You resemble my mother," I murmured for the girl's ears alone.

Alas, Emma also heard. "And mine," she couldn't resist saying. There was the expected accusatory glare. But, yes, April had had red hair, as I recalled.

I looked once again at the girl, who raised an eyebrow at me, a smile playing at her lips. Riley. It might grow on me. Riley London. Her name represented both sides of Emma's family, and I felt an unwilling twinge of respect for Emma. At least she hadn't given her daughter the last name of Finlay. Why honor the boy who impregnated you and let you waltz off with your unborn child?

Jason Finlay was a waste of cells.

"If we're done peeing on the kid to mark ownership,"

said Donelle, "would anyone else like a drink? I know I'm ready. Mr. Riley, what will you have, hon?"

He looked at her a minute. "A beer, please."

"You got it. Shaylee!" she bellowed. "Come out here."

Shaylee, that was it, the girl from town. Donelle gave her our drink orders. The child was offered soda but asked for water instead, and I was pleased. Better for the complexion, and no calories.

"Shaylee, please take the dogs and put them outside," I said. "No, not Minuet. She can stay." Shaylee, silent as a stone, herded the dogs out of the room.

"How many dogs do you have?" the child asked.

"Five. I'm rather a soft touch."

No one said anything. The point was made. Well. It was time to regain the upper hand.

"Riley, is it?" I asked, as if I hadn't hired a private investigator a month after Emma left. Riley Olivia London. "It's very nice to meet you, dear. This is Donelle, my housekeeper."

"And best friend," Donelle added.

"My companion," I said. "And a dear friend."

"It's nice to meet you both," Riley said. "Your home is beautiful."

I smiled. At least she had good taste.

"So this is Minuet?" she asked. "Hi, cutie! Can I pick her up?"

May I. "Of course, dear. She's three years old and quite friendly."

"You're adorable, Minuet! Mom, look! Isn't she sweet? You are, little fluff ball."

Emma glanced over and gave a stiff smile. She and Paul stood there, several steps behind Riley, like the Secret Service, protecting her from my nefarious plans.

"Would you like to wash up, Riley?" I asked. "Brush your hair, change for dinner?"

She smiled at me, clearly catching the hint. "Sure. Which room is mine?"

"I thought you'd enjoy staying in your mother's old room. Go up the front staircase, take a left and follow the hall all the way down. It's the pale pink room."

"Thank you." She put Minuet back on the window seat and left the room. Excellent posture, and none of that stomping so common in girls her age. Quite graceful, in fact, moving in that fluid way of a runway model.

"Does she take ballet?" I asked.

"Soccer," Emma said.

"I see." I took a deep breath and, for the first time, looked directly at my granddaughter. "Hello, Emma. You look healthy."

"As do you, for a woman dying of cancer. How *is* your health, by the way?"

None of your business, I wanted to say. "I'm doing well, thank you, but let's not discuss such a personal matter just now. Paul, you're more than welcome to unpack and refresh yourself in a guest room. A man of your age must be quite tired after the journey." I was older than he was, but why not go for a dig?

"I got a place in town."

"Have you?" *Thank heavens.* "I hope you'll be quite comfortable there. Charles will be happy to take you to your accommodations after dinner."

"I don't need your limousine, Genevieve. I'm only here for the summer to watch out for my girls and make sure you don't mess with Riley. She's a great kid, that one, so keep your hooks out of her."

"Why would I put hooks in anyone? I'm dying, Paul."

"Get on with it, then."

"Thank you for your concern."

"I'm not concerned. I'm eager."

Honestly. The man had hated me since we'd first met, and frankly, the feeling was mutual. He and his wife . . . Betty or Ellen or Joan, something plain . . . had been so smug, so *tender* with each other. Granted, she'd been in a wheelchair because of her ALS, but even so. They rubbed their coupledom in my face. And the way they talked about their daughter (before her death, granted), how *talented* and *creative* she was—she'd wanted to be a chef, I now recalled—how she had ambitions, how Clark should do more than work on his novels (as if Clark had any skills at all). They made it clear, however; April had dreams as well, and Clark should do more to encourage her.

I did think they oversold her talents. April cooked for me a time or two when I visited, and it was decent enough, but hardly Michelin-star quality. How creative did one have to be in order to be a cook? Helga was a cook, and I was quite sure no one ever used the word *creative* in describing her cuisine.

The truth was, I never got to know April very well before she died. Afterward, it was difficult to sympathize with someone who'd abandoned her child, especially when my child had been stolen from me. I knew depression was a legitimate illness; it was simply hard to imagine committing suicide when one had an eight-year-old.

I hadn't. I'd wanted to and I hadn't.

Once I had custody of Emma, Paul became quite the authority on raising children, when look how his had turned out. That didn't stop him from lecturing me on what Emma needed, a child I had never asked to care for, a child they were more than happy to let me take. The *advice*, as if I needed parenting guidance. Hadn't I been Sheppard's mother, after all? And then there was the pain, their grief, dripping out of them for all the world to see. *You aren't the only ones who've ever lost a child!* I wanted to scream. *At least mine didn't throw away her life!*

But, of course, those things went unsaid. Clark wanted me to take Emma; Paul's wife—what *was* her name?—had that horrible Lou Gehrig's disease and was wasting away, the poor thing. She, at least, hadn't been hateful. Naive and poorly educated, but that was hardly her fault.

"We gonna stand here all day?" Paul asked.

"Emma?" I asked. "Would you care to freshen up? I've put you in your father's old room, the one overlooking the wisteria bower."

"I'm fine," she said. We eyed each other a moment, and I kept my face neutral. So did she. Where was that drink?

"Is it strange to be back?" Donelle asked.

"It's like I never left," she said.

"Sorry to hear that," Paul said.

Shayla or whatever her name was finally brought me a martini. I sipped it and suppressed a sigh. No lemon. Young people today and their ridiculous drinks. I'd have to speak to her later.

"Just to remind you again, Genevieve," Emma said quietly, "I don't want you speaking to Riley about any possible inheritance."

Donelle sputtered. I ignored her.

"Of course not. That would be entirely too crass," I said.

"I wanted to be clear," Emma said. She stared at me, and there was something very different about her. A hardness. No, a strength. Oh, she might despise me for showing her the door all those years ago, but she had been too soft, too easily manipulated back then. Too much like her father. If she hadn't been, she never would've gotten pregnant in the first place.

Sometimes, a firm kick in the pants is what someone needs, whether they know it or not.

Riley came downstairs again, wearing a cheap knit black dress that was far too short. At least she had tried. I'd take her shopping. She was a London, and she should look like one. We'd visit the headquarters and she could have her pick from the showroom, Beverly Jane be damned. Riley's hair was brushed and gleaming, and my fingers itched to pull it back into a bun. She had a lovely neck.

"Mom, you should see my bathroom," she said. Then she laughed. "Oh, wait, I guess you have! I love the tub. It's huge. And there's a shower and the closet is practically bigger than my room at home. The bed is the size of a boat." She cut a glance at her grandfather. "Not that I need a bigger bed, Pop. You know I love mine."

He smiled the faintest bit, and I gathered there was a story attached to the bed. I imagined he'd made it for her, carving it like Joseph making a cradle for the baby Jesus, since martyrdom did seem to run in their side of the family.

"I'm glad you like it, dear," I said. "I'll give you a full tour of the house tomorrow, so you can appreciate its history."

Emma was quiet, looking at me. I drank more of my lemon-free martini. Thank God for gin. "Tell me about yourself, Riley," I said.

"Well," she answered blithely, "I'm the bastard child of a teen mother, as you know."

Donelle snorted; Emma and Paul smiled. Personally, I was not amused. "Do go on."

"I'll be a senior this fall, I'm an honors student, I play soccer and like to read."

"We have a library here. Just down the center hall on the left."

"Cool. Tell me about yourself, um . . . Genevieve."

How utterly refreshing! A child—a teenager, no less—asking an adult about herself! "I'm the founder and CEO of a design company, as I hope you know."

"Retired CEO," Donelle said. I cut her a look.

"I definitely do know," said Riley. "All my friends love your stuff."

As they should. "I also like to read, and I graduated summa cum laude from both Foxcroft Academy and Barnard. Are you planning to attend college, dear?"

"I am. I'm hoping to go to Notre Dame."

A pity. If she had the grades to get into Notre Dame, she could get into an Ivy League school. "Have you been raised Catholic, then?"

"Mm-hm."

I suppressed a sigh. A deliberate slap in my face, of course. Emma had *not* been raised Catholic. She'd been nothing till she got here, though her mother had been "technically Catholic." *I* had taken Emma to the United Methodist church every Sunday she'd lived with me.

"Are we ever gonna eat?" Paul said.

"How gracious of you to ask, Paul. Of course. Please, into the dining room. Helga made us something very special." What that was, I couldn't remember, though I knew I'd given her very specific instructions. Ah, well, it was sure to be an unpleasant evening, whatever was being served.

"Does this something special have arsenic in it?" Emma asked, confirming my prediction.

"Just the gruel and stale bread you grew up on," I answered pleasantly. "I knew you'd want your favorites."

"Interesting that you could get rid of your grandchild but not an incompetent cook." She pulled out a dining room chair and sat down hard. Paul blew his nose in a napkin, and Donelle was already half in the bag.

From the backyard, I could hear Mac howling. I knew exactly how he felt.

CHAPTER 9

Emma

Much to my surprise, I slept like the dead my first night at Sheerwater, waking when the sun hit my face. I opened my eyes and glanced at the clock. Quarter to seven. Too early. If her schedule hadn't changed, Genevieve slept till eight thirty every day like it was a commandment. She did not appreciate noise before she had her café au lait.

I sat up and looked around. Last night, I'd been too tired and tense to take in any details, aside from the half dozen dogs running around, farting, scooting their butts on the carpet, wrestling, snarling.

I had nothing against dogs. I loved dogs. In fact, I'd *begged* for a dog when I lived here, and guess what? The answer had been no. Sheerwater was far too impressive a home to allow dogs to ravage the place. Now, Genevieve had five. Five.

Everything she did felt like a slap in the face. Then again, why would that be any different now?

I'd been put in what had been my father's room, but Genevieve had changed it at some point in the past seventeen years. Whereas I remembered it being hunter green with white wainscoting, it was now the palest yellow, the window seat cushion upholstered in green, yellow and blue floral fabric, throw pillows in pastel shades. All my father's things—his model airplanes and Hardy Boys books, knick-knacks, Yankees pennant and an old musket from the Revolutionary War—were gone.

To be fair, he'd told me he never read the books. Funny that I'd remember that. In the ten years I'd lived with Genevieve, my father had visited only ten times: every Christmas Day. And while the house looked like a movie set, the holiday itself was always chilly.

I'd called Clark and told him I was coming here. Told him his mother was sick, which he hadn't known. He didn't seem all that concerned. "Guess everyone dies someday," he'd said, which was about on par for my father's depth. I'd long since stopped hoping he and I would bond, but it would've been nice to have an ally, the both of us united against Genevieve in some way. I reminded him that Genevieve was Hope's guardian, and he'd grunted. Nothing more.

"Is it okay with you if I become Hope's guardian?" I asked.

"I guess," he said, and I gritted my teeth and said a terse goodbye.

I didn't know why his lack of interest surprised me. He'd always been an absentee father. I wondered if he knew he was being cut out of Gigi's will . . . or if in fact he *was* being cut. Gigi had never liked her second son, but she was a stickler for tradition.

Genevieve. Not Gigi. Gigi sounded fun and lively, like a young-for-her-age grandmother who'd play hide-and-seek or make a fort on a snowy winter day.

I wondered how she was with Hope, if she cuddled her and read her books, or if she just looked on, her mouth a razor slash of disapproval. Well. Hope had me, and I'd be visiting her later today.

I went into the adjoining bathroom (Sheerwater had eight full bathrooms). Mine had been updated—maybe they all had been, and it was now a lesson in fabulosity—all white marble and tile, plus white towels, tiger maple cabinets and a deep soaking tub where I could sit and look out over the Sound. There was a glass shower, towel warmer, indented shelves on which sat potted white orchids and a copy of Genevieve's coffee-table book, *Life with Genevieve.* Ha. I should write a lurid tell-all. *She was a cold bitch, really. I don't remember a single hug.*

At least I'd be comfortable here. Physically, anyway. Maybe later I'd take a bath, but first, I wanted to check on my daughter.

That view, though. That was a good view. The sky was pure blue, the Sound behind it smooth as glass. The grass was emerald and lush, cut on a diagonal by Genevieve's gardener or yard service. Beneath me, the wisteria bloomed in what Genevieve called the bower—a huge trellis that sheltered an outdoor sitting area. I used to read there, curled into one of the wicker chairs, the smell of the blooms so sweet. If Genevieve found me, I'd get a lecture on posture and sitting with ankles crossed.

Sheerwater sat on the end of Bleak Point, jutting out into Long Island Sound. The lawn was probably at least a couple of acres, and the seawall was stone. There was a private dock, too. To the south of the lawn was the rose garden, set in a circle with rows extending like rays of the sun, and past that, a little forest of pine and oak trees. I used to be afraid of those woods, convinced someone would take me the way my uncle Sheppard had been taken. Or murdered.

I looked a little closer. Someone was out there. A man. He stared out at the water, hands stuffed in his pockets.

That was Genevieve's land, and she wasn't the sharing

type. Could it be Jason? Was he here to see Riley? If so, he was early; we were meeting for lunch.

My phone chimed. A text from a patient, asking if we could reschedule.

When I looked back out at the forest, the man was gone. I'd ask Genevieve. Or Donelle, who had actually seemed happy to see me yesterday. If he was a trespasser, someone should know, especially now that Riley was here.

I went down the hall. To think that my kid might inherit this place was overwhelming. This was Kardashian-level money. Well, not that, maybe, but a lot of money. The artwork in here had to be worth a ton in itself. The Turkish carpets (despite whatever dog secretions they were infused with), the signed first edition of *To Kill a Mockingbird*, the furniture, both the new and the antiques.

I almost hoped it *wouldn't* go to Riley. Money had a tendency to ruin people, to alienate them and isolate them and make them wretched and alone or, worse, surrounded by people who only wanted a piece.

Well, as Pop had said, Genevieve's true intentions wouldn't be clear until she was dead and the will was read. For a woman with a brain tumor, she sure looked healthy. Three martinis last night, and not a wobble in her step. I'd asked Calista for info and read up on her condition, but Genevieve would need to tell me the stage, the location, the plan of treatment. I planned to go to her doctor's appointments with her.

If nothing else, Riley would have a memorable summer of privilege. A summer away from those abruptly nasty girls.

For a second, I stood in front of my old room. When I'd first come here, a heartbroken eight-year-old, I'd had a lot of hope. After all, orphans fared okay, right? Annie of the brain-worm songs about tomorrow? Anne of Green Gables? Surely my grandmother would love me just as much as Anne and Annie had been loved.

I'd been wrong about that.

I opened the door. Riley was sprawled like a starfish on her back, sound asleep, and I crawled into the king-size bed and looked at her. Those perfect lips, so red and curved, open a little, as she was a mouth-breather when sleeping. The space between her front teeth I loved so much. Her freckles . . . When she was little and they began to pop up, I'd kiss each new little speck and tell her it tasted like cinnamon or chocolate. I loved the smell of her, a little salt, a little morning breath, her citrusy shampoo.

Dinner last night had been endless. The table was set with full pomp, a low flower arrangement of hyacinths, roses and ivy (the color scheme matching the china and dining room décor, naturally). A twentysomething woman had served without speaking as Helga, my grandmother's cook, brooded in the kitchen. Helga nodded when she saw me. That was all, which was exactly how I remembered her—silent, morose, a terrible cook, able to drain the flavor from every food group, every time. The server may have been under orders not to speak, or, knowing both Genevieve and Helga, mute. They'd prefer it that way.

Donelle had been lively, Pop grumpy, Genevieve and I warily staring at each other, or not staring at each other. Riley had been oddly at ease, asking both Genevieve and Donelle questions about the house, Connecticut, the town.

And Genevieve asked questions as well, each of them a veiled insult.

Do you have a beau, Riley? Your mother was quite precocious that way. Lest my daughter forget I was in high school when she was conceived. No blame for Jason, of course. It was as if I'd gotten myself pregnant.

You don't mind playing such a masculine sport? Concussion rates are quite high in soccer, I hear. That was directed at me, implying I didn't know how to keep my child safe. Ironic, coming from a woman who'd lost her child. Literally lost him. I raised an eyebrow a centimeter, just to let her know what I was thinking, and she'd looked away, coming back with another question for Riley.

And the one that got to me the most: *Do you mind having red hair? No? Good for you.*

My mother had had red hair, and I'm sure Genevieve remembered that. The implication was, *Hopefully that's all you inherited from her.*

Genevieve and I had a language all our own.

"Her hair is beautiful," Pop growled. "People stop her on the street to tell her so."

"Of course they do," Genevieve murmured. "It's quite distinctive."

My death grip on my fork tightened, and I stabbed my tasteless roast beef with gusto, wishing it were my grandmother's petrified heart.

But Riley answered blithely. Didn't want a boyfriend yet. Loved having red hair. Never had a concussion, knock on wood, and had started playing varsity her sophomore year.

I knew my daughter. She'd want Genevieve to like her, and Genevieve would like her just enough to stab her with disapproval as soon as Riley thought she was in. It had been the pattern of my life here.

Riley stirred now, groaning a little. Her thick red-gold lashes fluttered, and she opened her eyes a crack, smiled, then rolled against me. "Hi, Mama," she said.

Mama. The word nestled against my heart, warm and precious. "Good morning, angel. Did you sleep well?"

"Yes, but this creepy stalker lady was lying in my bed when I woke up."

I smiled. "I'll tell her to get a life and leave you alone."

Riley stretched and yawned. "This bed is the most comfortable bed I've ever slept in," she said. "Don't tell Pop."

Pop had made her bed himself. It was a twin, not like this king-size monster.

"Nothing but the best for Genevieve," I said.

"It's like the nicest hotel in the world."

"Want me to show you around before Genevieve gives you the historical importance tour?" I asked.

"Okay!" She bounced out of bed.

"We have to be quiet, though," I said, getting up as well. "Genevieve will be asleep for another hour and a half, and Donelle longer than that."

"Where are their rooms?"

"Donelle's is on the first floor. Genevieve has the master wing up here on the western side."

"Of course she does." Riley went into the bathroom, then poked her head out. "This bathroom is worth the whole trip, Mom."

A minute later, we went down the hall, whispering, our bare feet silent against the walnut floor and soft runners. "This is a Toulouse-Lautrec," I said, pointing to a sketch.

"That sounds very expensive," Riley murmured, and I smiled. She knew who the artist was, and the relief that she was being herself again—happy, cheeky, sweet enough to get out of bed to spend time with her mother—filled me with gratitude.

I had to hand it to Genevieve—she really did have excellent taste. Nothing was garish, nothing shouted money, not like the Newport houses with their solid brass chairs and ceilings painted with gold leaf. . . . the "I have more!" school of decorating. No, Genevieve was old Yankee money. Every piece of furniture was beautifully made but functional as well, with clean lines and the best materials. She'd updated the look since I left, bought some new pieces, renovated here and there.

It was still the loveliest home I'd ever seen, comfortable and welcoming (unlike its owner) . . . a true home and not a showplace.

"Another guest room," I said, opening a door. "Gloria Vanderbilt stayed here once. Genevieve's friend."

"Who's Gloria Vanderbilt?"

Ah, youth. "Anderson Cooper's mother," I said.

"Really? Cool!" The room, like all the others, was tasteful, warm and impressive, with views of the water from nearly every window. "Can we go swimming later?"

"Sure. It's cold out there, though."

"I don't care." She opened the next door. "Whose room is this?"

It suddenly dawned on me that I should've given Riley a fuller history on the lost son of Sheerwater. Then again, I didn't know a whole lot about him myself, not really.

When I was little, my father had told me that he'd had an older brother who had gone missing when Clark was five or six. Clark had no memory of him and didn't talk about him. But living here, I'd picked up on the bigger story. No one was allowed to say that Sheppard was dead. Apparently, he'd vanished without a trace. Genevieve never had told me more about her firstborn. All she said was for me to stay out of his room. Which I had done.

Riley went right in, and I leaned in the doorway.

The room was preserved, and exactly as I recalled. I remembered peeking in here as a kid; I'd loved the wallpaper, which had blue and red race cars on it. Once it was outdated; now it was totally retro chic. My uncle had liked dinosaurs, based on the number of plastic creatures on the shelves. The twin bed was made up with same blue-and-red quilt I remembered, though its color had faded somewhat. A desk with a green-shaded banker's lamp, a window seat, a red pedal car, a wing chair by the window.

I imagined Genevieve sitting there, staring out at the ocean, waiting for her little boy to come home, and my heart clenched with sympathy. I knew why she was the way she was, after all. It was a shame she'd only had room in her heart for one.

"This was my uncle's room," I said, clearing my throat. "Sheppard. He died when he was little."

"Really?" came that voice, and I jumped. Genevieve stood in the hallway, her white hair perfect, a navy robe wrapped tightly around her still-damn-good figure, the tiniest of the dog pack clutched in her arms. "Don't speak about what you don't know, Emma."

Anger radiated off her, her lips thin with it, her eyes arctic cold. The other, sloppier dogs charged down the hall, racing past us and clattering down the stairs.

"Just repeating what my father told me, Genevieve," I said.

"Your father is an idiot."

"So he's *not* dead?" Riley asked. "Sheppard?"

Genevieve took a deep breath. "His body was never found, dear. It's possible he was kidnapped."

"Whoa. I didn't know that. And you never found out what happened?"

"We never did." My grandmother's gaze slithered toward me.

"That's so sad. I'm sorry, um . . . Grandma."

She smiled a little at that. "You're very kind. And you may call me Gigi," she said. "Would you like a *proper* tour of the house? It's your home for the summer, after all." She paused. "I would ask that you stay out of this room, however. As you may be able to tell, it's very special to me."

"Of course." Riley looked at me. "Do you mind, Mom?"

Genevieve set down the tiny dog and tightened the sash of her robe. "Helga will make you breakfast, Emma. She's quite adept at an egg-white omelet." Translation: *You need to lose weight. Look at me. I weigh the same as I did on my wedding day.*

I'd warned Riley about my grandmother and her subtle ways of undermining self-esteem.

It's fine, Riley mouthed.

"Okay," I said. "Have fun."

I ate the tasteless egg-white omelet. I'd tried to make my own breakfast, was denied, and when I asked for whole eggs, Helga looked me in the eye as she separated the whites and dumped the yolks in the sink. Unbuttered toast. Skim milk, no half-and-half.

I spent the rest of the morning unpacking. Last night, I told Genevieve I'd need a room to work, and when I explained online therapy, she snorted. "People just love to indulge in their misery, don't they? Well, if it pays your bills, fine."

It did. Sort of. Barely. I had $96,475 in student debt, the cost of my shared office space, a car payment and upkeep, rent to my grandfather (at my insistence, since we'd lived for free for years and I worried about his own bank account). Groceries, two-thirds of our utilities, Riley's school expenses (activity fees and sports fees and the ridiculous list of school supplies each year). Health insurance. Car insurance. Gas. Saving for her college. Clothes for a teenage girl who was still growing. Cell phone and service. Internet. Credit-card-debt payments. The fees that covered my license to practice psychology, membership to the American Psychological Association, malpractice insurance. The conferences I was required to attend to keep my certification. Taxes.

Then there are the things you don't think about. Haircuts. Veterinary care for the "free" kitten we got when Riley was seven, only to find it had a heart condition and spend $750 that we couldn't afford on the poor little thing and have it die anyway. School pictures. Field trip costs. A new washing machine. Gifts for Riley's friends' birthdays, my coworkers' baby showers and weddings.

Life was expensive, even when you got child support. Jason worked in his family's construction business and made a fairly decent living, but he wasn't rich. I was proud that Riley had had a pretty normal childhood because of my financial savvy . . . especially given that we lived in Downers Grove, which had been a humble working-class town when Pop bought his house but had grown into a wealthy, desirable suburb.

Which was a long way of saying I couldn't afford to take the summer off and needed every client I could get.

Genevieve had granted me use of a room on Sheerwater's ground floor. The giant house was built on a slight hill, so it was essentially the walk-out basement but, as was the rest of the house, beautifully done. A home theater, gym, yoga studio (seriously), the dogs' playroom (again . . . seriously) and this room, my summer office.

While it was small by comparison to other rooms in Sheerwater, it was easily quadruple the size of my office at home. The room had a built-in desk that lined one wall, a couch and sliders out to the flagstone patio that was shaded by the main-floor deck. The patio had chaise lounges and a firepit, and the view of the lawn went all the way to the water.

I'd forgotten how very lovely Sheerwater was. In my memory, it was more formal; in person, it was simply perfect.

Hard to imagine my sixteen-year-old inheriting a mansion. I'd have to talk to a lawyer and probably hire a financial adviser, because this was out of my league.

I caught a glimpse of Genevieve and Riley walking across the lawn, my daughter's hair glowing in the sun. They were arm in arm.

Be nice to my daughter, old woman, I thought.

At noon, we were meeting Jason and his sons for lunch. His wife, Jamilah, and I had spoken a few times on the phone. She'd always been cordial, if a little . . . tight sounding. They had two boys—Owen and Duncan, ages seven and nine. They sent us a Christmas card each year—the perfect family photo. Jamilah was African American and gorgeous . . . Owen, the older boy, had green eyes and lashes to die for. The little one looked like mischief incarnate with dimples and curly hair. I rather liked the boys, based on the occasional sliver Jason would share with me, or the times Riley Skyped with them and I could hear them laughing.

The old familiar feeling of being on the outside, almost but not quite welcome, wrapped around my heart.

And then, after lunch, I'd be seeing Hope. That, at least, was one thing I was very much looking forward to. Being near her for the summer was a silver lining in this whole endeavor.

Well. Before any of that could happen, I had to deal with the Mastersons, who were trying to fix their marriage after Dirk had cheated with a younger woman. Amy wasn't willing to give up on the marriage just yet. Not before she ate his beating heart, I thought.

I set up my computer on the desk, checked to make sure my background wasn't too distracting, and smoothed my hair. Smiled my therapist smile and clicked their names. The gurgling of the connection sounded, and there they were, sitting next to each other, not touching, Amy's jaw tight, Dirk's gaze on the ceiling, already irritated.

"Hi, guys," I said. "How's this week been?"

"Shitty," Amy said. "Because he lied. Again."

"I didn't lie. I just didn't tell you because I knew you'd be like this." He looked at me . . . well, at the computer. "Dr. London, I didn't tell her I was getting drinks last night with my coworkers because I knew she'd think I was going to see Bailey again."

"Please don't say your whore's name in our house."

"Jesus, Amy. Calm down."

Great advice, Dirk. Like telling a cuckolded wife to calm down ever worked. "Before we get into details," I said, "let's back up a little. Dirk, we talked about how an apology means naming the thing you did wrong, taking full responsibility for it, acknowledging the pain it caused and discussing how you'll act differently. Have you given that a try?"

"Yes. Repeatedly."

"Yeah, well, the whole sincerity aspect isn't coming through," Amy ground out.

"Dirk? Do you want to address that?" I asked after a beat.

"Maybe I'm not sincere because I'm tired of being treated like a whipped dog."

That was the trick with marriage counseling and infidelity. One spouse had wronged the other—not in a vacuum most times—but to beat up the unfaithful spouse week after week made him less responsive to working things out.

Neither of them said anything, too busy clenching their sphincters. "A lot of couples come to marriage counseling to feel okay about getting a divorce," I said. "And some come to try to save the marriage. Where would you say you stand? Amy? Want to go first?"

"It's hard to want to stay married knowing he's a cheating scumbag," she said.

"Let's try not to call names, okay?" I said. "Dirk was unfaithful, Amy. It happened, and you can't change that. If you're going to work on the marriage, you're going to have to start letting that go."

"So the burden is all on me. As usual."

Dirk sighed, long and loud. "I *said* I was sorry. I *said* I wouldn't do it again. It's my fucking mantra. 'I'm sorry, Amy, I'm sorry, Amy.' How long are you going to punish me?"

"As long as I want, cheater. Asshole. Liar. Cliché. Dating a younger woman. Where'd you come up with that? In the middle-age-loser handbook?"

"Let's try to reframe that without name-calling, Amy. It's more helpful for you if you try to explain your feelings to Dirk. Maybe start a sentence with 'I am really hurt when I think of . . .'"

"I am really hurt when I think of you and that whore."

Dirk stared into the computer screen and rolled his eyes, trying to win me over.

"Amy," I said, "you're going to have to move forward, either with Dirk or without him. But you do have to move forward."

"Well, I wish I could move backward and be thirty again. Like Bailey, whose vagina is probably nice and tight because she didn't give birth to Dirk's two sons!"

I tried not to sigh. I felt for her, I really did. Amy had had a real problem with Bailey's age. Even more than the infidelity was the insult, she said. She was forty-five; Bailey was thirty. "Fifteen years younger than me!" she'd sobbed in our first session. She talked constantly about Bailey's figure—she stalked her online—her beauty, her skin, her hair, her half marathons.

The fact that Amy was fixated on Bailey showed her own insecurity and self-esteem issues. Those were harder issues than forgiveness for her.

One of the dogs—the biggest one, from the sound of it—clawed at my door and moaned.

"You okay?" Dirk said.

"You're so concerned about everyone," Amy snapped. "Except me."

"Sorry, that's my . . . my dog." The less clients knew about my personal life, the better.

"What kind?" Dirk said. "I love dogs."

"A mutt," I said.

"You're a mutt," Amy said, looking at her husband. "You're a nasty, filthy dog."

"Amy. The name-calling isn't making anything better," I said. "Let's change the focus here. What do you want from Dirk?"

"Honesty. Decency."

"And what does that look like in the day-to-day?"

She paused. "Not lying about where he is and who he's with?"

"Dirk? What do you think about that?"

"Yeah. Fine. But then she can't punish me for telling the truth."

"And what would you like from Amy, Dirk?"

"I'd like some respect, that's what. Home was like a

black hole where I couldn't do anything right. If I was there, I was in her way. If I was out, she was pissed because I wasn't home. If I was working, she was pissed because I wasn't making enough. If I worked more, she said I didn't care about her. If I suggested we do something without the kids, she'd give me this martyred look and tell me why she was too exhausted to leave the house. If I didn't, she'd ask why we never went out anywhere."

"First, that is so skewed," Amy said. "And second, now you being a cheating, lying scum is my fault because I was a shitty wife?"

He pretended to think. "Yeah."

Her face went blotchy with rage. Outside the door, the dog barked and clawed harder, sort of like a direwolf, but senile and less cool.

I cleared my throat. "I think we have to address the atmosphere at home if we're going to move forward," I said.

Amy looked at me. "Are you taking his side?" she screeched. "Is he somehow the good guy here?"

"No, no," I said calmly. "There's no good guy here. You both did things wrong, and you need to take responsibility for that."

Amy got off the couch and left my range of vision. Dirk raised an eyebrow and smirked. There was a smashing sound. A second later, she came back.

"I did *nothing* wrong," Amy said. "I mean, seriously, what else was I supposed to do, raising the kids when you were out being a big-shot lawyer?"

"Supporting our family, you mean? But since you asked, maybe you could've put out once in a while," Dirk suggested.

"Would you even want my saggy, baggy old body? I'm not Bailey, after all. I don't run 10Ks and go to the fucking salon to get a blowout and get my pubic hair ripped out! I'm sorry I'm not thirty anymore! My vagina has been stretched out with your two kids!"

"How would I know? We've barely had sex since Evan was born!"

Mac barked, then began to howl, possibly picking up on the Mastersons' mood.

Times like this, I was glad I'd never gotten married. As they yelled at each other, the screen froze, and I couldn't say I was sorry. A second later, it clicked back in. They were still yelling.

"Enough," I said loudly. "You don't have to do anything. You're welcome to get a divorce. There's nothing stopping you. Your children can grow up in two households, and frankly, that might be better for them in this case."

That stopped them dead.

"If you want to stay married, you have to do things differently. This isn't about Bailey, as much as it seems that way. This is about the two of you. You're here, you've made the time for counseling . . . that tells me, at least in part, that you want to stay married. So let's schedule another session for later this week, and we'll talk about what made you decide to get married. What you liked about the other, found interesting and exciting."

Amy opened her mouth, but I shushed her. "You've been married for sixteen years. According to what you said, you were happy for at least ten of those. You know how to be a loving partner because you were one. Think of a few things you do for each other that shows that. Little things, maybe. Amy, you said Dirk always scrapes your car when it snows. Dirk, you mentioned that Amy takes books out from the library that she knows you'll like. We're going to need to focus on the positive here. Otherwise, you'll just be in a spiral of bitterness and anger."

We talked for another few minutes and then clicked off, and I sat back, satisfied. Whether or not the Mastersons took my advice was up to them, but it had been good advice, and I hadn't pussyfooted around about the way they acted.

I opened the door to let Mac in, only to find that he'd left but not before shitting on the floor. With a sigh, I went to find some paper towels and clean up.

The Mastersons did not exactly inspire hope, not with Amy's fury and Dirk's simmering disappointment. But the intensity of anger they exhibited could only come after love. Maybe they would find their way back to each other.

Would I have been a good wife? Once, I'd pictured Jason and me together, first when we were in high school, later as I percolated Riley and then in the years of her toddlerhood. With every month that it didn't happen, I knew the odds were lower. It was like being swept out to sea by the Gulf Stream, seeing an island that looked so beautiful, but never getting quite close enough to swim to shore.

Besides Jason, marriage had never been a consideration. I'd been putting myself through school and raising Riley. I'd dated three guys in the past sixteen years, but none had ever gotten to the "meet my kid" phase. None had gotten to the third date, in fact. And that was fine. My life was plenty full already. I had Calista, a few pals from the grocery store, school, my colleagues and clients. I liked to ride my bike and, um, other things. Movies and books, sure. I belonged to a book club that, yes, I'd been neglecting, but I was in one.

When Riley went to college in a year and change, I'd be thirty-seven. Sometimes, that felt as if I'd be all alone in a vast, cold ocean, with no islands at all.

CHAPTER 10

Genevieve

won't tell you about my son's disappearance because, frankly, it's none of your business. Who wants to read about someone else's worst nightmare, anyway? I don't approve of this voyeuristic time we live in where everyone feels obliged to write a memoir about their drunken blackouts, their miserable childhoods, their cheating spouses. What good does it do, really? Social media is responsible for half of the misery in this world. All that *sharing*. Spare me.

That being said, I *will* tell you about how hope erodes. What it takes from you. You might view yourself as a strong person. You're from a good family with an excellent education. You think you have the ability and skills to handle life, make a home, a family, a marriage. And you're right. You are strong. Up until a point.

When the police arrived at our house to inform me that my son had "wandered off," I remained calm. They drove me to Birch Lake, and when I saw Garrison's too-wide eyes and Clark's dirty face streaked with tears, I wasn't afraid.

Sheppard had just found something fascinating. He had a singular ability to concentrate, my son. Perhaps it was a fox den, and he was waiting to see the kits. Surely it was something innocent. He would be firmly lectured so he understood the danger he could have faced, not to mention the worry he put his parents through. Being the sweet boy he was, he'd apologize. Perhaps he'd write a note to Garrison and me. We would laugh about it someday. "Oh, such a free spirit, our Sheppard! Did he ever tell you about the time he got lost at the lake? He scared us nearly to death!"

Even as I called his name, my voice clear and strong, I imagined that—telling his beautiful fiancée this story over dinner, just the four of us, candles flickering, the young woman laughing gently, putting her hand over Sheppard's, my grandmother's diamond winking on her left hand. She'd be the daughter I never had. We'd be fast friends, certainly. Garrison would smile at me, and Sheppard would say, "Mother, please, not that story again."

Within hours, the police brought in bloodhounds, and even then, I was positive the dogs would find him. The fox den theory had been replaced with a broken ankle, at least in my mind. But no, that wouldn't explain his silence, so I amended it to be that my son had slipped and hit his head on a rock, concussing himself. He would be fine. There was no other acceptable alternative.

Then came the divers . . . well, I suppose they had to be called, but I wouldn't tolerate that scenario. And I was right. They didn't find my son, because he was *not* in that lake.

When darkness fell that night, when there was no sound of a little boy calling out or crying, I still hoped. But now, a dark spot had wormed its way into my heart, like mold.

I went home from the lake sometime before dawn to check on Clark. It was only then, standing in front of Sheppard's empty bedroom, his bed neatly made, that I felt truly afraid. Fear dropped me to my knees, and I covered my head and bit down on the yawning, ravenous terror that wanted to swallow me.

But I had to be strong. This was taking longer than it should, but Sheppard would be *fine*. He wouldn't have fallen in the lake without Garrison noticing, for heaven's sake! He could swim! He was quite a good swimmer, in fact.

The next day, since the dogs had found nothing, and the divers had found nothing, they dragged the lake. And found nothing. Thank God, they found nothing. The silt was deep, though, they said. It was possible that— "No," I said firmly, calmly. "He's not in there. But thank you."

Ugly phrases were used. *Posthumous gases. Floating patterns. Facedown.* I ignored them all. My son was *not* in that lake. I knew it with all my heart, and mothers have a gift this way.

Sheppard was out there somewhere. Surely he would come home. He'd gotten lost. We walked, lines of us, through those woods, time after time, day after day, and still I hoped. No, I *knew* my son was alive. I would be the one whose voice woke him from his deep sleep. He would be scared but so glad to see us, and Garrison and I would wrap our arms around him and say, "All that matters is that you're safe now, darling. We're here. We've got you." He would be hungry and dirty, and I'd give him a bath and make potato soup myself, his favorite.

More than a dozen times, we walked the woods. There was nothing. No shoe, no scrap of fabric, no scent for the dogs to pick up. They dragged the lake again. Still nothing.

My theory became that someone had mistaken him for a lost child and brought him somewhere. He was in a police station in a town very close by, and it was bureaucratic incompetence that was keeping us from our reunion. I may have snapped at the police chief. I may have suggested his force was failing to do their job, that they were incompetent idiots. I seem to remember slapping someone's face.

The police were treating it as a missing person, then as a possible abduction. Garrison and I went on the news, pleading with the person who had taken our son, holding pictures of him. "Bring back my son," I said. "We love him so much. Please. Please."

A detective interviewed us and asked about any predators— the human kind. Had we seen anyone giving Sheppard any special attention? A teacher? A priest? "We're Protestants," I snapped. "And no! Of course not."

The days became a week. Ten days. Twelve. Two weeks. Nineteen days. Three weeks. Four and a half, and it was stunning that this was still going on. Stunning! Sheppard was listed in the registry of missing children, and I called in daily. Nothing. No one was reported as matching his description.

Nine weeks after he . . . went away, they found the boy in Boston, and my heart soared. I would make it all right. I would heal his wounds, soothe his fears, and we would be together again, and . . . and . . .

It wasn't my son. Someone *else's* son had been found, but not mine, and I hated that other mother who was granted such mercy, such joy. I hated her so that if I had seen her, I might have attacked her, screamed at her, begged her to give me her son so I could pretend he was mine. I hated God with all my heart.

We resorted to psychics who told us nothing. "I see a tree," said one, and it was all I could do not to slap her. Another said, "He's very close to water," but could not say whether she felt he was alive or dead. Another told us he was not in pain.

No one told us where he was.

Garrison accepted things in inches. I heard him sobbing in his bathroom, saw the emptiness behind his eyes. We held each other so tightly at night, the only time I could be honest, when I shook so hard my teeth chattered, and Garrison cried quietly. His hair turned white, and he started drinking three cocktails each night instead of two.

Three months.

Five months.

Seven.

A year. A *year*. Three news appearances, all starting with "Today marks the anniversary of the mysterious disappearance of Sheppard London, a beautiful little boy who went missing at Birch Lake in Stoningham. With us today are his parents . . ."

There were three calls after that first anniversary. All dead ends.

Grief is an ice pick, chiseling you to nothing bit by bit. All I could think of was my lost boy. When Clark came to me for his story time one night, *Peter Pan* clutched in his chubby little hands, I snatched the book and threw it in the fireplace. There would be no Lost Boys in my home. "Go to bed," I snapped. Then, later, when he was asleep, I climbed into bed with him and silently apologized to him for loving Sheppard more.

It seemed impossible that the days kept coming. How could there be a spring, an autumn, the holidays, when our boy was out there, somewhere? If he was dead, wouldn't I have *felt* it? Wouldn't he come to me in a dream, my angel, my son? I had loved him with every molecule in me. Wouldn't he do me that favor, at least?

Then Garrison died, and the last bit of my violated heart died with him. Or no, it petrified; it was there but utterly useless. I did my best for Clark, and it was a paltry effort. Thank God I hired Donelle, who loved him.

Every day, Sheppard's beautiful, perfect face filled my mind. My arms were useless without him to hold. My mind was constantly buzzing. I imagined him living with another family—foreigners who didn't speak English. They'd found him; he *had* fallen and hit his head and had amnesia. Desperate for a child of their own, they took him. At first he was frightened, but they treated him well. They took him back to their country—Portugal, I imagined—and Sheppard learned their language. They had children after that, and in my mind, Sheppard played with his dark-haired siblings as he had once played with Clark. The memory of his other life would fade away, but some long-hidden part of his heart was still with me.

I would accept that, I told God, if only I could see my firstborn again. Even if it was his bones I saw, I had to know. It would not be possible for me to die without seeing my boy one more time. As the years passed, this was the bargain I struck with God—I could live without my son so long as He let me know. Either I would look into those blue, blue eyes once more and tell my little boy, now a man, how much I loved him, how I never, ever stopped looking for him . . . or I would have his remains to bury next to Garrison.

I spent tens of thousands of dollars on private investigators who specialized in missing children. I had dogs flown in from around the world who were supposedly able to discern the tiniest bit of human remains. Four times a year, I walked those woods around Birch Lake. If my son had ended up in a shallow grave, I wanted to know. I would finally know.

With an empty heart and a shrewd eye, I founded my company. It was the one place I could concentrate on something that was not Sheppard, the place where the Missing stepped aside and I could escape the grief, the terror, the loneliness. Clark grew. Donelle became a fixture. My employees at Genevieve London Designs revered and feared me. I continued to hire investigators and cooperated with the occasional journalist who wanted to do a story, made all the more salacious now that I was a successful CEO, an important contributor to the fashion world.

More time passed. Years. Decades. When DNA testing became a way of finding people or identifying bodies, I gave the FBI a strand of hair from Sheppard's hairbrush. Nothing in their system matched. Ever. I hired artists to sketch what he would look like at fifteen, twenty, thirty, forty.

When Clark brought me his child to raise—Clark, ever useless, ever slightly stupid—I accepted. It was my duty, of course. I wasn't about to let my granddaughter go neglected or be raised by that other side of the family, the side that had produced April, a young woman so desperate and afraid that she abandoned her only child. Honestly, how dare she? Had *I* resorted to suicide, I who had lost a child? Did people think it hadn't been tempting?

Here was I, a mother who *still* searched the forest each year, decades after her child went missing, and Clark's wife had been given a healthy child and left her. Oh, I understood clinical depression and its lies, its reach . . . but could she not have stayed for that child? No. She left her daughter alone with Clark, of all people, my inept, spoiled son, he who was best defined by the word *incompetent*.

For a moment, when I saw Emma standing in the foyer, her hair greasy, her coat too small, something in my petrified heart stirred.

Then I realized she was one year older than Sheppard was the last time I'd seen him, and my heart once again turned to stone.

When Sheppard went away, he'd taken everything good with him.

I provided for Emma. I got her a decent haircut and bought her appropriate clothes. She appreciated living at Sheerwater, got decent marks in school. She was not unattractive, though she was timid and startled easily. She answered when spoken to but kept to herself.

Frankly, I was disappointed in her. After a year, one would've thought she'd have snapped out of her self-pity, but no, she seemed to view herself as a tragic orphan, and not the heir to Sheerwater, to the London dynasty. She didn't view herself as lucky at all, and it was both maddening and wearing at the same time.

Still, she was my grandchild. When she was thirteen, I sat her down and told her about sex, hormones, her menstrual cycle. I told her about birth control. I told her I expected her to remain a virgin well into college at the very least. I told her that at the first sign of depression, she was to tell me and we would take her to the finest doctors and therapists, that we would smite it. I talked about reputation, education, marriage.

I wanted to send her to Foxcroft Academy, but she made the case that Sheerwater was her home, and she'd just gotten comfortable here. "Please, Gigi," she had said. "Let me stay."

I did. In a rare error in judgment, I let her stay.

Though she wasn't quite the gleaming academic or social star I'd hoped she would be, she did well enough. With the money from my family and Garrison's, she could go anywhere, frankly. I would send her to Harvard, where my father had gone, or possibly Columbia, Garrison's alma mater. She could go to Bryn Mawr or Smith or Stanford and get an MBA, perhaps live in Paris or Copenhagen for a year or two, then join me at Genevieve London Designs, in marketing, I thought. Eventually as creative director and then, when I saw fit to retire, as CEO.

She never objected to these plans. She had the right pedigree and was on the road to success. I tolerated her dating Jason; at least she'd chosen a dimwit whose influence wouldn't last once she left for college. Smith had been her decision in the end, and I approved.

And then the stupid girl got pregnant a week before high school graduation and insisted on keeping the baby. I told her it was foolish. I was furious. A teenage mother? When she had every opportunity in the world waiting for her? How would she support a child? She had options—abortion, a grim choice, but better than throwing away her life. Adoption, even; I would send her to Switzerland or London for the duration, and she could defer college for a year.

No. For the first time ever, she stood up to me and said she was keeping the baby. It was not open for discussion.

I kicked her out. Oh, yes, I did. I hadn't *wanted* to raise Emma. I hadn't asked for her, this daughter of a sick, tormented woman and my useless other son. But I did, I took her in and gave her the best of everything, and she defecated on it all. Keeping the baby? Fine! If she wanted to pretend to be an adult, she could do it on her own dime, thank you very much.

It was much more peaceful without her.

Except it wasn't. Without Emma, Sheppard became my focus once more, the ten-year reprieve of Emma's care now over.

After Emma left, I ached for my son all over again. But I never broke. I never became a lush, though it was tempting, or addicted to sleeping pills or pain medication. I never needed hospitalization for grief, because I was a strong woman. I waited instead for Emma to come back, to beg for forgiveness and admit she was wrong, and I waited for something, anything, to change with Sheppard's case. I waited for God to grant me His side of our bargain—to let me see my son one more time.

Instead, I have a death sentence. It looks as if God left me, just like everyone else.

I know it wasn't fair to ask Emma back here. She had a point when she said I didn't deserve to meet her child. So I used what I always used when love failed me—money. And I know that wasn't fair, either, but by the time this all spins out, I'll be dead, and at least I won't have died alone.

CHAPTER 11

Emma

D ad!" Riley flung herself out of the car and ran up the steps to Jason, who opened his arms and gave her a big hug, laughing.

I got out more slowly. We were having lunch at a restaurant so Riley could meet her half brothers in person. Jamilah was there as well, just getting out of the car, and I suddenly felt self-conscious. After all, I was the dopey teenager who'd been careless with her birth control pills. Hey. We'd also been using condoms . . . except for that one time. One pre-graduation-party screw, and I was preggers. I somehow knew Jamilah would never have been that dumb.

Jamilah was beautiful, which I knew from pictures and the occasional glimpse of her on Skype. She'd shaved her head since I got the Christmas card, and she looked brilliant and sophisticated, which she was. A tech genius who'd graduated in the top 10 percent of her class at MIT.

Her boys were being introduced to Riley, shaking hands

sweetly, then hugging her as my child laughed. It was painfully wonderful to witness.

"Hello, Emma," Jamilah said, and I tried to assess her tone and failed.

"Hi," I said, running a hand through my hair. The wind blew it across my face. Should've thought of that. Also, I was wearing jeans and a sweater; Jamilah was in something long and flowing and white.

"It's great to finally meet you in person," she said, shaking my hand.

"Same here. Your sons are so beautiful."

"Mom!" said Riley. "This is Owen, and this is Duncan. My brothers!" They were clutching her hands, and it was adorable.

"Hi, boys! I'm Riley's mom. Remember when we talked on the computer last week? It's nice to meet you in person. How do you like your sister so far?"

"She's great!" Owen said. Duncan was swinging Riley's hand, and my daughter was smiling. Beaming.

"Hey there," Jason said, giving me a hug. He smelled good. Felt good, too, still lean, the same as ever. And gorgeous. Had I mentioned his looks?

"Nice to see you," I said, stepping back. Weren't we all so modern! Jason, his wife, their separation, their sons, our daughter, me . . .

"Are you staying for lunch?" I asked Jamilah.

"No, unfortunately, I have some work to do." She was an advisor to Google but, according to Jason, worked from home only a few hours a month. Her parents had a summer home in Stoningham, which was how they met. The summer Riley was six.

I wondered why they were separated.

"Okay, boys," Jason said, "shall we get your sister inside and feed her? And Emma, too?"

"Yes! I like cheeseburgers. Do you like cheeseburgers?" Duncan asked.

"I do! Who doesn't, right?" Riley looked at Jamilah. "It's great finally meeting you in person," she said.

Jamilah surprised me by hugging her. "You, too, sweet-heart. Don't let these boys talk your ear off, okay? See you soon."

She nodded to Jason, gave me a small smile and glided over to her Audi station wagon.

We were at Dockside, a restaurant where the views had always been better than the food. It hadn't changed much—a casual place with the expected fake lobsters and starfish hanging from the walls. The boys were firing questions off at Riley—why was her skin so white? Her hair was so red! Did she skateboard? Did she like video games? Would she take them swimming? Riley was eating it up.

"Man. This is great, seeing them together," Jason said. "I can't believe it's the first time. We should've made it happen sooner. That's on me." He sighed, then looked at me, smiling. "You look so good, Em. I've missed you."

"Thanks. You too," I said.

"Can we have our own booth?" Duncan asked, he of the mischievous dimples. "Please, Dad? We'll be good."

"I'd like to spend time with my girl," he said.

"You can have her later," Owen said. "We need her now."

"They need me now," Riley said, grinning.

Jason and I both laughed. "How's this?" Jason said. "You can order milkshakes, but when lunch comes, Emma and I will sit with you, okay?"

"Yay!" the boys said. They dragged Riley to a booth by the window, chattering like blackbirds.

"What lovely boys," I said.

"They're great. Here. Let's sit at the bar, where we can keep an eye on them. Want a glass of wine?"

"No, thanks," I said. It was only lunchtime.

Jason perused the drinks menu. "I'll have a Lonesome Boatman," he said as the bartender came over. "Thanks,

Jen. Hey, this is my . . . uh . . . my daughter's mother," he said. "Emma London, meet Jen, the world's best bartender."

"We went to school together, idiot," she said, flicking the towel at him. "How you doing, Emma?"

"Great! It's good to see you." Jen Pottsman, salutatorian of our class, now bartending. If memory served, she'd gone to Amherst. "How've you been?"

"Not bad. Your daughter's wicked cute."

"Thanks," Jason and I said simultaneously, then laughed. I guess I'd have to get used to sharing credit for her, at least for the summer.

"Anything for you, Emma?"

"Just seltzer water, please."

"You got it." She went off, and I watched as Riley ordered milkshakes for all three of them. You'd think she grew up with the boys, the way she was talking to them, laughing. She tapped Duncan on the nose, then proceeded to breathe on her spoon and press it against his, where it balanced for a few seconds.

I'd taught her that trick. Used to do it every time we went out, which, granted, hadn't been that often.

"One seltzer, one Lonesome Boatman," Jen said, setting down our drinks. "Want any food?"

"We'll eat with the kids," Jason said. "Thanks, Jen."

"You got it. Well, I bet you have a lot to catch up on, so I'll leave you alone. Good seeing you, Emma."

"Yeah, you too."

She went away, and Jason shifted so he could see me better. "You have not aged a bit," he said.

"Since December?" The last time he'd been to Chicago.

"I mean, you look like you're still eighteen."

"Please. I don't want to look like a dumb kid anymore."

He smiled. "At least us being dumb made a great daughter."

"There is that, yes." I watched as he took a long drink from his beer. "Lonesome Boatman, huh?"

"It describes me these days," he said with a wink.

"Except you're not a boatman."

"They didn't have a Lonesome Carpenter." Another grin. "Well, I guess I should tell you I'm not sure Jamilah and I are gonna make it."

"I'm so sorry," I said.

"She's changed."

Oh, boy. The cry of the idiot husband. "I am a therapist, if you'd like to talk about it. You can have the family rate and everything."

"No, no, it's fine. We did try that. Counseling. Anyway. The boys don't know yet."

"Where are you living?" I asked.

"With my parents." He grimaced. "It's just kind of expensive. You know. Child support for you—"

"For Riley, actually." My fingers tightened on the water glass. Every penny he'd ever sent went directly to Riley's needs. I'd never used a single dime of it. Not a penny, unless you counted groceries.

"Yeah, yeah. I'm sorry," said Jason. "Of course. For Riley. But we have the mortgage, and the boys are in private school, all that stuff. If Jamilah worked a few more hours a month, she'd make more than I do, but God forbid . . . Anyway, I won't bore you with that. The lowdown is I can't rent anything right now. How about you? You staying with Genevieve?"

"Seems that way. Riley loves the house."

"How is she, the old hag?"

"She's good. Stuck-up as ever."

"She always looks right through me when I run into her in town." He grinned and took another pull of his beer.

Jason was handsome, to be sure. Big dark blue eyes, thick lashes, a huge smile. Right now, he looked rugged with a few days of stubble, and his hair was dark and curly. Riley, too, had those coarse, irrepressible curls, though the color had come from my mom, also a redhead. Her eyes were sky blue . . . stunning if I did say so, and while I understood genetics, I never could guess where she'd gotten that shade.

I liked to imagine my mother would've loved Riley. She of the winter forts, the best cookies, the giggles at bedtime.

Why'd you leave, Mom?

The eternal question. One worn out from repetition, and one I rarely allowed myself as an adult. But somehow this odd reunion—Genevieve, Donelle, Jason and his family—had me thinking about it. And yeah, I knew all the clinical answers, but the eight-year-old in me still wanted more.

I still missed her. I would always miss her.

"So Genevieve is sick, huh?" Jason asked, bringing me back to the moment. "Always figured she was too mean to die."

"Me too," I said. "Guess not."

"Will you inherit everything?"

The question made me blink. Then again, we shared a daughter, so I guessed my finances were his business, sort of.

"No," I said honestly. "She's made that quite clear."

"Too bad. What with college coming up for Riley."

"Yeah, about that, Jason. We're gonna need your help."

He grimaced. "Sure. I'll give what I can."

"How about your parents? Did they save anything for her?"

He gave me a look. "What do you think?"

"So that's a no."

In a nutshell, Jason's parents were shits. Once, I had loved Courtney and Robert Finlay. Imagined them as my in-laws, spent more time at their house than at Sheerwater in my last two years of high school, stopping by on Thanksgiving when our own frosty family dinner had been endured, and basked in their solidarity—the aunts, uncles, cousins and, of course, Jason.

Courtney had adored me when I was heir to Sheerwater and the London fortune. She'd been big on compliments—how good I was for Jason, how sweet we were together, how smart/pretty/kind I was. And she had a mad crush on Genevieve. "I just adore your grandma's bags!" she'd coo. She had six or seven and always flashed them around town, especially in Genevieve's presence. "I couldn't resist this color!" she'd say when they ran into each other. "So good to see you, Genevieve! We should sit down with these gorgeous kids and have our families get to know each other!"

"I hardly think that's necessary," Genevieve would murmur. "It's quite infrequent that high school sweethearts stay together, after all."

It didn't have the chilling effect Genevieve intended. Courtney volunteered on every committee Genevieve was on—historical society, garden club, scholarship fund—and kissed up to Genevieve at every step, hinting about marriage (which was fine by me back then). She wanted access to Genevieve's world, and Genevieve was quite content to keep the secret handshake to herself.

Given its natural beauty and lovely homes, Stoningham attracted a few celebrities in the summer. We weren't the Hamptons (thank God) but we had a sighting or three each year. Many knew Genevieve through her company or charities. One year, Meryl Streep came for dinner at Sheerwater—she and Genevieve were on the board of some organization, and Courtney begged me to get her invited. When that failed, she asked for just five minutes so she could tell Meryl how much she adored every movie she'd ever made.

I tried. I loved Courtney, who gave me a glimpse of what it would be like to have a mother. "Gigi," I pleaded. "She loves Meryl Streep. It would make her *life* to meet her."

Genevieve, sitting behind her enormous desk, gave me a

pitying look. "You do realize that woman is trying to use you to get to me," she'd said, and honestly, the ego! The narcissism! The bitchery! "She is the very worst type of social climber."

"No, she's not! She's really nice. You should give her a chance."

Genevieve raised an eyebrow and said no more.

Turned out she had been a hundred percent correct. The second I'd been unceremoniously turned out of Sheerwater, Courtney cast me as an irresponsible slut who was trying to latch on to her son, steal his money and ruin his future. His role in impregnating me was dismissed with "you know how boys are."

Robert, who was what can only be termed a limp dick, fell into line. Jason would "do his duty," but I had better not expect anything from them. We knew where babies came from, and he was disappointed with us both. When Riley was born, they didn't come out. Didn't send a present. Pretended Riley—our beautiful child—didn't exist.

"By the way," I said now, taking a sip of my seltzer, "I'm not crazy about the idea of Riley spending time with your folks."

Jason frowned. "I was kind of hoping they'd get to know her a little bit."

"It's a no, Jason. They've had sixteen years to get to know her." My jaw locked. Fuck the Finlays. They didn't deserve her. Riley had had shit luck in the grandparent department—Clark, my mother, the idiot Finlays—but at least she had Pop.

He nodded. "True. Sorry. They're great with the boys, so . . . yeah. I see your point. Never mind." He finished his beer. "Well. I'm glad you're here. Both of you. I think it'll be a great summer. Why don't we go sit with the kids?"

"Sure thing," I said.

As I got off the stool, he stood and hugged me. "I've really, really missed you," he said.

I patted his back and stepped away quickly.

Once upon a time, I'd loved Jason Finlay with my whole heart. And when you've only had one experience with love, I guess it leaves a mark.

CHAPTER 12

Emma

Rose Hill had once been a small college for women. Forty years ago, it became a residential facility for children who needed care that their families, for a variety of reasons, could not provide. Most of the kids here were profoundly intellectually disabled, and many had physical challenges as well.

It was a private facility, staffed by a fleet of nurses and doctors and physical, occupational and speech therapists equipped with every amenity you could dream of—an accessible playground, four golden retrievers who were trained as therapy pets, a small stable for equine therapy. I imagined it was ungodly expensive. If not for Genevieve, I wasn't sure where my sister would be. With me, I guessed. Genevieve was too old to care for a special-needs kid, and my father . . . no.

Beth, my pal from high school, was waiting for me in the parking lot. Over the years, she'd met me here a few times and hung out with Hope and me. Sometimes, because she was such a good soul, she'd visit Hope just to say hi.

"Hey!" she said now, and we hugged. "I love your hair."

"And I love yours." It was an old joke—Beth's hair was the stuff of legend, long and chestnut brown and naturally curly, and being a woman, she hated it. Mine was straight and dark blond and unremarkable, and for decades, we'd wished we could trade.

"How's Hope?" she asked.

"From what I know, she's great."

We walked up the long, winding path to the main building. "Think there are any single doctors here?" Beth asked.

"I don't know. You're dating again?" She had a long history of terrible taste in men.

"Sort of. I just want a baby. Can't you give me Riley? All the hard work is done, and she's so great."

"Okay. Done."

"Seriously. I want a baby. I'm thirty-five. Why wasn't I smart like you? Should've gotten knocked up in high school so I could be the cool young mom."

"Oh, yeah. That's always a great plan. We teenage mothers have it made."

She shoved me. "Blah blah blah. Just keep your eye out. Maybe Jason will impregnate me. He makes gorgeous kids."

"Yeah, I met his sons today."

"Oh, right. I guess I should be sensitive and ask how that went."

"It was fine. Jamilah's . . . nice."

"She's amazing. How about her shaved head, huh? You watch. A dozen women will show up to yoga bald next week." Beth cut me a look. "Do you hate her?"

"No! I just . . ." I stopped to fondle a clump of deep purple petunias in a planter. Rose Hill had a crew of gardeners as well. "It's just that she's Jason's second love, and I was his first."

"You wanted to be his only."

"That was a long time ago. He's good to Riley and never misses a payment."

"Such a prince. Anyway, back to me. Keep your eyes peeled for my future husband."

"Your third," I couldn't help saying.

"And final. All I want is a baby. From a rich guy. Believe it or not, being a florist and part-time bartender hasn't put me in the one percent."

We went into the main building, where the kids played and did physical therapy and the like. "Good to see you, Emma," said Caridad, one of the nurses. She came over and gave me a hug.

"Nice to see you, too," I said. "Do you remember my friend Beth?"

They smiled at each other. "Also," I went on, "you'll see me quite a bit this summer. My daughter and I are staying with Genevieve for a bit."

"Are you? How wonderful! There's nothing like family."

Beth snorted. "Mm," I said.

"How's that sweet girl of yours? Riley, right?"

"Yes. She's great. She's with her dad at the moment, but she'll be coming later this week. Where's Hope?"

"She's right down the hall. Working on motor skills. She'll be so happy to see you."

"I'll let you two visit," Beth said. "I'll just wander around."

"Best of luck," I said, raising an eyebrow.

Caridad led me down the hall. The sound of construction was a dull roar in the background.

"Are you expanding?" I asked.

"We have your wonderful grandmother to thank for that," she said. "They're putting on the new wing."

"Oh, wow. That's fantastic!" Maybe Genevieve could've mentioned that last night, rather than shooting insults across the Limoges china.

"And over here is the new saltwater indoor pool."

"It's beautiful."

"Yeah, the kids hate the old one. Too cold. I don't blame them. And the chlorine! It takes days to wash the smell out of your skin." She opened a door. "Miss Hope! Look who's here to see you!"

My sister was with an aide. She didn't look up, trying to put differently shaped plastic pieces in their correlating box—the circle in the round box, the triangle in the triangular box.

"Hope, you have a visitor," the aide said. She was new.

I went over and knelt down in front of Hope. "Hi, sweetie," I said, and then her face lit up, and she leaned against me.

"I missed you," I said, my eyes filling even as I smiled. "Hi, I'm Hope's sister, Emma," I said, reaching a hand out to the new aide even as I held Hope.

"Nice to meet you. I'm Dakota." She stood up. "I'll let you guys have your visit."

"See you later, Emma," Caridad said, and both women went out.

Hope was smiling now, humming her happiness in the sweetest way. "How's my girl?" I asked. "Are you wonderful? You are. You're a sweet, sweet girl." I kissed her hair and hugged her close.

Hope had drawn the short stick with her condition. She didn't talk, and while she could follow some simple instructions, it was clear that she would need to be cared for her entire life, however long or short that might be.

She looked up at me, smiling. Fifteen years old, but she looked much younger. "Who loves you?" I asked. "Guess what? It's me! I love you, honeybun."

Her eyes were bluish-green and beautiful, with irises that looked like they were made up of pieces of stained glass. Then, because Hope was a creature of habit and it was kind of our thing, I took her hands in mine and started clapping them and singing "Rubber Duckie" from *Sesame Street*. Her face lit up.

It was our song, after all.

Beth poked her head in about an hour later, informing me that she had seen only one male and he had failed to meet her criteria for baby daddy. She stayed to roll balls around with Hope and me, then left, giving my sister a kiss on the cheek and me a pat on the head.

I stayed until dinnertime, when Hope went to eat with her fellow residents.

This was definitely one of the best things about the summer, I thought, watching Dakota lead her down the hall, my sister's gait uneven. I could see Hope as much as I wanted. I'd get Genevieve to make me her guardian. Financially, Genevieve had said, Hope was set for life, and while Genevieve might have done it out of a sense of patrician duty, I had to admit I was grateful.

I stopped to check out the new wing. Jeez Louise, it was going to be gorgeous, according to the architect's drawing displayed on the door. More residential space, plus the heated, super-salinated pool to increase buoyancy and the benefits of aquatherapy. It would be open to the public on Sundays, too, for a fee. If it was finished this summer, Riley and I could come and float around with Hope.

At the bottom of the sign, under the architectural firm, was another logo.

Finlay Construction was building the addition. Jason hadn't mentioned that, and he obviously knew my sister lived here.

Well. He had other things on his mind, I guessed. But it was a pretty plum job. The company must be doing well.

I'd have to look into that. A sense of unease settled in my stomach. I didn't want to have to dig around into Jason's finances. I knew he wasn't legally required to pay for college, but still.

I had the uncomfortable feeling he was hiding something.

CHAPTER 13

Genevieve

A week into their visit and much to my surprise, I found that I quite liked Riley. I hadn't expected to *hate* her, of course, but neither had I foreseen that she would be so . . . lively. Intelligent. I certainly hadn't anticipated that she would be an excellent conversationalist, not with her mother's own teen years of milksop ways and accusatory sighs. Honestly, Emma had been *so* morose, and I had little tolerance for people who indulged in self-pity.

Even now, with my fragile medical state, Emma's resentment was thick enough to taste, like an acrid fog. Aside from dinner each night, I barely saw her. Twice she'd asked for details of my health, which I had no plans to provide. Otherwise, she'd take Riley into town, or swimming in the pool or the Sound. Sometimes I'd hear them in the morning, as they seemed to have a habit of climbing into each other's beds and talking before breakfast, which made jealousy flare in my stomach.

Sheppard used to come into my bed if Garrison was

traveling. When he was very small, he was afraid of his father being away, and I'd cuddle him close and reassure him, and I can still remember how his face would light up when Garrison called, how big the phone looked next to his perfect face as he chattered to his father.

Clark, too, had come into our room occasionally, but after Sheppard went away, I honestly couldn't bear it, and I'd leave Garrison to do the work of comforting our other son.

That phrase . . . what was it again? Oh, this wretched failing, these holes where words are supposed to be. What was it? That thing people do when the Missing is so huge, so cruel and sharp that even your skin feels as if it's tearing . . . tearing, yes. Tearing your hair out. That. That's what I'd wanted to do when Clark came in, fat tears rolling down his face, his lower lip trembling. I'd walk out of the room and go down the hall to the cedar closet, push aside the clothes, sink to the floor and grab fistfuls of my hair and pull until it burned, the scream welling up inside of me.

These memories served no purpose. I had to stop. Just because I was a sick old woman didn't mean I had to behave like one, lost in the fog of the past, boring people to death with stories of a grief too deep and personal to be voiced. Honestly, I wished other people were more like me. Too many loved ripping off their scabs in public, gleefully shoving their tragedies down the throats of the rest of us. Miller understood, the dear man. He never talked about his wife, and I was grateful. It was the appropriate way to mourn. Stoically.

Today, Riley was with that Jason, which I supposed was fine. At least he'd owned up to fatherhood, though he certainly hadn't offered to marry Emma, which would've been the right thing to do. In my generation, if one was irresponsible enough to get pregnant out of wedlock, one married and dealt with it. Not that Jason had been a prize, mind you. But neither did I want Emma to be a single mother.

I got dressed with care, as I did every day. Those yoga-pants women or, worse, those who proudly touted the fact that they were in their pajamas all day . . . I did not understand them. Today, since the weather was fine, I wore a crisp white blouse, cream trousers, sassy patent-leather orange heels of my own design and a red-, orange- and blue-printed silk scarf from my spring collection a decade ago. A classic scarf was every woman's friend.

Too bad Emma didn't care about things like clothes. Style was one's invitation to the world to judge you. Her invitation said, *Ignore me.* Solid colors, usually in shades of blue. Jeans. Most days, she didn't wear jewelry, and her hair, which was an ordinary color, length and style, was often pulled into a ponytail. I yearned to make her over, but those days were gone. Even when she was sixteen and I took her to a salon in Manhattan, she barely cared.

Riley, at least, had a little flair. Not the kind I personally enjoyed, but I'd called Beverly and told her we were coming into the showroom later this week, and my great-granddaughter was to be treated like royalty (by which I meant she was to be allowed to take whatever she wanted). Beverly had paused before answering, but then said, "Of course." Which was the least she could do.

"Donelle!" I called, picking up my handbag (bottle-green tweed with brown leather accents). "Are you ready?"

"I've been ready for an hour," she called from the kitchen. She and Helga straightened up from their whispering as I came in.

"Very well, let's go, then," I said. It irked me that Helga and Donelle were friends. I supposed I couldn't blame Donelle, since she, too, had been the help once, but Helga was such a dour thing, both in looks and personality. "Have a lovely morning, Helga. We won't need lunch, but please include asparagus on tonight's menu. My granddaughter enjoys it."

"Your *great*-granddaughter," Helga said, sticking her tongue in her cheek most unattractively. It was a reprimand, perhaps her way of telling me I'd slipped, or chastising me for caring more what Riley liked than Emma. Not that Emma and Helga had been fast friends back in the day, mind you.

"Asparagus, Helga," I said. "Thank you."

Donelle and I got into the car and headed out of town. Already, traffic was picking up for the summer season. Someone waved to me at the corner of Water and Bank Streets, and I waved back, unsure whether I didn't recognize him because he was someone I barely knew or because of my condition.

I drove to Palmer Farm, which had been owned by the same family for generations and was now being sold into lots for tacky, poorly made McMansions and the new-money people who would inhabit them. Then again, I didn't know what would happen to Sheerwater once I died, did I? The thought made my chest ache sharply. The house had been in Garrison's family for a century. I'd completely redecorated it three times. It was part of me. One of the best parts.

I turned off the road into the drive that led to the gracious old farmhouse, now empty. Had this property been in the historical district, I would've fought to keep it pristine, perhaps making it into a park for the town, or at least conservation land. But the greedy Palmer descendants had no attachment to it and could only see the benefit to their bank accounts. No one lived here, and no one had for the past ten years, ever since Jacob Palmer had gone to that dreadful nursing home. He'd finally died last winter, thank God. Dementia was a horrible thing to endure.

Visiting him each month had only reinforced my resolve to die on my own terms.

"I can't believe we're doing this," Donelle said as I parked the car behind the old stone barn.

"Oh, hush. Practice makes perfect."

"Think about what you just said."

"I'm simply scouting locations, Donelle. As you well know."

"For your suicide."

"Yes. For my suicide." And what could be a more lovely place than a field on a high summer day, the blue sky deep azure?

"How can you do that to that poor girl?"

"Riley barely knows me."

"I was talking about Emma."

"I doubt she'll miss me," I said.

"Her mother committed suicide, dummy." Donelle scowled. "And what about Clark? How's he going to take this, huh?"

I sighed. "When they learn about my condition, they'll understand. Perhaps even be grateful."

"Grateful that you shot yourself in the head?"

"Not in the head, Donelle! I would never do that." I paused. "In the heart." I didn't want a ghoulish scene, after all. The first responders in Stoningham were all volunteers. I'd heard that Archie Baker fainted at a car accident last week. A gunshot to the head would ruin him.

A bullet to the heart. It couldn't hurt more than Sheppard's disappearance, and all the agonizing hours since then. I might not die right away, according to the answers I found on the Internet. (I shuddered to think I was relying on Google for my end-of-life decisions, but assisted suicide was still illegal, unfortunately.) But a gunshot wound to the heart would do the trick. I'd be in shock, and I'd bleed out quickly. If it hurt, it wouldn't for long.

I took a thick flannel blanket out of the trunk, removed my pumps and slid on my wellies, which I'd brought for just this reason. Donelle and I walked up the hill to where a lovely maple tree was in full leaf. Birds sang and fluttered, and the wind rustled through the long grass. I shook out the blanket and lowered myself to the ground, trying to ignore the pain in my hip, my wrists, my left knee. I should've used the bathroom one more time before leaving the house. Old age was such an indignity. The ground was uneven with roots, and they stuck into my spine. I might even bruise.

Next time, I'd bring padding of some sort, if this did prove to be the spot. There was no reason for me to be more uncomfortable than necessary, even in my final moments.

Donelle lay next to me, grunting a little. It took her longer to get settled, but when she was finally done muttering and sighing, the loveliness of the setting enveloped us. The dappled sun warmed my legs, and the breeze was gentle and kind.

"Not a bad place to die," Donelle admitted. "Which doesn't mean I approve, obviously."

I tried to imagine coming out here, alone, with my .38 Special. I'd have to set things up so I'd fall onto a forgiving surface, making it easy for the coroner to tell what happened. The blanket would be ruined, of course, but I deserved to die on something nice. How much blood would pool under me? Would I have a few seconds, staring at the sky? Would I see my body from above? I'd want to die on a sunny day, when the sky was the same color as Sheppard's eyes.

The same color as Riley's, too.

"What if a bird craps on you?" Donelle asked.

I closed my eyes and sighed. "Must you?"

"You know what I read? You'll shit yourself. Your bowels just liquefy and that's how you'll be remembered. Genevieve London, lying in her poop. The fire department boys will talk about the smell of shit and blood, and everyone will know. That's not what you want, is it?"

What was the phrase the young people used? "You're really killing my buzz, Donelle."

"Of course I am! I'm your best friend! I don't want you to shoot yourself! What will happen to me, huh?"

"You'll be fine. There's some money set aside for you and Charles and Helga."

"Oh, *fuck* you," she said.

"Language, please."

"Fuck that! You can't kill yourself, Gen. You really can't. It's not the worst thing in the world, getting old, is it?"

"It is this way. I'd rather shit myself, as you so delicately put it, once, rather than daily as my brain rots away when tied into a wheelchair in some kennel."

Donelle snorted. "Like we'd let that happen to you."

I looked at her. It was true, she was my best friend. I didn't have a lot of friends, not like Donelle. My throat tightened.

"This will break Hope's heart," Donelle said, playing the ace up her sleeve.

I couldn't think about Hope. "She won't know. You'll visit her, won't you?"

"She'll know." Tears were leaking out of Donelle's eyes, slipping into her gray hair.

I took her hand. "I'm dying. It's already started. I need you to be on my side with this, Donelle. Someone has to understand."

"When are you gonna talk to Emma?"

"Soon. I don't know."

"Tell her the truth. Don't die under this tree, Gen."

The truth was, I didn't want to. I wanted to slip away, to fall asleep gently, without pain, surrounded by my loved ones . . . well, by Donelle. Emma. Clark, if he had to be there.

That wasn't many. Losing Sheppard had cut me off from loving people. Who else would be there for me? Miller? The Drs. Talwar? There had been my lovely assistant who'd been so capable and respectful for so many years, ever cheerful and efficient. Melissa, who went by Mel. Would she come? It probably wasn't appropriate to ask her, but she'd been such a lovely woman. I'd wished frequently that Emma had been more like her, working with me, my right hand. Then again, Emma was the one who'd thrown it all away.

Whom else did I love? What was love, anyway?

It would be nice, perhaps, if Riley were there at the end, if it wouldn't be too traumatic. She seemed both innocent for her age and in possession of an old soul.

Her name was growing on me.

Perhaps over these next few weeks, I'd have another chance to love a child, albeit a teenager. Perhaps, this time, I could get it right.

I had finally pried permission from Emma to bring Riley to New York, and the day after my scouting mission, we were all set to go. Suspicion still bubbled out of Emma like a toxic steam; I was afraid she'd insist on coming (though she could do with a makeover). Frankly, I didn't want her to come. Riley seemed to like me, and having her mother there, poisoning the atmosphere, would make the day sub-par. Also, I imagined Beverly would lecture me for bringing in two people to raid the showroom. Sometimes, I thought she forgot just who founded this company. The company was called Genevieve London Designs, not Beverly . . . Beverly . . .

I'd forgotten her last name. Panic swirled in my stomach. Jenkins? No, no, that wasn't it, though the name was familiar. James? Jennings?

I glanced around. This was my bedroom. I was home. Why was I here? What was I supposed to be doing? Was it bedtime?

There was an abrupt static in my brain, like a poorly tuned radio station. I was standing in front of my mirror. I was dressed. Should I put on my nightgown? Why was I standing here? Was everyone else already asleep?

I started to unbutton my blouse, but my fingers were clumsy. They didn't seem to be mine, even. Was that my ring? Were these my hands? They looked so old!

There was a noise in the hall. "Who's there?" I called, abruptly terrified. My voice sounded loud.

"It's me, Gigi. How do I look?"

A girl stood in my doorway. Her eyes were . . . they were so blue. Like someone else's eyes. Someone I'd loved. Someone I'd loved very much. A boy. A little boy with blond hair. Sh . . . Sheh . . . Sheppard. My mind grabbed onto the name like a lifeline, and it was as if I were swimming up toward the light. Sheppard was my son. He'd gone away. A long time ago.

This girl was his child. No. His . . . niece? That was almost right. I had another son, not as good as the first. Clark. This was Clark's child. Grandchild.

She had a last name for a first name. She had red hair like someone else, someone who had died.

Then I was back. Riley stood before me. Red hair like Emma's mother. Emma, my granddaughter.

All the pieces fell into place, and I knew where I was. It was morning. We were going to New York so I could show my great-granddaughter my empire.

"Forgive me," I said. "I was thinking of something else. What did you say, dear?"

She smiled. "How do I look? Is this okay for the trip?"

"Well. Hm." She wore the same cheap black dress she'd had on the first night here. (See? I could remember everything now, brain tumor or not.) Over that, a denim jacket. Brown leather sandals. Her hair was in a ponytail. "You definitely have a sense of style," I said generously, "but why don't we take a look in my closet? Do you mind?"

"Are you kidding? I'd love that!"

My granddaughter—great-granddaughter, rather—was tall and slim (thankfully, she took after me in that regard, and not her mother, who wasn't exactly slender and was four inches shorter than I).

Though my earlier fog was gone, my heart still pounded. I took a deep breath, trying not to let Riley hear. We walked through my bedroom and into the hall that led to the bathroom and dressing room.

"Now this is a closet," she said as we went in.

"Dressing room, dear." It was, complete with an ivory couch, jewelry cabinet (with safe), ten racks and twenty drawers.

"Dressing room. So cool."

"Clothes are important. The way we dress is an invitation for how we want others to view us," I said, which *Vogue* had used as a headline when they interviewed me ten or twelve years ago. Or fifteen years. A long time ago, back when I was still at the top of my game.

Riley fondled the sleeve of a silk dress. "People must view you as, I don't know, Khaleesi or something."

I didn't know who that was, but I knew it was a compliment. I perused the racks, which I organized by color. Riley sat on the couch and watched.

I chose a black sleeveless sweater, which, though a decade old, had never been worn, since I was of the opinion that women should dress appropriately for their age. Despite my very respectably toned arms, I was still eighty-five. A black-and-white-polka-dotted circle skirt, strappy kitten-heeled shoes of my own design in cheery red, and a cropped silk Chanel jacket, patterned in black, white, blue and red and edged with a metallic silver material.

"What do you think of this, dear?"

"I love it!" Much to my surprise, she pulled off her jacket and dress right in front of me. She wore a blue bra and cotton panties—not a thong, thank heaven.

Her skin was as white as milk. So smooth and perfect. She was perhaps a bit too thin. I would speak to Emma about it.

She pulled on the clothes and spun around in front of the mirror. "What do you think?"

"Marvelous!" The clothes made Riley look both elegant and youthful. She'd look darling if she cut her hair.

"Wow," she said, staring at her reflection. "You have the best taste, Gigi. Can I take a picture?"

"Of course, dear," I said. "Send it to your friends and give them my best regards."

Her face fell a little. "I just meant for when I'm home. I'll try to imitate this look."

"My dear, the clothes are yours. Don't be silly. Can you picture me in this outfit?"

"Actually, yes," she said. "You'd rock this look, and you know it." Then, quite unexpectedly, she hugged me. "Let me go show Mom, okay?"

"Of course." She left the dressing room, and I picked up her cheap dress. I'd burn it, perhaps.

Beverly *Jane*. Of course. That was it. The CEO of Genevieve London Designs.

By the time I got to the foyer, Charles was waiting in the hall, and Emma was talking to Riley in a low voice, no doubt warning her about my shark-like teeth, detachable jaw and cannibalistic habits. She hugged Riley, told her to have fun and then said, "A word before you go, Genevieve."

"Of course. I'll meet you outside, dear," I said to Riley, and Charles and she went out. "Yes, Emma?"

"Don't spend too much money on her."

"Isn't that why you're here?"

"No. It's not. I'm giving you a chance with my daughter, and against my better judgment," she said. "Riley had some . . . issues with friends, and I thought a summer here might be helpful. But you can't buy her love, and I don't want you to try."

"I have no intention of buying anyone's love, Emma."

"Good. It's not for sale."

We eyed each other a moment. "I noticed Riley seems a bit thin. She seems to eat well, but . . ." I let my voice trail off.

"She grew almost five inches this year," Emma said. "It's not an eating disorder." She paused. "But thank you for your concern."

"Of course." There was an odd sense of neutrality between us. A cease-fire of sorts. "Do I have your permission to leave now?" I asked, ruining it.

She rolled her eyes. "Be home before ten, please."

"Have a lovely day." I checked my reflection—were I

going to live a bit longer, I might have some injections done—and left.

But it seemed Emma's lecture had infected Riley, for once Charles pulled onto 95 South, she asked, "Why did you kick my mother out when she got pregnant with me?"

I suppressed a sigh. "I didn't exactly kick her out, dear. I gave her a choice. If she wanted to keep you, then I felt I wouldn't be doing her any favors by continuing to support her so she could pretend to be an adult."

"She was all alone."

"That's not true. She had Jason and the Finlays, and her father, and her grandfather Paul."

"But you raised her. Also, my dad's parents are jerks."

"True enough. And I did raise her, and I'd raised her to be smarter than to get pregnant while still in high school."

"So you wanted her to abort me."

"I suggested abortion, yes, but I also suggested that she give you up for adoption." I felt a flush of shame, for some reason. "Your mother had a very bright future. She was smart—"

"She still is."

"Yes, I'm sure, but please don't interrupt, Riley. It's rude."

"It's also rude to toss someone out because she's pregnant."

I did sigh this time. "Things are very black-and-white when you're young, Riley. I forced your mother to address the consequences of her irresponsibility. Birth control is very effective. Somehow, your mother and Jason got it wrong. Coddling Emma was not going to improve her life." I didn't mention the part for which I felt the most regret.

"She worked as a cashier, you know," Riley said. "At a grocery store on the night shift. She worked up until the day I was born and went back two weeks later."

That was not a pleasant image. "There's no shame in hard work," I said. "I imagine she learned a great deal."

Riley was silent, but her gaze said much.

"I was going to pay for her college, you know," I said. "And graduate school. I wanted her to come work with me, to pass my business down to her. She made her choice, and it was you. I doubt very much she's sorry."

"She's not. We have a good life."

"I'm glad to hear that."

She huffed. "It's just sad. You're dying, and only now do I get to know you. You could've called, you know."

"She told me not to."

"Can you freaking blame her?"

I could not. Truthfully, I'd thought Emma would call *me*. I thought she'd break, even living with that Paul. I thought she'd ask for money, and of course I would have given it. I was anxious to give it, frankly.

But she'd never called. Not once. And while I knew where she was, I had never been able to bring myself to simply send a check. I should have, but I never did.

"Why don't we try to have a nice day in the city?" I suggested. "I'm eager to introduce you to the staff and have you enjoy yourself. They're excited to see the next generation of Londons. Can we do that, dear? I was thinking you might enjoy getting a haircut and makeover."

Her face lit up before she could help herself. "Fine. But you can't think that throwing some awesome purses at me is going to make everything okay with my mom."

"I know that."

"But you're gonna try? To make things right?"

"Of course."

I had no intention of trying. Emma had painted me as the Evil Queen a long time ago, and I simply didn't have the energy to fight with her.

Riley was looking at me, and once again, the resemblance cut through to my heart.

"You okay, Gigi?" she asked, her voice kinder now.

"Oh, yes. It's just . . . your eyes are the same shade as my son's," I said.

"Sheppard?"

"Yes."

"Did you ever get *any* information about what happened to him?"

"We did not, unfortunately. There were leads, but none ever turned out." Summer blue. That's how I used to think of Sheppard's eyes, as clear as the summer sky.

"Maybe," Riley said, "maybe we can do something to find him this summer. I mean, not find him, maybe, but figure out what happened to him. I listened to a podcast about that once. We could do a DNA test. And register you on one of those genealogy sites? Maybe there's someone out there related to you that you don't know about. I'm really good on the Internet. Stalking and stuff. Maybe I could find something."

Unexpectedly, there was a lump in my throat. The child had just offered more than anyone had in decades. "That would be so kind, dear."

Soon, the Missing would end. That was the only thing I was looking forward to in suicide . . . seeing my son again. Surely God would grant me that.

I felt a hand in mine.

"Don't cry, Gigi," Riley said softly.

"I never cry," I said, squeezing her hand. "Now. Tell me about your friends back home."

CHAPTER 14

Emma

had a bad feeling about the trip to New York. Genevieve wasn't being honest with me, not that this was a big surprise. But surrendering Riley to her for an entire day made me nervous. The best thing I had going for me in life was that my child loved, respected and liked me. I knew Genevieve shouldn't be able to touch that, but the idea of my grandmother telling my daughter what a loser I was—in much more elegant prose, of course—made me feel a little sick.

We'd only been here a week, but it felt like an eternity. Genevieve seemed to like Riley. That made me nervous, too, because I remembered all too well how it felt to win that woman's approval, only to have it yanked away. But when she gave a small smile, or said, "Well done," it had been like winning an award in front of a thousand people.

I shouldn't worry so much. Genevieve was different with Riley. If she wanted to spoil her a little bit, that would be fine. In essence, that *was* why we were here this summer . . .

to get Riley away from the bitchery of the little coven and, yes, be able to claim her name. Genevieve London's great-granddaughter. The only one.

Possibly the heir to all this.

It was a clear, bright day, and the rooms of Sheerwater were drenched in sunlight. I had to give it to Genevieve—she'd balanced sophistication with hominess, and while the house was a mansion, it felt . . . comfortable. Friendly and posh, the way I used to picture Garrison London.

I went into the formal library. I had some clients scheduled, but not until later.

Genevieve had updated almost every room since I lived here, and now the chestnut bookcases were lit from within, which made them glow, the books magical. White birch logs were stacked artfully on the fireplace irons, and there were a few photos on the mantel—Genevieve and my grandfather on their wedding day, looking happy and wealthy and in love. Her dress was the best of the fifties—white satin covered by handmade lace, a Grace Kelly type of gown.

I suddenly remembered Genevieve had told me I could wear her dress on my own wedding day. I'd been maybe . . . nine? Still unsure if I'd be staying in Connecticut, still hoping my father would come back for me. For some reason, I'd been crying . . . Maybe my other grandparents had called and I was homesick for Downers Grove? I remembered Genevieve had come home from work, taken one look at me and brought me up to the cedar closet, which was big enough to be a bedroom. Took out a giant box lined with tissue paper and held up the dress.

"This was mine," she said. "It was one of the best days of my life. Someday, you'll find a wonderful man like your grandfather and marry him, and you can wear this dress. It will never go out of style."

The memory was so vivid I could smell the cedar. And she'd been right about one thing, anyway—her dress was a classic. I wondered if it was still in that closet.

I wished I'd met my grandfather. Life would've been a lot better for my father, and probably for me, if Clark had had a good male role model.

Here was another picture of Garrison, smiling into the camera. A nice face. A photo of my father, perhaps twenty, on the deck of a boat, also good-looking but without the confidence that shimmered in Garrison's pictures.

Another photo of Clark and Sheppard, their arms around each other, Sheppard taller, my father still chubby with baby fat.

Poor Gigi. Losing a child, especially without any sort of closure, had to be brutal. An image came to me of a younger Genevieve, waiting by the phone, praying, calling her son's name in the woods for weeks.

I had never counseled someone who'd lost a child. Twice a colleague had recommended me, and twice I'd recommended someone else. Maybe when I was more experienced. Maybe when Riley was grown. I was so paranoid about her safety that I'd practically had a chip put in her ear. Honestly, why didn't they do that? You could track your dog, but not your kid?

I texted her. How's the ride going?

She texted back. Fine. Don't worry. Charles is a good driver. Better than you! LOL!

I smiled. Let me know when you get there, okay? Send pictures!

Okay! Have a nice day! I might get a haircut if that's okay.

A haircut, huh? Riley had the most beautiful hair known to humankind. Who would cut it? People would sell their souls for long, curly red hair!

I sighed. Parents had to pick their battles, and hair wasn't going to be one of mine. Whatever you want! Love you so much!

Love you too, Mama!

Mama. Love swelled in my chest. I sighed. It was only 9:37, and she wouldn't be back for twelve hours.

Maybe I relied on my daughter too much, our girls'

nights watching *Project Runway* or *The Bachelor*, our bian-
nual trips to Wicker Park and the fabulous thrift stores
there. These past two years, when she started to have more
of a social life, when I assumed she'd be home on Sundays,
only to have her tell me she had plans . . . it had been something of a shock. Of course I wanted her to have a good
social life, a nice group of friends, but I hadn't realized that
I'd feel a little bit . . . abandoned.

We all have our issues, I knew. Being left was mine.

I needed a hobby while I was here. I only had twelve
clients a week. Maybe I needed another job. Maybe the grocery store was hiring.

Maybe Pop would want to have lunch with me in town.
He and I always had a vegetable garden, a really big one that
took up about half of the backyard, and I missed digging
and staking tomatoes. Oh, man, the tomatoes were so good.
On Sundays in the summer, we'd make tomato sandwiches
with Miracle Whip. Don't judge—in the Midwest, Miracle
Whip is used in 90 percent of all recipes. We'd sit there, the
three of us, and Pop and I would have a beer, the sound of
lawn mowers and music filtering in from the street.

He'd been awfully good to come here with me. Then
again, he was the best man in the world. He never talked
about my mom—his only child—but when Riley was born,
and he saw the glow of her hair, his eyes welled up, and he
kissed her head so gently. He'd come over for lunch the
other day to see Riley and me and to exchange jabs with
Genevieve.

I took out my phone and called him. "Hey, you want to
grab lunch today, Pop?"

"I can't, honey. I'm a little busy."

"Doing what?"

"None of your business, that's what. How about dinner?
I'll cook for you."

"Dinner would be great." Better than eating here under
the baleful gaze of Helga.

"Six o'clock?"

"Sounds perfect. See you then, Pop."

So. Still nothing to do. I could swim in the pool, except I didn't want to. Genevieve would inevitably hear about it from Helga, and later make some snide comment about my workload, or my use of the pool, or how there were bathing suits designed for chubby women.

I knew what I'd do. I'd start a vegetable garden. I'd passed Gordon's Nursery the other day when I took a drive, and I could buy some tomatoes and basil, peppers and parsley. Genevieve had more than enough room, and it would give Pop and me something to do here.

I went outside into Sheerwater's impressively landscaped backyard. The scent of wisteria and lilacs was thick in the air, and the wind was strong enough to make the flagpole rope twang against the metal pole, making me glad I wore a cotton sweater and jeans. A rabbit hopped along the base of the stone wall, where there were two Adirondack chairs overlooking the sea.

I couldn't make the garden too close to the house, because Genevieve would think it was very déclassé to be growing one's own food. Roses, yes. Beans, never. Still, she had ten acres. I'd scout a location.

I went to the gardening shed and got a shovel, then continued past the pool, which had been upgraded from the aquamarine of my childhood to some dark gray stone. I walked through the gate on the west side, into the wilder part of Genevieve's land, where the pine trees grew and the towering rocks were covered with moss. I used to play here, making fairy houses or pretending that I was a baby wolf. Then Genevieve found me and scared the life out of me with tales of people who took children, or children who got lost or fell into the sea and drowned, or children who had fallen and hit their heads and were now brain damaged.

So. My love of the forested part of Sheerwater ended, until I was sixteen, and Jason and I would come out here and look at the stars and kiss, the slippery fabric of a sleeping bag underneath us, our breathing shallow, our bodies pressing against each other's.

Those were happy, horny times. Maybe the time when I felt most secure, in some ways. Secure that Jason loved me, which he had. Secure that even if Genevieve didn't, she put up with me and would continue to do so. Secure in my future, which, though blurry at that time, seemed drenched in sunshine.

God laughs, as they say.

The pine needles crunched gently underfoot, and a blue jay announced my presence to the other wildlife. The sun was warm on my hair, and I was abruptly aware of how stinkin' beautiful it was here. As a state, Connecticut never got its fair share of love from outsiders, but those of us who lived here kind of preferred it that way.

There. A sunny spot on the eastern side of the point, where there was an open space in the trees. It would get plenty of light but be safe from the harsh afternoon sun in high summer. I'd grow tomatoes that smelled earthy and warm, and even Genevieve wouldn't be able to resist them. Peas and basil and parsley. Maybe even mint for her to put in a pitcher of ice water, the only thing she drank other than booze and coffee.

Then again, Genevieve might be dead by high summer.

I wish she'd let me talk to her doctor. I'd snoop, but I was a healthcare professional, too, and I'd never be able to violate HIPAA. Still, my grandmother allegedly wanted me here to take care of her and do my duty; if she wouldn't tell me what that was, it was going to be harder.

I set my shovel to the ground and shoved it into the dirt, which was soft and yielding.

"What are you doing?" came a voice, and I shrieked a little. "Stop it! Jesus!"

A man stood behind me.

"Who are you?" I asked, my hands gripping the shovel.

"This is private property." Did I have my phone? Should I call 911?

"Who are *you*?" he demanded. "And what the hell do you think you're doing?"

"I live here."

"No, you don't."

He looked . . . familiar. Then again, I'd grown up here, so a lot of people looked familiar. But wait. I knew him. "Miller?"

"Yeah."

"Emma. Emma London."

Recognition dawned on his face. He ran a hand through his black hair, and a few strands of silver caught the sunshine. "Sorry. How are you?"

"I'm good. How are you? It's nice to see you."

Miller Finlay was Jason's cousin, older by five or six years. I'd met him a few times, since Jason and I had dated all through high school. Jason had idolized him—the cool older kid who'd take him out sailing, or to a bar in New London to hear a band. In fact, Jason had been in Miller's wedding; it was why he hadn't been at Riley's birth. Granted, she'd been two weeks early and my labor lasted all of four hours, so I couldn't blame him for that.

Miller wasn't quite as handsome as Jason, but he was nice-looking just the same. His face was angular and somewhat plain and he looked older than . . . what? Forty? On closer inspection, I recognized the boy Jason had loved so much. They worked together at Finlay Construction, the business their fathers had started.

"I guess I heard you were coming to visit for the summer. I must've forgotten," he said. "How are things? How's your daughter? Riley?"

"Yes. She's great. She and Genevieve are in the city today, so I thought I'd make myself useful and put in a vegetable garden."

"Not here, though," he said.

"Why's that?"

"My wife is buried here."

I flinched. "Oh, God. I'm so sorry, Miller. I didn't . . . I don't think I knew that."

Had I even heard that his wife died? Did Jason forget to tell me? I think I would've remembered something so huge.

Miller looked away. "Genevieve got permission from the town. She, uh . . . Ashley, that is, she didn't like cemeteries. And she loved this place. Loved Genevieve, too."

Ashley, yes, that was it.

I had a flash of a memory of a Christmas party at the Finlays', Miller and Ashley sitting cuddled together on the couch. They'd just gotten engaged, and it made me so happy, the idea that high school sweethearts would end up together, as Jason and I hopefully would. Miller saw me staring at them, the perfect couple, and winked.

I definitely would have remembered if Jason told me his cousin was a widower now.

"I'm so sorry," I said again, and my voice was husky. "How long has it been?"

"A little over three years."

I knew better than to ask how it happened. If he wanted me to know more, he'd tell me. The blue jay called again, watching over us, and a seagull dropped into the water, emerging with a small fish in its beak.

"Do you have any kids, Miller?" I asked, a little surprised I didn't know the answer.

"Yeah," he said. "Tess. She's three."

My heart dropped before my brain caught up with the math.

His wife must've died right after the baby was born. Oh, God! How could Jason not have told me about this? The whole family must've been devastated. Ashley—in my limited experience with her—had been really, really great. Funny and friendly, even to someone who was not quite in the family.

"Well, Riley's sixteen now, so if you need a babysitter, she loves kids. And, uh, so do I. You know. I mean, I'm sure you have plenty of help, but we're here! If you need anything! But you're probably an old pro."

Hard to believe I was a therapist.

"Thank you," Miller said.

"It must be very hard," I said, managing to remember *something* from all those years of training.

He didn't answer for a second. "It is. Well, I should go. I'm sure I'll see you again. I, uh . . . I come to Genevieve's cocktail parties sometimes. On Fridays."

"Good! Good. It'll be good to see you." Three *good*s. Jesus.

"Have a good day," he said. Four.

"You too."

I watched as he walked away, hands in his pockets, head down.

Broken.

There, just at the edge of the forest, was a bench I hadn't seen until this minute. A plaque was mounted on the back.

In memory of Ashley James Finlay
Cherished wife, mother and daughter
Loved by all who knew her.

CHAPTER 15

Miller

Childbirth classes were the most fun Miller had ever had with his wife, and that was saying a lot. Their marriage had been, in a word, perfect. Yes, she ground her teeth at night and it made his blood run cold. Yes, he talked too much about how many laps he swam every time he went to the pool. No, he didn't really get along with her dad, and yes, she hated Thanksgiving at Uncle Rob and Aunt Courtney's house and always got a little drunk to counter Aunt Courtney's endless stream of meaningless chatter.

Ashley had terrible taste in television, weeping over the schmaltzy and predictable network shows. She hated his taste in music, a genre that was best described as Another White Guy Who Loves Rap. She was a clean freak and couldn't relax if a pillow was out of place; he was unable to fold shirts according to her exacting requirements.

But every day, they were so *happy* together. Every day they touched, kissed, hugged, said I love you, did something nice for the other. Every day, he felt lucky. Miller didn't understand men who complained about their wives. He couldn't imagine someone other than Ashley, with her smile that could lift his heart, the way she'd fill up his phone with deliberately unflattering selfies, how she laughed harder than anyone when he cracked a joke at a party.

All those years together, and he still felt his heart rate kick up when he pulled into the driveway every night. Sex, which had always been great, only got better the more years they spent together. They loved to travel, strolling hand in hand through strange towns, whether it was an hour away or on the other side of the planet. Every time he cooked her pad thai, she lit up like a little kid on Christmas morning.

That was what made marriage great. The ease of it, the connection, the appreciation. The companionship. She was his best friend bar none, and she told him everything, every bit of gossip about her friends, her job—she was a civil engineer who specialized in water runoff, and the way she talked about it made Miller wish he'd gone into it himself. She would laughingly torture him with the details from her grandmother's phone calls—how many times the old lady had pooped, what she ate, how gassy the dog was.

He loved their life. He loved it. Every frickin' day, he was grateful.

Their only sorrow was not being able to get pregnant. They'd put off trying a few years; they'd gotten married young—twenty-three, both of them—and wanted to travel, have sex in the living room, drink a bottle of wine on a Saturday night without having to get up at dawn with a baby. They were young and healthy. Infertility? It never crossed their minds.

Until they learned they were infertile. They'd expected Ash to get pregnant in the first few months. After eight months without so much as a late period, they went for workups. Nothing was wrong, the doctors said. Nothing that they could find. Try not to stress over it. It would happen when it happened.

The months of trying turned into a year, then a second year, then a third. Ashley went on Clomid; Miller had his sperm count checked three times. And even then, with that sense of failure starting to loom, even then they felt lucky. They loved each other more, because in not getting everything handed to them . . . well, Miller thought it brought a depth to their love. After all, the stars were most brilliant against the darkest sky. Their infertility was the darkness, making every happy moment all the more brilliant for it.

And there were so many happy moments. Simple, unfettered, easy moments. The way he'd put Luigi the cat in their bedroom, since he got up first, and she'd smile without opening her eyes and say, "Thank you," and the cat would curl against her stomach and purr. The way she'd bake just before he came home sometimes, so the house would smell like bread or cookies. How they held hands without thinking, how she always invited him to feel her freshly shaved legs, which always led to sex. How she was so grateful that he set the timer on the coffeepot so she'd have her cup seconds after stumbling out of bed.

The failed adoption was the darkest time. Well, Miller *thought* it was the worst. He was still naive back then. They'd come within an hour of being parents. An *hour*. Sitting in the hospital waiting room, clutching hands, trying not to bolt into the room to see the baby who'd been promised to them. He could still hear Ashley's wail when the social worker came out and told them that the teenage mother had changed her mind.

Their hearts broke, but they broke together, and when one of them lost it, the other would comfort, and they'd take turns in their grief, putting on a brave front for the world, fielding the stupid, well-meaning comments about what was meant to be and next time and all that shit.

And then God smiled on them. In a month that was no different from any other, long after they'd stopped doing temperature charts and checking cervical mucus, Ashley's period was late. It was six days before she even wondered, and he failed to notice she wasn't power-eating Ben & Jerry's, as she always did on the twenty-ninth day of her cycle.

Without telling him, she just went into the bathroom, peed on one of the old pregnancy tests, and came out, eyes wide, cheeks flushed, and showed him.

After years of telling himself that it was just fine if they never got to be parents, Miller's knees almost gave out at the wonder, the miracle, the perfection of what that stick showed him.

They would be a family. Not just a couple, though that was everything—but a *family*.

Though it had taken years to get pregnant, Ashley was clearly great at gestating. She really did glow. Her cheeks were pink, her hair was shinier, her stomach was beautiful, her breasts even more gorgeous than usual. She felt great, had more energy, and when he tried to take care of her and pamper her, she'd laugh and swat him away. Still, he insisted on nightly foot rubs with peppermint lotion. He cooked for her—kale and salmon, roast chicken and new potatoes. He assembled sundaes piled with real whipped cream and hot fudge he made himself, sent her to the spa for prenatal massages, rubbed coconut oil into her beautiful round belly and worshipped her amazing, miraculous body that could grow an entire human. Their daughter. Their little girl.

The childbirth classes were like an exclusive club they'd been longing to join for years, and unlike most clubs that make you wait to join, this one wasn't a disappointment. They sat on the floor in a yoga studio with the other blessed couples, Ash between his legs, leaning back against him, Miller's hand on her stomach. He could feel the baby rolling and pushing, and if that wasn't proof of God, he didn't know what was.

The class covered things like physiology and pain management—"Manage this, pal," Ashley had whispered, shaking her fist at him with a grin. Positions and transitions, massage and relaxation, breathing and Kegels. After class, they'd go out with the other three couples—Sasha and Joe, Victoria and Maggie, Dominic and Hannah. They'd drink nonalcoholic beers or seltzer water and laugh and talk, and it was the happiest time in his happy life.

Ashley and he made their birth plan. They decided that it would just be the two of them in the delivery room; her mother would fret, her father would faint, and his mom had moved to Arizona after his father died. The thought of a crowd in the waiting room . . . it just wasn't them.

Besides, it had been just the two of them for so long, always a little separate from everyone else, first because they'd gotten married the year after college, then because they truly liked each other more than they liked anyone else . . . and then by the sorrows of infertility.

So just the two of them it would be.

They went through the downloadable checklist for a happy birth, snorting over terms like *squatting bar* and *hot therapy.* "Sounds like how we made this baby," Miller said, and Ashley laughed so hard she had to run to the bathroom.

Her death was not discussed. There was no check box for "Please choose if you would like to be in the room when your wife is given CPR."

In the ninth month, however, as they were lying in bed—or, rather, as Miller was lying in bed and Ashley was stuffing pillows under her stomach, between her knees and against her chest, she suddenly stopped what she was doing and looked at him.

"Yes, my empress?" Miller said.

"If something goes wrong in there, I expect you to pick the baby over me."

"You got it. I've had my eye on a younger, hotter wife anyway, so thanks for making it easy."

"I'm serious, Miller. Promise me you will."

"I'm not going to have to choose anyone, honey. Nothing will go wrong." As if he had *any* right to say that. He had no knowledge, no authority, nothing. God, the fucking *arrogance* of that statement. "And even if there are complications," he added, taking the old whistle-past-the-graveyard approach, "the odds are huge that you'll both be fine."

"I know," she said cheerfully, and went back to punching her pillow. "Just wanted it out there."

She went into labor at three fifteen on a Tuesday afternoon, a day after her due date, and called him right away. In a rush of adrenaline and fear and joy, Miller drove home, fast but not dangerously, and found her beaming and deep-breathing at the door. "No hurry to get to the hospital," she said. "Why go there when I can torment you here? Oh, God, here comes a contraction! Honey! Feel!" She grabbed his hand and pressed it against her stomach, and Jesus God in heaven, it clenched like a rock, and Ashley's expression became sharp and focused as she inhaled slowly, held her breath and then exhaled as the contraction released.

"Amazing, right?" she said.

"You are," he agreed.

At first the contractions were erratic—every fifteen minutes, then every ten. After a couple of hours, they got stronger and more regular, though not closer together. But Ashley was sweating and making low moaning noises, so he called the doctor, was instructed to come in, and got the smaller suitcase, which had been packed for a month. For a second, he paused, touching the baby's outfit. A little white fuzzy thing with lambs on it.

By the end of the day, his child would be in this world.

The thought made his heart ache with love. His baby. His little girl. He already loved her so, so much.

"Let's go meet our little one," he said, and her beautiful eyes filled up with tears of happiness, and she gave a wobbly smile. He hugged her gently, breathing in the flowery smell of her shampoo, and kissed her neck.

It would be the last time he held her.

The ride to Westerly Hospital took fifteen minutes. Ashley's contractions hadn't changed much.

At the hospital, Dr. Dunn met them cheerfully, checked for dilation. Only three centimeters. "It's gonna be a long night, kids," she said. "Ashley, do you want anything for the pain?"

"I'm good," she said.

"Okay. If you change your mind, there's no shame in that. Anything that makes this easier on you is a win."

There were terms discussed by the nurse and doctor: fetal monitoring, advanced maternal age (Ashley was thirty-seven), but Miller was locked in on his wife. She held his hand and stared into his eyes as she breathed and he counted, riding out the contractions, smiling when she could. She rolled on her side; he rubbed her lower back. When a few tears slipped out of her eyes, he brushed them away and kissed her forehead.

"You're a superhero, you know," he said. "I love you."

Labor became more painful, the contractions stronger, and Ashley's moans were low and guttural. Miller wondered why everyone was so calm, why his wife had to go through this, why it was taking so long. The soundtrack they'd made had played four times already. Every time her face whitened with pain, his heart felt like it was being pulled apart.

When Ashley dozed off around eleven p.m., Miller asked the doctor if everything was okay. If the baby was doing all right, stuck in there for so long.

Dr. Dunn laughed gently. "The baby is just fine. This is Ashley's first delivery, so I'm not surprised it's taking so long. No two babies come the same way," she said, patting his arm. "It's normal to worry."

He was normal, then. Maybe he was just paranoid, but it felt like something was . . . off. That the baby *wasn't* going to be okay, that the ultrasound has missed something, and even though the fetal monitor showed a fast, regular heart rhythm, a sense of doom had crept into Miller's bone marrow.

Please, God, let the baby be healthy. Please. They'd waited so long. If she had special needs, that would be okay. Ashley had a cousin with Down syndrome; Miller had grown up with a kid who had brain damage from a car accident. They'd talked about this. It would be fine.

So long as the baby lived, they could handle anything.

It never occurred to Miller that his wife was the one who'd needed the prayers. He figured they'd put in their time, their heartache. Ashley was healthy and strong. She'd done yoga all the way through, even that morning. Truly, it had been a beautiful pregnancy unmarred by morning sickness or heartburn or swollen ankles. Her hips were wide, perfect for pushing out babies. Or, if they needed to do a C-section, that was okay, too. Ash was in great shape.

The night slipped by, measured by contractions, by Ashley's soft groans, her grip on his hand tightening and easing.

When the transition came to the third stage of labor, they asked Ashley which position she preferred for pushing. She wanted to sit with her feet in the stirrups, and Miller stuck by her side like a burr. "You can do this, babe. You're almost done."

"I better be," she said, gritting her teeth.

She'd been in labor for twenty hours. He had to wonder how she could keep going. How the baby was still okay, squished in there for almost an entire day.

"One . . . two . . . three . . . ," he said. "Doing great, honey. You're amazing."

She pushed. And pushed. And pushed. Miller understood why women had babies, because he would've been a whimpering wreck begging for death by now. But his wife . . . she was otherworldly in her strength. An Amazon.

Half hour. Forty-five minutes. An hour.

Why was this taking so fucking long? How could the baby survive? He knew how, but it didn't seem right.

"You're making great progress," Dr. Dunn said. "I can see a little bit of the head. Reach down and touch your daughter, Ashley."

And so, before the baby was even out, Ashley became the first person to touch her. It would haunt him for the rest of his life. She looked up at Miller with an expression of such joy, such love and wonder, that he knew everything would be fine.

He was wrong.

She suddenly fell back on the bed. "I'm cold," she said. "I'm freezing." Another contraction gripped her and she tried to push again, but she was weaker this time.

The nurse, Chelsea, got her a blanket, even though Ashley was covered in sweat.

"You okay, babe?" he asked.

"Fine." Her eyes were too wide.

She didn't look fine. She was abruptly white. Her teeth were chattering, and her muscles were shaking.

"Ash. Ashley," he said. She didn't answer. "Doc?" Miller said. "Is she okay?"

"This is normal for the third stage," the nurse said, glancing up from between Ashley's legs. "Her muscles are in overdrive."

"Get . . . the baby . . . out," Ashley said. "It hurts . . . a lot." It was the first time she'd complained about anything.

"A few more pushes, and you'll have your girl. It's a little late for an epidural," the doctor said, looking between Ashley's legs. "This baby will be out in five minutes. You're almost there." She glanced up. "You good, hon?"

"Yep." There was a grimness to her voice, but when she looked at him, Miller's heart started a sick, rolling thump.

"Doc," he began.

"Next contraction, I want you to bear down, the best push yet, sweetheart," Dr. Dunn said, and Ashley did, hard. Her teeth were chattering, and her tremors had turned to almost violent shaking. This couldn't be normal.

"Almost there, honey," Miller said. He felt like crying, and not with joy.

Ashley nodded. Tried to take a deep breath and then coughed. It was a deep, nasty, evil sound.

"Babe?" he said.

Ashley's eyes rolled back in her head, and she was suddenly limp. The monitors began to bleat.

"Ashley?" the doctor asked. No, yelled.

"Oh, shit," the nurse said.

Miller heard a wet splat. "Ashley? Honey?" She didn't stir.

"Ashley! Ashley! Wake up!" the doctor barked. "Fuck! Get a crash cart in here and call the NICU! Massive transfusion protocol, stat! She's coding!"

The words flew past in a blur, and terror bottomed out in his stomach. All he knew was that his wife was not awake. He pressed his forehead against hers. "Ashley," he said. "Ash. Wake up! Wake up, honey, our baby's almost here! Honey! Wake up!"

Then someone was dragging him by the arm, pulling him away from her. "Stand here and don't move," the person said, and he stood alone in the corner, stunned as if he'd just been clubbed. There were so many people around Ashley, and everyone seemed to be yelling. The bed was lowered so she was flat, and they were ripping open her johnny coat.

They were giving her chest compressions. Chest compressions! Miller's mind went to a white roar of fear. There was so much noise, the monitors blaring, Dr. Dunn yelling things like "Suction, suction, where's the transfusion team, goddamnit?"

Was that *blood*? Was that a puddle of *Ashley's* blood on the floor? What the fuck was happening?

The doctor's hands were in Ashley, pulling the baby out; how could they do that to her? They were going to tear her in half! "Is the tube in?" Dr. Dunn said. "If this is AFE, she's got a probable PE."

"Ashley," he said, but it came out weak, like a question.

"Chelsea, push on her stomach or we'll lose the baby, too," Dr. Dunn said to the nurse, who was grim faced and way, way too rough.

What did that mean, "lose the baby, *too*"?

"Please," he begged, out loud or silently. "Please, honey. Please. Please. Please."

A bluish, blood-soaked alien was pulled out of his wife and handed to a team of four or five people draped in gowns, who fled the room. Blood poured out of Ashley, and now a doctor was straddling her, pushing so hard on her chest Miller heard a pop and distantly realized a rib had just snapped.

"Get the fuck off and shock her!" Dr. Dunn yelled.

Was this really happening, or was this a dream? "Wake up," he said, to himself and Ashley both. "Wake up now."

This was not how it was supposed to be. They had a tube in her mouth. "Doll's eyes," someone said, and yes, her eyes were sliding around the wrong way.

Like she was dead. Like she wasn't there anymore.

Miller stood there, arms dangling like pieces of sea-weed, useless and weak, at his side. "Ashley?" he said, more loudly this time.

"Get the husband out of here," someone said.

"No," he said. Or something. He said something.

"You're in the way," a woman said. "We can help her better without you in the room. Your baby needs you."

"Please save her," he whispered.

"We're doing everything we can," she said, and her eyes were kind and sad.

Then a different person—a man this time, wearing a uniform. There were so many people! A guard? Yes, a security guard led him down the hall. "You need to pray now, mister," the man said. Miller looked at him, uncomprehending.

There was a waiting area, and the man guided him to a chair and then stood in the doorway, looking down the hall. More people were running to Ashley's room, talking, yelling, barking at each other . . . but Miller's mind could only hold the one sound, the splat of blood on the floor. Only one sight—the bluish, bloody *thing* being pulled out of his wife.

Pray, the man said. He had forgotten how.

"I'm the hospital chaplain," a woman said. "Can I call someone for you?"

He looked at her. "What?"

"Can I call someone to wait with you?"

"Oh. No." Why call anyone now? He would call when there was good news. When the doctor came out and said, "Man, that was crazy! She's doing fine, Miller. You can go in now."

The woman took his hand. "Lord, we ask for your strength and comfort for this man. Watch over his wife and child."

Save her. Save her. Save her.

Ashley, that was. She was the only one who mattered. The baby was immaterial now.

The chaplain's mouth was still moving. The man was still standing in the doorway, head bowed, lips moving. That was nice. The man was praying for him. That was very kind. Miller thought he might pass out. But no. He should stay here for when Ashley woke up. Sure, she might be sick for a little while, but he would take care of her. He always had. It was his job. His calling. He was a great husband.

Time had stopped. The world had stopped, really. Eventually, a nurse came in. "Your baby's doing fine," she said, and her mouth wobbled as she tried to smile. "Do you want to see her?"

"No."

The nurse looked at the chaplain. They stood up and talked. "Miller, come this way, please," the chaplain said, and they took him into a room where they told him to sit, and then the nurse went to a plastic bassinet and took out a bundle. She put it in his arms.

It was a baby. He supposed it was his baby, his and Ashley's. It had a pink face and its eyes were closed. "Your little miracle," the nurse said, tears in her eyes. "Perfect Apgars," and Miller did not give one rat's ass. The baby was wrapped tightly in the blanket, like a burrito. There were bruises above its eyes, and a smear of blood on its forehead.

Ashley's blood.

The chaplain stayed but stopped speaking.

A long, long time later—hours, maybe, Dr. Dunn came into the waiting room, white faced. She sat next to him, tears in her eyes, and said she was afraid she had very bad news. Ashley hadn't made it. In a very rare complication, it seemed amniotic fluid got into her system, and it caused a catastrophic event, an embolism to her lungs, massive hemorrhaging and cardiac arrest. They'd tried to revive her for more than an hour, but her condition was simply too dire. Dr. Dunn was very sorry. So sorry. Such a rare event, so sorry it happened to Ashley. She reached out and put her hand on Miller's knee.

"So she's . . . she's not alive anymore?" he asked.

"I'm so sorry for your loss, Miller."

Ashley hadn't made it. Was that right? She was dead? The word sat there like a boulder, crushing the air out of his lungs. Dead. Ashley was dead.

That didn't seem possible. More likely, it was a mistake. "Are you sure?" he asked.

"I'm afraid so."

"Could you just answer the question with one word, please? Is my wife dead?"

Dr. Dunn's mouth wobbled. "Yes."

There was just white now. White and quiet. He actually might pass out, he thought distantly.

Ashley was dead. It . . . they wouldn't lie about that. It must be . . . it must be true.

"Can I see her?" he asked.

"Of course."

He went back down the hall with Dr. Dunn, to the room he and Ashley had walked into so happily the day—really? just a day?—before.

His wife lay on the bed, covered in blankets, only her head showing. The floor was smeared with her blood, though Miller could tell someone had tried to clean it up. He was grateful for the attempt.

The nurse, Chelsea, was crying, and a tech was wiping Ashley's face. A tube lay next to her throat. The tech took it away, then turned off the monitor, which showed only flat lines.

One by one, they left in silence, leaving him with his wife's body.

The baby was still in his arms. He'd almost forgotten. He could've dropped it. They shouldn't have left him alone with a baby. He was clearly not father material.

But Ashley was born to be a mother.

"Ash?" he whispered, because surely she would open her eyes when she heard his voice. "Ashley? Please, honey."

There were miracles, after all. Remember the baby who had died, then they put him on his mother's chest, and an hour later, the baby woke up? Also, that Christmas special of *Call the Midwife*, where the dead baby was in the leather bag with the hot-water bottle and then it wasn't dead anymore? He and Ashley had avoided that show until she got pregnant, then spent an entire long weekend binge-watching it and eating spaghetti. So yeah. Miracles. *Lazarus, come forth!* He remembered that Bible story, he sure did! Best one in the whole book! Total miracle. So how about one now?

I believe, Miller prayed. *Please. Please bring her back.*

It seemed that his prayers went unheard, or ignored, or God just side-eyed him on the request. Ashley's eyes remained closed. Her chest did not rise or fall. Her hair spilled out on the pillow behind her, her beautiful honey-colored hair. Her freckles stood out, because her face had no color now.

The baby stirred.

Right. The baby.

He unwrapped it—her—and placed the baby on his wife's chest, skin to skin, and folded her arms around the baby. Ghoulish, that, but the baby didn't seem to mind. Should he take a picture? Jesus, no! Where did that thought come from?

Was her soul close by? Was she waiting for him to say something?

"The baby's fine," he said, not recognizing his own voice. "You did it, Ashley. She's fine, and I'll . . . I'll take good care of her."

After a while, the baby started to fuss, then cry, then scream, furious that her mother was dead. He didn't blame her.

Miller just sat there, looking at Ashley. Eventually, a nurse came in and gently rewrapped the baby. "Let's get her down to the nursery," she said, and guided Miller out of the room.

He stopped in the hall and turned around, going back in for one more look.

He realized this would be the last time he saw her face, felt her hair.

"I love you," he said, and kissed her. Her lips were not hers anymore. They were just layers of dying cells. He rested his head against her cool forehead. His tears slipped from his face to hers, into her hair. "I love you," he said

CHAPTER 16

Clark

Clark London grew up with the understanding that he was supposed to have been better. A better son. A better student. A better athlete, artist, musician, conversationalist. He should've had a better body, a better face . . . His was nice-looking, but bland. He resembled his father, but a paler, more generic version. A weaker chin.

But you get what you get. No use trying to change nature, right? Sheppard had been the good son, the perfect child. Even before his older brother disappeared, Clark could remember that feeling of being less than. Maybe it was age; maybe if Shep hadn't died (or "gone away," as his mother still said, which made Clark grit his teeth every time), he wouldn't have felt so inferior. But as it was, Sheppard's death intensified things a thousand percent.

He didn't remember much about his childhood, to be honest. He'd loved his father, who, even though he was brokenhearted over Sheppard, still smiled at Clark, still threw him the football, still cheered him on as he did tricks in the swimming pool. When his father died, it left a huge blank space in his life. Clark, alone with his mother, her iciness, her unbreachable heart. Even years after he'd passed her in height, he felt small around her, and fearful, as if she might slap him, though she never had.

Like most boys, he filled his spare time with TV, the pool, some friends who were kind of jerks but not that bad. Sometimes he'd take the sailboat out and just float on the Sound, glad to be away from his mother, watching the clouds float across the sky, thinking about how his father was with Sheppard now instead of him. Always second. Always the B-list son.

Every night, he and his mother sat down for a joyless dinner during which he was criticized. "Honestly, Clark, must you scrape your knife that way? Must you?" He mastered the art of tormenting her—manipulating a bit of food on his upper lip and leaving it there, pretending not to notice until she snapped at him to use his napkin. Or he'd slosh his milk just a tiny bit so that she couldn't see, and the milk would drip down the glass and through the tablecloth, staining the antique cherry table. If he could manage it, he'd fart when he walked past her, not flush the toilet in the downstairs bathrooms, pick his scabs just because it bothered her. *Sheppard* would never have done that. Of course not. *Sheppard* was perfect.

He stopped pretending to listen to her or make her like him when he was about ten. By then, Donelle lived with them. She was so much nicer than his mother. Donelle let him watch TV in her little den when Genevieve traveled, which always caused Helga to go to her room in a huff. Donelle played video games with him and asked him about his friends. She knit him a blue scarf in the softest cashmere and said it brought out his beautiful eyes. She'd never met Sheppard, so she didn't know *Sheppard's* eyes were the beautiful color, that startling blue that leapt out from photographs even now.

As for his friends, well, they weren't real friends. They were just boys he hung around with. The truth was, Clark didn't know how to be with people very well. Still, his money, his family history, his mother's instant fame in the fashion world couldn't be ignored by the other kids, who weren't as wealthy, whose houses weren't as beautiful as Sheerwater, who didn't have a three-bedroom apartment in the city waiting for them. His family had donated libraries and hospital wings. A driver picked Clark up from school every day. So even if the other kids didn't like him that much, they knew better than to say it to his face. Unlike his mother.

"You have to stop being so weak, Clark," she said to him. "You're thirteen. It's time to start being a man. Show some interest in life, for God's sake."

But what was there to be interested in? Lacrosse was okay, he supposed. He liked action movies. He could sail, but it had been way more fun with his father. He liked shooting at the Rod and Gun Club. He liked *Playboy* magazine and jerking off. He read comic books, waiting for the day when, like lucky Batman, his mother would die, and he would inherit a fortune and start being heroic.

When he finished eighth grade at Stoningham Country Day School, he went off to Choate, where you could buy really good weed, get by on a fifth-grade knowledge of math, skip half of your reading assignments and still get into an Ivy League school, which Clark proved by getting into Dartmouth. The fact that there was a building there with his grandfather's name on it didn't hurt.

He floated through six years of undergraduate studies in New Hampshire, changing majors three times, popular by way of his name, wealth and, of course, his mother's business.

The college finally expelled him after a drunken episode when he set a fire in the Rauner Special Collections Library. It was *funny*; they had no sense of humor, those snotty academic assholes. Who really read Shakespeare, anyway? It was the final straw, the dean said. Clark didn't care. He was bored anyway.

He returned to Sheerwater for three weeks before Genevieve informed him he had a job and an apartment in Manhattan, where he'd be moving the coming weekend.

That was fine. He was *supposed* to be a titan of some kind, and why not? Born to an impressive family, the finest education, blah blah blah. This was what happened to kids like him—they knew people, or their parents did, or they joined certain clubs at certain Ivy League schools, and bam! A seat in the House or Senate, or a job with an impressive title, a huge salary and a corner office, regardless of ability to do the work. Sorry, everyone not born with a pedigree. That's how real life works. You can be a self-made man, like . . . like Spider-Man or something, or you could do it Clark's way.

Career-wise, all Clark had to do was show up. His job was with FHK, the advertising agency that handled his mother's empire. Vice president of customer relations, whatever that meant. Starting salary, $400K a year. Six weeks' paid vacation, an office overlooking St. Patrick's Cathedral, a smokin'-hot secretary fifteen years older than he was who knew more about the accounts than he ever would and made a tenth what he did.

His apartment was fantastic. His mother had furnished it (of course); an Upper East Side flat on the thirty-second floor, two bedrooms, giant living room, kitchen, three baths, terrace. Leather couches and soft towels, a maid service twice a week, a fully stocked bar, probably expensive artwork on the walls.

He deserved it, because he was a London, an almost-graduate of Dartmouth College, and he knew his way around sailboats. That was his job, apparently. Taking clients out on the company sailboat. Buying them cocktails at the Standard. Golfing in Westchester County. Treating them for dinner at Peter Luger's or whatever restaurant had a Michelin star, then out to a high-class strip club, depending on the client's taste. Clark would sit in a conference room while a minion threw around terms like *ROI* and *attribution* and *media buys*, and he would fantasize about screwing his assistant. That was his birthright. Sorry, suckers.

He knew he was hated at FHK—by those above him, who'd naively thought he'd bring a little more to the table, being Genevieve's son, and now found themselves with an employee they couldn't fire; and by those beneath him, who had to do all the grunt work and *know* things and have *talent*. Clark knew it wasn't fair—he had nothing to offer other than a few choice stories about his mother, or some of his more colorful shenanigans at Dartmouth. He knew he was a shell. That he'd be nothing without his name. He knew his mother wished he'd been kidnapped and/or murdered instead of St. Sheppard. Try living with that legacy. "And this is Clark, the son we *wish* we'd lost." The disappointing second. The never-as-good-as-Sheppard son.

Too fucking bad, Mother.

One day a couple of years into his employment (so long as Genevieve used FHK, they had to keep him), the firm sent him to Chicago for some reason he wasn't clear on . . . take some client to dinner and schmooze them, which Clark did, the entire night wondering just what it was that the client made and what FHK was supposed to do for them. Didn't matter. The client was about his age—James or Jay or Jack—Clark just called him J-Dog.

They met at a ridiculously overpriced restaurant, Clark taking out his reliable stories. "Yes, *that* Genevieve London is my mother. Don't make me tell you about the New Year's Eve when she rolled naked in the snow with Ruth Bader Ginsburg!" The fact was, if RBG had visited Sheerwater, Clark wouldn't have known who she was. He knew she was tiny and old and women loved her. Something to do with government.

When the tab had been paid by the FHK Amex and Clark had glad-handed the Jay or James or Jack to the door, he felt an unexpected loss. J-Dog had liked him. The sommelier had *loved* him, given that he'd ordered three bottles of wine costing eight hundred bucks each. The waitress also liked him, because she'd gotten a $500 tip. She was pretty and friendly without sucking up to them, and she didn't interrupt every ten minutes asking how things were.

But now the night was over, and Clark had nothing left to do. He went back to the table, figuring he'd finish the last of the wine and see if there was a late movie playing somewhere close by.

"Can I get you anything else?" the waitress asked when he sat back down. Nice rack. Redheaded, too. He liked redheads.

"Join me for a drink?" It was closing time, after all. The waitress, who had a month for a name, checked with her boss, then sat down. They ended up talking for another hour. With all the alcohol in his system, Clark felt happy and relaxed and . . . well . . . kind of cool. After all, she didn't know what he did or didn't do for work. She didn't know whose son he was. He was just a wealthy customer, young for an executive, in the city on business.

"Are you free tomorrow night?" he asked when the manager started turning off lights.

She was. She took him to a dive bar and, three hours into their date when he called her June, laughed till she cried.

"You're two months off," she said, and when he didn't get it, she added, "April. My name is April." She said it nicely, too, not making fun of him.

She wanted to be a chef, was working at the restaurant to make contacts, was in culinary school part-time, had dreams of owning her own establishment someday.

He invited her to see his suite at the Drake, where she laughed more and told him it was twice the size of her apartment. She opted not to sleep with him but said if he asked her out again, she'd probably say yes.

He extended his stay in Chicago for a few days, then a week, then ten days. April was too great to leave. She was happy and energetic and great in bed. She borrowed a bike for him so they could ride through Chicago, which he abruptly loved—Grant Park, the lake, tea at the hotel with all the old ladies, April giggling away.

On the eleventh day, his boss at FHK told him to get his ass back to New York or lose his job, and by the way, she was about to cancel his company credit card.

"I quit," he said unexpectedly. But yes! He didn't need those ass pains at FHK. He was tired of the thinly veiled contempt, the attitude, the resentment at his Brunello suits, his swanky apartment, his Porsche. They hated him and wished they could be him in the same breath, the hypocrites.

He would be a novelist, he decided. Why not? Six years at Dartmouth had probably taught him to be a great writer. Besides, with his last name, the publishers would be falling over each other to get to him. It would be a fictionalized memoir of his life—his sad childhood, stories of his horrible, unloving, impressive mother, his adventures with pot and drugs and women, the stupidity of his job in New York, his previously undiscovered genius with words.

The redheaded April thought it was a great idea. Clark was young, after all. If he wanted to write a novel (he didn't mention the memoir part, not sure if she would approve), what better time was there? He should go after his dreams.

She was his dream. Sure she was. He suddenly wanted to be married, to live with her, this happy April, to be normal and loved and have kids and cut the grass, then go into his den, because he would have a den, of course, and write what would clearly be a great American novel, like . . . like . . . like that Hemingway book about fishing. Or *Mommy Dearest*, because who hadn't read that one?

April was his muse. She was vibrant and fun and naive, unlike the Dartmouth girls who'd looked down their perfect noses at him, the New York women who didn't even pretend they weren't interested in his money, asking if he owned his apartment, dawdling in front of Tiffany's, whining about wanting to go to Turks and Caicos. April was different. She loved her really boring but normal, nice parents. She wanted to have kids and own a restaurant, and she wasn't shy about it.

A chef and a novelist. How cool was that? Wouldn't they be the best people on the block? Everyone would want to know them, come to their parties, admire how happy they were. They'd summer in Europe and their kids would be really well behaved and maybe there'd be a nanny so April wouldn't have to take care of them all the time and could still be really hot and beautiful.

Genevieve was icily furious when he told her he quit, but hey. The Upper East Side apartment was in her name. She could do what she wanted with it.

Two months after he met April Riley, Clark proposed. He'd been writing furiously, had rented a comfortably furnished town house—it was nice, being like the normal people. He swept April off her feet. It was easy, since he had the trust fund. He could send her flowers, buy her pretty things, ask for her help picking out a car.

He listened more than he talked, because honestly, he didn't have too much to say, and it was fun listening to her chatter energetically about work and food and her family. She didn't really understand who his mother was because she didn't shop in those circles, and she thought his silence and smiles were because he was smitten. Which he kind of was.

She said yes. After all, what woman would not love this new Clark, so creative and driven and happy? He'd lost some weight, was better-looking than ever, went with her to the Art Institute and wandered around, making jokes about some of the art, standing in feigned awe at others (they were just pictures . . . some scribbles, some almost as good as photos). It made her happy, and the guy who made April happy had to be a pretty great person.

Her parents thought they were rushing, but Clark and April didn't care. They got married at city hall and bought a house in the burbs. When he called Genevieve to tell her the news, there was a long silence.

"When may I meet my daughter-in-law?" she asked. She flew out the next weekend, and April hugged her and said she hoped they'd be friends.

"Wouldn't that be nice?" Genevieve murmured, and April was too naive to realize she'd just been rejected. "Did she sign a prenuptial agreement?" Genevieve asked when April was out of the room.

"I don't believe in those," Clark said, though the truth was, it hadn't occurred to him. His mother rolled her eyes. *Too bad, Mother! You don't get a say about everything!*

He took great pleasure in showing his mother their house, an ordinary two-story in an ordinary neighborhood in an ordinary town outside Chicago. His trust fund had bought it, and while he could've afforded more, he wanted to rub the banality in her face. The neighborhood was everything he hadn't had as a kid—close-knit and noisy, people's children riding bikes and playing tag . . . utterly, beautifully ordinary. Clark almost wished he were a kid himself, because the trick-or-treating would be killer around here, and Genevieve had never let him go. It was too common, she'd said. Candy made in a factory somewhere? How garish.

Marriage was mostly nice. April was in school part-time during the day, worked at night and cooked great meals when she was home. Sex was fantastic. Granted, she irritated him sometimes; she'd ask about how his book was going, or if he'd done the laundry or picked up groceries, and obviously Clark was too busy for that.

"You're home a lot more than I am," she said. "You have to do your share, Clark." She didn't want a housekeeper, which was his solution. She said it was silly, there were just two of them, and they should save their money and be self-sufficient. Typical midwesterner.

So Clark lied about writing, said he had to be out of the house to be productive, said the public library was better, and told her he had meetings with a few agents who were already interested. The library proved to be boring, and writing was harder than it looked.

> *My mother always loved my brother best, but he disappeared when he was seven and I was five, and she was never the same after that. If I ~~cried~~ was upset about it, my father would come in my room and ~~cuddle me~~ sit with me. Then my father died, and that really ~~sucked~~ was sad. He was a good dad. Not like my mother, who was a cold woman.*

He didn't like writing about Sheppard, though his brother's disappearance was probably the most interesting event of his life. He'd doodle pictures of Genevieve with horns or a penis, then see if the library had any comic books, because his love for them had never died. Sometimes, he took a nap in a worn chair in the stacks.

He joined a writers' group that met in the library. Keep at it, they said, those other members. Writing was harder than most people knew! Maybe he needed a break. Refill the well. When two people in the group got published, Clark stopped going. They were irritating, anyway. Thinking about writing was fun, but they were kind of show-offs, talking about page counts and contracts.

Sometimes, Clark went to the movies; sometimes he went out to eat. Then he joined the Park Ridge Country Club. Didn't mention his membership to April, because she really wasn't a country club girl—totally different world from her middle-class upbringing. She didn't even play tennis. Clark was immediately at home, though. The golf course was fantastic, the tennis courts beautiful.

There were also a lot of hot women. Tennis moms and college-age daughters, second and third wives wanting to prove they belonged, single women using membership as a way to network.

So, sure, he had affairs. That was what men did. Chances were his father had cheated on his mother, and who could blame him? Clark bought a sleek condo in Park Ridge so that when he did want to sleep with someone, it was easy. Life was good. Out here, he was out of Genevieve's shadow at last. His own man. The fact that he lived on the money from his trust fund didn't matter. Once the book came out, he'd make millions. Once he sold it to Hollywood, more millions. Maybe he'd be a producer. Write the screenplay. How hard could it be?

When April got pregnant, he wasn't thrilled. Marriage had kind of lost its shine, frankly. April wasn't as happy as she used to be. Not as interested in him, either. But hey. A kid would be fine. A son. Maybe he'd name him Sheppard, if only to piss off his mother.

Sheppard . . . sometimes, a memory stabbed at him while he was dozing . . . the way his heart had lifted when Sheppard asked if he wanted to play. Clark seemed to remember that Shep had helped him brush his teeth at night. But Sheppard hadn't been perfect, though Mother would stab herself in the heart before admitting it.

When he and April visited Sheerwater over Christmas, he paused at the pictures of him and his brother. "A handsome boy," April said, slipping her hand in his.

"Yeah."

"You must miss him so much."

"Yup." He wished his brother hadn't died. Ditto his father.

"Let's not talk of painful subjects, shall we, April?"

Genevieve said, frost in her voice. "Clark, do tell me about your . . . book." She always paused like that, as if she knew he was really fucking tennis moms or falling asleep in movie theaters or playing golf and drinking at eleven a.m.

"Book's going great," he said.

"It's going up for auction in Hollywood," April said, and Clark winced internally. April would buy that kind of lie; Genevieve would not.

"How very thrilling for you," she said.

"Yeah, well, they want a second book," he said, "plus a proposal for the third, and that's almost done, so we should know pretty soon."

Genevieve lifted an eyebrow, managing to convey that she knew he was lying through his butt. Yes. If the baby was a boy, they'd name it Sheppard, and it would make Genevieve furious. There was only one child named Sheppard in the world, and it was hers.

The baby was a girl, unfortunately. He floated Sheppard as a girl's name, but April said no. Her heart was set on the name Emma, so whatever. That was fine. The kid was cute enough. Genevieve visited and pronounced her "quite the Riley." The insinuation was clear . . . Even his kid wasn't good enough.

A month after the baby, April's mother got sick and it was bad, one of those long, wasting diseases with no cure. April was sad, of course, and that got tiring pretty fast. Actually, maybe she was sad before, too. The postpartum depression thing, maybe? It *was* depressing, that was for sure. No laundry done, the house a mess, smelling like breast milk and sour diapers. Her mother getting sick sure didn't help. He hired a cleaning service and a private nurse for his mother-in-law, but even that didn't cheer up his wife.

When Emma was about four months old and sleeping through the night, Clark told April he had to travel for "research."

"You can't go!" April had wailed. "Are you crazy? I'm barely holding it together, Clark!"

"I have to," he snapped. "Who do you think pays the bills around here?"

"Your family's money!"

"You think that covers everything?" he said. "You're wrong." Total lie. "I've been doing some consulting in the city, and I *have* to, since you want to stay home with the baby." Another lie. No one would hire him, for one, because FHK had sued him for breach of contract just to be spiteful. The trust fund could pay for an entire life for the three of them, though, yeah, he'd spent a lot in the past few years. Not that April knew about that.

They fought. It just made leaving easier.

God, he'd forgotten how much he loved traveling! Everything was new when you traveled. Every time you saw a street you'd never seen before, where no one knew you, where you could be anyone, where you had no history . . . what was better than that?

He went to LA, because you never knew who you might meet, especially when you stayed at the coolest hotel in town. Clark dressed the way he thought a writer would—black T-shirt that cost $350, distressed jeans ($900), Converse high-tops (cheap), the $5,000 briefcase his mother had given him when he started at FHK. Monied (i.e., successful), but still cool. He lingered in the hotel lobby, saw Denzel Washington come in with three or four other people, thought about asking for an autograph but then decided to simply pretend he knew him.

"Denzel, my man!" he said, jumping up to shake the actor's hand. "Clark London. Great to see you again."

"You too," the actor said with a courteous nod as he continued into the restaurant with his people.

"Take care!" Clark called, then regretted it. But it was okay. It was great! He'd met Denzel Washington! They'd talked. They were both in the hotel on business, and they'd talked, so this was definitely a step in the right direction. He found himself saying to strangers at the various bars he frequented, "Denzel and I were talking a few days ago at the Bel-Air when we had drinks . . ." And they *had* had drinks. Not together, but practically.

He loved it. Stayed away for three weeks. When he came home, April was different. Her eyes told him she knew what he'd been doing. He lied, said the consulting had been just fine, and guess what? The books had been optioned and were going into production soon . . . He and Denzel Washington— yes, really—had talked about him playing the lead role of, um, Pierre (April knew nothing about what he had or hadn't written).

"Is there any money associated with this?" she asked.

"As a matter of fact, yeah. I'll have the check this week."

Her face changed. "Clark, that's great," she said, hugging him. So he had to take a huge chunk of money out of his trust fund—Jesus, the fines they charged, it was robbery— and gave it to his wife. "My advance," he said.

That turned out to be a big fucking mistake. April spent the money—just about all of it—on an experimental treatment for her mother at the Mayo Clinic, and for about a year, Joan felt better and could walk again. But she gradually slipped back, and when they tried the treatment again, it didn't work, and Joan was back to dying and the money was gone. Clark guessed he could see why April would do that—desperation, whatever—but it was a waste just the same.

Another trip was required for sure. And another after that, and another after that. Since he'd lied and given her the money, April wasn't as suspicious, so why not? Plus, she'd spent the money the way she wanted to . . . on her mother. It was his turn now.

The women . . . God! The tennis moms from the club were one thing, but he'd have to see them again, and it could be awkward. But the Portuguese woman who'd stayed in the suite across from his and knocked on his door, stark naked? The French woman who came up to him at a bar and said, "Would you like to fuck me?" in that dead-sexy accent?

Maybe he'd write a travel column for the *New York Times* or Condé Nast. "Where to Get Laid in Europe." "The Best Places to Eat in Scandinavia." "The Most Beautiful Women in the World." "Best Cocktails on the Continent." Hey, that last one was a good one. He'd have to pitch that to an editor or something.

When Clark took the occasional look at his trust fund, he'd flinch a little. Traveling first class to, say, Australia could run in the tens of thousands of dollars, let alone doing all the things he liked to do. Five-star hotels and restaurants. Spas. Golf. Scuba diving. Sometimes he'd make friends or be invited to join a group of people, and he loved picking up the tab. He'd rent a boat and throw a party, and it felt so good, having friends. Sometimes he'd "entertain" a woman (his little term for cheating) and sometimes, sure, he paid for it. Nothing like a high-class whore.

But the money, which had once been self-sustaining because of royalties or interest or other financial things he'd never tried to understand, was shrinking with alarming speed.

Well. There was always more if he needed it. Genevieve wouldn't let her son and grandchild live in squalor. She wouldn't expect him to travel coach. Maybe he'd even work for her. Sales or something. The fact that he'd already failed at that wasn't important. He'd cross that bridge when he came to it.

When Clark was home, he tried to be a good father, but it really wasn't for him. He read a few books at bedtime, gave Emma piggyback rides, bought her a trampoline for the backyard, which April made him take down when Emma cut her head falling off it. The kid was cute and nice, though she really did look like April's side of the family. She had blond hair, at least. That she got from him.

But April . . . Jesus, she was kind of a train wreck. Her mother got worse and worse, her father was heartbroken and trying not to show it, and April was a mess. He told her to go to a shrink, get on some meds, whatever she needed. He'd sit with her on the couch every night for a few weeks between trips, watching stupid television shows, fold the laundry to show he cared, take her out for dinner, and she'd cheer up a bit. Or not. Then the itch would become too great to ignore, and off he'd go again.

"Babe, I have to. It's important."

He couldn't wait to get out of there. After all, he was Clark London. He grew up in a mansion on the water. Their little neighborhood had lost its charm and become boring. Ordinary. And he wasn't. He was his father's son, or so he liked to think. Garrison London would've wanted Clark to have everything, see everything, *especially* because of what happened to Sheppard. Clark deserved the best things in life. His father would've insisted.

Joan got worse, in and out of care facilities. It was sad. One time, she got pneumonia and almost died, and let's be honest, Clark was kind of hoping it would just end. His father-in-law was stoic, at least. But April would go wild with grief, crying, literally pulling out her hair, and it was fucking scary.

"Honey, you know she's going to die," he said, and she punched him in the *face*. Why? What was wrong with her? Joan *would* die. April had to get used to the idea.

He sent her away to a spa in Arizona that had yoga and shit and told her to rest and relax, then called his mother and told her April had been checked into a psychiatric facility.

"Good," Genevieve said. "She worries me."

"Can you come out, Mother?" he asked. "Emma would love to see you."

"Fine. I'll be there tomorrow."

She was horrified by the state of the house, the mess, the grubbiness that Clark had stopped noticing. By the end of her first day there, she'd hired painters, a garden service and a cleaning lady, and had ordered meals from a local caterer. Clark couldn't help thinking this was exactly what April should've done with the money he gave her.

He told her the facility was expensive. "I'm sure it will be worth it," she said, and thank God, she wrote out a fat check.

In a rare moment of admiration, he said, "You never fell apart like this, and things were a lot worse for you."

She gave him an inscrutable look. "Thank you," she said. "But we're not all as strong as we'd like to be."

Translation: *Your wife is weak and useless.* Clark agreed.

After two weeks, April came home, Genevieve left and things were a little better. But there was still something off. They hadn't had sex in ages. Maybe more than a year, now that Clark thought of it. *He'd* had sex, of course. Just not with April.

April's regular doctor prescribed antidepressants. That helped. She took good care of Emma, and Emma was a happy enough kid.

But the sunshiny, fun, optimistic girl he'd met and married was a long way off from this pale, tired version who only seemed happy from 3:35 to 8:00 p.m. . . . the hours when Emma was home and not asleep. Weekends were tough, because April was in overdrive—make a fort! do crafts! go ice skating!—and it exhausted her. He told her to take it easy, that Emma would be fine just reading or watching TV.

"I have to make up for you," she snarled.

They never talked anymore. She didn't ask when the movie of his (unpublished, unwritten) book would come out. Sometimes he would catch her looking out the window, and her eyes were so sad it made him want a divorce.

Yeah. A divorce. That would help. She'd get a big fat settlement (from Genevieve, because the trust fund was, hello, almost gone). Free from April's moods, he'd really come into his own. Write that book, or get that job as a travel columnist, penning witty observations from faraway places.

When he couldn't take home another minute, Clark booked a trip to Seattle. Such an awesome, artsy city, a place where he really belonged, not like flat, predictable Chicago. A week there, he told April. Scouting sets. Yes, he had to go; he was a consulting producer.

The city smelled so good, all that seafood, the fresh air from the Pacific, the dark, rich scent of freshly ground coffee. He booked himself into the Fairmont Olympic, told the bartender he was a movie producer, and found himself with a bunch of new friends, a lot of good weed and seemingly endless possibilities. He was thirty-four, and he felt both young and mature in this city of perpetual men-children. It was the money, he decided. His success, or at least the perception of his success. His last name. His *legacy*.

At the last minute, Clark decided to change his flight, choosing a ten p.m. flight instead of the morning flight he'd scheduled. Just one more day before he went back home, one more round of sex with Moira, a street artist who, aside from not shaving anywhere—not even armpits—was stunning (and a wild, furry animal in bed). So what if he came home at night instead of at noon?

It was one day. Hours, really. He'd tell April that his flight was canceled or, better, his cab had a flat tire, because she couldn't track that one. But he wouldn't call her, because then she'd be mad or sad or depressed or all three, and he just didn't want to hear it. He'd been gone twelve days; what was twelve more hours? He totally deserved some extra fun.

So he stayed.

Obviously, if he had known his wife was planning to

commit suicide, he would've come home earlier. It was horrible that Emma had been the one to find her. Horrible. So selfish of April, he was surprised. Yeah, yeah, if he hadn't bumped his flight for one more fuck with Moira, *he* would've been there to find her, but April should've planned on something coming up.

Her note said she couldn't keep going, and she wanted to leave when Emma would still have good memories of her. That she was sorry but this was the only choice she had. That Emma would be better off without her. That she couldn't let her daughter watch her fade away, and the fading just wouldn't stop. That she'd been drowning, and dying felt like a life raft. It was as if she didn't exist anymore, and she was terrified something would happen to Emma and she wouldn't be able to help her. That, by April dying, Emma would be safer, and though she'd be sad now, it would be better for her in the long run. Her parents would understand, and her father needed to focus on her mother now, and she was so sorry.

No mention of Clark.

What the *fuck* was he supposed to do with that? Talk about having the rug yanked out from under you! His wife had been *suicidal*, and she hadn't even said anything? Who did that? Oh, and now Paul was telling him she'd struggled with depression since she was a teenager. Nice to know now, after ten goddamn years of marriage!

That's when his father-in-law punched him in the face, and God, it hurt!

"Maybe if you'd been around more, you would've noticed," Paul growled, shaking his hand. "You think she didn't know what you were doing out there, when you were supposedly writing a book or making a movie or any one of your damn lies?"

So. His fault again, same as he'd been blamed for not being the one who *went away*.

A month of single parenthood, a tear-stained little kid

with snarls in her hair, the Rileys' palpable grief for April and hatred for Clark . . . it was impossible. A widowed father who had to do *everything*? Being the parent was hard! Emma was supposed to see a shrink and go to the regular doctor and get shots and do projects for school, and she was a Girl Scout and also played soccer. (Did eight-year-olds really have to do this much?) Then there was the homework, the laundry, the notes from the teachers talking about how Emma was struggling, the school counselor who wanted to talk, the other moms who had loved April. There were groceries and cooking and cleaning up and bills and taxes to be paid and, frankly, fuck it.

This was not who he was. This was not good for anyone. If his mother-in-law hadn't been shriveling away; if the Rileys had had any money; if they hadn't been so fucking sad and ruined, maybe Clark would've left Emma with them. Maybe, if Paul hadn't punched him in the face, he would have, even with Joan dying in bits and pieces. If he could've hired a nanny, a cleaning service, a chef, a lawn service and not have to do the grunt work of life, maybe he would've kept his child.

The money, unfortunately, was gone. Millions and millions of dollars, squandered in ten years.

But Genevieve . . . she had an endless supply. If she was taking care of Emma, maybe she'd soften toward him and give him some more. Yeah, Genevieve would see that Emma was a good kid. Maybe she'd put him on the payroll or, better yet, just cut him a check. She had piles of it, the hateful old bag.

Emma would be happier in Connecticut, at Sheerwater. Fucking huge house, staff, the pool, the Sound . . . better than the little shitbox where her other grandparents lived. They could visit her if they wanted to.

It worked. Genevieve gave him money and off he went again. Was it hard to say goodbye to Emma? Sure, but that would pass. He knew he was supposed to feel more for her.

He just didn't. He blamed Genevieve. How many shrinks would agree that she'd basically ruined him after Shep died?

He came back at Christmas to collect his check and see his daughter and be criticized by his mother and see Donelle, who told him Emma was a good kid and he was right, it was better for her here.

Even so, he felt ashamed. To drown out that feeling, that echo of not good enough, he did what he always did. Traveled. Drank. Lied. Avoiding thoughts of his daughter became habit. Days passed without his thinking of her. She became a small fact in his big life.

But sometimes, in the middle of the night, he'd remember his own father, and how Garrison had made him feel safe and loved and . . . enough.

Clark had given his child away.

Then he did it again.

Years later, millions later, when apparently he was a grandfather, he had another daughter. And this one . . . she was sick. She had problems. Bad problems. He was a middle-aged man, for Christ's sake! He hadn't been equipped to take care of a regular baby, let alone Hope with all those issues and needs and special care. The money it would take to keep her healthy and safe was a gut punch. Even with the allowance from his mother, he didn't have it.

But Genevieve did. Always her weapon, the mighty checkbook. Back he went, and it was horrible, telling her about Hope, her prognosis, telling her that he needed her money again, knowing he had failed on every front a man could. He cried as his mother looked at him in disgust.

It didn't matter. Hope would be cared for. The mother, Kellianne, who had clearly seen Clark as a meal ticket and lied about birth control, was more than happy to sign away her maternal rights.

Funny that he had sobbed uncontrollably when they took Hope to Rose Hill. That he finally knew what love felt like, and it sucked, literally sucked the soul out of you.

He had failed Emma years ago, and Emma had become a cliché, a teenage mother, living with Paul Riley in Chicago. He failed Hope months after she was born. Oh, it would've been great to think that finally he could've become a gentle, kind, selfless man, caring for his special-needs child.

But he just couldn't, not after all the years in his emotional wasteland.

That just wasn't how life worked.

CHAPTER 17

Emma

I always thought Jason and I would get married. Right up until he told me he was engaged, I thought we'd be husband and wife.

Color me stupid.

We'd dated from the age of sixteen, starting at the tail end of our sophomore year, losing our virginities to each other over the next Christmas break. By then, I was so in love I could barely see straight. Every night, I fell asleep with the phone tucked against my ear. Every day, my heart walloped in my chest at the sight of him. He was so *happy* all the time. So sweet and fun, up for anything from rock climbing to swimming in the Sound to watching Brat Pack movies from the '80s. More than anything, Jason was blissfully . . . uncomplicated.

Given my family history, there was a lot to be said for that. My memories of my mother told me she'd been happy, so they obviously couldn't be trusted. I hated and loved my mother so much that it was hard to think about her . . . the woman who had sung during my baths, made the best forts, colored with me for hours and then one day decided to kill herself and let her eight-year-old child find her body.

My father had seemed like a good enough dad when she was alive. Granted, he was away a lot, but he'd bring me toys from his travels, give me the occasional piggyback ride . . . but when I needed him the most, he simply dumped me at his mother's. When he came to visit every Christmas for his annual twenty-four-hour visit, most of his time was spent arguing with his mother and sighing when he looked at me. After the initial year of waiting for him to come get me, I realized he wasn't . . . and by then, I didn't want him to.

The day my mother died, my father had been delayed at the airport or something. He didn't get home until hours after our neighbor Mrs. Fitzgerald made me call 911, and I was in shock. Pop had gone to the morgue, and Grammy had me wrapped in a blanket, and she and Mrs. Fitzgerald were talking in gentle voices.

Then my father came home.

Rather than take me in his arms and comfort me, he just fell apart, making the worst day of my life that much worse. To see him sobbing, shaking, crying so hard snot ran down his face, saying, "I'm sorry, April, I'm sorry!" when even I knew that she couldn't hear him. Later, when I heard the term *drama queen*, I always thought of my father in that moment.

It was Pop who'd said, "We'll get through this, honey," even when his face was gray and his eyes teary. My grandmother, who could still hold me on her lap at that time, stroked my hair.

Genevieve came out for the funeral. Told me to "be strong" and made me wear the black Mary Janes that were too tight.

For the first few days, my father and I stayed with my mother's parents, sleeping in my mother's old bed. We went home the next week, and everything was different. Everything was wrong. My once-cheerful room where my mom had read to me and made my stuffed animals talk in squeaky voices . . . what had happened? She'd loved me, and she killed herself! The kitchen where she'd made such delicious food now smelled like hot dogs and burnt toast, courtesy of my father. Papers piled up, and everything was sticky and grimy.

I wanted to move in with Pop and Grammy, but after a few weeks, my father told me I'd be visiting Connecticut.

He left out the word *forever*. He left out the words *by yourself.* He neglected to say goodbye, but instead just said, "Try to be brave."

So. I had no plans to forgive him for abandoning me, and he didn't seem to care much. Why? How did a person not care about his child? I mean, yes, my father had suffered, losing his brother, his father and then his wife. But you'd think (or so I thought, as a child, then as a tween, then as a teenager swamped with feelings 24-7) that those losses would make him love me all the more.

They didn't.

As for Genevieve, she was utterly inscrutable. She was doing her duty by me, and she made sure I knew it. Things that I thought would make her happy didn't. For instance, when I was put on the varsity swim team my freshman year, she told me to stop gloating; I had an unfair advantage, since Sheerwater had a heated pool we kept open eight months of the year. She'd go for days without speaking to me for no apparent reason, Donelle simply shrugging if I asked why Genevieve was mad at me. Then again, I sneaked in after curfew at least once a week after I started dating Jason, and she never said a word. One time, when I thought I'd be grounded for sure, since it was after one a.m., she said only, "Make sure the door is locked, won't you?"

So *uncomplicated* was a joy. Uncomplicated meant I could breathe. My shoulders would drop an inch when I was with Jason, and my teeth, which I clenched at night, didn't hurt as much. Jason's eternal good cheer, good looks, good kissing . . . what more did a teenage girl need? His parents liked me, welcomed me into their home, and all the love I gave Jason was returned right back to me.

He wasn't like other boys. He never was crass or rude or gross—no fart jokes, no filthy bathroom, no crude comments about women or sex. Instead, he'd tell me I was beautiful. I was fun. I made him so happy. He loved me.

You have to understand . . . no one said those things to me. Donelle was kind, but not loving in the way a parent might be. Pop was gruff, more after my poor grammy died. I *needed* someone to love. Anyone, really.

Jason filled that gaping hole in my heart. We didn't go for more than half a day without speaking, and with few exceptions, we did something every weekend and several times a week. On the appropriate holidays, he'd get me something lovely—a delicate bracelet or a journal or fancy chocolates. He held my hand all the time, in the halls of school, in front of my grandmother. We were voted cutest couple and prom royals.

Almost three years of blissful first love without a single fight, without tears, without drama. After all those years of feeling lost, I'd finally been found.

Then my period was late. I told myself it was the stress of graduating from high school, though we'd basically been killing time since Memorial Day. But I knew. One time without a condom, even with me on the Pill, which I forgot to take one time. One time.

When I was ten days late, I told Jason, and he came over with a pregnancy test he'd bought two towns over. We didn't say much; Genevieve was at some luncheon in New York, Donelle was repainting the laundry room, and Helga was banging around in the kitchen, brewing coffee, a smell I usually loved and now made me want to puke.

Jason, pale and silent, sat on my bed. I went into the

bathroom like it was a prison cell, pulled down my pants, prayed that the test would be negative and peed on the stick. Before the waiting time was even up, the two lines showed loud and clear.

My heart thudded against my ribs. I was pregnant, all right.

Not real convenient.

In August, I was supposed to leave for Smith College to double major in marketing and economics. My times had qualified me for the swim team. I was going to live in Cutter House, a special-interest residence where we'd only speak French. My roommate and I had coordinated our comforters. Even Genevieve approved of my future.

Which did not include a baby.

Oh, God. What was I going to do?

Suddenly, I wanted my mother so, so much. Forget that she'd killed herself. I wanted her, hugging me, stroking my hair, telling me it would be okay. I wanted the mother who'd tucked me in so perfectly every night, folding back the covers the perfect amount and kissing my forehead, nose and lips, then doing the same to Cookie Monster, who slept with me every night.

I put my hand over my stomach, where cells were burgeoning and reproducing, practically tap-dancing with life.

I was pregnant. God! This was *terrible*. Almost laughably wretched. Jason, too, had a bright future . . . well, a good solid future. He planned to major in business and go into his family's construction company. He wasn't a twit, but *mature* wasn't a word that leaped to mind when I thought of him. Fun. Happy. Nice.

Young.

So I should probably make things easy and not stay pregnant. My brain—and heart—bounced away from the uglier words.

My mother's face flashed before me, smiling, her freckles and pretty red hair blowing in the wind. The smell of her, always so comforting. The way we'd held hands and she'd let me wear her rings on my thumb.

This baby would be a piece of her, too. Her grandchild. Granddaughter, because I suddenly knew it was a girl. I believed in a woman's right to choose. I knew this could be over in a day. I knew life would be a lot easier if I followed the plan of college, staying in Genevieve's good graces, not becoming a teenage mother.

And I knew with abrupt certainty that I was choosing this baby. This clump of cells, this little zygote, had my mother in its DNA.

I loved Jason. I wanted a family with him, though I'd always thought it would be at least seven or ten years down the road. I'd always wanted kids, ever since I was about thirteen and started babysitting. Jason wanted them, too. Just a few weeks before, we'd gone out for breakfast, and the server's name was Meghan, and he'd said what a nice name that would be if we had a daughter someday.

I went into the bedroom. "Positive," I said, and Jason looked like he was about to burst into tears.

"Okay," he whispered. "What do you want to do?"

"I want to keep it," I said.

Jason closed his eyes. "Your call, obviously." Not exactly a reassuring answer.

"We can do this," I said more firmly. "It's a few years ahead of schedule, but we can do this."

He grimaced a little, then fixed his face. "Yeah. We can. You're right. We love each other, and we . . . well, we'll figure it out, I guess."

At that moment, though, sitting on my bed with Jason, our combined ages making us all of thirty-six, I was naive and selfish and right. Having Riley would turn out to be the best thing I ever did, and ever would do.

When Genevieve came home, Jason and I sat down with her in the formal living room and told her. She ordered Jason out of her house and, within the hour, cut me off and kicked me out. We told Courtney and Robert, and they were dismayed, betrayed and disappointed in both of us (me especially, those pesky eggs of mine seeming to bear more blame than Jason's sperm).

We talked about me going with Jason to the University of New England, but Courtney asked who'd pay my tuition, sliding Robert a murderous look when he opened his mouth. It didn't make a lot of sense, she said, and Jason nodded. Better if he went to college so he could support us.

"You can stay here, I guess," Jason said. "Take some classes, have my mom help you out." Courtney didn't have a job outside of homemaker, and now her only child was leaving for school. I looked at her hopefully.

"No," she said, her chirpy voice suddenly hard. "I'm sorry, I have to agree with Genevieve. You took this chance, Emma, and now you have to pay the piper."

I took the chance. *I* had to pay. Jason's life would be pretty much the same, it seemed. Four days before, Courtney had told me it felt like I was her daughter when she took me for a pedicure. Of course, four days ago, she thought I was heir to a considerable fortune.

So I called Pop and told him the news in a whisper. "Guess you better live with me," he said, his voice gruff. That was all, but it was so much.

"I'll come out to Chicago all the time," Jason said. And once it was settled, he returned to being his uncomplicated, happy self. "College seems so stupid, but I guess I'm not much good for you two without a career."

Besides, his mother had insisted he finish school. Insisted. And Jason rarely disappointed his parents. Knocking me up was bad enough. Dropping out of college before he started (or at any time) wasn't going to happen.

The fact that *I'd* had to put college on the back burner wasn't discussed.

So Jason flew me out to Chicago, told Pop he'd support

me and the baby, already had a job lined up on campus, thanked him for taking care of us and didn't seem to mind the fact that Pop said not one word to him.

We held each other and sobbed when it was time for him to leave. "I miss you both already," he said, and I knew he meant it.

But already I was growing up. I wanted Jason to live up to his promises, but there was a tiny kernel of knowledge in my soul, and it told me I was just another single mother about to be disappointed by the baby daddy.

I ignored it. I had to. As I grew bigger and more awkward, when stretch marks made it look like I'd survived a werewolf attack, when the baby pressed against my sciatic nerve and I could barely sit on the stool the grocery store provided, I had to think Jason would come through. We'd be a couple. We'd make it. The picture of our happy future cradled me when the lady at the community college told me that my check bounced, when the store manager yelled at me because I dropped a bottle of corn syrup and it broke, and he made me clean it up, even though I could hardly bend over because I was nine months pregnant, when my car broke down on the highway and no one stopped to help.

Later, I'd think long and hard about the selflessness and heroism of girls and women who go through pregnancy and give up their babies for adoption. Later, I'd realize I had no business having a baby without the means to support her, without any real knowledge of what it took to raise a child or even keep one alive. Later, I'd know the odds of Jason and me being a married couple were almost nonexistent.

When she was born two weeks early, my poor grandfather was at my side, trying not to see too much—Jason was at Miller and Ashley's wedding.

It didn't matter. When I first saw my daughter's beautiful face, I made a vow. *I'll do my best. Every day, I'll do my best.*

She had red hair. If that wasn't a sign from heaven that

my mother loved and watched over me, I didn't know what was. I named her Riley in honor of my grandfather. Olivia for a middle name, which had also been my mom's.

I honored my vow. Every day, every hour, I did the best I could to take care of my baby, love her and care for her, to try to deal with the exhaustion, the fear, the terror of being a single mother. That instant love I felt for her wasn't pretty or besotted; it was primal and fierce. I'd die for her. I'd *kill* for her. Later, it would gentle into the gift it was—the shimmering, wonder-filled love for my favorite person, my daughter, my treasure . . . my reason for being.

But I still kept imagining a future with Jason. When I figured out just how damn painful nursing was and broke out in a sweat when Riley clamped down, when she cried nonstop every afternoon for six straight hours until she was four months old, when she had her first fever and was so limp and sick, I held on to that vision. Pop was still working (he had to, with me and the baby), and calls from Jason were a lifeline.

"You're amazing," he said. "I love you so much. This will all be worth it, honey, I promise."

I wanted that to be true so much. I imagined a path toward a happy life out here. We'd have a little house. Sometimes, on a Sunday, I'd pack Riley into the little front carrier and go to open houses and imagine a couch here, a crib there.

Jason came to see his daughter, of course. He came every few months, which was not nothing. He made much of how he suffered for fatherhood, the only freshman in his dorm to be a dad, how the other kids at school couldn't believe it. He complained about how he had to take the bus one time since his parents wouldn't give him a plane ticket, making his trip seem Odyssean. He was often tired on the visits to Chicago and slept more than I did.

Pop would give me a look and say nothing, but I knew. I felt it. Over the months, then years, it became clear that

Jason was a perpetual boy, whereas I'd become an adult the day I saw those two lines on the pregnancy test. From that moment on, everything I did was for the good of my baby. My needs, wants, dignity, health, pride, everything . . . they were a far-distant second.

Meanwhile, Jason got Cs at the University of New England, would call to tell me about a party his fraternity had hosted where thirty uninvited girls had crashed. He told me he loved me but didn't think he could make the trip out over spring break because he'd been fired from his on-campus job. The ten hours a week had proved too demanding.

He contributed. I might've been naive, but I wasn't stupid. I sent him a list of our expenses each month, and he sent a check to cover half. I knew the money came from his parents . . . not that they ever acknowledged Riley.

It was crushing, but I didn't have time to wallow. I waited, yes. Boys matured more slowly than girls. I knew that motherhood was the strongest urge in nature. I knew Jason would've chosen an abortion.

But hope. That thing with feathers, right? Like a stupid pigeon who crashes into someone's windshield on I-90 and then flies off, not realizing that all its flapping isn't recovery . . . it's a death knell.

I *needed* that dying pigeon. When Riley spent her entire fifteenth month with a stomach virus so bad her butt was raw and she cried at the sight of food, I pictured being a "real" adult. Pictured Jason walking in like a man this time, not a skinny college boy, telling me it was time for us to be together, his parents and college be damned. That he'd bought a little house a few blocks from Pop, and it was waiting for me and Riley, and I'd plant tulips along the stone wall and we'd get a puppy and his job would support us, and I could take classes more regularly and wouldn't have to fall asleep with my head on a cash register, an open textbook in my lap.

It was like being a kid and believing in Santa. What's the upshot of knowing the truth? Why not hold on to the magic a little longer? Why not, when my days consisted of childcare, laundry, working, cooking, studying, little spurts of sleep that only reminded me how tired I was? Why not picture a fricking ring and a small but tasteful wedding, a swing for the baby, a blue couch where Jason and I would sit each night, his manly arm around me, the two of us unbreakable?

He had his moments. When I learned I was a sister and flew out to meet Hope, Jason came down from Maine, not telling his parents, and paid for the hotel. He brought Hope a stuffed animal and was kind to her. I cried when I had to say goodbye to her, and Jason took me to a tiny restaurant in Norwich, and I felt cherished as he listened sweetly and told me I was a good person.

Never once was he harsh or cruel. He was just . . . young.

Every time he came out, he'd kiss me, carry Riley on his shoulders, bring presents. The pigeon of hope continued to flap once in a while. I waited. I made excuses. I didn't want to imagine anything but that little house, that blue couch, the yellow tulips and Riley's swing.

When Jason graduated, I asked him when he was coming to visit. For the first time ever, his voice became uncharacteristically cool. "You've been riding me to get a job all these years, Em," he said. "Now I have one. I need to do it."

Me? Riding him? I'd been ridiculously accommodating. "I think I've been kind of amazing, actually," I said through gritted teeth.

"And I think I've done a lot more than most guys would've in my shoes," he said.

It was a threat. And yet, it was also true.

Two months later, he came out for a visit and everything seemed fine. He was happy to see us, kissed me, swung Riley around and called us his little family. The child support increased without my having to ask, which was good, because Riley was starting nursery school, and even at that age, there were extra costs.

At Christmas, he came out again, with a bike for Riley that she'd have to wait three years to ride, it was so big. On Valentine's Day, he sent me a card that said, *You treat me like a unicorn when we both know I'm an ass.* Not exactly romantic. In March, he came out, rented an unremarkable hotel "suite" that had an alcove with a twin bed for Riley, and invited me to stay over.

I did. We had quiet, not-great sex while our child slept. We were each other's first love. And, I told myself, sex, even not-great sex, showed we were still a couple. It was a fragile, fraying thread, but a thread nonetheless. He never mentioned a girlfriend, and I sure as hell didn't have the time or inclination to date. While the sex wasn't what it used to be, it was at least comforting.

The truth was, Riley was the love of my life now. The terror of being a mother had subsided when she learned to talk, when she got past the Year of Tantrums. Now her sunny, sweet personality was a gift. I was so used to our setup—my daughter, work, school, home life with Pop— that the vision of the little house got harder and harder to picture. Sometimes I'd take it out and dust it off, and try to imagine the day when Jason and I would get married. We were still so young, I told myself. There was no rush.

And so it went for two more years. Jason would visit, call once a week or so, mostly to talk to Riley, making her laugh and giggle. He'd send those checks. We'd see each other when I visited Hope—two nights in a hotel together. I figured out that talking about the future made him glum, so I only mentioned things that didn't involve him—what classes I'd be taking next semester, that kind of thing.

He never invited us to Stoningham. It was just as well, given how horrible his parents had been. Fuck 'em. Same with Genevieve. Not a word, and certainly not a check. So it was just Jason, Riley, Pop, Hope when I could see her, and me. My family. At least we had each other.

Then, when Jason and I were twenty-four, he came out

and asked if we could have dinner in the city without Riley, who was then five.

"It's always hard to talk when your grandfather is standing there like the angel of death," he said.

True. Pop had never warmed to Jason, but he begrudgingly agreed to babysit; he loved Riley. It was me going out with Jason he didn't care for.

Jason made a reservation at Gibsons, and I took my time getting ready, because I didn't have a lot of chances to eat out. Especially not at an iconic steakhouse. Especially not on a date with the father of my child. I bought a pair of barely used shoes at a secondhand store—black suede with three-inch heels, my first indulgent purchase since becoming a mother. I wore a black dress I'd had since high school and a silver necklace. Put my hair up, because Jason had always loved my neck, back in the olden days when we were teenagers.

I figured he was going to propose. He didn't. He did talk about marriage, though. He waited till our appetizers had arrived—shrimp for me, oysters for him, and we were on our second glass of wine. "I'm not sure how to say this, Emma," he said, and then I knew.

He'd met someone. She was really smart and nice. I would like her a lot. So would Riley. It was pretty serious. They, uh, they were thinking of getting married. But he wanted my blessing first.

"It won't change anything with Riley, of course," he said, covering my hand with his. I looked down. I'd painted my nails with clear polish that afternoon. They looked strangely nice.

He was marrying someone else. Jamilah, her name was. I waited for heartache and rage and . . . and . . . well, something.

"Are you going to want joint custody?" I asked, just before my throat clamped shut. An image of me putting my fiery-haired first grader on a plane flashed in front of me, and then I did feel something. A knife in my heart.

Jason pulled his hand away. "No! No, of course not. I wouldn't do that to you."

Such a giver. And yet, I was glad, because for a second, I thought I might stab him if he said yes.

"I do love you, Em," he said. "Just not romantically."

"Yeah. That's fine." I took another bite of shrimp.

Riley would stay with me. That was all that mattered.

No house with a stone wall. No blue couch, no puppy, no swing in the backyard. No tulips. The pigeon, who'd flapped intermittently all these years, finally gave up the ghost. I'd known all along that Jason would never come through. It was time to admit it.

When Jason dropped me off later that night, after I'd had filet mignon and scalloped potatoes and crème brûlée and was slightly drunk from the wine and the dessert martini and more than happy to stick him with the enormous bill, he opted not to come in. "I'll see you and Riley tomorrow, okay?"

"You bet," I said. "Thanks for dinner."

I wobbled inside on my unfamiliar heels, kicking them off the second I went through the door. Pop was sitting at the kitchen table, doing the crossword puzzle.

"You gettin' married?" he asked.

"Nope. But Jason is," I said, sitting down across from him.

He filled in an answer. "Good," he said, not looking at me. "You deserve a lot better than that idiot."

I swallowed, the first tears of the night finally gathering in my throat.

"You gonna cry?"

"Nope."

"That's my girl." He flicked a glance at me, patted my hand. "I need a six-letter word for a work-shy person."

"Skiver," I answered.

"Smarty-pants," he muttered, filling it in. "Riley's staying with us, I take it?"

"Yes."

"Good."

"Yep."

"Go to bed, sweetheart," he said. "Sleep tight. You're better off, you know."

"I know. Thanks, Pop."

I went upstairs, regretting the twenty dollars I'd spent on those shoes, and feeling very, very old.

Because I was a mother and always had to do what was right for my child, I told myself I'd be friends with Jason, good friends. I'd never give him reason to step further away from Riley. I wouldn't bad-mouth him to her, I wouldn't talk about money in front of her, and I'd be cordial and friendly and decent and let Riley love her dad.

But for that one night, I would let myself cry a little bit, because even though I'd known for a long time that my little house with the blue couch and the yellow tulips was just a fantasy, it had been so precious just the same.

CHAPTER 18

Genevieve

On Friday afternoon three weeks after Emma and Riley had arrived, I was in my yoga studio, trying to hold warrior one without wobbling as my rather handsome trainer instructed me to extend my breath.

I'd designed the studio myself on the ground floor of Sheerwater some decades ago. *Home gym* was such an unpleasant term, and besides, I still walked a mile each day (most days) and lifted small hand weights to maintain my bone density. The studio had an open glass wall to the patio. The floors were bamboo, and there was a rice-paper screen that hid the mats, blocks and other accessories. A large bamboo tree sat in the corner. I even had a small statue of the Buddha surrounded by candles and usually played traditional Indian music to honor the art.

"Warrior two," John said, and I obeyed. "Deepen your stance."

I tried. My knee flared with pain, and I had to adjust. Additionally, I could hear Emma yammering away with her clients, as her office was across the hall from the yoga studio, and we both had the windows open. Idiotic phrases floated to me on the breeze—"Let's unpack what you just said" and "What do *you* think it means?"

It was hard not to roll my eyes. "Let's call it a day, John," I said. "Thank you. I'll meditate without you."

"Anything you want, Mrs. London. This is your time."

I'm well aware, I wanted to say, but he was a nice young man, and a veteran.

I had just gone into child's pose when I heard a sharp rap on the French doors and looked up.

Ugh. It was that wretched Paul in all his scowling misery. I pushed back into downward-facing dog, then halfway lift, then tree, stretching my arms upward until my cartilage creaked, just to make him wait.

He rapped again, then opened the door.

"What, Paul?" I snapped. No namaste for him.

"I want to talk to you," he said. His eyes scanned me critically, and really, the man had no manners. I wore a very tasteful outfit—wide-legged, loose-fitting pale gray pants with a tangerine-colored long-sleeved cotton shirt over a white tank top. Fashion was for every moment of life, after all, and Lululemon was so common.

I took my water bottle and walked barefoot out of the studio. I had no desire to overhear Emma's "calls" or have her overhear her grandfather lecturing me, as he was no doubt preparing to do. The grass was delicious and thick under my feet, which had been sore lately. I should've had that bunion surgery ten years ago, but there was no point now.

Without addressing my interrupter, I walked to the beautiful linden tree, which was more than a hundred years old. Under its generous spread of branches were a teak table and two chairs. A pair of chickadees were singing, and the sunshine was warm after a rather chilly week. I breathed in the salt air and tried to regain my peace of mind.

Paul sat without being invited. He was dressed like the handyman he was, work boots and jeans and a denim shirt over a Cubs T-shirt.

The buzzing started in my brain.

The Cubs . . . not the bear type, but something else. Something I used to know and didn't anymore. There were the Cubs, and there was another group, and they had something to do with . . . with that city. The one on the lake. I felt the cold, fast rise of anxiety. What were the Cubs? Why was Paul wearing a shirt with that word on it? The knowledge lingered at the edge of my brain, but the strange buzzing sound kept interfering with my ability to grasp what it was.

It didn't matter, it wasn't important, I should let it go, Dr. Pinco said. Think of something familiar. My birthday, which was April 5.

Running? There was something about running and cubs. Not the grizzly bear kind. The noise in my head was deafening.

Baseball. *Got you, damn it,* I thought viciously. Baseball. The Cubs were a baseball team, and the White Sox were the other.

The noise, and my anxiety, slid away.

Paul Riley was looking at me suspiciously. Had I said something? I didn't think so.

"Why are you here, Paul? Visiting Riley, I assume?"

"She's with her father today," he said.

"Indeed." Perhaps Riley had told me that. I didn't remember.

"Between him pretending to be her father this summer and you taking her to New York to fill her head with nonsense, I'm a bit worried about her."

I sighed. "I didn't fill her head with nonsense. I showed her my company and bought her a few things."

"She got her hair cut!"

"Is that why you're here? To protest a teenage girl's hair choices?"

"It was beautiful hair!"

"It's still beautiful. Let her express herself, Paul. Small rebellions will quell bigger rebellions."

He leaned back and squinted at me. "Don't act like you know anything about raising children, Genevieve. From where I sit, I can't see that you did such a great job with anyone."

How dare he? "Right back at you, Paul." My voice was icy.

He jolted forward. "Don't you dare talk about my girl. April had . . . troubles. We tried to help her. And we raised her just fine. She wasn't spoiled, not like that idiot Clark."

Perhaps it was because this was my last summer on earth, but I said, "On Clark, we are agreed. And I know April was troubled. I asked Clark to make sure she got help. Many times."

He settled back, his face a mask of pain, and I regretted descending to his level.

"I did my best with Emma, you know," I said. "Not that I feel compelled to justify anything to you, but I did."

"You could've loved her a little more."

I rolled my eyes. "Is my lecture finished? I'd like to clean up before cocktail hour."

"You really leaving all this to a teenage girl?" he asked, gesturing to the house.

"That's none of your business."

"You think it'll help her, inheriting millions? Because it sure didn't help your worthless son."

"Hi, guys." Emma walked up. "Still fighting after all these decades?"

"Hush, you," Paul said.

"Are you finished soothing the souls of the self-obsessed?" I asked.

"I'd happily counsel you for free, Gigi," she said, unruffled, and I felt a stir of pride that she hadn't let my barb land. She kissed her grandfather, and the pride turned to envy at their easy bond.

Once, I'd hoped Emma would be like a daughter to me.

"It's funny," she said, tilting her head as she sat down with us. "I've never heard a kind word between you, and yet you both lost children. You both helped raise me. You have so much in common."

"And so little at the same time," I said. Paul huffed in agreement, and for a second, our eyes met in amusement.

He was a rather nice-looking man, in that blue-collar way. Thick white hair, mustache, gravelly voice.

Emma's phone rang. "Another soul to soothe," she said, giving me a significant look. "Enjoy your chat, and no hitting, you two."

She got up and put the phone to her ear. "Dr. London here. Oh, Jim. How are you? What's going on?"

Paul's gaze followed her as she walked away, the pride unmistakable. "Dr. London. That has such a nice sound to it."

"She could've been a surgeon."

"She's never good enough for you, is she?" he said. "She put herself through three degrees, raised that beautiful kid, and all you do is pick at her. Give her some goddamn credit."

"Why are you here again, Paul? Trespassing, was it?"

He narrowed his eyes at me. His eyebrows could use a trim. "Your friend invited me for happy hour."

"Cocktail hour. Happy hour is for beer-swilling, nacho-eating troglodytes."

"Sounds good to me."

"Which friend?"

"Do you have more than one? Donelle."

I stifled a sigh. "How lovely for us all, in that case."

He settled against the wooden chair. I had to get new cushions. The wood was too hard for my bones, and though I'd been warm a few minutes ago, I was chilly now in the sea breeze and shade of the big tree.

Eighty-five years old, my body betraying me by the minute. I wondered if Garrison would even recognize me.

Paul was taking off his denim shirt. He handed it across the table. "You're cold," he said.

"How very gallant of you, but no thank you. I have many wraps inside."

"Well, we're not inside now, are we? You gonna shiver for the rest of the conversation?"

"I was hoping against hope that we were finished."

"Can you just drop the dragon-lady bit? I want to talk to you without the usual bullshit."

The breeze stirred again, and so I slid my arms into his shirt and was glad for it.

"How sick are you?" he asked. "You seem pretty god-damn healthy to me, doing all that yoga and whatnot."

"I will be dead by the end of summer," I said.

"Why aren't you getting treatment?"

"There is no treatment."

He looked down. There'd been no treatment for his wife, either. ALS. Such a dreadful end.

"It's not easy, getting old, is it?" he asked.

"No."

"I came out this summer to make sure the girls would be all right. She won't admit it, but Emma loves you, even if you don't deserve it. And I'm begging you, don't mess with Riley. She's had a hard year."

"She alluded to that. Friend trouble?"

"She's not like other girls. She's better. Got a good heart, that one. And it'll go unappreciated until she's older, I'm afraid."

"Are you concerned she's depressed?" I asked.

"I've been on the lookout since she was two." He swallowed, and without thinking, I leaned forward and covered his hand with mine.

Two old hands, age spotted and gnarled, his rough, mine wrinkled.

I took my hand back. "I quite like Riley," I said. "She's

a delightful, smart young woman. I won't mess with her, as you so delicately put it."

"Don't ruin her with money, either. After you're gone, I mean. Be smart about it."

"She won't be ruined."

The baby birds in the hedgerow began their furious twittering as the mother robin came with food. We listened for a second.

"I was very sorry when your wife died," I said, apropos of nothing. "And April, of course."

He didn't answer right away. "It's a terrible thing, to outlive your child. I don't know how you've done it all these years."

His words were like a spear in my heart. "We never knew what happened to Sheppard. He may well still be alive."

The kindness—and pity—in Paul's eyes was like a Molotov cocktail on a simmering fire, and I was suddenly furious. How dare he feel sorry for me? My son *disappeared.* Paul's daughter had felt so worthless she took her own life.

Irony slapped me in the face.

I was hoping to take my own life, too. And soon.

"Well," I said, standing up. "I must change for cocktail hour, and I'm sure you'll want to do the same. See you at five." I took off his shirt and tossed it on the chair behind me, angry for no good reason.

CHAPTER 19

Riley

'm gonna find out what happened to Gigi's son.

Being sixteen has its advantages. Who else knows how to work the Internet better than a teenager?

Okay, backing up a little—against my will, I kind of adore Genevieve, even if she kicked Mom out way back when. Let's face it: My parents were totally stupid, and sure, Mom had it hard, but look at me now. Pretty well adjusted, high honors student, varsity soccer, and if the bitches formerly known as my best friends ditched me, I'm better off without them.

That sounds really badass, right? I'm faking. The truth is, I miss them. A lot. The *old* them, before they became a pack of mewling coyotes, as Gigi called them.

Second thing—I am surrounded by old people here, not counting my brothers, who are wild demons (and I totally love them for it). So I need something to do other than look at Donelle's big toe and see if her nail fungus is gone yet, and if not, would I smear it with Vicks VapoRub. I'm serious. This happened. The struggle is real. Pop and I went fishing the other day. That killed four hours. He's working for my father's company doing handyman stuff. My seventy-eight-year-old grandfather is totally living the midwestern work ethic.

Third thing—I don't have much to do here. It's been three weeks, and aside from that fabulous, fabulous trip to New York, I watch the aforementioned wild demons, swim in the heated pool, do yoga with Gigi sometimes and reassure my mother that I'm fine. I'm a little bored. It's nice to be bored in paradise. I'm not complaining. Life at Sheerwater has been pretty incredible, I'm not gonna lie. Living in a house with a name, a cook (even a bad one), a driver (Charles is super nice), a pool, an ocean view . . . *incredible* is the exact right word.

I've discovered stuff I didn't know existed. A heated towel rack so I don't catch a chill getting out of the soaking tub (soaking tub, another richie-rich thing). My closet has revolving racks. There are warming drawers in the kitchen, a cold storage pantry, a dry goods pantry (who knows?), and a fridge just for wine. There's a wine cellar. An outdoor kitchen and bar by the pool, because one *must* have that, mustn't one?

Every day since we got here, I've had this tingly feeling in my stomach, like coming down the stairs on Christmas morning. I just wish Mikayla, Jenna and Annabeth could see this. Especially Mikayla, who always managed to work how much money her parents had into every conversation. I've been posting on Snapchat and Instagram here and there. Let them see.

I try not to think about them, but I have too much downtime. My father is busy working, though he took me to a construction site the other day (not really my thing, but it made him happy to introduce me around). Mom is taking every client she can get through the interwebs, and when she's not, she's trying to oh so subtly take my mental health temperature. Gigi works every day in her office and takes a nap every afternoon from four till five. I take care of Donelle and her toe, but she's kind of addicted to the Home Shopping Network, so I limit my time there. Helga hasn't said a word to me since the first night, so I think our bonding is pretty much complete. I hang out at Jamilah's house as much as I can, but as nice as she is, I don't really want to push it there. I mean, I'm a stranger, and she and my father are separated, so having me taking up space might not be her happy place.

She's really cool, though. I asked if I could take a selfie with her and the boys, and she said, "Of course, honey!" and put her arm around me. It was a nice picture, though my skin looks like goat cheese next to theirs.

Anyway, I need a project, and finding out what happened to Sheppard is a pretty big one. And I might even ask Jamilah to help me, since she works for Google, and Google knows everything about everyone.

A project would be good.

I honestly didn't know how I would've gotten through this summer if we hadn't come here. Mom said mean girls "harbor a deep sense of self-hatred and low self-esteem." Gigi called them coyotes. I liked that better.

But I still get a lump in my throat thinking about them. I know I shouldn't miss them, but I miss them anyway. Not the coyote version . . . the old gang. The four of us. I'd give a lot to time travel back to last summer, which was the happiest, best, funnest time of my life.

I don't know what happened. I seriously don't. One week, we were the same as we always were. The next week, I was out. Little things, like them all getting to lunch first and already engrossed in conversation when I got there. It used to be that Jenna and I walked together, since our lockers were on the same hall. All of a sudden, she was already gone. Annabeth and I always sat together on the bus, but then her mom was driving her. No explanation.

In a blink, the three of them were different people. Annabeth seemed to feel at least a little guilty, but by the end of week one, she'd gotten over it. She always took orders.

I just didn't see this . . . alienation . . . coming. I didn't see the meanness, and I feel so *stupid*. In some ways, it had been there all along . . . Jenna with her funny-but-mean comments about Mr. Stebbins and his hairpiece. Mikayla with her obsession over designer clothes and "jokes" about Lissandra, who had been her best friend in middle school. Annabeth, who's always been such a follower, had stopped wearing purple because Mikayla told her it was an ugly color.

I just didn't think it would happen to *me*. I never dreamed I'd be *jumped* by my three best friends in the bathroom. I knew it was over by then, but even so, I didn't expect it to be so awful. I cried so hard on that bathroom floor I thought I would break.

And still, I miss them. My mom would die if I admitted that. She'd talk for days about how what I was feeling was *normal*, and *okay*, and *everyone* had these experiences, and the important thing was to *learn* from them. Don't get me wrong; I love my mom, but her double duty as shrink and mother can be hard to handle.

Genevieve, though, she understood. In the car going down to the city, I found myself telling her everything. She didn't give me any advice or quote *Psychology Today* articles at me. Instead, she asked me some questions. How were my grades? (Stellar.) Was I getting recruited by any colleges? (A little? Stanford had been sending me e-mails about visiting, but didn't they do that to everyone?) Had I been singled out for any academic awards? (Yes . . . Chemistry and Trig Excellence Awards.)

"But that's how it always was," I said. "I tutored them. I've always been the dork of the group."

"Dear, don't use that word. It's so pedestrian. You've always been the *intellectual* of the group. The one who's being recruited by the finest colleges. The one with flawless skin and remarkable eyes."

Mikayla had posted a picture of me on Snapchat with the caption tinted contacts make u look like an alien. Except I didn't wear tinted contacts. *Remarkable* was a nicer way of thinking of it.

"Your former friends are jealous, Riley dear. Last year, you weren't a threat, since college wasn't looming on the horizon. Last year, you hadn't blossomed, I imagine. This year, they see you as you are—superior. Therefore, they've banded together like a pack of mewling coyotes, sensing that you're the timber wolf in their midst, and trying to make you feel like a rabbit instead of what you are."

I liked the way she called me *dear*. And *timber wolf*. Yes, I liked *timber wolf* a lot.

"Did anything like that ever happen to you?" I asked.

It had. She told me all about it, admitting she'd been a bit of a snob herself at Foxcroft. (I snorted . . . How could you avoid being a snob at a place called Foxcroft Academy?)

"I wouldn't have classified myself as a coyote," she said, "but looking back, I can see I never really gave some girls a chance. Which is different from turning on a friend, mind you."

"Were you ever . . . cut out?" I asked. I thought she might think it was a rude question, but she tipped her head, considering.

"After Garrison—your great-grandfather—died, my friends would visit, or invite me to lunch, but I was never invited to anything to do with their husbands, or anything with couples."

"Because you were gorgeous and single and loaded," I said.

"Gorgeous and widowed and well-to-do, dear. Choose your words more carefully. They make such an impact. But yes." She took a pair of sunglasses from her purse and put them on. "When I founded my company and began garnering a lot of attention, some of the other, more established designers became catty. A few started a whisper campaign about the treatment of my workers, or claimed I'd stolen their designs, or called me an imposter with too much time on her hands." She paused. "Once, Giuliana Camerino got up and moved when I sat next to her at a fashion event," she said. "It was quite hurtful at the time. And quite a public snub. It made Page Six."

"What did you do?" I asked.

She lowered her sunglasses and looked at me. "I excelled," she said, arching her eyebrow.

I smiled. She *was* kind of awesome, this Genevieve London person.

I didn't want to like her *too* much, because of how she stranded Mom way back when and suggested an abortion. But I understood. Mom had been eighteen. Genevieve knew life was going to be hard, and she wanted to give Mom a way out that didn't involve supporting her (and me).

And my mom was the *best*. The youngest, the prettiest, the smartest and nicest mom of anyone. I knew how hard she worked to get through school, and it made me proud. She was so cute when she went into the city to her office, asking me if she looked okay, what jewelry she should wear.

My mom was kind of perfect, to be honest. Overprotective and a little heavy on the advice, but hey. At least she cared. She was my best friend, and hardly anyone had a mother like that. Maybe that wouldn't have happened if we'd stayed here on the Sheerwater tit, so to speak. Maybe Genevieve knew what she was talking about.

And maybe—though I knew better than to ask—maybe she'd leave my mom some money. It'd be nice to have Mom be able to breathe a little. When she'd finished her PhD, Pop and I bought her a leather satchel from this really cool boutique in Wicker Park, and she cried when she saw it. She didn't have a lot of nice things, and she never seemed to mind, but seeing how Gigi lived . . . well.

Anyway, back to Sheppard. When I'd mentioned doing some research the other day, I knew I hit a nerve.

So far, I'd done the following:

1. Did a Google search for people who suspected they'd been force-adopted.

2. Asked Gigi for a saliva sample (you should've seen her face). We used three different testing companies. You never know. Maybe Sheppard *was* out there, looking for her, too. Gigi said she had already given a DNA sample way back when, but now it's kind of a fad, so more people might be doing it. And why not, right? She has plenty of money.

3. Read all the old articles on Sheppard's disappearance. They didn't say much . . . just that he was missing, and it rained two days later, which didn't help. There were no persons of interest in a kidnapping. No suspicious vehicles reported, no leads, nada.

I can't imagine what it would've been like to be Sheppard. I mean, there's not a real good outcome in his case, is there? I listen to enough true crime podcasts to know he's probably dead. I remember being seven . . . second grade, Mrs. Schoenberg, my teacher, dressed like a duck on Halloween, and Mom had made me a chick costume that year, and it felt so special, matching the teacher. That winter, we had a big snowstorm, and school was closed for days. Pop and Mom and I went sledding at Caldwell Woods, and we got cocoa after.

It was easy being seven. Seven was a nice age. You could read by yourself, but you were still little.

I hope Sheppard didn't suffer. I hope he wasn't molested. At best, he was kidnapped and raised by some person who just really, really wanted a kid.

I don't think the odds were in his favor, though.

I planned to go out to the woods near Birch Lake, where he'd last been seen. And I wanted to go through his room, but only if Gigi gave me the okay.

It would be awfully nice to have someone to do this with. A friend, even if just for the summer. Everyone in the neighborhood seemed to be in the over-seventy crowd, or these stressed mothers lugging bags from Whole Foods into their gorgeous houses.

I saw a boy about my age at the library, but he had headphones on and we did that awkward thing where just as we made eye contact, I looked away. Boys were way too hard, unless they were gay. Couldn't really see going up to him and saying, "Hi! Are you gay? No? Okay, never mind."

I sighed.

"Honey?" My mom poked her head in my room. "You coming down for cocktail hour?" She pulled a face.

"Yes, I'll have a martini," I said. "Extra dry."

"Or a Shirley Temple. Or water. Or milk."

"Or formula," I said. "I was just kidding. I'm gonna change first, though." I paused. "Is anyone else coming? Anyone under fifty?"

"I'll be there."

"Anyone else?"

She laughed. "I don't know," she said. "Come down with me so Gigi can't criticize my clothes."

I looked her up and down. Jeans and a boring blue oxford. "You could use a little pizzazz," I said.

"Don't you start," she said, hugging me. "One fashion critic in the family is enough."

CHAPTER 20

Genevieve

After my talk with the wretched Paul, I spent some time in my office, Googling suicide options under the guise of assisting Beverly with some issues on next year's spring line. The truth was, Beverly hadn't e-mailed me since I brought Riley down to the city, and I felt snubbed. She was supposed to update me twice a week.

Then again, we hadn't put anything in writing. It was really a courtesy, and we both knew it. The only thing Beverly wanted from me was my name. When we'd been in the showroom, she was lovely. But when I asked her if she'd like a few sketches for next year's fall line, she gave me a look and said, "I think our team has everything well under control."

At least Riley had been in the dressing room and didn't hear.

I was no longer relevant to the company I founded.

How many meetings had I granted Beverly to explain

my corporate culture, my aesthetic, my hopes for the company? I was proud to have hired her myself out of a very distinguished pool of applicants. Obviously, I'd wanted a woman to take over, and I was doubly proud to pass the baton to an African American woman. One of the stipulations of selling the company had been that I'd choose my successor. The board of directors was wild about her, and profits were higher than ever.

I supposed I hadn't expected her to make the company so much *hers*. I didn't blame her; I admired her. She'd been president of the company for fourteen years; the business was thriving.

But Genevieve London Designs was founded because I'd needed something to walk alongside the Missing. It was founded after I'd crawled out of the cedar closet, so weighted down with grief over my son and husband that I could not even stand. My first designs were sketched in the middle of the nights when I woke up, terrified that Garrison was dead, then stunned when I realized it was true . . . and Sheppard was still out there, unfound. I shoved the Missing aside to do research on leathers and hardware and lining. I toured vacant factories in Newark, wanting my products to be made in America. I started a training program for craftsmanship for at-risk youth at Newark high schools and offered a job to every one of them who finished.

I had been a *visionary*.

Now I was just an old woman who was no longer needed at the company that bore my name, Googling articles on the best ways to die.

Would Dr. Pinco prescribe me something on which I could overdose? He was clever, that one, and so far had only given me sleeping pills five at a time. How could I ensure that I wouldn't simply do more damage to myself and end up exactly where I feared I'd be—a vegetative state, tied to a wheelchair or hospital bed in a nursing home? Cutting my wrists sounded ghastly, but if I had enough gin in my system, could I do it? It would be better than a gun, wouldn't it?

Drowning seemed to be my top choice. A few seconds of panic—ten? twenty?—then surrender. Drowners (who survived, obviously) describe a warm feeling of acceptance. One man even said it was the most wonderful feeling he'd ever experienced. A "lovely sense of peace," he'd said. I could use a little of that.

Also, drowning could be passed off as accidental, so that if I took out a life insurance policy, the suicide clause wouldn't be invoked, and I could make Riley the beneficiary. I clicked around on Google for a few minutes. Unfortunately, insurance for a person my age only covered burial costs, and I already had that under my current plan.

If people thought it was an accident, Emma wouldn't have to experience another suicide. Not that I felt she would mind, really. It was one thing when she was eight and her mother was young and healthy. She had loved her mother. I don't think she'd flick an eyelash toward *my* corpse, frankly. One would think I'd locked her in the basement those ten years. So far, she and I had avoided any intimate conversations, which was both a relief and a burden. I supposed I had to say something to her eventually. She'd been quite nosy about my health.

When I read the obituaries, which becomes quite a habit as one ages, I lingered over the descriptions of the final moments. *Surrounded by her family, so-and-so went home to her Heavenly Father* or *After a courageous battle, so-and-so died peacefully at home, her family at her side.*

My preferred death would be simply a massive stroke or heart attack, the way Garrison had gone. In that scenario, I'd die here. Maybe even in that same Adirondack chair, looking out over the Sound. Perhaps in bed, wearing the pink silk pajamas with black polka dots. Minuet would be cuddled at my side, looking mournful. No. I didn't want my dog to suffer.

There it was. The sum of one's life. I didn't want my *dog* to suffer any grief, since my other son was a wastrel. One granddaughter wouldn't mourn me, and the other wouldn't know I was gone. My great-granddaughter barely knew me. Donelle would be sad, but she was so matter-of-fact it was hard to picture her saying more than, "Welp, you had a good run, Gen. See you on the other side."

The person I really wanted holding my hand as I breathed my last was, of course, Sheppard.

Where was he, my little boy? Was he alive? Did he remember the days with me, with us, the love and adoration that infused every moment of his first seven years? Did he feel betrayed and abandoned? Had he cried for me to help him?

The Missing bit down hard, its teeth still razor sharp.

God had failed me. *You promised*, I thought. *You promised I would see him again, and You lied.*

Then there was a knock on my door. "Gigi?" It was Riley.

"Come in, dear," I said, clearing my throat.

She did, wearing one of the outfits we'd bought (taken) in New York. She looked like a true London.

And she had the eyes.

She came over to me and spun around. "What do you think?"

"Beautiful," I said. "Iconic."

Her smile faded. "Are you sad, Gigi?" she asked, putting her hand on my shoulder.

"You need a manicure," I said. "Your cuticles are a disgrace. A woman of class should always keep her nails tidy."

"That's what Mom calls deflective conversation," she said, not moving her hand. "It's okay if you don't want to answer the question, but don't insult me."

How different she was from Emma, who, at that age, would've left the room or cried.

Then again, Riley had a mother who loved her and, from what I'd judged, had raised her well. Very well.

"I am a little sad," I said, patting her hand. "Thank you for caring."

"Do you want to talk about it?"

How could I tell a teenager about the Missing? Looking into her blue, blue eyes was hard enough. Sheppard blue. I had an entire line of blue purses and accessories, but none had ever captured the perfection of his eyes. Of Riley's eyes.

"No, dear. Tell me why you're all dressed up. Are you going out with friends?"

A look of confusion crossed her face. "No, Gigi. It's cocktail hour."

"Is it?" I sensed I was supposed to know something about it.

Then the buzzing began in my head, and suddenly, I wasn't sure if it was winter or spring. Had someone just asked me something? What had I been doing? Why did I feel so . . . sad?

A large dog nudged my hand. It was rather ugly and didn't smell very good. "We should have this beast washed, shouldn't we?" I asked . . . ah . . . I asked the girl.

Her name was gone. Completely gone, and yet I *knew* I was supposed to know her.

April? No, it was the *month* of April. Wasn't it? I glanced out the windows. All the leaves were on the trees, so it must be later than April. May. June. August?

"He's so pretty," she said, kneeling down. "Aren't you, Mac?"

Mac. The dog's name was Mac, and apparently, he lived here with me, which was strange, because I didn't even like dogs. Mac. Mac. *Don't forget his name. Mac. Mack. Macintosh.*

Why was I thinking of a computer?

I no longer remembered the dog's name. He might've been this girl's dog. He might've been mine.

"Don't slobber on me, boy," the girl said. "These clothes are way more than you can afford." She looked up at me, and I felt a rush of love for the freckles smattered on her nose. Could she be my niece? Didn't my sister have a daughter? "Are you ready?" she asked. "I love your outfit."

Which outfit was I wearing? I glanced down. It was a three-piece white ensemble, with wide-legged pants, a silk blouse and a flowing white sweater with subtle silver trim.

I didn't remember the outfit. Was it new? I had no recollection of buying it. Was it even mine? When had I gotten dressed? I wasn't sure where we were going.

There didn't seem to be anything in my brain, no thoughts to hold on to. I felt like clutching this girl and begging her to help me, but something prevented me from saying anything.

"I'm ready," I said, and let the girl take my hand and lead me out of the bedroom, which, I assumed, was mine. It was lovely but unfamiliar. Down a long hall. There was a painting there . . . an oil abstract, purple and cream.

Wait. I knew that painting, I did. I'd bought it at auction because the colors had been so rich and lovely, the shapes so organic and comforting, almost like gentle flame . . .

It was a Peter Lobello, that was it. I'd bought it when I was dating Gerard, the appraiser for Christie's. I'd paid $35,000 for it, and that was some time ago.

And this redheaded girl was Riley, Emma's little girl. April's granddaughter. That's why April was stuck in my head; she'd had red hair also. I felt a ridiculous sense of triumph at putting the pieces together.

Mostly, though, I was simply grateful to be back in my own head again.

Dr. Pinco had told me that, at first, these spells would pass. But as my condition worsened, it would become a permanent state.

I could deal with pain. I'd proven that for decades.

But losing myself . . . that was unbearable. I didn't want this girl to pity me.

I might love her, after all.

Tomorrow, I'd go for a swim and test the waters, literally and figuratively.

CHAPTER 21

Emma

When Miller called to say he couldn't get a sitter for his daughter and would therefore miss cocktail hour, I told him to bring her.

"She's going through a rough patch," he said. "It'd be better if we stayed home."

"Oh, come on. I love kids. My daughter does, too. She babysits all the time back home." There was no answer. "Unless you don't want to come," I added.

"No, I'd like to. I love Genevieve. But Tess is a handful."

"We'll double-team her," I promised, though my brain paused on the phrase *I love Genevieve*. "Triple-team, even."

"Okay. Thanks, Emma." I thought I heard a smile in his voice.

Miller's story had stayed in my head. Donelle, who knew everything that went on in town and didn't view gossip as a moral failing, as Genevieve did, had told me that Ashley died in childbirth. "Just like Tyrion Lannister's mother," she said. "Or Sybil on *Downton Abbey*. I saw that coming, I tell you."

"Ashley? Was she sick?"

"I'm talking about Sybil. The second she had a headache, I was like, 'Oh, she's a goner.'" Donelle stretched. "I don't know the deets on Miller's wife. Your grandmother won't let me ask."

I was glad Miller was coming. I still felt awkward about almost planting tomatoes on Ashley's grave.

I'd had eight clients today, and I could use cocktail hour. My brain was a little sore. Pop was already here, nursing a beer, idly petting Valkyrie as she gnawed on his hand. We were in the conservatory (or sunroom, as Riley had mistakenly called it)—a giant, beautiful room complete with an iron-paned glass dome and floor-to-ceiling windows, which were open to the soft evening air. There was a fireplace in the corner, a walnut bar and half a dozen huge ferns and potted palm trees. The floor was polished stone, and in the winter, it resembled a Russian palace. It had been my favorite room as a kid.

Riley and Genevieve came in, and my daughter smiled at me. She looked so grown up, dressed to kill, holding on to Gigi's hand, and a lump came to my throat. She was kind, my child. So patient with my grandmother.

"About time," said Pop. "I thought you said five thirty. It's quarter till six."

"Paul. So glad you began without us," Gigi said.

"I brought my own."

"I'm well aware," she said, her voice as dry as she liked her martinis. "Old Milwaukee is not a brand with which I'm familiar. Donelle, would you kindly see if the girl is ready to serve hors d'oeuvres?"

"You bet, Gen. Shaylee!" We all winced as Donelle bellowed from the couch.

The bell rang. "I'll get it," I said, and went without waiting for permission. Down the hall past the library, the formal dining room (not to be confused with the breakfast room or eat-in kitchen, where Helga lurked like a gargoyle), into the vast foyer.

When I opened the door, I blinked. "Jason! Hi."

"Hey, Emma," he said, leaning in to kiss my cheek. "You okay with me being here? Riley asked me to come."

"Um, sure. I don't mind. Come on in."

We heard a scream from the driveway. "Jesus, what's that?" Jason asked.

Miller was getting out of a Volvo station wagon. "I'm guessing that's your cousin and his child," I said.

"Oh, God, you haven't met Tess yet, have you?" Jason said with a grin. "Run."

"By the way, you forgot to tell me Ashley died, Jason."

He blinked. "No. I couldn't have. It was horrible." I gave him a pointed look. "Seriously? I didn't tell you?"

"Seriously. I would've remembered. I loved them."

"Yeah. The golden couple." His handsome face was regretful, and his hand went to my back, idly rubbing between my shoulder blades.

Miller was still hunched over, trying to get his child out of the car. More screams filled the air. "Go see Riley," I said. "I'll help with the baby."

"Great idea. See you inside." He kissed my cheek and left, and I went down the path.

"Hey, Miller," I said, the shells of the driveway crunching under my feet.

He straightened. "Hi, Emma." He needed a haircut and a month of sleep.

"I not going! I not going!" the child inside shouted.

"Hi," I said, leaning down to see her. "What are you yelling about?"

"I not going!"

"Not going where?"

"Here!"

"That's too bad," I said. "There are five dogs inside."

"I hate dogs." She kicked the back of the passenger seat.

"There's also a secret fort," I said, referring to the cedar closet, which was bigger than my bedroom back home.

"I hate forts."

"Tess," Miller sighed, "please don't say 'hate.'"

"Why don't you go in, Miller?" I suggested. "Tess and I will stay out here." I gave him a nod. "We'll be in soon."

"No!" said Tess. "I go *home* soon."

"You sure?" he asked.

"Yep."

"Okay. Come get me if she . . . if you need me."

He went up to the front door, glanced back over his shoulder, then went inside.

"I'm Emma," I said. "And you're Tess."

"No, I not."

I smiled. "Really? What's your name, then?"

She looked around. "Driveway."

"Oh! What an interesting name! Nice to meet you, Driveway."

She narrowed her eyes at me, unsure of my game.

"What's your favorite color?" I asked.

"I hate color."

"So white, then. I like red myself. Do you want to come inside and run around and play and hide and maybe eat some food?"

"No."

"Okay." Being three was hard (though Riley had been an angel, quite frankly). Kids had little control over their lives, so tantrums were usually an expression of that frustration. Accepting her answer (because in this situation, I could) was a way to let her feel she had some control. "We'll just stay here." I sat in the front passenger seat.

"Where my daddy?"

"He's in the house."

She craned her neck to look, her little brows furrowed. She was awfully cute, if a little grimy.

"I like sitting here," I said. "Thank you for wanting to stay in the car."

"I *don't* want to stay."

"Oh. Okay. Well, there are nine doors to get inside," I said. "Would you like to pick the one we go in?"

She looked at me, trying to figure out how I was tricking her. Smart kid.

"Or we can just stay out here," I offered.

"We go in now," she pronounced.

"Great choice," I said, unbuckling her.

"What you name?" she asked.

"Emma."

"I hate that name."

"I'm not wild about it, either," I said.

She started to get out of the car, but I blocked her. "Hold hands, please."

"No."

"The ocean is close," I said. "I'd like us to hold hands so we don't fall in it and get cold," I said.

"No!"

"Okay. Back in the car seat, then."

She stuck out her lower lip.

"Car seat, or hold hands," I said.

She didn't answer—that would be conceding too much power—but she let me take her little hand. I tried not to smile.

Once she was out of the car, I got a better look at her. She was quite the combination of her dad and Ashley— dark eyes like her father (I seemed to remember Ashley's were green or blue). Her hair was curly, like Ashley's had been. And snarled, unlike Ashley's. Practically dreadlocks. We walked around Sheerwater until she stopped and pointed at Door Number 4, which went into the kitchen.

Shaylee the Silent was taking a sheet of mini-quiches out of the oven as Helga scowled. "Shaylee, Helga, this is Tess Finlay," I said.

Shaylee nodded our way, reinforcing my idea that Helga had scared the ability to speak out of her (or cut out her tongue).

"Get that kid out of my kitchen," Helga said.

"*You* get out," Tess said. "You go now."

"What a brat," Helga said.

"*You* a brat."

I kind of liked Tess. "See you later," I said, leading Tess through the kitchen and into the conservatory.

Tess lurched to a halt.

It was a sea of legs, after all, from her point of view. In the time we'd been outside, the other guests had arrived . . . ten or so adults, all talking, plus Riley, who was five eight. "Want me to pick you up so you can see?" I asked Tess.

"No," she said, but she reached her little arms up to me, and I picked her up.

She didn't smell great; she could use a bath, and my fingers were itching for a comb. But the feeling of a little one in my arms . . . it was awfully sweet.

Riley saw us, said something to her dad and came right over. "Hi, kid," she said. "How's it going? High five?"

And just like that, Tess high-fived her. "Riley, this is Tess. Tess, this is my little girl, Riley."

Tess stared at Riley for a minute. "Your hair pretty," she said.

"Thanks," Riley said. "Want to touch it?"

Tess did, then smiled.

Kids always seemed to possess an instinct for who was another kid, no matter how tall they were.

"Want to go play?" Riley asked, and Tess nodded.

A boy with dark hair and beautiful liquid black eyes came over. "Oh, Mom, this is Aarav Talwar. His parents live here in the summer."

"It's so nice to meet you," he said. "I go by Rav."

"Emma London," I said. "Riley's mom." He was maybe her age, maybe a little younger. "What grade are you in, honey?" Riley rolled her eyes at the endearment. Sue me.

"Tenth. Just finished," he said.

"Where do you go to school?"

"Mom," Riley said. "We're gonna go entertain the little kid, okay? Save the interview for another time, maybe?" She nudged my shoulder with hers, letting me know she didn't really mind.

I smiled at them both. "Just make sure it's okay with her dad. Miller. Your father's cousin."

"Yeah, we met at a job site last week. He seems nice." I handed Tess over to Riley, and the kid didn't protest. "Hey, Miller," Riley said. "Is it okay if we take Tess upstairs?"

"Uh, yeah. If she'll go. Tess, do you want to play with Riley?"

She didn't answer her father, too busy fondling my daughter's hair.

"Want to see my room and play with my stuff?" Riley asked her. Tess looked at Rav. "Don't worry about him. He's nice."

"We go," Tess decided.

"Come get me if you need me," Miller said, his eyes a little wide with wonder.

"I no need you, Daddy. We never coming back."

"Harsh, Tess," Riley said, reading my mind, but she smiled. "We'll definitely come back. See you in a bit!"

With that, they left, my daughter and Miller's, and the handsome boy.

My heart felt like warm caramel. Wouldn't it be so nice if Rav and Riley became friends! And how sweet that they were both going to play with Tess! (Or smoke pot. Or meth. Or give each other homemade tattoos. Or have sex. Or lose Tess.) I let the familiar stream of maternal doom run through my head. I knew my child, and I trusted her. She adored kids and had been babysitting since she passed the Red Cross test when she was twelve.

It reminded me of my own days babysitting for some of the summer families, or the children of Genevieve's guests. I'd always been more comfortable that way, anyway. More the Silent Shaylee type back then.

"Your daughter is sort of . . . magical," Miller said. "Wow. Tess usually hates babysitters."

"Well, we're in a strange place, so she probably feels a little off-balance and in need of an ally." *Enough psychobabble, Emma.* "And you're right. Riley is really great with kids."

"She is," Jason said, suddenly at my side. "You should see her with her brothers. Got you a drink, Em. Cosmo, Grey Goose, your favorite."

"Thanks," I said. It hadn't been my favorite for a while, but it was thoughtful of him.

"How are you, Jason?" Miller asked.

"Great! Good. How are you? The kid's gotten awfully cute."

"Thank you. Takes after her mother."

"She does. Yep. Yeah, Riley's great with her brothers. You should definitely come over sometime, Miller. Mom and Dad would love to see you."

Okay, this was . . . odd. They were cousins. I'd imagined they'd be closer. I'd yearned for cousins as a child. Still did. "Don't you guys work together?"

"We do," Jason said. "I do the boring office stuff, though. Miller runs the sites."

Miller nodded, looking at his drink.

"Your grandparents are totally not happy I'm here," Jason said in a conspiratorial tone. "They still hate me for knocking you up."

"Well. I was a pure and innocent teenager, after all."

"So was I." He grinned.

"But your life went pretty much the same," Miller said,

not looking up. "Whereas Emma had to move and raise the baby and do all the work."

Jason's face froze, and Miller gave himself a little shake. "I'm sorry. I don't actually know what I'm talking about. Didn't mean to be rude, Jase. I'm not getting a lot of sleep these days."

"No, dude, it's fine. You're right."

"Spot-on," I said. "Which is exactly why my grandparents resent him. But Genevieve resents me, too, so we can be a club, Jason." As usual, I offered the olive branch, then wondered why.

"Emma, would you take off my sock?" Donelle called. "I can't reach it, honey, and I want to show Dr. Talwar my toenail."

"Duty calls," I murmured, going to Donelle's side and taking off her sock. Both the good doctor and I recoiled.

Donelle's big toenail didn't look like something that grew on humans. It looked like a tree fungus, greenish and curling around into a tube, with a whitish ooze coming out. I would never look at a cannoli the same way again.

"Let's put this sock right back on, shall we?" I said, trying to do the job without actually looking at the foot.

"Hold on there, Emma," Donelle said. "Dr. Talwar—what's your first name?"

The female doctor looked slightly terrified. "Saanvi. I'm a thoracic surgeon, so I'm afraid I can't—"

"Don't worry. I'm sure you're smart enough to figure this out. Look. Is that fungus or what? Also, can you prescribe some medical weed for this? Wait. Is pot legal yet?"

Dr. Talwar covered her mouth with her fist. "Your toe does require attention, yes. I'm fairly certain you can't get medical marijuana for it, though."

"Good God, Donelle," I said. "Put it away. Here. Let me help."

"I've been having the kid smear it with Vicks VapoRub," Donelle said. "Think it'll work?"

"You know, I don't recall Vicks as a therapy for that, ah, condition," Dr. Talwar said, backing away.

"I'll cut it back for you," Pop said, cocking his head. "Got some pretty sharp hedge clippers that should do the job."

"Are you flirting with me, Paul?" Donelle asked.

He smiled begrudgingly and didn't deny it.

"Seriously, Doc, what's your take on it? Surgery?"

"Donelle, for heaven's sake, stop harassing my guests." Genevieve arrived, martini in hand. "We have discussed the state of your hideous foot more than enough. Saanvi, I would love your opinion on a new color for the front parlor. Do you mind? Donelle, darling, put your sock back on and let Emma visit. Emma, dear, have you met the other Dr. Talwar? Vikram, this is my granddaughter, Emma London."

There it was, the magical Genevieve London hospitality. Even Donelle's hideous, bark-like toenails couldn't faze her. For a moment, our eyes met, and I felt an unwilling tug of admiration.

"Very nice to meet you," I said to the guest.

"And you," he said. "So nice for Genevieve to have you and your daughter here for the summer." His phone chirped, and he looked at it. "I'm so sorry. I'm on call tonight and have to take this."

"Of course." The other guests seemed to know each other—three women and a man, all laughing, all very well dressed, preppy with a little extra—the diamond stud earrings, the Patek Philippe watch.

For a second, I felt the urge to go upstairs and hang out with the kids. But Riley was making a friend (I hoped), and I should let her.

Always on the fringe, that old familiar feeling.

"Em. Come on out here and play with people your own age." Jason waved me over to the deck. Miller was already there, looking out over the lawn toward the water. The birds had begun singing their evening songs, and a blue heron made its way slowly across the sky, looking prehistoric as it flew.

"Tess seems like a very bright girl," I said, sitting down on a lounge chair next to Miller.

"I think she is," he said. "Thank you."

"If you ever need someone to talk to," I said, "I'm a psychologist and all that."

Really great sell, Emma. He looked at me and smiled a little, his sad eyes crinkling, and for a second I remembered the slight crush I had on him back then. He'd seemed so much older and more together than Jason.

"Thank you," he said.

"He's got us, too. You know that, right, Miller?" Jason sat down on the other side of me.

"Of course," Miller said.

"So things are going well, Em?" Jason asked. "We should have dinner and really talk. We have so much to catch up on."

We didn't, to the best of my knowledge. We talked almost every day since I'd gotten here and had never gone for more than a couple of days without some communication.

He was being a little . . . weird. Possessive. Something.

The sun sank behind the pine trees, and the water sparkled with gold and red.

"Did you start that garden?" Miller asked me.

"I did," I said. "Over behind the garage, on the south side. If you want fresh tomatoes in a month or two, you know where to raid."

"I love fresh tomatoes," Jason said. "You put in any basil?"

"A few plants, yep. Parsley, dill."

"Cool. We have a garden, too. Well. I guess Jamilah has a garden, even if I did all the work putting the plants in." He waited. Miller was staring straight ahead, so I asked the question Jason seemed to be waiting for.

"And how are things with you and Jamilah?"

He sighed. "Hard to say. Jamilah's a very high-maintenance woman. I mean, I don't know what she wants. She's always looking at me like I'm a huge disappointment, but when I try to talk, she won't say anything. You can't win for losing at this marriage game. I mean, she says I need to take more responsibility, but she won't say at what. You know what I miss? Having fun together. Not to mention sex. When did sex become such a chore for her? Let me tell you, her head almost exploded when I said that. Is that such a crime? I'm telling you, it's a game. A game that's fucking rigged against you."

Well. That was quite the outpouring.

"I'm gonna go find Tess," Miller said. "Nice talking to you both."

He left, and I turned to Jason. "Hey. Idiot. His wife is dead."

Jason closed his eyes. "Fuck."

"Yes! Maybe now isn't the time to bitch about your perfectly perfect wife. And in front of me, no less."

"Why not in front of you?"

I may have growled. "Because I thought you and I were going to get married, Jason. Remember? We had plans."

"Yeah, well, we were kids, Emma. We were eighteen. How often does that work out?" He patted my hand, and I jerked it away.

"Did you ever really think we'd end up together?" I asked. "Because I did. I know we were young, but I . . . yeah. I thought we'd make it." It still caused a weird pressure in my chest to think about those early years of parenthood, when the little house with the blue couch fantasy had been my lifeline.

Jason ran a hand through his hair. "I think I was too young. You were more mature."

"I had to be."

"I know. And, Emma, you've been the best mother. You *are* the best mother. I can't tell you how much I see that, and how much I appreciate it. Really. Riley is incredible, and it's all because of you."

"You're right." Remembering my old promise not to

spar with my child's father, I took a few breaths and a pull of my drink. "I thought you and Miller were closer."

"Well, we were. Sort of. When Ash died, he just closed himself off."

"I'm sure it was devastating."

"It was."

I hesitated. "How did she die?"

Jason sighed. "Something went wrong during the delivery. She died before the baby was even out."

"God." My eyes filled with tears. "Does he have help? A girlfriend or anything?"

"I don't think so. Ashley's parents are around and they help out a lot. He had a nanny for a while."

"He seems lonely."

"He is."

"Do you guys go out, ever? Do you have him over for dinner? I'd hope that your parents would—"

"We try! We're not monsters. Jamilah and I gave him a ton of stuff the boys had outgrown. One of those baby knapsacks, the high chair . . ."

"There you are," Genevieve said, her tone frosty. "Emma, Saanvi wanted to speak with you. If you're not too busy."

"Not at all," I said, getting up and coming back inside.

It was darker now, and the lights were on in the house, low and tasteful. In the fireplace, white candles flickered, and Shaylee was making the rounds with another tray of food.

"Emma," Saanvi said, "your grandmother said you're a therapist. I consult at Rose Hill, and we are looking for a family counselor, as ours went out on paternity leave. Part-time, but perhaps you would consider looking into it?"

Genevieve pulled her head in, disapproval radiating from her.

Whatever. "I did an internship with children and family systems at Lurie Children's Hospital in Chicago," I said.

"I'd have to think about it, since obviously I have a personal relationship with the place. But thank you for the tip."

"Wonderful," Saanvi said warmly. "I am not on the search committee, but I'll suggest your name to the director, whom I assume you already know."

"Of course," I said. "I visit as often as I can."

"Your sister is lovely," she said, smiling. "I'm afraid we must be off, Genevieve, but as always, it is so wonderful to see you. Thank you for your hospitality. You must come for dinner this week. You too, Emma, and your charming daughter. No excuses this time, Genevieve. We are all busy women but we must eat."

Oh, I liked her.

She called up the front staircase, and a second later, her son came gallumphing down, all legs and arms. Soon after, Riley did as well, Tess holding her hand. Riley looked away when I gave her the *is he nice?* look, but her cheeks turned pink.

So he *was* nice. Thank God.

Miller followed behind them.

Cocktail hour was breaking up; the other guests whose names I hadn't quite gotten were saying goodbye, and Pop gave me a chin jerk and motioned that he'd call me. The Talwar family left after securing a dinner date, Saanvi reminding me to call Rose Hill. Jason left, too, getting a frosty nod from Genevieve, who then swept into another room, disapproval thick as oatmeal.

Interesting that Genevieve hadn't mentioned the position to me. I was sure she knew about it. She was on the board of directors.

"Time to go home, Tess," Miller said, reaching for her.

Tess jerked back, and almost fell, but Riley caught her just in time.

"No! No, Daddy, no!" she screamed, wrapping herself around Riley. "I hate you! I want to stay! No!"

"Enough, Tess," he said firmly, prying her arms off my child's legs.

"Time to go with Daddy," Riley said.

"No! No! No!"

After a minute, Miller and I got Tess off of Riley. "Bye, Tessie," my daughter said. "Don't be sad! I'll come play with you again."

Tess's screams were reaching 911 level. "I'm just gonna leave," Miller said over the noise. "Please tell Genevieve thank you for me."

"Take care," I said as he tried to keep Tess from kicking and biting him. I closed the door after them, her screams fading as he walked across the lawn.

"Yikes," Riley said. "My ears are ringing."

"Me too. Thank you for never being like that."

"Aw, she's sweet. I mean, until now, she was sweet. Well, sweet's not the right word. But she's so funny, Mommy. She loved hiding on Rav and me, and we had to pretend not to see her little legs sticking out from under the pillows. I tried to brush her hair a little, but we didn't get too far."

"And how's Rav? He seemed nice."

"He is. Don't get that look. He's nice, and he's a dork who plays video games and gets straight As."

"Sounds hauntingly familiar."

"He might help me on a project, if that's okay."

"What project is that?"

"Um, a summer thing."

"For school?"

"Kind of. Extra credit."

Teenagers needed their privacy, I knew. Still, I hated when there was stuff I didn't know. "So long as I know where you are at all times, there's at least one adult in the house with you, doors open, no bedrooms, phone check-ins every half hour."

"And of course we'll both wear our chastity belts." She

pulled a mock-serious face. "You sound slightly suspicious, Mother."

"It's the checklist they gave us in Mommy School."

"He just seems nice, that's all. It's refreshing to talk to someone born in this millennium."

"Oh, burn," I said.

"It's so cute when you try to be cool, Mom. That word is really passé, by the way. I'm going to my room to read, okay? I'll say good night now." She hugged me, and I breathed in her sunshiny smell, my heart vibrating with love and relief. The dark cloud that had shrouded her this past winter and spring seemed to have truly evaporated.

And Genevieve was—for now—surprisingly good for her. I watched as Riley went into the living room, where Donelle and Gigi sat, fresh drinks in their hands. They had the livers of Ernest Hemingway. Well. Genevieve did. I swear they taught cocktail consumption at Foxcroft. Donelle was a bit looser, a bit more giggly.

Riley kissed them both on the cheek and said a few words, and they both gazed after her as she left the room.

"Don't skulk there in the hall spying, Emma," Genevieve said. "Join us."

I did, curling up on the velvet armchair. "You have nice friends," I said.

"Don't sound so surprised. And please get your feet off the chair."

With a pointed sigh, I obeyed.

"Why are you always picking fights with her?" Donelle asked. "Give her a break, Gen."

"Who invited Jason?" Genevieve snapped, ignoring her. "Your grandfather is one thing. Your *impregnator* is another. He ruined your life. I don't want him as a guest in my home. Especially after the way his mother treated you. Such a climber, that woman."

"First of all," I said, my voice tight, "if Riley's father

isn't welcome here, *you're* going to have to be the one to tell her. Secondly, he didn't ruin my life. He gave me Riley, who is everything to me, and someone even you seem to care about. And thirdly, I agree with you about Courtney, but she was taking her cues from you, Genevieve. You kicked me out first, after all."

"Boom," said Donelle. "She got you there, Gen."

"You needed to learn a thing or two," she said.

"And lastly, though you seem damn healthy to me, you're allegedly dying. You've been playing with me for weeks now. I want to talk to your doctor, and if you don't sign over Hope's guardianship by the end of the week, Riley and I are going back home."

"This *is* your home."

"No, Genevieve, it's not. You made sure of that. Now, I'm going for a walk," I said. "Good night, Donelle. Genevieve, sleep well in your casket."

Donelle cackled. "Casket! Like you're a vampire, Gen. You're funny, Emma."

"You so enjoy judging me, don't you, Emma?" Genevieve said, her voice deceptively calm. "And yet I took you in after your mother killed herself and your father didn't want you, and those other grandparents with whom you *wanted* to stay were too overwhelmed. I gave you every opportunity, and you threw it out the window in order to have sex with some ridiculous, shallow boy. I did nothing wrong."

Where had that speech come from? The honest emotion in it seemed out of character for my grandmother. Had she really forgotten what she said? How she had all but cursed me? I looked at her for a long moment. Was there a point in arguing with her? Would she really care about anything I had to say? Should I try now, while Donelle was idly peeling her moldy toenail and holding shards of it up to the light?

"Well?" my grandmother said. "Speak your mind or take your walk."

"I just wanted you to love me, Gigi," I said, surprising myself with the words.

"Love is overrated," she said.

I took a slow breath. "It's ironic," I said. "You lost a child, and years later, you were given one. I wasn't Sheppard, but I was scared and lost and afraid, just the way he was."

"Do *not* bring up my son," she hissed.

I let the silence sit there until she finally looked away.

"I'll take that walk now," I said. "Good night."

CHAPTER 22

Emma

I remembered some things about the day my mother died with perfect recall. It was raining, and I finally got to use my new umbrella—pale pink with hundreds of brilliant butterflies and flowers on it. My mom had bought it for me as a going-back-to-school present, and then it didn't rain for twenty-seven days. Otherwise, third grade had been perfect so far, and I'd already gone on three playdates *and* I sat with the nice girls every single lunch *and* was learning double Dutch at recess.

Then, finally, it did rain, and I always wondered if the rain was connected somehow to what happened later. I woke up that morning elated, the rain hissing through the leaves outside my window. Everything was normal; Daddy was away, and Mommy let me have Cap'n Crunch for breakfast and didn't even make me eat a banana. I remembered that she zipped up my raincoat and handed me my backpack. "And don't forget your pretty umbrella!" she said. She hugged me extra long. Or maybe I made that part up. Maybe I just hoped she hugged me extra long.

I think I said, "I love you." I didn't specifically recall that part, but the memory is there. I did love my mother, and we told each other that a lot. Every day, the same as I did with Riley.

I remembered the stiff plastic of my slicker and the new smell of my umbrella. I remembered that I had peanut butter and honey for lunch, and I ate with Rachel and Taylor. On the way home from school, I sat with Drake Fitzgerald from down the street, who was a year older than I was and very nice, even though he was a boy. Our bus stopped at the end of our dead-end street, and half a dozen kids got out, which was why I was allowed to walk the half block home by myself.

As the other kids scattered and ran because of the rain, I took my time. A gust of wind caught my umbrella, and for a second, I thought I'd blow away, whisked into the dark, wet sky, carried above the clouds, over Lake Michigan, and what a fun and happy adventure that would be! I wanted to have adventures, like the girl who got the seven-league boots, like Pippi Longstocking, like the cousins in *The Wolves of Willoughby Chase*.

I remember all those thoughts.

Mommy always told me to come right home from the bus stop, but that was silly. I wasn't little anymore, after all. I was eight, almost eight and a half. Besides, she almost always waited for me on the front steps. I didn't see her there that day—the rain, probably—but I was a big kid compared to the kindergarteners, who were so tiny. The rain made such a loud patter on my umbrella, and the air smelled like copper. Rainwater gurgled in the gutters, carrying the first of the fall leaves along on a happy ride. The weather, my new coat, my beautiful, fancy umbrella. All the other girls in my class had loved it. Even Jake Nydvorst had said it was pretty.

Our house looked nicer that day, for some reason. Maybe it was just because I was happy to be in the pink-tinged world under my umbrella. I jumped in a puddle, and the water splashed onto my pants, and it felt warm and icky, like pee. It looked like I had wet myself, too, but I was almost home; I would take an early bath and get into my jammies, and maybe Mommy would make pancakes for supper, which she often did when Daddy was away.

I was glad, because it was more fun without him. When he was home, Mommy was sadder. Even though I felt bad about that thought, I knew it was true. Daddy worked, but not like other fathers. He wrote books and flew around the country a lot, doing research, he said. I had never seen one of his books, because they weren't finished.

In order to make my special rainy walk a tiny bit longer, I passed our mudroom entrance and went in the front door. Plus, that's where the closet was where we put the umbrellas. It was quiet inside, with a faint sound I couldn't quite identify. A sound like the dryer, but not the dryer. I took off my red boots and carefully closed my umbrella, wrapping the strap around it tightly, making sure the snap was secure before I put it in the closet. I hung my slicker up, even though it was hard to reach the hangers, and went to see what was for snack.

The kitchen was empty. I called for my mom, but she didn't answer. She wasn't in the kitchen, or in the dining room folding laundry, or watching TV. I went upstairs, because Mommy took naps, though she was always awake when I came home. Maybe she was taking a bath? Sometimes she did that at odd hours, which always struck me as strange, as if grown-ups should have more important, grown-uppy things to do.

She wasn't anywhere in the house. I called down to the cellar, a little afraid to go there by myself, but she didn't answer. Then I looked for a note, because I was eight years old and I could read, of course, and maybe she had left me a note. Even though she had *never* not been home before. She was *always* home.

She didn't have a job like some of the other moms, and that was fine with me, because even though she hardly ever dressed up and sometimes was a little stinky, she was always home. BO. That was a new term I'd learned on the bus. Body odor. But my mom's BO wasn't that bad, and when she took a shower, she smelled so nice.

Besides, my mom didn't *have* to work. I knew from hearing my parents fight that we were a little bit rich from my grandmother who lived far away and came to visit every once in a while, which made my parents' voices tight and hissing. So my mom got to stay home, and even if it meant she was sloppier than other moms and had BO some days, I didn't mind. I liked taking care of her, making her a cup of tea, climbing into bed with her to watch TV sometimes. I could always cheer her up, she said. She cried sometimes but she was sad about Grammy being in a wheelchair, which Grammy didn't seem to mind. She was always so nice, Grammy, and Pop pushed me really high on the swing in their backyard, so I didn't know why my mother was so sad.

So my father traveled and was important, and my mom was always here, and I liked it that way. The only times Mommy wasn't home was when she had her appendixes out, and then Daddy was here. Drake from the bus had told me that you only had one appendix, but my mother's had grown back. When I asked about it, Mommy told me it wasn't common, but it could happen. Drake didn't know everything, even if he was in fourth grade.

I couldn't find a note. Maybe she was taking a walk. Which was a little rude, since she should have been home when I got there, especially because she had all day to take a walk, and I wanted a bath and pancakes. And her. I wanted her.

She wouldn't have gone out, because her car was broken

in some way. Last week we'd taken a taxi to the movies, and it was really fun. I liked taxis.

Maybe she took a taxi to the grocery store.

I waited on the couch for a little while. The house was very neat and clean that day, which was nice. I had stopped biting my nails for third grade, but I wanted to bite one now. I chose my pinkie finger and nibbled the nail down to the quick.

My happy umbrella feeling felt like a long time ago.

I had a bad feeling in my stomach, and I knew I should do something. Mrs. Fitzgerald was nice, both Mommy's sort-of friend and also Drake's mom. Their number was by the phone for emergencies. It was strange to call a grown-up, and when she answered, my heart started thumping. "Hello?" I said. "Mrs. Fitzgerald? Is my mommy there? It's Emma London."

I hadn't meant to say *mommy*. I meant to say *mother*, but *mommy* slipped out, and my voice sounded small and weak.

"No, sweetie, she's not. Are you home alone?"

"Yes. My daddy's away for work and I don't know where she is." I felt like crying suddenly.

"I'll pop over. I bet she had to run out."

Thank goodness. Mrs. Fitzgerald was so nice. She was always dressed in regular clothes, too, and smelled good. I hoped she wouldn't tell Drake I was a baby who needed a grown-up, but I *wanted* a grown-up with a sudden, all-consuming wave.

I turned on the kitchen light. For some reason, it made the quiet of the house more noticeable.

The noise—that thrumming, not-dryer noise—was still there. Louder here in the kitchen. Now that I thought of it, it hadn't stopped since I'd gotten home.

It was coming from the garage.

The dread welled up in me, even though I wasn't sure why.

Suddenly, I realized why I'd thought our house had

looked prettier. The garage door was down, and it was usually up. The opener was broken, and Daddy hadn't fixed it because, the truth was, he wasn't good at that kind of thing. It had been stuck open for a while now. The house looked nicer when you couldn't see the trash cans and boxes and Mommy's broken car.

There wasn't a good reason for a noise to be coming from in there.

I did *not* want to open that door. I hated our garage. One time, when I was little and it was Halloween, Daddy had hidden in here with a mask and jumped out at me when Mommy and I were just getting back from trick-or-treating. I screamed and felt the hot rush as I wet my pants. Mommy had yelled at him, and I cried, and he felt bad. He said he was just trying to have fun, and Mommy said, "She's four, Clark! For God's sake!" I loved her for protecting me and also felt bad for Daddy, because he was always wrong in some way.

He'd had an old man mask on, the skin gray and leathery. I still remembered how ugly that mask was, with heavy wrinkles and a sagging, wobbly mouth. The hooded, uneven eyes.

Somehow, I was very, very afraid that an old man was in the garage now. Not just Daddy with a mask.

The garage was connected to the house by a breezeway. I went down that hallway slowly. The plants Mommy had out in a little wicker stand were dead, I saw. The African violets she loved and that usually bloomed in such fat, happy clumps. Why hadn't I noticed they were dead?

Yes. The noise was definitely in there. Was it the car?

"Mommy?" I yelled, suddenly angry. Why would she be in the garage all this time when I was home? Why was she scaring me by not answering? She knew I was afraid of the garage! She never made me take the trash out if it was dark. She was so nice that way, when Daddy always told me not to be a baby.

I felt like a baby now. "Mommy!"

Open the door. Open the door. Some older, sadder part of me told me what to do, and with a great rush of terror, I flung it open.

Her car was in there. Running. The garage was foggy, but I could see she was in the car, and I was terrified before I knew why.

"Mommy!" I screamed, because she wasn't moving and her eyes were closed, and I knew I had to save her, but what if the old man was there, the Halloween man, what if he had started a fire and that was why there was smoke in here? It smelled bitter, coating my throat.

I yanked open the passenger-side door, and my mother tipped toward me, sliding out and to the ground.

I felt a hot rush down my legs, and I screamed, a thin, helpless sound. Grabbing my mother's arm—it was cool, she was chilly—I pulled as hard as I could. Did the old man kill her? Was she asleep? Sick?

"Mommy! Please!" I shrieked.

And then Mrs. Fitzgerald was there, grabbing me around the waist and practically tossing me back out of the garage. "Call 911!" she said, and then dragged my mother into the breezeway. She slammed the door to the garage, and my mother . . . my mother's face was gray, like the Halloween man.

"Call 911, Emma," Mrs. Fitzgerald said again, more gently this time.

"I wet my pants," I sobbed.

"It's okay, honey. Call 911." Then she bent over my mother and breathed into her mouth.

From that point on, I only had flashes of memory. The ambulance lights. Mrs. Fitzgerald helping me into clean pants and driving me to the hospital. The relief of seeing my pop and grammy come into the waiting room, how I felt like everything would be okay then.

But it wasn't.

My mother had died in that garage. On purpose.

I didn't have memories of her funeral. I knew that I didn't go to school. Gigi came out and shook her head at the sight of me and had many whispered conversations with my father. She stayed at a hotel because Daddy and I were staying with Grammy and Pop, but Gigi came over every day. She told me not to cry, but I did. She told me to be strong, but I wasn't.

Grammy and Pop tried hard to be cheerful around me. But their eyes were so sad. Grammy looked old, and Pop had to stand in the backyard for long periods of time after dinner. Grammy was sick and needed a wheelchair, and Pop worked and couldn't skip his job like my father. Pop yelled at my father one night, and Daddy took me back to our house, and we watched TV and ate pizza, and I cried for my mother.

After a while, my father told me we were going to visit Gigi. We got on an airplane and flew to Connecticut, where I had never been. My dad rented a car and drove us to my grandmother's house, which was huge and pretty with lots of blue flower bushes. It was like a castle on the water.

"Stay here," my father said, leaving me alone in the big front hall. There was a lot of hushed talking, then some sharp voices.

When Gigi came into the front hall, I had to pee so badly I was afraid I'd wet myself, same as I had the day Mommy died. My grandmother looked at me, her lips pressed tight.

"Donelle will get you settled," she said, and another lady picked up my suitcase and led me upstairs where, finally, I got to go to the bathroom.

When I had washed my hands with the lemon-scented soap and dried them on the softest towel, I came back out. The lady was gone, but my things were unpacked. I sat on the bed and looked out the window. That was the ocean, I guessed.

I sat there for a long time before the woman, Donelle,

came back to tell me it was time for dinner. My father had already left, but Gigi said he'd come back to visit.

It took me a long time to realize my father had deserted me. That I'd be living here permanently.

To be honest, I was glad not to have to live alone with my father, who had drunk a lot of yucky-smelling brown stuff and didn't know how to do laundry. I wanted to live with Grammy and Pop, but I understood that wasn't happening.

I yearned for my mother with an ache so big and powerful I didn't have words for it. At night, I was afraid to go to sleep, of the tears and shaking that would envelop me. I missed my old life, missed sitting next to Drake on the bus, missed recess with Rachel and Taylor. No one at my new school could double Dutch; there weren't even jump ropes given out at recess. I missed our house, the smell of pancakes, my old room.

Gigi was sort of famous, I learned. The other kids at school all knew her, but this didn't help me make friends. Now I lived in a house with a name and servants (though Helga terrified me, Charles would play checkers with me sometimes in his house over the garage).

I tried to be brave. I was a little scared of Gigi, but she was my grandmother. She would love me.

That's what I expected. But it never quite happened.

CHAPTER 23

Miller

Tess was in her crib, finally, and Miller was holding an ice pack on his jaw, thanks to her head-butt. She was winding down, only screaming every six seconds now instead of with every breath. He watched the footage from the surveillance cam he had in her room, which showed her still standing at the bars, so tired she was nearly falling asleep between screams.

He wanted with all his dead heart to go into her room and pick her up, kiss her sweaty curls and say, "It's okay. Daddy's here. Go to sleep now, little bunny rabbit," or whatever normal fathers said. But experience had taught him that this would only cause a surge in adrenaline, enabling Tess to stay awake and enraged for hours more. Hours.

So he had this. A surveillance camera so he could make sure she wasn't hurting herself, so that he could see the moment she finally would sit, then flop to her side, then fall asleep for a few hours.

Fatherhood, once removed.

He'd found a nanny last week, a somewhat resigned college girl. Kimmy wasn't a monster by any means, but she let Tess run wild while she was glued to her phone. At least she took Tess outside for a few hours in the fenced-in backyard. But she didn't love Tess, didn't try to win her over, or read to her, or give her a bath. She just kept her from hurting herself. And while Miller understood that philosophy quite well, he did want more for his child. Someone to love her.

But today had been a good day. Or a good evening, anyway. At Genevieve's, he was amazed at how Tess had taken to Emma's daughter. Riley. The girls were sort of related; second cousins or something like that. Ashley would've known; she loved genealogy, the only person he'd ever met who knew what *second cousin once removed* actually meant.

Going to Genevieve's house for cocktail hour over the past couple of years had been Miller's only social outings. It was the only place where no one would try to fix him up, and the one place where he wouldn't be asked the inevitable "How *are* you?" He didn't feel like such a failure with Genevieve; they'd gotten to know each other when he did some construction on Sheerwater five years ago, sprucing the place up, replacing the roof, some of the windows, putting in a French drain. He'd been under the impression she was going to sell the place, but apparently not.

"You're not the wastrel I expected," she said when he was done. "I wouldn't have hired your family, but I like to keep my business local. You were a pleasant surprise."

He remembered laughing with Ashley over the comment. Like everyone in town, Ashley was fascinated and awed by the great Mrs. London and had pumped him for every detail of the house, her shoes, her outfits. That night, they'd made love, and Ash had said, "You were a pleasant surprise," and he'd pressed his forehead against her heart and laughed and laughed.

Genevieve had come to the funeral, and rather than the usual drivel people said at funerals, she'd held his hand for a minute, looking him in the eye, and said, "This is a horrible tragedy."

That was all. A few months later, he got a written invitation to come to cocktail hour, and he'd gone. That was back when Ashley's parents still offered to take care of Tess, and Miller felt insane with grief that day, afraid to take care of Tess, so tired his hands shook. He'd gone, and Genevieve made him a drink strong enough to make him weave on his feet. He woke up in a lounge chair some time later, covered by a soft throw, and she'd had her driver take him home.

Since then, he'd had a standing invitation every Friday. He tried to go at least once or twice a month. Being around people his own age was too hard. And Genevieve had suffered great losses, too—her son, her husband. He admired her and was grateful to her . . . She never gave advice, just kissed him European-style and talked about town news or books. Occasionally, she'd ask for a recommendation—who'd do a good job plowing her driveway, who was the most ethical boat salesman. It was rare that Miller felt normal, but in Genevieve's presence, he did. Donelle was a hoot, and the guests at the cocktail parties were always very nice. No one pried. He wondered if Genevieve had coached them, and if she had, he was grateful.

Tonight, being with Emma and Jason had been tough, Ashley's ghost so close he could almost see her as he gazed across Sheerwater's lawn toward her grave. When Jason started talking about how hard marriage was, he'd had to leave or he would've punched his cousin in the face.

But Tess had been so cute with Riley, and Emma, too, and that had outweighed his anger and loneliness. Moments like that—Tess going upstairs to play without screaming or kicking, letting herself be held by someone—gave him hope that his daughter might be normal.

On the iPod screen, Tess's legs finally gave out, and she crumpled to the mattress, asleep. He watched for a minute to make sure she was breathing, then poured himself a finger of single malt and went to sit on the front porch, Luigi on his heels. The cat jumped up on his lap, purring.

"Hey, buddy," Miller said, stroking the cat's fur, which was considerably softer since his Desitin treatment. Latin music from the next-door neighbors drifted up, and he heard laughter. They were a happy family, the Oliverases, and Miller tried not to resent them for it. Sometimes, Mrs. Oliveras left food on his porch. It was always delicious.

For a builder, Miller didn't have the most impressive house. His parents had, back when they lived in town, a sprawling McMansion with a four-car garage at the top of a hill in a development, appropriate for the owner of a construction company, Miller supposed. It had been more than comfortable growing up, but Ashley preferred older houses, and whatever she wanted, he did, too. They'd bought a fire-sale house, literally; a Craftsman bungalow that had been seriously damaged when the owner left a frying pan on the stove. Who better than a carpenter to reclaim it? They'd restored it, put on an addition with plenty of room for kids (pause for bitter laughter). Really good insulation, too, and double-paned windows, which kept the Oliveras family from reporting him to DCF, since they didn't have to hear Tess's screams.

He'd thought about selling the house a thousand times since Ashley died, but her spirit was here, her touches, the paintings she'd chosen, the ugly lamp shaped like an Easter lamb, her books, her cat. Tess would at least have something of her mother in this house.

Besides, he couldn't bring himself to leave. "You don't want to move, do you, Luigi?" he asked the cat, who answered by curling his claws gently into Miller's leg. "I didn't think so."

The front porch was his favorite place—snug and deep with two comfortable chairs and a coffee table. Fat rhododendrons grew in front of it, hiding it from the road, from the sidewalk. In the summertime, he and Ashley used to sit out here. She'd offer commentary on the summer folks who liked to stroll and look at the houses. Back before she died, their front yard had had quite a garden, and it wasn't unusual for people to take pictures of the flowers, not realizing the owners were sitting there, watching. Sometimes, Ash would fake a sneeze to scare them, which never got old for her. Now the garden was in sore need of weeding and pruning. He should get on that.

The air was cooling down, and the wind rustled the leaves, bringing the scent of moonflower and roses, both planted by his wife. Joe Oliveras was playing guitar, and one of his daughters was singing softly.

Miller sometimes wondered if he was the loneliest man on earth.

A woman stomped by, her pale shirt glowing in the dim light from the streetlamp.

It was Emma.

"Hey," he said. She didn't stop. "Emma."

She turned. "Hello?"

"It's me. Miller." He suddenly felt stupid.

"Oh! Hi! I didn't see you there."

"Yeah. It's . . . I'm lurking."

"Is this your house? Or do you just sit on random porches at night?"

He smiled. "The former. Come on up. Unless you're going somewhere, that is."

"No, I was just taking a walk." She came up the path and took in the house. "What a nice place."

"Thank you. Have a seat. Would you like a drink?"

"Um . . . sure. If it's no trouble."

"Wine? I have both colors. Or scotch."

She smiled, and he remembered that he'd always liked her. "I'll have a glass of white."

He went in and poured from a bottle he must've opened a month or two ago, hoping it wasn't vinegar. On the monitor, Tess hadn't moved and was still breathing.

He went back outside. Luigi had taken up residence on Emma's lap, and was purring loudly.

"I like cats," she said. "This one seems extra nice."

"He is. Luigi, meet Emma." He handed her the glass. "Hey, thank you for tonight. For dealing with Tess and, uh, for having a great kid."

She smiled. "She *is* pretty wonderful. Yours is, too."

"She's a terror, but thanks."

"She's sleeping, I assume?"

"Don't curse it, but yes."

They sat there a few minutes in the near dark. "So why are you out walking the mean streets of Stoningham?" he asked. "You seemed like you might have been . . . stomping."

"Oh, I was," she said with a sigh. "Genevieve and I have issues, and she likes to slip in the knife whenever possible."

"What issues?"

She glanced at him. "She kicked me out when I got pregnant."

"Really?" He tried to remember if he'd known that. Three years of sketchy sleep had wreaked hell on his memory. He knew Jason had knocked up his girlfriend and that she moved to the Midwest. Oh, yeah. "Riley was born on my wedding day," he said. "I remember now." Jason, in a tuxedo, crying happy tears. Eighteen fucking years old. Ashley had hugged him and told him congratulations.

He hadn't realized Emma had been banished.

"That must've been really hard," he said.

She shrugged. "It was. It was harder that she never called or sent a card, but hey. People are complicated."

"You would know, I guess. Being a therapist."

"Yeah." She laughed. "Somehow, though, I'm not immune. I make the same dumb mistakes as everyone."

"Don't we all."

A car drove past, the bass thumping from the radio, then the quiet settled in again. Joe Oliveras had put his guitar away, apparently.

"You know what I hate?" Emma asked. "I hate when people say stupid but well-meaning things."

He glanced at her.

"Like right now," she went on. "I'm sitting here, thinking about how nice Ashley was and how I always felt special when she talked to me at a party, and how much you must miss her. Which of course you do."

"Yes. I do. But thank you. She was . . ." *Everything.* "Special." He took a sip of the whiskey, feeling it warm its way past his cold, dead heart. "But you know what it's like. You lost your mom. People must've said stupid and well-meaning things to you, too."

"They did," she said cheerfully. "'She's watching over you' was a personal non-favorite. I mean, I would've preferred she was still here and watching me live and in person, you know?"

"I do. People say that to me, too."

"Do you also get 'Be strong'?"

"God, yes. I hate that one."

"I was eight when my mom died. I didn't even know what being strong meant."

"Of course you didn't."

"And then when I had Riley, people would say, 'You're so strong, Emma.' I felt like saying, 'No, I'm pathetic and weak and my boobs hurt and please take my baby so I can sleep, and also do you have a few extra thousand dollars lying around?'" She laughed and rolled her eyes, and Miller found he was smiling a little at her honesty.

"'Heaven's got a new angel,'" he offered. "That one makes me homicidal."

"That is a *particularly* horrible thing to say. Wow."

He liked the emphatic way she talked. "Your turn," he said.

"Okay. Um . . . 'You'll meet again someday.'"

"Gah." He shuddered. "How old were you again?"

"Eight. Your turn."

"Oh, here's a good one. 'It was God's plan.'"

"You're allowed to slap someone who says that, I'm pretty sure."

"Thanks. I'll do that next time."

"I'll post your bail." She took another sip of wine. Miller's whiskey was gone, and he was tired and knew he should ask her to go so he could try to sleep.

But it was nice, sitting on the porch with a pretty woman, one who wasn't coming on to him or offering parenting advice.

"You and Jason get along pretty well," he said.

"Yeah, we do." She sounded noncommittal. "Although you were completely right about our . . . dynamic. He's not a bad father, but his life didn't change that much. He went to college, got a job out here, fell in love and got married, and I did one thing. I had Riley."

"And got a couple of degrees, I hear."

"Sure. But without my grandfather, I don't know where we'd be."

"I guess I don't really know too much about what happened to you. I'm sorry."

"Oh, it's fine. Um . . . your aunt and uncle didn't want much to do with me. They've never met Riley, in fact."

"Are you shitting me?"

She looked at him. "Nope."

"I . . . wow. Emma, you must hate us. I always thought you went to . . . where was it?"

"Chicago. Downers Grove, to be specific."

"I thought you went out there because you wanted to."

She laughed a little. "No. I wanted to marry Jason and live here."

"Are you bitter?" Listen to him, asking all the Oprah questions.

"Well, sure! I mean, have you met Jamilah? She's stinkin' beautiful." But he could tell by her tone that she wasn't bitter, which was fairly amazing.

"You're a good kid, Emma."

"I'm thirty-five and feel a lot older most days."

"I'm forty and feel a hundred."

"Yeah. I bet you do." She set her wineglass down on the coffee table, causing Luigi to jump off her lap. "I should head home. It was nice talking to you."

"You too."

"I'm around if you need help with Tess. And Riley is not gainfully employed this summer, so if you need a sitter . . ."

"I kind of do."

"Call." She put her hand on his shoulder for a second. "Nighty-night."

"Need a ride home?"

"Nah, I'll walk. It's gorgeous out. Bye, Miller."

"Bye."

He watched her go down the street until she turned the corner.

Then Tess began to scream, so, with a sigh that wasn't quite as defeated as usual, he got up to see to his child.

CHAPTER 24

Genevieve

Five days after I was so rudely given the ultimatum by Emma, she and I went to my attorney's office to fill out the paperwork while Riley waited in the foyer with Charles. Apparently, they played Words with Friends together.

Riley was a wonderful girl. I wished Emma had some of her sunniness. Granted, I heard them laughing together in the mornings. The natural affection that flowed between them, the way they hugged and touched each other, the compliments and little jokes that only they got . . . it constantly reminded me of what I didn't have and had never been able to create with either Clark or Emma.

I'd thought—hoped—that once Emma went to college, matured a little—that she would see me differently and come to respect and admire me. I hadn't enjoyed being Clark's mother, we all knew that, and I hadn't enjoyed having a ruined little girl thrust on me without warning, either.

But I'd hoped Emma and I might be friends one day.

Donelle, who had finally agreed to see a doctor about the small ecosystem growing out of her toenail, had reminded me of that just this morning in the breakfast room.

"You don't have much time left, Gen. Do or die. Do *and* die, as the case may be." She slurped up her cereal off the spoon, making the most horrible noise.

"She's never receptive," I said in my defense.

"Right. And you're so warm and welcoming. Helga, can I have more coffee? My toe, you know?"

Helga got her a refill without comment, glanced at my empty cup and failed to ask if I needed anything. Honestly. I should fire her.

At any rate, here we were in the very tasteful office, waiting for my attorney to finish with another client in the conference room. Unlike too many lawyers' offices, which were stuffed full of law books and piles of paper, Brooklyn (what *had* her mother been thinking?) had chosen a soft color palette to suit the bright and airy space. The walls were white, a lush gray carpet was on the floor, and her desk and bookcases were a honey-colored tiger maple. Several green glass sculptures sat on the shelves. A bit too modern and severe for my tastes, but very chic nonetheless.

Her Smith and Yale diplomas hung on the walls. "She went to Smith," I said, in case Emma hadn't noticed, and because apparently I couldn't help myself. "Graduated a year after you would have."

Emma turned her head and gave me a look.

"It's simply a fact, Emma. You needn't look so wounded."

"I'm not wounded. I'm curious. It's been seventeen years. Shouldn't you be over it by now? I went to college. I have a doctorate in psychology."

"From a no-name school, and such a silly degree. Therapist. You might as well be an Internet-ordained minister."

"Trust me, Genevieve. You could use a shrink. *And* a minister. Speaking of that, do you have any funeral plans you'd like to share?"

I felt an unwilling burst of pride at her quick repartee. "Brooklyn has all the details."

"Should we talk about the will while we're here?"

"Don't be crass."

"If I have to sell Sheerwater, I'd like to make some plans."

"You're not the heir, are you? I fail to see where it's your business."

"The heir is sixteen and therefore a minor child. Do you want her in charge of millions of dollars, that house and all your belongings at her age? That's a brutal responsibility. All that money could lead to a lot of trouble. Are there trustees until she's twenty-five or something like that?"

I felt my face warming, much to my chagrin.

"Good morning, ladies!" Brooklyn came in, mercifully interrupting. I took in her outfit automatically—St. John sleeveless knit, a classic. The white fabric looked smashing against her dark skin and clung to her figure in a way that showed it off without coming across as trashy. She wore a wide gold cuff on her wrist, a gold necklace, no earrings. Too bad Emma still refused to dress herself well.

"Sorry to make you wait. Lovely to see you again, Genevieve. Ms. London, I'm Brooklyn Fuller." She shook hands with Emma. "So nice to meet you."

"Same here," Emma said. "And it's Dr. London. I have a PhD in psychology."

"My apologies, I didn't know. Dr. London, then." Brooklyn sat behind her desk. "Before we get started, Genevieve, I just have to show you this." She opened her desk drawer and pulled out a buttery brown leather purse. "From your spring line. My favorite one yet!"

I suppressed the irritation. I had not designed the spring line. Granted, the purse was beautiful. But it wasn't mine, no matter whose name was spelled out on the small gold tag.

Brooklyn smiled, put the bag back and opened the file.

"Down to business. I've got all the paperwork here, and my assistant has filled out the basics. Really, the only question you need to answer is this one." She read from one of the pages. " 'Explain the change in circumstances that led the guardian/temporary custodian to file for resignation.' " She passed the papers over to me.

The change in circumstances. Could I say brain tumor? That sounded the most noble. I hated to say *health* . . . It sounded weak. *No longer able to care for* . . . Also demeaning. *Old age*. Please.

"And, Emma, these are for you. A petition for temporary guardianship here, and appointment as a trustee here." She passed more papers across her impressive tiger maple desk. "The Department of Developmental Disabilities will have to do a study, so they'll be contacting you to schedule that."

"Got it. I've been asked to help on some of those back in Chicago."

"Fantastic. Where'd you get your degree?"

"Rosalind Franklin's where I got my doctorate. My undergrad and master's were at Chicago State."

"My cousin got her MD at Rosalind Franklin. She's a pediatrician in Milwaukee now."

"What a great field," Emma said, looking up with a smile.

How very pleasant that they were bonding. I gave Brooklyn a frosty look, which she correctly interpreted as *let's get back to the issues*.

She cleared her throat. "So you're familiar with the process, Dr. London, which makes everything easier. Genevieve, has Hope's father waived his parental rights?"

"No," I said. I'd been unable to convince him to do that.

"He's never even been to see her," Emma said, and really, did she *have* to air our family secrets? Clark was an idiot and a terrible father, yes. Nevertheless, Emma didn't have to hang from her cross and shout it out to the world.

"I just want to make sure he won't be able to access

Hope's trust," Emma continued. "Or any inheritance she might be getting. Can he contest my grandmother's will?"

Brooklyn's head jerked back the slightest bit. She glanced at me. "Uh . . . no, everything is ironclad regarding Hope's trust. And I don't . . . foresee a problem with anything else."

"Great. Thank you." She turned her attention back to the papers.

I looked down as well.

Oh, no.

The words swam before my eyes. The too-familiar panic rose fast and hard in me, pulling me under like a riptide. The buzzing was deafening. Was it really in my head, or was there a fire alarm or . . . or . . . something? The other women didn't look perturbed. Why was I here? Where was I? Why was the black woman looking at me?

"Gigi?"

I glanced at the young woman to my right. "Yes?"

"Are you all right?"

"Y-yes."

She looked at me another minute. I knew her, but her name wouldn't come to me. The black woman . . . I *didn't* know her. She was a complete stranger! Why were we here? Were they about to take me somewhere? Was I going to the . . . the . . . the place where they put old people? The jail? The asylum? What was it called? The kennel? It was like a kennel for old people, and I was old, wasn't I? There were age spots on my hands, and I was very tired, and from the corner of my eye, I could see that my hair was white. White! When I'd always been blond before.

Tears came to my eyes. I hated this. I hated being afraid.

The white woman squeezed my shoulder, her eyes kind. She'd take care of me, I knew instinctively.

"I think we'll finish this at home, Brooklyn," she said, and the name meant nothing to me. Were we in Brooklyn?

Why? "It gets a little emotional whenever we have to make a decision about Hope."

Why was she talking about hope? What were we hoping for? Or dreading? Because I felt filled with dread.

The black woman said something, and the white woman answered, but I couldn't hear properly.

We got up, and I remembered to take my handbag. I was dressed well, at any rate. For some reason, that reassured me. If I was going to the home—the nursing home, that was it—at least I looked put together.

In the waiting room were two other people who both stood when we came out. "I totally killed Charles with 'zygote,' Mom," said the girl.

"It's true. I'm dead," said the man.

"Yay for AP Biology," said the kind woman. Emily. That was her name. Or, no, not quite.

Those were jokes. I didn't understand why they were funny, but at least I could hear again. I pretended to smile, terrified that someone would find out. I knew to pretend I wasn't confused. I smiled at the redheaded girl, feeling fond of her, and swallowed the panic. I hoped they wouldn't hurt me. I was fairly sure they wouldn't, but I felt like crying just the same.

This would pass. This would pass. Someone had told me that; I had to believe it was true.

"Ready to see Hope?" the redheaded girl asked.

"I am," I said, and let her take my hand and show me hope, whatever that looked like.

At some point, I started to come back to myself. I had faked my way through the minutes (or hours) that spooled out, and little slices of the world came back into their rightful place. I knew Rose Hill, and then suddenly knew the names of the three girls—Emma, Hope, Riley.

Catching and holding on to the information was like trying
to knit together wisps of drifting fog. Was Emma their
mother? No, not quite right. Emma was Hope's brother. *No,
stupid, not* brother! *The other one! The girl version of*
brother.

My hands looked so old! Were they really mine? Those
rings were familiar, the diamond engagement ring, the
simple gold band, a wide, plain silver ring on the other hand
that looked out of place on these wrinkled, crooked fingers.
How embarrassing, that chic and stylish ring having to sit
on that old finger! I wanted to cry. The horrid buzzing
ebbed and flowed, sometimes drowning out other sounds. I
wanted to scream, "How can a person think with that
noise?"

If only I had someone to comfort me, to hold me and tell
me I was fine. I knew I had a sickness in my brain. Cancer,
perhaps. Where was Garrison? He would tell me . . . but no,
he was long dead. Instead, I sat there on a wooden bench
that hurt my hips and spine, and watched the girls play with
a large ball.

Sisters. Emma and Hope were sisters—half sisters—and
they were both my granddaughters. Olivia . . . no, not Olivia . . .
what was her name? Olivia was her middle name, I was sure.
Riley. That was it. Riley was my great-granddaughter. Emma
and she were staying with me for the summer, because I was
sick. The man who had driven the car . . . I knew I'd known
him a long time, and I employed him. Was he my bodyguard?
The notion seemed absurd.

Sweet Hope. She came over to me for a hug, fitting right
against me. She smelled so familiar. She laughed with
Emma and Riley, too, and as the foggy wisps drifted together, I realized that they'd been to see her. Many times.
A tightness clamped around my throat. I couldn't remember why Emma wouldn't come see me, but I knew that she
hadn't.

We ate lunch, Emma helping Hope with her food, Riley, too, wiping Hope's chin when the child laughed and food spilled out. We looked at one of those . . . those holes in the ground that are filled with water for swimming. A constructed lake. A pod? Almost, almost. A pill?

Pool. A pool. We looked at the pool at Rose Hill, where Hope lived.

By the time we were in the car with Charles (for heaven's sake, of course it was Charles), I'd checked my leather-bound planner (a Genevieve London design, of course, and one of my own making), and seen that we'd had an appointment with Brooklyn Fuller, my attorney, at ten, before spending the day with Hope. It was five o'clock, and for nearly all that time, I'd been out of myself, and lost. No episode before had lasted so long.

Getting home had never been such a relief. Thank goodness I had Charles. What if I'd had to drive myself?

"And how is Miss Hope?" Donelle asked, hobbling in to greet us.

"She's great," Emma said. "How's the toe?"

"Still oozing."

"I'm afraid I have a terrible headache," I said, which was the truth. "I'll take a tray in my room, and, Donelle, would you kindly make me a martini as well?"

"No," she said. "Because I'm an invalid, can't you see?"

"I'll do it," Riley offered.

"You're sixteen," Emma said. "What do you know about making a martini?"

"That's why the Internet was invented," she said. "Also, it's a useful life skill, Mom. I can bartend through college."

I made my way upstairs slowly, gripping the railing, too tired to talk to anyone anymore.

The mirror showed an old, well-dressed woman who still had her height, though my shoulders were caving inward. Mother would've been horrified. Then again, she

CHAPTER 25

Riley

Helga made some grayish meat for dinner, so instead of giving that to Gigi, I made scrambled eggs with cheese and sourdough whole-wheat toast that Mom and I got at the farmers' market the other day. Helga wasn't happy, but I didn't really care. From where I sat, she didn't deserve this job, so screw her.

I buttered the toast carefully, then got a rose from the garden and put it in a little bud vase.

When I was little, I used to play waitress with my mom and Pop. All I could manage was toast with jelly, and they always made such a fuss over it. I kind of missed living with Pop. Maybe I'd sleep over this weekend and we could watch *The Hunt for Red October*, his favorite movie. I also wanted to go to the library and do some digging about missing children who'd been found in the years after Great-Uncle Sheppard disappeared.

Also, Rav had texted me and said he'd be there on Saturday, so maybe we could hang out. I'd been really chill about it and just texted back saying sounds cool, not sure what our weekend plans are, but probably yes.

He might like me. Even if he was a little bit younger, I didn't even care. No boy had ever liked me before, and Rav was super good-looking. When he was twenty-five, he'd be drop-dead gorgeous.

I also thought I would bike out to Birch Lake and take a walk around. Not that I was going to trip over a skeleton, but just to kind of immerse myself in the scene. That's what all the detectives did on the BBC, after all. They stared out and brooded. I'd seen *Broadchurch* three times and was fairly sure I could pull off a David Tennant–worthy brood.

I slid the eggs on the plate. "I'm available for cooking classes, Helga. If you want to learn the basics."

I'd say she glared back, but she always glared. Oh, the martini! I made it carefully and added it to the tray—how fun was it to make adult beverages?—and went through the living room. Mom was talking on the phone.

"Headache. And these . . . lapses, where she gets very quiet. No, not that I've noticed, anyway. Just quiet. She wouldn't tell me if she did, and she won't let me talk to her doctor. Nope, she has a driver. Please, Calista. Of course she does."

So Mom was doing some digging of her own. She saw me and waved. I smiled back and kept going through to Gigi's private staircase. (Who invented things like that?) Calista was Mom's best friend back home, and a neurologist. She was fabulous. One of those adults who didn't talk down to me about med school and said I could shadow her when I was eighteen if I still wanted to be a doctor. I sort of did. It was hard to say; when you're good in math and science, everyone thinks medicine, right? Mom said there are a thousand things I could do, and I shouldn't pigeonhole myself into any one thing until I was older.

I told you she was kind of perfect. Most kids who are

smart in Downers Grove (and everywhere) have parents who are hovering over them, writing their college essays and seeing a shrink if the kids don't make high honors. My mom just said to do your best and be happy.

Come to think of it, I was really happy these days. Maybe I'd go into fashion. Follow in Genevieve's footsteps. Start the Riley London line, which, come on, how cool did that sound?

Down the long hall of the master wing to Genevieve's bedroom. The door was closed almost all the way, and I knocked with my elbow and went in.

Gigi was sitting in a chair by the window, looking at a photo album.

"Dinner is served," I said, setting the tray on the table next to her.

"Oh, aren't you a dear," she said, sounding a lot better than earlier. She looked at the tray, with its cloth napkin and flower and my dorky little note that said *Feel better, Gigi!* "This is lovely! How kind you are, Riley." She smiled up at me, and I felt myself blushing, dorkishly proud.

"Well. You seemed down before. At Rose Hill."

Her gaze flickered. "A bit, yes. I've been Hope's guardian all her life. I worry about her."

"My mom will take good care of her, Gigi. And so will I."

"She's your aunt, isn't she? How strange."

"We visit every year. Mom goes twice a year."

"I know. That's very good of her, especially given her father's lack of attention. I would understand if she had nothing to do with Hope."

"Then you don't know my mom at all."

"Touché, darling, and good for you for standing up for your mother. Sit down, dear."

I sat in the comfy chair opposite her. The sky outside was pure blue, and the leaves on the fat maple tree were still. It was hot today, but never too hot here by the water.

Gigi took a bite of her toast, then cut into the omelet. She ate the European way, fork in her left hand, knife in her right. It looked very classy, and it made sense, rather than switching back and forth the way we Americans did.

"Is it hard, knowing you're going to die?" I asked. "Sorry. Is that rude?"

She took a sip of her martini. "Delicious, dear. And yes, it's a bit prying."

"I'm sorry," I said again.

"I appreciate your interest." Another bite of toast, a dab of her lips with the napkin. "Yes. It's hard. On the one hand, I've had a remarkable life. On the other, I lost two people I held most precious, and the idea of seeing them again is . . ." Her voice grew husky. "Rather wonderful."

"Are you scared?"

She handed me a piece of toast, and I took a bite. "Yes. I am. Not so much of dying, but of how it will be in the last hours. Or days."

"My mom's friend? Calista? She's a neurologist. I bet she could tell you what it's like. Maybe give you a second opinion, too."

"I don't need another opinion, dear, but it's a kind thought."

"I don't want you to die, Gigi. I'm just getting to know you."

Her eyes filled with tears. "Yes. And for that, I'm very, very sorry. You're a lovely person, and I'm quite grateful to have you this summer."

"Right back at you."

"Excuse me?"

"You're a lovely person, too. Sort of." I smiled so she knew it was a joke. She arched an eyebrow at me and continued eating. Ate the whole omelet, but only half a piece of toast, so I ate the rest.

"Watch out for carbohydrates, dear," she said. "They'll catch up with you. You're naturally slender, and an athlete as well, but even so."

Like healthy eating hadn't been drilled into my head since I was six. "Good advice," I said.

"Do try to speak in complete sentences, dear. One sounds so much more cultured when one does."

"That was excellent advice, Great-Grandmamma," I said, over-enunciating. "Thank you terribly much!"

Gigi laughed, then looked out the window for a few beats, her smile fading. "I don't suppose your DNA sites have turned anything up."

"No, which is a total disappointment," I said. "But I do have some questions, if that's all right with you."

"Go ahead, dear."

"What do *you* think happened that day?"

She sighed, then sipped her drink. "They'd been fishing," she said. "Garrison was putting the poles and tackle box back in the car, and he turned around and Sheppard was just . . . gone. It was so unlike him, too. He was a remarkable child, Riley. So attentive and smart. And charming! He could speak so well for a little boy, and yet he had this innocence about him that was utterly . . . pure."

"So for him to wander off . . ."

"Very uncharacteristic. Something must have caught his attention. Maybe he forgot something—his shoes or a lure or a book, and went back for it."

"Did you ever wonder if . . . well, if . . ." No. That was way too harsh.

"If my husband hurt him?"

I nodded.

"Of course I did. I had to. The police asked immediately, and when a few days had passed and we still hadn't found a trace of him, I asked him myself."

"What did he say?"

"He was ruined, Riley. Sheppard's loss ruined him. But I had to ask." She took a long breath. "He didn't hurt Sheppard. Nothing ever indicated that, and I knew it in my bones."

"I guess he was force-adopted," I said.

"That's my hope." She sat there, her hands playing with the sash of her robe. "Once upon a time, I made a bargain with God. I could bear the loss of Sheppard and Garrison if only I could know what happened. If only I could see my son, or bury him, I could get through life and take care of Clark, and I wouldn't kill myself or become a drunk. But here I am, at the end of my life, and God has not held up His end."

I was quiet for a minute. "I think you're pretty amazing, Gigi," I said. "And I'm sorry it's been so hard."

"I wasn't a very good mother to my other son," she said. "Clark. Your grandfather. Maybe that's why God didn't help me. I tried, but . . . I was dead, too, you see."

"I'm sure you did your best," I whispered, because I was crying a little bit.

"It wasn't very good," she admitted. "I just threw money at him. Sent him away to school the minute I could, and kept throwing money at him to keep him happy. I should've made sure his wife was under a doctor's care. I knew she was struggling. I just didn't know how much."

"Well. Neither did her own parents. And you're not God, Gigi. Even if you think you are some days."

She snorted a little. "Shall we change the subject? Tell me about young Aarav. I saw the two of you got on quite well."

And so, for another half hour, I talked to her about boys, how I'd never been kissed, wasn't sure I wanted to be, how some girls said I was a lesbian but I didn't think so, even though I would be okay with that if I was. I told her about school and my former friends, about Mom and how hard she worked and how much I loved her, and all the things we did together, and how Pop was the best.

"You should come visit us in Illinois," I said. "I have a trundle bed. I'll sleep on the pullout, and you can have my bed. It's really comfy."

She reached out and put her hand on my knee. "Thank you," she said, and I hugged her then, resting my head on her bony shoulder.

Because everyone needs a hug. Even—especially—a mean old lady who didn't know how to be with people.

CHAPTER 26

Emma

By week five of my stay in Connecticut, things were settling into a rhythm. Genevieve had granted me the use of one of her cars, an aging but once-sporty Mercedes. I needed it, since I'd started at Rose Hill and had been seeing two families who were dealing with all the emotional issues that went along with needing this facility.

I'd found out a few other things, too.

Rose Hill was endowed so that, like the famous St. Jude's children's hospital, no family would ever be turned away because of the inability to pay.

"But of course, you knew that already," said Tom, the executive director, with a wink. "We are quite grateful to"—he made quote marks with his fingers—"'anonymous.'"

I gave a small smile back. No, I hadn't known, and I was more than a little dazzled. That was quite an act of generosity on Genevieve's part. And anonymously at that! It was . . . selfless. Go figure. Gigi usually liked the London name spread far and wide, engraved in marble if at all possible.

Being at Rose Hill three afternoons a week meant I got to spend more time with Hope. Her seizures, which had been well controlled for a long time, seemed to be coming back, and her neurology team was adjusting her meds.

I had always known that Hope's life expectancy was up in the air. Her disorder was complex; Hope had tumors, hundreds of them, all benign, on her brain, heart, kidneys, liver, eyes. She'd had two brain surgeries so far and might well need another. Being her guardian wasn't going to be easy, but I was so, so glad I'd forced the issue. Genevieve could've picked her attorney or, God forbid, even my father.

Most children at Rose Hill didn't have tuberous sclerosis, which was a rare genetic disorder. There were about eighteen kids here with a variety of conditions—traumatic brain injury, microcephaly, severe autism, neurodegenerative disorders. I'd been reading as much literature as I could get my hands on, talking to Calista, getting referrals to doctors at the children's hospitals here in Connecticut so I'd be better informed.

My first session at Rose Hill was with the family of a beautiful four-year-old boy with so many medical complications that he needed 24-7 medical care and supervision. They'd done their absolute best, but the medical bills were killing them, and he needed more care than they could give. The parents broke down, sobbing at the thought of not living with their son, and suddenly, though maybe it broke some therapy rules, I was on my knees in front of them, hugging them, and found I was teary-eyed, too. "There's no easy way to do this," I said. "No easy way."

"Thank you," whispered the mom. "Does anyone get okay with this? Do you know any of the family members here?"

"Actually," I said, "my sister's a resident here." The director and I had talked about bringing up my own issues, which I felt would only be okay if asked directly. "She's fourteen and has been here since she was three. She's really a happy kid, and this place has been great for her."

Their faces brightened a little, and I knew it had been the right thing to say.

I'd always been tentative around my clients when they were in extreme pain. And what could be more painful than leaving your child, no matter how beautiful the facility, how wonderful the staff? It was brave and horrible, acknowledging that, in some cases, your child needed more than you could give.

Some parents, like my own father and whoever Hope's mother was, were relieved not to care for their kids anymore. Clark might not have signed away his rights the way Hope's mother had, but he was a nonperson to my sister. I did wonder why he hadn't abdicated his rights, too. He'd always been more than happy to foist his children off on Genevieve. Not that I was bitter. (Hint. I was.)

On Friday afternoon, I left Rose Hill after smooching up Hope, who was a little sleepy from her meds, and headed back to Stoningham. My grip tightened on the steering wheel as I followed the car's directions. I was going to Jamilah's, because Riley was having a sleepover weekend there. Both nights. Helga had gone to visit her sister—I pictured them in a dark forest together, their house on chicken legs, like Baba Yaga's, surrounded by a fence made of bones.

Not only that—Genevieve and Donelle had decided to go to the city (I wasn't invited) for "one last pub crawl," in the words of Donelle. When I asked Genevieve if she was up for the trip, she predictably snapped at me, told me to mind my own business, not to bury her just yet, etc.

But I was getting used to her ways. Being an adult (and a therapist) let me see her differently—a woman fearful of losing her status and power, afraid of acknowledging her mortality. I could sympathize, even if I still didn't like her a whole heck of a lot.

But she was wonderful with Riley. Maybe it was the generational difference. I had to admit I kind of loved seeing them together, my daughter amiably sparring with the woman I'd once called the Gorgon, and more than holding her own. Gigi was more affectionate with Riley, too; she'd smooth her hand over Riley's hair, and Riley would say, "I should charge for this."

At any rate, Sheerwater was mine for the weekend. Me, and twenty-some-odd rooms at my disposal. The upshot of this was I was having my own sleepover party. But first, I had to talk to Jamilah.

Jason and I had had dinner the other night, just the two of us. It had been nice . . . sort of. We talked mostly about Riley and her wonderfulness, how good she was with her brothers. I told him she'd been helping Miller's nanny with Tess, and he said yes, Riley had texted him a picture of her and Tess. I hadn't gotten that picture, but hey. I'd always been glad my daughter and her father had a solid relationship. If he wasn't in her life enough to be a proper role model, he liked and loved her, and that was more than a lot of people got, myself included.

I steered the conversation to college, and he said he'd give whatever he could. "I was kind of hoping for a number, Jase," I said. "We'll be filling out the forms soon, and they ask for that kind of thing."

"Gotcha," he said. "Well, we'll see what kind of scholarships she gets first, right?"

"Wrong. First they determine need, so we won't know how much we need until we know how much she has."

"I meant academic scholarships. Or sports! I mean, she's good at soccer. We played with the boys the other night down at the high school."

"She's not good enough to get a D1 scholarship, Jason. And even if she gets a merit scholarship—"

"Why don't we talk about it when I'm at my computer?" he said. "It's hard to know where I'll be next year, financially speaking. Of course I want my daughter to go to college, and of course I'll help, Em. Don't worry so much."

That was a line he'd said a lot in the past sixteen and a half years, and as usual, it irritated me.

Then again, the therapist side of me murmured in the gentle, soothing voice that he had a point. The mother part of me wanted to kick him and demand a check for a quarter mil, but what could you do?

But then he leaned forward and filled me in on some gossip about one of our classmates. He was a good story-teller and bore more than a passing resemblance to Jake Gyllenhaal, and we were coparents.

And now my daughter was staying with his not-quite ex-wife. I turned onto their road, drove up to the top of the hill and pulled into their driveway.

Jason had neglected to tell me he lived in paradise. Sure, I'd Google-stalked their address, but as Jamilah worked for Google, the picture was blurred out for privacy reasons.

It was a sharply modern house, white stucco and lots of glass. Perched on the hill as it was, it had killer views of Long Island Sound. The front yard was landscaped with precisely trimmed boxwoods and a single Japanese maple bearing rich red leaves. The walk was blue flagstone set in polished cement, and the light fixtures were art deco. On the porch hung three huge Boston ferns. Not a dead leaf on them.

The cool factor was choking me. I knocked.

Almost immediately, Jamilah opened the door, wearing a long, flowing red dress with spaghetti straps. I guess motherhood hadn't done to her boobs what it had done to mine. Her earrings were simple, thin gold strands. Did she have to be dazzlingly beautiful *and* stylish on top of every-thing else? (Also, where could I get that dress?) "Hi," she said.

I fixed my face. "Hey! How are you? What a lovely home! It's amazing! So tasteful." *Muzzle it, London*, I said to myself.

"Great to see you, Emma," she said. "Come on in. I've made us tea."

Of course she had. I didn't even like tea, but I suspected I would soon be converted.

"Where are the boys?" I asked.

"They're at karate," she said. "Jason will bring them home by six, but of course, Riley is welcome anytime."

"Uh, yeah, um . . . I guess Jason will swing by and get her? Or I can drive her up."

"No need for you to make another trip," she said. "Unless you want to. Um, I guess you want to make sure it's okay for her to stay here?"

The house was just as gorgeous on the inside. "I'm sorry to be a dork about this. It's just that we don't really know each other that well . . ."

"I'd do the same thing," she said. "Have a seat."

I did. "You have two sons and a white couch. Are you magic?"

She laughed, and I felt the tug of liking her. A tea tray was set on the coffee table, as well as a plate of pastel-colored macarons. "Sugar?" she asked. "Milk, lemon, honey?"

"Just black is fine."

She poured me a cup. "I'm a little nervous," she said. "Sorry if I'm overcompensating."

"No, no! It's fine. It's great. It's lovely. Genevieve would heartily approve."

Jamilah looked up and smiled a little. "I guess I want to impress you."

"Really? I want to impress you, too!"

She smiled. "Well, you've raised the world's most perfect child, and you're Jason's first love, so . . ." She raised an elegant eyebrow at me, and I wondered when I'd last plucked mine. They tended to resemble large, scary caterpillars if I went too long.

"That's very nice of you," I said. "You're pretty damn

impressive, too, Jamilah." I took a sip of tea. Yes. It was delicious, damn it. "I guess I just wanted to ask the usual questions for sleepovers. You'll be here the whole time?"

"Of course."

"Any other adults?"

"No, just me." She sipped her tea. "We don't have any guns in the house, and we have a cat but no dogs. The pool has an alarm on it in case anyone falls in. No drugs in the house, maybe half a bottle of white wine, and we don't use Tide Pods."

Well. That about covered it. I felt a little stupid.

"Let me show you around," Jamilah said, and so I saw the guest room where my daughter would stay. There was already a framed picture of her, Owen and Duncan on the bureau, and a framed print of Paris—Riley was taking French. She had her own bathroom. The boys shared a bedroom, appropriately sloppy but clean. There was a finished basement with a huge TV.

"I limit the boys to an hour of TV and another hour of screen time," Jamilah said. "On school nights, they can't watch TV, but in the summer . . ."

"Sure. Loosen the rules a little."

"Do you think that's too much?"

She was asking my opinion! "No, that sounds good. What about you, though? You work for Google, so you must be on the computer all the time."

"Yeah," she said. "I only work part-time, though, and I try to compartmentalize it so I'm not always checking."

"That's very healthy."

We nodded at each other, that awkward moment when we'd run out of compliments. "Well. I guess I'll be going, then."

"Did Jason tell you why we're separated?" she asked.

Ah. The good stuff. "No, not really. Just that things were . . . hard."

She looked out the window and toyed with the ring on her finger. The huge wonking diamond engagement ring on her finger, to be exact. I wondered how much tuition that would cover. "He had a . . . what did he call it? An emotional affair."

"Oh, fuck." *Bad answer, Emma!* "Sorry. I mean, that must be hard."

"I like your first answer better." She sighed. "It's so embarrassing. A Facebook affair with his college girlfriend."

I flinched, then pushed my hair back to cover.

I had been Jason's college girlfriend. Or so I'd thought. Not the only one, apparently.

"I probably shouldn't have told you that," Jamilah went on, "but I didn't want you to think it was over something frivolous. I mean, your daughter is part of our family, even if she's not here. If Jason and I divorce, that will still be true."

"That's very kind of you. She likes you a lot, Jamilah."

"I don't believe in evil stepmothers. She was here first. I mean, I hope Jason and I will get through this, but . . ." Her eyes teared up, and on impulse, I gave her a hug. She smelled fantastic (of course).

"Thank you," she said, hugging me back. She stepped away and got a tissue and wiped her eyes. "I hope it's okay that I told you. I wanted Jason to tell you, but I said if he didn't, I would. I guess he took the easy way out."

"Wouldn't be the first time."

"God, of course! Who do I think I'm talking to? Honestly, I think you're a saint for being so generous with him."

"I also think I'm a saint." She grinned. "Hey, Jamilah, there's one thing. Courtney and Robert have never met Riley, and I'd like to keep it that way."

"Totally understandable. I can't believe the way they've treated her. Or not treated her. And believe me, I've given them a piece of my mind about that."

"Really!"

"Of course! They're horrible. Courtney is so fake. For years, I thought if I just kept scratching away at the surface, something else would be there. Nope. She's all surface. You know what she calls Owen and Duncan? 'My black grand-children.' I'm always introduced as her black daughter-in-law. You know. Just in case someone might miss that. It's like it ups her social status to whip out my race whenever possible. In case people are blind and can't see for them-selves. My parents hate her."

"She's always been a climber. When I was a teenager, she would try to crawl so far up my grandmother's butt . . ."

"She still does. She tries to make it seem like she and Genevieve did their best with you, agonized over your wild ways and tried to woo you back home, but you were ex-tremely selfish and out of control.'"

"I was a pregnant grocery clerk living with her grandfa-ther, going to city college part-time."

Her mouth dropped open. "You and I need to go out for a glass of wine."

I smiled. "I think that's a great idea."

From the kitchen counter, her phone chimed, and she picked it up. "Jason's on his way with all three kids. You're welcome to stick around."

"Actually, I'm having a sleepover myself. My friend from Chicago is coming, and do you know Beth Guida? The florist?"

"Sure."

"Of course you know her. You live here. She's my bestie from high school, and we're going to take advantage of Sheerwater." I paused. "Too bad you can't come."

She tipped her head. "Do you mean it?"

"Yes! Is there any reason Jason can't spend the weekend with his three children?"

She smiled. "Give me five minutes, and I'll pack my bag."

If there was anything better than four women sitting on a deck, drinking margaritas and watching the sunset, I didn't know what it was. Minuet sat on my lap, curled into a tiny cinnamon bun shape. Mac was in the side yard, barking at nothing, and the other three dogs were elsewhere, farting and shedding and doing their thing.

"I can't believe you walked away from this house," Calista said. "I could live here with Satan and be happy."

"With Justin Bieber, even," Beth said. "Or the Kardashians."

"I love the Kardashians," Jamilah said. "Don't judge me."

"Too late. I'm sorry."

Everyone snickered.

"Calista," Beth said. "Have you met the staff? Sheerwater has a staff. A cook and a driver and a live-in housekeeper. And a fleet of purebred dogs."

"No butler? Sad," Calista said. "I should've been born an heir. Would've made my student loans a lot easier to pay off."

"Okay," I said, "first of all, I'm not an heir, and my student loans will be smiling at me when I'm on my deathbed. Secondly, the cook hates people, food and cooking, so it's not what it sounds like. The meat is gray, the soup is Campbell's, and she'll bite you if you try to make something yourself," I said.

"Is it hard, being the one percent?" Beth said, and we all laughed.

"Thirdly . . . are we on three? The housekeeper sits on the couch and makes Riley nurse her infected, fungal toenail—"

"No!" Jamilah said. "Give me custody. That's clearly child abuse."

"—and hasn't used a vacuum cleaner since the nineties. The many dogs, some of whom humped you when you came in and are even now peeing on your suitcases, rub their butts over the carpets, puke and poop everywhere. Watch where you step." I paused. "The driver is kind of awesome. And single, Beth."

"And gay, Emma," she said.

"He is? Shoot. I didn't know."

"He's been dating the postmaster for at least ten years. Where have you been?"

"Chicago," I said, and maybe it was the tequila, but we all thought that was hilarious.

"So, Emma," Calista said, "you haven't asked me if you have Ebola or leprosy or exploding head syndrome since you came out here. Did you retire from being a hypochondriac?"

"Oh, no! There goes my hobby!" It was true. Maybe because I was around someone who *did* have a brain tumor, but I hadn't been testing my neurological function as much as I usually did. "Speaking of that, what do you think about Genevieve?"

"Hard to say, since I haven't met her."

"Based on what I told you, though."

"Really hard to diagnose over the phone, hon."

"What's going on with Genevieve?" Jamilah asked. "Is she sick?"

"It doesn't seem that way to me," I said. "But I was summoned here this summer because she said she has cancer. A brain tumor, specifically. She said she was dying."

"Well, if that's what dying looks like, I wish I were dying, too," Beth said.

"No more margaritas for you," I said. Another round of giggles floated up, and I felt utterly, completely happy.

"Jamilah, how are things going with Jason?" Beth asked.

She shrugged, glancing at me. "We'll see. He's a great father, and the boys really miss him, so that kind of sucks. Being the only parent is *so* much harder than when you can pass the kids off to someone." She closed her eyes. "I'm sorry, Emma. That was insensitive."

"Don't worry. It's true. Single parenting is brutal." I sipped my drink. "He and I were never together, not really. Not after high school." Beth and Calista, who knew the inside scoop on that, side-eyed me but didn't contradict.

"What makes a great father?" Beth asked. "Because I'm

looking. I want babies so bad my ovaries spontaneously triple in size every time I see a picture of Lin-Manuel Miranda."

"Happens to us all," I murmured.

"Is Jason a great father to Riley?" Calista asked. She had a grudge against him, which was easy to do, since she'd never met him and encountered his easygoing charm and Jake Gyllenhaal eyes.

"He is," I said generously. "He's never forgotten a birthday, and he always gives Riley the best presents. He calls or texts a couple times a week, and he visits at least once a year. And then he always takes her somewhere cool or does something amazing with her. Rock climbing or sailing or *The Lion King*. She adores him." I paused. "Thank you for making that easy, Jamilah."

"Oh, God," she said. "It's nothing. He just needs a nudge."

I tilted my head. "I meant, thanks for being so understanding," I said. "What did you mean, he needs a nudge?"

"Uh . . . nothing."

I looked at her a minute. Her cheeks flushed, and she played with her ring.

"So that's all you?" I asked. "The calls and the visits and remembering her birthday?"

"Well . . . I put a reminder in his phone to call her. And of course her birthday is on our family calendar." She pressed her lips together.

"Do you schedule the visits?"

She winced.

"And pick out her gifts?"

She grimaced. "I . . . yeah. It's me."

"Are you kidding me?" I asked. "I mean, well done and thank you. But really? It's not him?"

"Surprise, surprise," Calista muttered.

"He absolutely loves her," Jamilah said. "I just . . . I didn't want her to ever feel second-best, you know? When we got married, I told him I wanted her to be a priority, and you know he's kind of scatterbrained, and—"

"It's okay," I said. "It's fine." I swallowed. "It just makes me like you more, in fact."

"And like him less, we hope?" Calista said. "No offense, Jamilah."

"None taken. We're separated. Does anyone here really like Facebook? Because it's ruining my marriage."

The conversation swung around to social media, how ridiculous it was, how no one would get off it, how everyone felt worse for being on it.

My mind was busy recalculating. All those years, Jason never said a word about his wife having a hand in his . . . fathering.

"Here's an idea," Beth said. "I'll move in with you, Jamilah. We can coparent those beautiful kids of yours. I won't even ask for sex unless you beg me."

Good old Beth. We all laughed, and the tension was broken. In fact, I felt a little relieved. Jason wasn't quite as perfect a father as he pretended to be (and as I'd believed him to be). And my daughter's stepmother loved her. Life tooketh with one hand and gaveth with the other.

"No one has provided me with a man, by the way," Beth said. "It's been five minutes. You don't know anyone?"

"Move to Chicago," Calista said. "I've got at least four interns who could use an older woman to help them grow up. They're children, but they have high earning potential and good hearts."

"A cougar," Beth said thoughtfully. "I like it."

The doorbell rang. "I'll get it," I said, and hauled myself off the chaise lounge.

"Bring more guacamole," Calista ordered.

"Yes, my liege," I said.

"See, she gets our dynamic," Calista said. "I tell her she doesn't have Huntington's, she makes me guacamole."

"Completely fair," Jamilah said.

I was still smiling as I went into the foyer and opened the door.

It was Miller. "Hey!" I said. "How are you?"

"Hi. Nice to see you."

"You too. What can I do for you?"

"Uh . . . it's cocktail hour?"

"Oh! Um . . . Genevieve's not here. She's in the city with Donelle doing a pub crawl. Which, given the state of that toe, is an accurate description. But come in, come in. We're having girls' night."

"Shit. She did leave a message, and I forgot. I'll go. I don't want to interrupt."

"Miller. I assume you have a babysitter, right?"

"Right."

"So get your butt in here and have a margarita and hang out with us for a little while. We'll kick you out when we start talking about periods."

He almost smiled. No, he did smile, and suddenly I realized that he was . . . well . . . kind of hot in that tragic, manly way. Jason was the looker of the two, but Miller had a quiet appeal that was . . . well . . . very appealing.

Perhaps I should also stop with the margaritas.

"We're on the deck," I said.

"No," Jamilah called. "We're in the room with the stone floor because the mosquitoes were killing us. Oh, hi, Miller! How are you, hon?"

"Jamilah." He gave her a kiss on the cheek. "Hey, Beth."

"Hey, hottie."

"Miller," I said, "this is my best friend from back home, Calista Daniels."

He nodded. "Nice to meet you."

"Miller is Genevieve's friend and Jason's cousin, Calista. He's got a three-year-old named Tess, and Riley's helping take care of her here and there." Like I hadn't given Calista the details already.

"Nice to meet you." She winked at me, sort of blowing my cover.

"How about a margarita, Miller?" I asked.

"I'll take a beer. I'll get it, though," he said.

"You forgot the guacamole, princess," Calista said.

Miller and I went into the kitchen.

No doubt about it. Miller *was* a hottie, and I was a little surprised I hadn't noticed it earlier. I mean, there had never been anything wrong with his looks, but age had made him more attractive. His dark hair was graying a little in a way that made my ovaries squeeze—the tragedy of the widower was shamefully sexy . . . so much cleaner than a sloppy divorce. And his sense of duty got me right in the feels, because a father who put his daughter first was not something I'd seen a lot firsthand.

"How's Tess?" I asked, handing him an IPA from the fridge.

He shrugged. "She's fine."

I sliced an avocado carefully. Helga did have very sharp knives. "Riley adores her."

He gave a half smile, and my ovaries stirred again. "Riley is amazing. She knows all these cool things to do that keep Tess interested. Little things, too, like pulling all the pots and pans out of the cupboards and giving her a wooden spoon and whisk and letting her bang the hell out of them. Or the other day, she filled up the sink with water and put dish soap in and just made bubbles and splashed. This morning, they put rocks in a bucket for forty-five minutes, and Tess was happy the whole time. Where do they teach that stuff? All my time with Tess is spent trying not to get her to break things and hurt herself."

I smiled to myself. Riley had learned those things from me, because I'd done them with her. My mother had done them with me. "Well, it's a lot easier when your job is just to entertain someone. You have to do all the work, too. Cooking, laundry, cleaning, taxes, doctor's appointments . . ."

He picked at the label on the beer bottle. "Does it ever get easier?"

"Hand me that cilantro, okay? And yes. It does." I mashed up the avocado, added the cilantro and some jalapeño and red onion. "You're a good dad, Miller, and you've had extraordinarily hard circumstances."

"I'm not really a good dad," he said, and there it was, his deepest fear, out in the open. I could tell both from his tone of voice and the way he was so carefully studying the remains of his beer label.

"Do you hurt her?"

"No! Of course not."

"Do you feed her?"

"Yes."

"Do you keep her safe?"

"Mostly."

"Do you take her to the doctor when she's sick?"

He rolled his eyes. "Yes."

"Do you try your best, even though she's a fiery little demon, and tell her you love her?"

He sighed. "Yeah. Even when I don't mean it."

"Then you're a good dad, Miller. Trust me. I've seen bad fathers. You're not even in the same neighborhood."

Suddenly he met my gaze. "Sometimes I think I hate her. Ashley died because of her." He looked away and took an unsteady breath. "Shit. I never said that out loud before."

I put down the fork I was using to mash the avocados, rinsed my hands, dried them, then set his beer bottle on the counter and held both his hands in mine. They were workingman's hands, and I held them tightly and looked into his dark, dark eyes. "That's a perfectly normal way to feel," I said. "It doesn't make you a bad person. It makes you a grieving husband."

He looked at me, too, his eyebrows drawn together. Then he was hugging me, and God, it felt good, because in that moment, I knew I'd said the right thing at the right time, and it hit him in the exact right place.

Poor guy. Poor, sweet, kindhearted guy.

He was lean and warm and smelled like sunshine and salt air, and he was taller than I thought. My face fit against his shoulder.

"Shit, is there romance brewing here?" Beth asked, and we broke apart.

Miller wiped his eyes in that way men do, one-handed.

Beth leaned on the counter. "Did I interrupt? If you guys need to start kissing, I can just stay here and watch in a totally non-pervy way."

"We were not kissing," I said.

"Yet," Beth said.

"Make yourself useful and grab the chips, Beth." I patted Miller's arm (his biceps was rather gloriously hard and full) and took the guacamole into the conservatory.

Miller didn't say much, but he made a fire in the fireplace, as it was getting chilly, and I lit a bunch of candles and kept the windows open. Got a few Genevieve London cashmere throws, and we sat there, laughing and talking and drinking wine and eating my very good guacamole. Amid stories about how Calista and I had met (me falling off my bike and thinking I had a hematoma and not just a bruised ass), and how Beth and I had met (first day of fourth grade, fell off the monkey bars and got a legit concussion, and Beth walked me in to the nurse), I found myself looking at Miller more than a few times.

He wasn't boyishly good-looking, the way Jason was. He was a man, and his battles showed on his face—the grief, the responsibility, the weariness. But there was intelligence there, too, and when he smiled, it felt . . . profound. Not just a knee-jerk reaction, but an affirmation that life still held beautiful things.

We talked about traveling, kids, books, television shows, what our parents were up to (I sat that one out; I wasn't sure whether my father was even in the country or not). It was lovely, really.

"Well, I should get going," Miller said eventually. "I told

the babysitter I'd be home before ten. Thanks for tolerating me, ladies."

"It was tough," Calista said. "You're rude and ugly and we don't like you at all."

There was that smile again.

"I'll walk you to the door," I said, standing up.

He thoughtfully grabbed his beer bottle and the now-empty bowl of chips and put them in the kitchen. We passed through the formal dining room, where there was a painting of the sea over the fireplace.

"Is that a Winslow Homer?" he asked.

I squinted at the signature. "Yes."

"Holy crap. It's gorgeous." We went into the foyer. "This is such a beautiful house," Miller said.

"It is," I said. "I heard you did some work updating it a few years ago."

"Will you have dinner with me sometime?" he replied, then looked away, rubbing the back of his head with one hand. "Sorry. Not exactly a date, but just . . . well, maybe a little bit of a date. Except you're Jason's ex and it might be weird for you, and I'm not exactly firing on all pistons these days, kind of a mess, really, and—"

"I'd love to."

He looked up. "Yeah?"

"Sure."

He gave a crooked smile, and my heart squeezed a little.

It had been a long time since I'd felt any kind of way about a man other than Jason. A *really* long time. I shushed the warning voices in my head and smiled back.

"Great," he said. "I won't kiss you or anything."

"Don't make promises you can't keep." I winked, then cringed internally—*leave the winking for George Clooney, Emma*—and kept the smile firmly on my face. "I'm kidding. Dinner will be really nice."

He looked at me another minute, still smiling. "Okay. Bye." He nodded and went down the walk.

That warm, tight feeling in my stomach stayed.

I went back into the conservatory.

"Someone has a boo," Beth said, and they all laughed their tipsy heads off.

I didn't deny a thing.

CHAPTER 27

Genevieve

On a sunny afternoon the week after Donelle and I had had one last trip to New York, I decided to practice suicide by swimming. My original date for this endeavor had been postponed due to weather.

The trip to the city had been everything I hoped. I'd booked us a day at Great Jones Spa, where Donelle's grumbles of "how the one percent lived" turned into groans of joy with the aromatic towel massage and Italian blood orange sea salt scrub and lemon verbena manicure. She even drank a green smoothie.

It was a true pleasure to see her so pampered, swathed in a luxurious bathrobe, being fussed over by angelic creatures with soft voices. Not that she'd worked terribly hard for the past fifteen years, but even so. Where would I have been without her?

After the spa, we went to a posh cocktail bar in the West Village, where, much to my delight, I'd been recognized by the bartender. He made us a special cocktail with gin, sage, honey and lemon and dubbed it "the Genevieve," took our picture, posted it on social media and said it would be a permanent fixture on the menu. For the next round, he made "the Donelle"—a gin and tonic with rhubarb, lemon and a slice of jalapeño, "because I can tell you're a handful." Obviously, she was delighted.

We avoided the Genevieve London store on Madison Avenue. Why bother? I doubted Beverly would let me raid the racks the way I had with Riley, and besides, Donelle knew those weren't my designs anymore. In fact, she was the only one, aside from my attorney, who knew everything.

Once I died, she was going to Scottsdale, Arizona, to live with her sister. I wished I could've found a way for her to stay at Sheerwater, and yet, the thought of her here without me filled me with a heavy melancholy.

At any rate, today was a good day to practice. Emma was off at Rose Hill—which made me a little uncomfortable, as she was wont to spread family gossip, and Rose Hill was *my* territory. Riley was helping at Miller's with his precious child.

I went into the den, where Donelle, surrounded by the dogs, was tapping away at her laptop. "What are you working on?" I asked. "Ordering a new bra?" She had dozens, each promising miracles that none delivered.

"I'm writing my book. It's a tell-all about you." She looked up. "Just kidding. I was online, looking for a girlfriend in Arizona. There are a lot of my kind of women out there."

I ignored Carmen as she dragged her hind end across the carpet. We had just been to see Anne, the veterinarian, who cheerfully diagnosed her with "itchy butt" and nothing worse.

"Are you a lesbian now?" I asked. Anne and her partner were, and Donelle did quite like them both.

She shrugged. "May as well try it, right? Men don't interest me anymore. Life is all about change, blah blah. I've always thought boobs were gorgeous. And the downstairs lady bits are much prettier than a drooping twig and berries. Stop laughing."

"Oh, Donelle. You're too much."

"What are you up to?" she asked.

"I'm going for a swim," I said, bending to pet Allegra, who was snuffling my foot. "To test the waters."

"Clever. So you're gonna practice offing yourself?"

"Must you be so blunt?"

"Have we met?"

"Regardless. Would you like to come?"

"To kill myself?" she all but shrieked.

"To swim, Donelle. I'm not going to kill myself today."

"When are you?"

"So eager for me to go?" I asked, linking my hands behind me and stretching, pleased that I still could.

"So eager for you to tell the truth, missy. Tick tock." She glanced at her foot. "You going in the Sound? Maybe the salt water would be good for my toe."

"Or maybe a sea creature would bite it off. Either way, a win. Mac, come here, boy, and gnaw off Donelle's toe."

"It'd be a mercy, Mac." She closed her laptop. "I don't have a bathing suit. Besides, me and Helga—"

"Helga and I."

"*Me* and *Helga* are going to the outlets. Want anything?"

Sometimes I did go with them. Genevieve London Designs had a shop there, and it always thrilled the staff when I showed up. That being said, it was always a little depressing to see my name but not my designs any longer. "Thank you, no. I'm off, then."

"Us too. Should I alert the Coast Guard?"

I sighed. "I'm just swimming to the buoy and back. I'll be fine."

I went upstairs to put on my swimsuit, by far the most difficult garment for a woman of age. Even though I'd worked hard to keep my figure, there was no hiding certain truths of being eighty-five years old. The skin on my thighs was crepey, and veins could be seen like routes on a map snaking through my calves. My arms and chest were spotted with discolorations I couldn't pretend were freckles and that laser treatments couldn't outpace. My feet, though I'd just had a pedicure last week, looked old. The bunion on my right foot looked worse than it did in the spring, and hurt more, too.

Then there was the actual putting on of the suit. I'd given up bikinis in my fifties when my skin began to lose its elasticity. This modest black maillot had a special material that held things up and in, and getting it from my ankles into place required a physics degree and a crane.

Finally, breathless from exertion, I allowed myself to look in the mirror. Minuet barked in appreciation and wagged her tail, bless her sweet heart.

I looked so *old*. Would my own mother know me? Though she had been dead for decades, I suddenly yearned for her. When was the last time someone had taken care of me who wasn't paid to do so? When was the last time I could rely on someone? The last time someone else was in charge?

I was so tired. Not physically, not today . . . just tired of living.

Get busy living, or get busy dying. That's what Red said in *The Shawshank Redemption* (my recall was perfect today), and that's what I would do now.

Unfortunately, I had to go to the bathroom first, even though I'd just gone ten minutes ago, which would require another wrestling match with my bathing suit.

Such were the indignities of old age.

Fifteen minutes later, I was down at the dock, dabbing a toe in the water. The sun was strong, and it was muggy out today, the green flies circling and buzzing.

The boys used to jump off the dock here, Sheppard running, his feet pounding the wood, little Clark bobbling behind. Both boys were fascinated at my ability to dive straight into the water at high tide. I'd promised to teach them.

But Sheppard had gone away, and I'd never gotten around to teaching Clark. Everything I'd wanted to be as a mother withered away that year, when each day dragged me further from my beautiful boy.

I would see him soon if I ever managed to kill myself. If he was dead, that was. If not, I'd have to keep waiting. That was, if the afterlife existed. It damn well better.

That was all the impetus I needed, apparently, for the next thing I knew, I was slicing through the water, the salty brine familiar and bracing. The waves were almost nonexistent, the breeze gentle. My shoulder creaked a bit, and my ankles felt stiff, and my knees would punish me later, but I was swimming, turning my head every third stroke for a breath of air. Goggles protected my eyes, but I'd forgotten a swimming cap. Ah, well. My hair would survive.

I'd forgotten how much I'd loved swimming in the ocean. Or the Sound, as the case may have been. It was better than the ocean, even, as there were no riptides, no sharks or squid. I wondered how far I'd have to go before it would be too late to turn back. I was a good swimmer, and the water was warm, so hypothermia would take quite some time. I passed the end of the point, where I'd let dear Miller bury his wife, and kept going. The sails of a few boats dotted the horizon, but otherwise, I was alone.

I swam underwater for a few strokes. Could I do this? Could I just . . . stop? Wasn't breathing something the body fought for at all costs? Would I have to load my pockets with rocks? A school of small fish swam beneath me, silver and flashing in the clear water.

Once, Garrison and I had taken the boys to Southern California, and we'd swum with seals and sea lions, and the fish had been so beautiful, their colors brilliant in the Pacific. Clark had been three and stayed on the shore with the nanny we'd taken along, but we had to nearly drag Sheppard out of the water. He'd been such a natural at everything.

I looked around now, wondering where the rocky cliffs were. Shouldn't I be able to hear the sea lions now? Where was Sheppard? Where was anyone?

This wasn't right! Where was I? There was something swimming at me. It seemed to be a golden sea lion. Very rare, I thought. Or was I imagining it? This didn't look like the Pacific one bit. Or did it?

Suddenly, my head was underwater, and I wasn't sure what to do. I was sinking. Sinking! The water was green, and I could see paws above me. It wasn't a sea lion. It was a dog.

Kick, said a voice in my head, and I did, and then I was above water again, gasping. The dog barked at me and swam closer, and I grabbed onto its collar. There. Over there. A floating object nearby, a green and yellow thing with a rope on it. I couldn't remember the word—boy?— but I knew to swim to it. I grabbed on, and it held me up, bobbing and slippery. The dog came with me and swam around in circles, barking.

Why was I out here? Who was watching me? Who would help me? Whose dog was this?

Had Sheppard drowned? Where *was* Sheppard? Was I supposed to be looking for him? He was lost, wasn't he? Had he jumped in with me? How did I get here? "Sheppard!" I called, but my voice was weak.

"What the hell are you doing?" came a gruff voice, and I looked behind me to see a small boat—a Boston something— approaching.

"Paul," I said, and then I was back in myself. It was summer, and I was old, and this was Emma's grandfather, and we didn't like each other because . . . because of a baby.

The dog barked again. He was mine. Maximilian. Mac. The dear, senile thing had swum out with me.

"Need help?" he asked.

"No," I said, then immediately regretted it. "Actually, yes. I've got a . . ." The word was gone. "A crink."

"A cramp, you mean?"

"Yes. That's what I said."

"Fine." He turned off the engine, the boat bobbing dangerously close to me, and reached a hand over the side, his lined face scowling. "Come on, you idiot. Why the hell you'd go for a swim all by your lonesome is beyond me."

"I have the dog for company, don't I?"

"Yeah, well, where's his boat?"

His hand felt wonderful, warm and solid. "Pull me in," I said.

"You gotta help out, Genevieve. This is gonna be a group effort."

My teeth were starting to chatter. "Just pull, Paul. I'm a bit weak from exertion."

"Well, you shoulda thought of that before you swam a mile, shouldn't you? Hate to break this to you, but you're old."

"Just help me on your damn boat, Paul, and save your lecture for when I'm not about to drown."

"I wish you *were* about to drown. Maybe you wouldn't be talking so much."

He had all his hair, which was nice. It was completely white, like mine, and his beard made him look like the perfect New England fisherman.

"If you don't get me on your boat, I'm pulling you in with me," I said.

Finally, he heaved, and I was able to grab the side of the boat. However, my legs were not cooperating. "Just swing over," Paul said.

"If it were easy, Paul, I'd have done it already," I snapped.

He reached down and grabbed me—my inner thigh, his hand right where it shouldn't be!—and hauled me on so that I fell onto the bottom of the boat in a rush of water and humiliation.

"There," he said. "Welcome aboard."

"You put your hand between my legs!" I gasped.

"And I didn't draw back a bloody stump, so we both win," he said.

"How dare you."

To my surprise, he laughed. He *laughed*. I felt my own mouth twitch a little bit.

"Guess we have to get this monster in, too, don't we?" he said. "Couldn't it have been the little rat dog?"

Together, we wooed Mac close enough to the boat to grab his collar and haul him in. Once aboard, he shook violently, then turned in a circle and lay in the puddle at the bottom of the boat.

"Two lives saved in one day," Paul said.

"Let's avoid self-aggrandizing statements, shall we?" I said.

"Yes, Your Majesty." He took off his ubiquitous flannel shirt, revealing a blue T-shirt, and handed it to me. I used it to wipe my face, removing my goggles, and then put it on and sat on the seat of the Whaler.

"Thank you," I said.

"You're welcome. Can I take you home?"

"Please do."

He started the engine and sat on the seat next to me, smoothly guiding the boat in a circle and heading back to Sheerwater.

"I've always loved the view of the house from here," I said.

"It's a looker, all right. So what were you doing out here?"

"I believe it's called swimming," I said.

"Looked like drowning to me."

"As I said, I had a cramp."

"You said crink, actually." He cut me a look. "Losing it, are you?"

"I have a brain tumor, in case you forgot. Occasionally bungling a word is a symptom."

"Maybe people with brain tumors shouldn't go swimming alone. Just puttin' that out there."

"Point taken." I glanced at him. He was an attractive man, his face weathered and wrinkled. Lovely crow's-feet. I'd always liked that on a man. He looked a bit like that actor, the one with the deep, deep voice and mustache. Sam Elliott, that was it. That being said, Paul's eyebrows were out of control, and tufts of hair stuck out of his ears. One could tell he was unmarried. A wife would've taken care of that. Those little, personal, rather endearing things that were only between a husband and wife.

How I missed Garrison.

"Would you like to stay for lunch?" I asked.

"Who's cooking? That German woman who hates food?"

I huffed out a laugh. "No. She and Donelle are shopping."

"In that case, yes. Is Emma home?"

"No. She's working at Rose Hill today, and Riley is at Miller's house."

"That little one is quite a terror, isn't she? I stopped by the other day. I've been doing a little work for Miller here and there to keep busy."

"Have you?" I felt miffed that I didn't know this. Miller was *my* friend. Then again, I did respect Paul for not sitting idle as so many people our age did.

"She is a terror," I agreed. "Adorable, though."

We were at the dock now, and Paul tied the boat up with a dexterity that bespoke experience. Mac jumped out on his own, apparently energized from his swim and brief nap.

"I gather you have a boat on Lake Michigan?" I asked.

"I did," he said. "Sold it when the wife was sick."

"Ah. I'm sorry."

He got off and extended his work-roughened hand, which I accepted. As I stepped onto the dock, I stumbled, and he instinctively grabbed me, close enough that I could feel his warmth.

It had been years since a man touched me, other than a doctor. Decades, perhaps.

"Thank you," I said, letting go. We walked up to the house. "Go on in," I said, punching in the code at the back door. "I'll rinse off and join you in a few moments. Make yourself at home."

The outdoor shower was lovely; Miller had redone it a few years ago, and it contained a dressing room stocked with bath gel, shampoo and conditioner (Gilchrist & Soames Fresh Citrus collection), loofahs, razors, plush towels and two Genevieve London Spa Edition bathrobes (Beverly's team's design, but lovely Egyptian cotton). I'd forgotten what a pleasure it was to shower with the sun beating down. I washed my salty hair twice, breathing in the lovely scent of the shampoo. When I was clean and fragrant, I wrapped myself in one of the robes and went upstairs to change.

Putting on makeup seemed too much of an effort. My face was flushed from sunshine and exertion, and while my eyebrows had been gradually disappearing these past fifteen years, I just didn't have the desire to sit down at my dressing table and put on my face. Instead, I brushed my hair back into a bun and pulled on a snug camisole to keep my breasts from rambling around like disobedient puppies. Chose stylish, loose-fitting, pale blue pajamas. I was sure Paul wouldn't notice that they were actual pajamas, or care. They were very snazzy. What was the phrase Riley used? On fleek.

Paul was sitting at the kitchen counter, where I never sat, already eating (no manners, honestly), and indicated my plate. What appeared to be a grilled cheese awaited me; no napkin, no side salad, not even carrot sticks.

I took a bite and closed my eyes in pleasure. Paul had a point. Helga did hate food. This simple sandwich was delicious, abundant with melted cheese, a little hint of mustard and a few thin slices of tomato.

"Delicious," I said.

"Emma's favorite thing when she was pregnant." He took another bite. "Still her go-to comfort food."

The reprimand was gentle but there.

"I always thought she'd come back," I said. He glanced at me. Brown eyes. I'd never noticed before. "I wanted her to," I added.

"You never called. You never visited. You didn't even send a Christmas card."

"It was her move."

"No, Gennie. It was yours." His voice was neutral for once, not accusatory. Also, he called me Gennie, and no one had ever done that. "Especially after what you said to her. You owed her an apology. Still do."

"You're right."

"Why *didn't* you do anything?" he asked. He was looking at me intently now.

He was finished with his sandwich, and I was nearly there as well. I took another bite, not eager to have this conversation. I'd have to make grilled cheese sometime. Mac had gotten inside somehow, but not without rolling in the grass first; his pale gold coat was tinted with green. I gave him a bit of crust, since he'd tried to save me, the dear thing.

"You gonna answer?" Paul asked.

"I'm not as good as you," I said quietly. "I'm too proud. And, I'll admit, I was embarrassed. She was eighteen years old, and we'd talked about unwanted pregnancy, and—"

"Did it ever occur to you that the pregnancy *was* wanted?"

I jerked a little. "She had her whole life in front of her. A *wonderful* life, Paul, with every opportunity waiting for her. Education, travel, whatever career she wanted, all the money in the world—"

"She wanted someone to love, Genevieve. And she wanted someone who'd love her back."

Oh, the endless judgment! "I *did* love her."

"Yeah, right. She was the burdensome child of a woman who committed suicide and the son you didn't care about. You were ashamed of her."

"I was not!" I barked, slamming my fist on the counter. It hurt considerably. "Granted, she was the daughter of a troubled woman, and Clark isn't exactly the son one dreams of having, but I loved Emma. I took her in and did my best, Paul Riley, and how dare you accuse me otherwise! The real problem was my best wasn't good enough. I knew that. I'm half-dead inside, and I have been for fifty-five years. I did my best, damn you, and when she went back to *you*, her *real* family, her *perfect* grandfather, I could hardly beg her to come back here, could I?"

My heart was pounding, and I felt slightly ill. I couldn't believe I had said all that out loud, and to this man of all people.

Paul looked at me a long minute. "Feel good to get that off your chest?"

"Oh, for heaven's sake. It's time for you to go. Thank you for pulling me out of the water." I stood up, and so did he.

"I like you better when you're not so fuckin' polite."

Then, shockingly, he kissed me. Briefly, just long enough for me to feel the warmth of his lips and the scrape of his scraggly beard.

"See you around," he said, and then he left, his footsteps loud in the quiet house.

The kiss hadn't been long enough for me to judge its quality.

Still . . .

He'd *kissed* me.

Greenish Mac woofed and wagged.

"Would you like a treat?" I asked, petting his big, damp head.

The other dogs heard the word from their various locales and came running, and so I doled out pieces of bacon that Helga made each morning just for them.

Then I poured myself a glass of dry Riesling, took the bottle with me into the conservatory and sat in the big leather club chair, my feet on the matching ottoman.

I had been kissed. At the age of eighty-five, no less. And, in retrospect, kissed rather well.

CHAPTER 28

Emma

n mid-July, Genevieve hosted her annual neighborhood bash. If ever a property was meant for such a party, it was Sheerwater.

She'd been a little quiet this past week; not sick, but a little inside herself. Uncharacteristically peaceful, too, which made me suspect something was up. But the party cheered her. A tent was set up on the lawn, and caterers had been hired to provide all the food except for dessert, which Genevieve allowed the guests to bring. Riley invited her brothers and Rav, and they chased each other around with the other kids from the neighborhood.

Miller came, too, with Tess. His in-laws were invited as well, and when I introduced myself to them and said I'd known Ashley a little, Mrs. James started to cry and had to go in the house, Mr. James at her heels, giving me a baleful look over his shoulder.

"Well, crap. Sorry about that," I said to Miller.

"It's not you," he said. "Tess, please stop kicking Daddy."

"Tess, do you want to go swimming?" I asked.

"I hate swimming," she said.

"Okay. Well, I'm going swimming. You can watch if you want."

"I love swimming," she said.

"She actually does," Miller said with a slight smile.

"Come with me, princess. Miller, we'll see you at the pool. Why don't you get a drink first and maybe some food? We have to change, right, Tess?"

"Yes, Daddy. You go away now."

His faint smile dropped, but he handed me the backpack with Tess's stuff.

It was awfully nice, her sticky little hand in mine. Brought back all the wonderful memories of Riley as a little one, when we always held hands. It was something I never took for granted. Truth was, we still held hands, and God, I was grateful.

This summer had been so good for her, taken her out of herself a bit and let her remember who she was. She radiated a sense of pride . . . not because she was staying in this house or because she was the great-granddaughter of Genevieve London, but because she was needed, by Gigi and Donelle, her brothers, and Tess and Miller.

Maybe, in all my years of ultracareful parenting and watchfulness, I'd forgotten to let Riley grow up a little bit.

Tess and I changed without too much difficulty, though she was jumping up and down the whole time.

"I see Wiley! I want Wiley!" she kept saying. The straps of her bathing suit fell off her shoulders, so I tied them up with a hair ribbon. When we went downstairs, Miller was out by the pool, talking to Saanvi Talwar.

"Go away, Daddy!" Tess commanded, and his face lost all expression. He kept talking to Saanvi, though, and she gave me a little wave.

Tess was tough, all right. I took her over to the wisteria bower, where no one else was.

"I want swimming!" she said.

"Tess, when you told Daddy to go away, that made him feel bad," I said.

"So what?" Her lower lip pushed out, and she looked away, telling me she knew she'd done wrong.

"What if I told you to go away, Tess? Or if Riley told you to go away? It would make you sad. Wouldn't it?"

"No. Yes." The lip got poutier.

"So why don't we go up to Daddy, and you can say you're sorry, and then we'll go swimming with Riley?"

"I go swimming now."

"No. You go swimming after you say you're sorry."

"I *not* sorry." She stamped her little bare foot.

"You made your daddy feel sad. That's not a nice thing to do. You say you're sorry, or we can go upstairs where there's no swimming."

She scowled at me.

"Would you like to go swimming, Tess? Riley and some other kids are in the pool right now."

"Yes. I go swimming with Wiley."

"Then let's say sorry to Daddy." I scooped her up and carried her over. "Excuse me, Miller. Tess wants to say something."

"Sorry, Daddy. Sorry."

The way his face changed was remarkable. It softened with surprise, and his dark eyes widened a little. "Thank you, Tess."

"I go swimming now."

"Have fun."

"We will. Thanks," I said, smiling. "Great job, Tessie," I whispered as I carried her to the pool's shallow end. "You made Daddy feel happy."

"Tess! Hooray!" Riley said. "Come on in here and play with us!"

Duncan and Owen were swimming around like eels, playing some kind of game with Rav, who was clearly their hero.

I went in and kept an eye on Riley's supervision of Tess. Kids in the water always made me a little nervous, a left-over from the tale of Uncle Sheppard.

I wondered how my father would've been different if his big brother hadn't disappeared. If he would've been better, stronger, more morally grounded.

I glanced over at Genevieve, who was talking to my grandfather (and, shockingly, not appearing to be irritated). Both of them had lost children, and both stories were almost unbearably tragic. Yet here they stood at a party, decades into their grief.

Please, God, I said silently. *Please, Mom. Please, Grammy, and Grandpa Garrison, and Uncle Sheppard if you're up there. Don't let anything ever happen to Riley. Or Tess, or Duncan, Owen and Rav.*

It was ridiculous, I knew. Children didn't disappear or die because the parent hadn't prayed enough. But there were no atheists in foxholes, as the saying went, nor in the hearts of parents.

When the kids got out of the pool, Riley and Tess and I went upstairs to her room to change. Tess's hair was again almost dreadlocked with snarls. "Let's see if we can do something here," I said to my daughter. "Got a brush?"

"I no brush my hair," Tess said firmly.

"Really? I do," I said, doing just that. "It feels nice."

"Your hair looks very shiny, Mom," Riley said, grinning. "Want me to put some conditioner in it?"

"Sure!"

And so we were able to woo Tess into letting us put conditioner in her hair, combing out the snarls and even putting it in braids.

"How's Rav?" I murmured as I French braided. I was an expert, having done Riley's hair most of her life. Now that it was short, I missed this job.

"He's a nice kid," she said. "We might ride our bikes out to Birch Lake and hike a little this week, if it's okay."

"Oh. Um . . . let me think about that."

"Mom. To hike, not to have S-E-X."

"S-E-X," Tess echoed, and Riley covered her mouth with her hand to smother the laugh.

"It's probably okay. I just need to think about it." I paused. "That's where my uncle, uh, went away."

"I know."

"I'll talk about it with Saanvi," I said.

"Okay. Be protective. Come on, Tessie-bear, you look so cute! Look in the mirror. Aren't you cute?"

"I cute," she agreed.

"Let's go show your dad," Riley said. "I'll give you a piggyback. Giddyup! Look, Mom! I'm Tessie's horse!"

"She my horse!" Tess confirmed, hugging Riley's neck tightly.

My heart swelled with love for my girl. Once, I'd been so afraid she'd reject me when she became a teenager (and there was still time). When she was tiny, I was afraid I'd love her less as she grew out of her infancy, toddler years, little-kid years.

It hadn't happened. Every day, I loved her more. Every single day.

"Get that look off your face, you big softy," Riley said.

When we found Miller, his jaw dropped. "Tess! You look so pretty! And clean!"

"I'm going to find the boys," Riley said.

"I come, too," Tess said.

"Okay. You have to hold my hand, though," Riley said.

Off they went, looking damn adorable.

"I can't . . . I don't know how she does it. Riley. She's so good with her," Miller said.

"She loves little kids."

"You do, too," he said. "That thing you did with her straps so they wouldn't fall down, and combing her hair . . . She won't let me near her with a brush."

I patted his arm. "I have the advantage of being a glamorous stranger."

He smiled a little. "How do you learn all that stuff?"

"You just do it. Dr. Spock says you know more than you think you do about taking care of your kid. And it gets easier when they learn to talk about how they're feeling. Tess is bright. It won't be long."

"I hope you're right." He glanced at me. "You hungry?"

We got some food and sat at a table, swatting the occasional mosquito as we ate. It seemed that every time we started to talk about something, someone would do a double take when they saw Miller, and say, "So good to *see* you!" or "How *are* you?" or "You look *wonderful!*"

"Sorry everyone's giving me the Sad Widower treatment," he said after one woman had hugged him a little too long.

"They're glad to see you," I said.

"I don't get out a lot. Grocery shopping is the height of my social life."

"Don't knock it. I worked at a grocery store for years. It was my lifeline to the real world."

He laughed a little, and my heart squeezed.

I really liked this guy.

When the fireworks started, we found the kids, all sitting on a blanket, Tess sitting on Riley's lap, Rav flanked by Duncan and Owen. All of them gazed up at the sky over the Sound as the fireworks lit up the night, and truly, if there was a more perfect moment, I didn't know what it was . . . those five kids, all still young enough to be awed by the fireworks, their faces perfect in the glow.

Afterward, the guests started to leave, all of them stopping to thank Genevieve, who stood there like the queen. I chatted with some of the guests, most of whom mentioned how lovely Riley was, with which I fully concurred.

I waved to the Talwar family as they walked past. Saanvi indicated that I should call her, and I nodded and smiled. Rav waved, too. He seemed like a sweet kid. Miller emerged from the crowd, Tess wriggling like an otter in his arms, whining. His hair ruffled in the breeze.

"You want to have that dinner tomorrow?" Miller asked over Tess's complaints. "Kimmy said she'd babysit. I meant to ask earlier, but things got a little backed up at work."

I was glad he said so, since I'd been wondering when he was going to make good on that invitation.

"I'd love to have dinner," I said.

"No! No dinner!" Tess said. "I hate dinner!"

"You're not coming," Miller said, wincing slightly as she caught him in the side of his head with her elbow. "Just Emma and me." The corner of his mouth pulled up in a smile, and there it was again, that warm squeeze of attraction. It had been a long, long time.

"I better get this one home," he said.

"No! Not home, Daddy! We not leaving!"

He ignored her despite her struggles. He just held on tight and kept looking at me, that faint smile on his lips.

God. There was something about him.

Just then, Jason came bounding up. "Left off the invite list to the biggest party in town yet again," he said with a grin. "Keeping my record pure, at least. How were the boys?"

"From what I saw, they were great," I said.

"Is it okay if I leave them with you and Riley tomorrow?" he said. "I have to do something."

"Um . . . actually, I have plans tomorrow. And they've been here since four."

"Right. Hey, can we talk for a sec?"

He hadn't acknowledged his cousin yet. "Sure," I said. "Miller, it was great seeing you. Bye, Tess! Can I give you a hug?"

"No."

"Okay." I knew better than to ask a child to accept physical contact if she didn't want to. "It was fun playing with you."

She let out a wail that made my bone marrow vibrate. Miller gave us a nod and left, Tess writhing as if she were on fire. "Daddy, you hurt me! You hurting me, Daddy!"

"Jesus, that kid," Jason said.

"She's going through a rough stage," I said, feeling protective of the little demon.

"Yeah, well, at least Riley never did."

"Not that you would've known."

He pulled back, wounded. "That's not fair. I was there as much as I could be, and a hell of a lot more than most guys would've been."

"You're right. Where's that medal I've been meaning to give you?" I pretended to pat down my pockets.

"What's gotten into you?" he asked.

"You're very judgmental about Tess, and Miller's your cousin. You could be nicer."

"You've always had a thing for him, haven't you?"

"No, Jason, I never did. But I can recognize that he's heartbroken and lonely and exhausted, and his family seems to do jack shit for him."

"Okay, fine, whatever. Listen," Jason said. "Jamilah and I are trying to get back together. I wanted to take her out for dinner, you know? Can you please help out? I mean, Riley can watch them here, right? There's a whole staff in this place, plus Genevieve."

My spine stiffened. "Genevieve's *staff* is not a fleet of babysitters, Jason. They're all well past sixty. She's made it clear the boys are welcome to visit, but they're little and pretty wild themselves. If you want to ask Genevieve yourself, go right ahead."

"I don't want to talk to her. She hates me."

"Well, I can't give you permission. It's not mine to give."

"So you're mad, is that it? Because Jamilah and I are getting back together?"

I counted to three, then five, then ten. "I wasn't aware that you were getting back together, for one, and for two, why would I be mad about that?" The honest answer was because, from what I'd observed, Jamilah deserved better, but I didn't voice that opinion.

"Because you've always hoped *we'd* end up together. You said so."

"That dream died when I was about twenty-three, Jason."

My grandmother glided over, wearing white silk pants (at a picnic, really showing off), a yellow blouse and a peach-and-yellow-floral-printed summer cardigan. "Jason," she said in that regal, frosty tone. "I wasn't aware you were here. Let me have someone fetch your boys so you can leave."

Man, she was good.

"Hi, Mrs. London, nice to see you, too."

"Did I say it was nice to see you? I don't recall saying that."

"You didn't," I said.

"Genevieve," Jason began.

"Mrs. London will do nicely," she said.

"Mrs. London, would it be all right if my boys came over tomorrow night and hung out with Riley?"

"Of course," she said. "Your sons are lovely and well mannered. Your wife is to be commended on raising them so well."

"Yeah, well, I did have a *little* something to do with that," he said, smiling. His charm didn't work.

"I'm sure you think so," Genevieve said. Boom! "Emma, dear, come with me, would you? I don't think you had a chance to chat with Amy and Anne. Good night, Jason. The boys will be right over."

Emma, dear. She hadn't called me that since I was eighteen. As we left Jason behind us, I said, "You know, Gigi, you do have your moments."

"Thank you for noticing," she said. "Ah, there they are. Owen, Duncan, your father is waiting for you by the wisteria bower. Riley, darling, would you be so kind as to escort them?"

"Boys, please let me escort you," she said, taking their hands as they giggled and tugged at her. Gigi and I watched them go.

"That girl is absolutely lovely, Emma," she said.

My mouth dropped open. "Thank you," I managed.

"Well. Don't just stand there. Anne and Amy are waiting. You have something on your shirt, by the way. Perhaps someday you'll learn to eat without soiling yourself."

But the words were said without the usual bite. With a faint smile, I followed her across the lawn to meet her friends.

CHAPTER 29

Riley

After Mom and Mrs. Talwar had, like, eleven conversations, Rav and I finally got permission to ride our bikes out to Birch Lake with instructions not to go swimming, since there were no lifeguards there. Which was ridiculous, because it was a perfect spot for swimming. But it was a state park or something, and budget cuts, the usual.

Rav and I both had backpacks on; mine had sunscreen (try being the color of milk in the summer), two bottles of water, two turkey sandwiches I made while Helga glared, and a couple of apples. He had a blanket in his, and some food his mom had packed. We'd had dinner at his house the other night, Gigi, Donelle, Mom and me, and man, it was fantastic. I wished *we* were Indian. The food was incredible.

The weather was perfect again; it had been muggy for days, but a thunderstorm last night cleared everything out, and the air was dry, which was great, because when it was humid, the mosquitoes found me like I was painted in blood.

We rode across town, away from the shore, taking the roads our mothers had mapped out like we were going to Mecca or something. The entrance to Birch Lake was a wide dirt road; the parking area was about ten yards down, so everyone had to walk down a path to get to the actual water.

Rav and I locked our bikes together.

He was nice. And cute. And almost as tall as I was. His eyes were so brown they were almost black, and his eyelashes were insanely long. But he was fifteen (and ten months) and I was sixteen (and seven months). I was going to be a senior; he was going to be a sophomore. When we'd been with other people, the age difference didn't seem to matter. Right now, it did.

"It's pretty out here, isn't it?" I asked.

"Sure," he said.

"Do you come here a lot?"

"Not really," he said with a shrug. "My parents aren't outdoorsy."

"Do you like being an only child?" I asked.

"Yeah! I mean, I don't know what it's like not to be, so I better like it, right? Do you?"

"I'm not an only child. But I guess I sort of am."

"Is it weird, having brothers who live so far away?"

"Yeah. But it's nice. They worship me." I gave him a sideways glance.

"Of course they do." He smiled.

Crap. I *liked*-liked him. My first crush ever, and on a younger man.

"So show me where this kid disappeared," he said.

That, of course, was why we were here. To track Great-Uncle Sheppard's last known location.

"The articles all talk about Otter Point, which is this way," I said, and we walked down the path, side by side, our shoulders bumping occasionally. We could hear other people laughing and yelling—the ubiquitous *Mommy, watch me!*

"Do you get along with your parents?" I asked. "I mean, it seems like you do."

"They're the best," he said. "Seems like you do, too."

I nodded. "My mom is amazing. She was a teenager when she had me, you know."

"Seriously?"

"Yeah. Single mom, worked her butt off, put herself through school but she was always around. Came to all those dopey parent things at school. Science Night. Math Night. Girl Scout stuff."

"She seems fun," Rav said, and it was so *nice*, having a conversation about how great our parents were! Mikayla, Jenna and Annabeth back home loved to dis their parents. You'd think they were chained in the basement or something.

"How about your dad?" Rav asked.

"Yeah . . . he's a good guy, too," I said. I picked up a tiny pine cone, examined it and put it in my pocket, a souvenir for when I was back in Downers Grove. "He's kind of . . . I don't know. Childish. Childlike? Not in a bad way, really, but my mom seems so much older and wiser."

"Do you like your stepmother?"

"Oh, she's all kinds of fabulous," I said. "And she's incredibly nice to me."

"Why wouldn't she be? You're pretty great, too."

I felt my cheeks getting hot. No hiding a blush when you're a redhead. "Thanks. Oh! Here we are."

A faded wooden sign said *Otter Point*, and underneath that was a newer sign: *Swim at Your Own Risk. No Lifeguard on Duty.*

Given the purpose behind our trip, the words were creepy.

This side of the lake was farther than the other swimming spots and little beaches. No one was this deep in the park just yet, having taken the beach spots closer to the parking area. Plus, it was only around ten in the morning, still early on a summer day. It was definitely pretty here, with big pine trees and huge gray rocks. A blue jay called, and a crow clicked and clucked nearby.

I told Rav what I'd been able to find out. I knew my grandfather and his brother had been playing while Garrison London packed up the car. He called the boys, and only Clark came.

"So Sheppard probably drowned?" Rav asked.

"They dragged the lake four times and never found anything," I said. "But the bottom of the lake is really mucky, so . . ."

"Wouldn't he float?"

I'd done a lot of reading on that. "Yeah. In almost all cases, bodies come up. That's why Gigi thinks he was taken."

"Man. That's grim."

We looked out at the lake, which seemed ominous now. I was glad our moms had forbidden us to swim, because I had an excuse not to.

Sheppard might have drowned here. Almost all bodies came up . . . but not all.

Or he'd been kidnapped and raised by someone else, like in that movie I'd found when I Googled "forced adoption."

Or he was just taken and maybe raped and murdered. It happened way, way too much.

This view might've been the last thing he saw. Poor Sheppard. I hoped he hadn't been scared.

"Was there anyone else out here that day?" Rav asked.

"Not according to what I read. I guess my grandfather thought there might be someone in the woods, but he was only five."

"What did he say?"

"I barely know him. I think I've met him, like, twice in my whole life." Rav had told me all four of his grandparents were coming from India to stay with them for two months. To say I was jealous wouldn't have been a lie. The Finlay grandparents had ignored me all my life (and all summer).

That was fine, because if I saw them, I might've flipped them off.

But I had Pop, and now Gigi and Donelle. I was hardly a pathetic orphan.

"Let's climb up there," Rav said, pointing to the giant rock at the edge of the little beach. "See what we can see." He went first, offering me his hand, and when I clambered up, he didn't let go right away.

I could feel my heart thumping. Man, all those clichés were embarrassingly true.

The view was gorgeous. Across the lake, we could see the bright little specks of color, people having fun with their families. I wondered if they knew about Sheppard.

"Want to look around in the woods?" I asked. "Not that we're gonna find anything after all these years."

"That's why we're here, right?"

We climbed down and went along the narrow little path into the woods, side by side. I wished he'd hold my hand again, but maybe he'd just been helping me up. It had felt so nice, though.

"This is a deer trail," Rav said.

"Cool."

"I wish you were staying here," he said, looking at the ground. "I never met a girl I liked so much." He looked up. "Sorry if that was weird."

"No," I said. "That was . . . that was nice."

Then, before I could think too much about it, I leaned forward and kissed him, just a quick kiss on the lips, just enough to feel that his were soft and warm.

Then we looked at each other. "You have the bluest eyes I've ever seen," he said, his voice cracking a little.

"And you have the darkest." I smiled, then he did, too, and we kept going, wandering in the woods, pushing back branches, climbing over rocks.

My first kiss. His too, I'd bet.

It was nice. It was more than nice. It was exactly right.

We didn't find anything relating to Sheppard, of course. We checked in what might've been fox dens, and under fallen trees, but there were no skeletons, no fifty-five-year-old scraps of clothing, no lonely little shoe. And I was glad. I wanted Gigi's scenario to be true—somewhere, far away, her son was a grown man with a happy family.

At some point, Rav and I held hands again, and he killed a mosquito on my arm. Chivalry. We surprised a deer and stood in awe for a second, so close we could see its eyelashes and the veins in its ears before it bounded into the woods.

I got two texts from my mom, asking how it was going and reminding me to reapply sunscreen. Rav got three from his, mostly the same, but with a reminder that he was a gentleman and there would be hell to pay if he put a toe out of line, and she had her ways of knowing. We laughed a lot over that one.

We didn't kiss again. We didn't have to. Instead, we ate our food, talked about school, movies, normal stuff. I told him about being iced out by my friends, and he said, "They sound like bitches," and for the first time, the thought of seeing the girls again didn't make me feel anything other than bored.

When we got back to Sheerwater, he walked me to the door. "You want to do something this week?" he asked.

"Sure. Anything."

He smiled, and my heart felt weird and hot and stretchy.

"Thanks for coming with me," I said.

"Thanks for letting me. Bye!"

And that was that, no big deal, except I felt incredibly happy. Just pure, clear happiness, because a nice boy liked me back.

CHAPTER 30

Emma

Riley helped me pick out clothes for my date with Miller; she'd become quite the little fashionista since living here. "Color, texture and pattern," she said, sounding way too much like my grandmother.

"And here I thought jeans and a T-shirt was fine."

"It is fine. You just don't have the right jeans and T-shirt. Too bad you're too busty for Genevieve's clothes." She rustled in my closet, sighing from time to time.

"It's just dinner, honey. Not the Oscars."

"It's a date, isn't it?"

I felt my face getting warm. "Um . . . maybe? Kind of?"

"I'll take that as a yes." She popped out of the closet with some clothes in her hand.

"What time are your brothers coming over?" I asked.

"Seven. Listen, Mom. I wanted to wait till we were alone, but . . ."

"What's wrong?"

"Nothing!" She sat on my bed. "I kissed Rav today."

Be cool, be cool, I told myself. "How was it?" *Don't cry, she's sixteen, it's fine, it's normal.*

She smiled. "It was nice. No tongue, don't worry."

"Honey—"

"Please, please, please don't tell me about you and Dad. I know where I came from, okay?"

I swallowed. "Okay. So . . . tell me about it." Was that the right response? What would I tell a client? Was I screwing this up?

"It was very . . . quick. But it was a legit kiss just the same. He said he liked me a lot, and I just leaned in and kissed him. And we held hands for a little while." She blushed and picked at the fringe of her shorts. "That's all."

"It sounds really . . . romantic."

She beamed at me. "It was, Mom. It was legitimately perfect. I mean, I'm not in love. But I'm in crush, I think."

"And he's a nice, kind boy? He seems like it, but . . ."

"He is. Don't worry, Mom. You taught me well."

Had I? Not by example, at any rate. "Thanks. Just . . . take things slow, okay? And talk to me about anything, no matter how personal or embarrassing. I'll always give you my best advice. I love you, and I'd never steer you wrong on purpose."

"See? You say these things, and I'm like, 'I have the best mother in the world.'" She hugged me, and I tried not to cry. Then she pulled back. "Aw! You're crying! You're so cute, Mama. Okay, back to your clothes. Then we'll do your makeup. You older women need to embrace highlighting, you know."

"I'm thirty-five."

"Like I said, highlighting can be your best friend."

A half hour later, wearing jeans and a T-shirt and a little jacket, sandals, borrowed earrings and with my hair sprayed with argan oil and with a solemn promise not to put it in a ponytail, I was deemed fit for a date. Riley led me into the den, where Donelle, Gigi and the five dogs were relaxing (or slowly dying) in a fog of canine gas.

"Ta-da! Doesn't she look great?" Riley said.

"Gorge," Donelle said. "Hope you get a little some-some, sweetie."

"Donelle! Gross! That's my mother we're talking about! Gigi, what do you think?"

"I think Donelle should stop aborting words in order to sound youthful," she said, flicking a glance at me. "You look much better, Emma."

"Thank you, Genevieve." I rolled my eyes.

"You look quite nice," she amended.

"Thank you," I answered without eye rolling.

The doorbell rang its multi-toned chimes. "I'll get it," I said.

"Oh, we're all coming," Donelle said, and so I greeted Miller with my three womenfolk and five dogs. Allegra mounted his leg, and Mac attempted to jump on him.

"Let's run for it before these dogs get rapey," I said. "Bye, girls! Have a fun night!"

"Bye!" they called, and I have to say, it was kind of sweet, all of them watching, Riley holding Minuet, Mac barking at the hydrangea bush, Donelle making gestures that probably meant *get a little some-some*, Carmen squatting to pee, and my grandmother giving us a regal wave.

"How are you?" I asked my date.

"Great," he said, not sounding particularly happy. "I thought we could go to Mystic, okay?"

"Sure."

"I just don't want . . . well, basically, everyone in town will talk if they see us together, and my mother-in-law is already upset because you brought up Ashley at the party."

"I . . . yeah. I felt bad that she . . . felt bad."

"It wasn't you."

He was driving in jerks and sprints. "Hey, there. Relax, okay? We're gonna have a nice dinner. That's all."

"Okay."

Not in the most talkative mood . . . "How's Tess?"

"She was screaming and naked when I left."

"So, normal, then?"

He didn't smile. "Sorry. That was rude. I was trying to lighten things up."

"It's fine."

I was fairly carsick by the time we got there. "Miller," I said as he closed the car door, "if you want to go back home—"

"No. I don't. I'm sorry. I just . . ." He sighed and rubbed the back of his head. "This is the first date I've had since Ashley died. The last first date I had was when I was fifteen."

I nodded. "Should we call it something other than a date, then? Like, dinner between friends?"

"No. Let's call it what it is. A date."

This did not appear to make him happy. "Okay! Super!" *Easy on the jolliness, Emma.*

We went inside the restaurant, which was one of those kitschy "guess what? we're near the ocean!" places with nets and mermaids and shells for décor. A wooden pirate with a hook for a hand and a patch over his eye stood next to the maître d' stand.

"Uh . . . this place was different the last time I came," Miller said.

"It's cute!" I said. "It's fine!" Exclamation points seemed to be my stress go-to.

"G'day, mateys," said the hostess in a toneless voice. She was dressed like a porno version of a sailor—a shirt tied under her breasts and a skirt that barely covered her butt. On her head was a little white hat with red horns. "Can I get ye a table by the water, me pretties?"

"So much wrong with this picture," I murmured.

"If you want to go somewhere else, we can," Miller said.

"Please don't!" the girl said. "Hardly anyone comes here, and I really need this job. Please, please, just look like you're having fun. Don't leave."

Miller looked at me.

"It'll be super fun!" I said.

"Thank you. I mean, thanks, my hearties. Or something. Do you have a reservation?"

"Finlay," Miller said.

"Right. Okay. Welcome aboard, then," she said. "Right this way, mateys."

The poor girl. It was chilly tonight, and she was barely dressed. Plus, she was wearing three-inch heels. "Are you cold, honey?" I asked as we sat down.

"Freezing," she muttered. "Here's our grog list. Avast, me fine beauties."

"Poor girl," I said as she walked away. "I hope you speak pirate, because I'm a little lost."

If there'd been a stage, this place would've passed for a strip bar. The servers were all women, all dressed like the hostess, and all having about as much fun. The lighting was dim and red, the tables adorned with plastic parrots and lanterns. Miller was rubbing his forehead.

"Hey," I said. "It'll be fun. It's different, right?"

"Right." He tried to smile, then looked at the grog list.

"Blimey!" barked someone, and we both jumped. "What can I get ye to slake yer thirst?" It was our server, a pretty girl with a fearsome glare. Clearly, no one worked here of their own free will.

"I'll have a Treasure Chest," I said, picking the first cocktail that appeared.

"Me too," Miller said.

"Don't get yer scurvy selves hornswoggled," she said loudly, then lowered her voice. "I don't know what that means. The drinks are strong, that's all."

The restaurant was largely empty, aside from a family with about six children seated not far from us. The parents were ignoring them as the children chased each other around the tables. There was also an elderly couple by the window, eating in silence, not looking at each other, just shoveling in their food. The portions looked massive.

"How was your day?" Miller asked, and thank God, because I thought he'd never speak.

"It was pretty good," I said. "I had a few clients online this morning, and then I went up to Rose Hill and did an intake session with a family." It had been really emotional. And kind of beautiful. And heartbreaking. But beautiful.

Truth was, my work at Rose Hill was a lot more rewarding than working with clients online. There was really something about being face-to-face, being able to give someone the occasional pat on the shoulder or, in this case, a hug.

"It must help the families, knowing that you're one of them. That Hope is there."

"I only tell them if they ask," I said. "But I think it helps me understand them a little better. I mean, I'm her sister; most people are the parents, so it's different. But it does help."

Our drinks arrived, and good God, they were huge.

"Ye ready for yer rations?" our server asked.

"Uh, not really," Miller said. "Can we have a few minutes?"

"Aye." She rolled her eyes and went away. I caught a glimpse of the hostess, now wrapped in a blanket. I sipped my Treasure Chest, then winced. It was apparently every alcohol known to pirate-kind thrown in a blender.

"I feel like I should tell you something," Miller said. "I . . . shit." He took a few swallows of his drink.

"Easy, big fella," I said. "Our serving wench didn't lie. They're strong."

"Yeah, I need the liquid courage. So. Here goes. Uh . . . I've never been with anyone other than Ashley. Never held hands with, kissed, slept with, loved anyone but her. So I'm not sure how this goes. Also, you're Jason's . . . something, and I don't want that to be a thing. And you know, I'm a widower with a horrible child and I work a lot and have kind of a shitty home life. So I'm not really much of a prize." He took another pull of his drink. I would be driving home, it appeared.

I looked at him a long minute. "How about if we just kiss now?" I suggested. "Get it over with. If it's horrible, we can just eat our fried clams and go home and be friends, no hard feelings."

He pondered this. "Okay," he said.

I laughed a little. This was so weird. Then I got up, slid to his side of the booth and sat down next to him. "You ready?"

He looked utterly wretched. "Yeah."

"You're not really inspiring confidence on my part," I said. "If this is on par with, say, walking the plank"—I started to laugh—"or being keelhauled, you can pass. Matey."

He smiled. "Go for it."

I did.

For a second, he did nothing. But then he caught on.

Oh, kissing. Kissing was so great. Miller's hand went to the back of my head, and he kissed me back, the pressure of his lips just right, and warm and wonderful. He tilted my head a little, making the kiss last longer, and when it was done, he rested his forehead against mine.

"Better than keelhauling," he said, and kissed me again, briefly. "Thank you."

"That's gross," said a voice. One of the unsupervised kids, about six, and damn cute, his blond hair sticking up straight, one tooth missing.

"Go back to your parents," I said.

"Kissing makes babies."

"No, it doesn't. Go."

I looked back at Miller. "Date, or friends?"

He touched my chin with one finger. "Date," he said.

I let out the breath I didn't know I was holding. "Good."

We smiled at each other for a dopey minute. "I'm going back to my side of the table now."

"Okay. Bye."

I was guessing that Riley and Rav had more game than Miller and I did, but who cared?

"Okay, so getting back to your list of failings," I said, "um . . . I'm not really experienced in the dating world, either. And that's been fine. I mean, Jason and I were together in my head longer than we were in reality. After he got married, I had a couple first dates. And two second dates. And maybe a third, but I stopped trying about five years ago because it just didn't seem worth the effort."

"Does it now?"

"It does."

"Even with a fucked-up widower and his horrible child?"

"You sell yourself so well. But yes. I like your horrible child."

Suddenly, there was a crash. The man by the window had fallen out of his chair. "Call 911!" his wife shouted.

The random kids started screaming. "He's dead! He's dead!"

"No!" said the wife. "Oh, God, please!"

"He's dead!"

"Shut them up!" I barked at the parents, dashing over to the fallen man. He was wheezing, grabbing at his throat. "Are you choking?" I asked. He was a big guy. The Heimlich or CPR would be hard. He shook his head.

"Oh, God, save him! Please, Jesus, please! Lord Jesus, save him! Save him, Jesus!"

"He's *dying*!" one of the kids wailed. "Just like Lucky! I miss Lucky!"

"Tanner! Get off the table!" the father yelled.

"I miss Lucky, too!" cried another kid.

I checked the man's pulse, which was fast and weak.

Miller was already on the phone with the dispatcher.

"The pirate restaurant. Moby's? The one with the pirates! Come on! It's right on fucking Main Street!"

"Please, Jesus!" cried the wife. "Don't fail me, Jesus! Calling on you, Lord! Come through for me, Jesus!"

The man was flailing at his pocket, his breathing so tight and hard it was a whistle. I felt his pocket—something hard and tubular—and pulled it out. An EpiPen.

I ripped off the cap and plunged the needle into his thigh. One of Riley's friends had asthma, and I'd done this once before on a field trip, years ago.

"She stabbed him! That lady is killing the man!"

The server was leaning over, too, her boobs nearly falling out. "Is he all right?"

"I don't know."

"Ambulance is on its way," Miller said.

The man's breathing was easier now. Easier still . . . the whistling turning to a wheeze, and then to normal. He lay there, panting, his color going back to normal. He reached down and pulled the EpiPen out.

"Are you okay?" I asked, abruptly feeling my own heart thud.

He nodded.

"He's dead!" one of the kids sobbed.

"No, he's not! He's getting better!"

"*Lucky* is dead, dummy! Dead!"

"Honey, are you okay?" the prayerful wife asked.

"Oh, boy," he said. "Was there shellfish in that dish?"

"Are you allergic? To shellfish?" the waitress asked. "You could've mentioned that!"

"Sorry," he said.

"You're allergic to shellfish and you came here?" Miller asked. "Here? To a seafood restaurant?"

"This happens all the time," his wife said. "Get up, sweetheart." Sure, she was calm *now*! She could've maybe mentioned the EpiPen while she was talking to God!

The fire department trooped in. "Hey, there, sir, how

you doing?" they asked, and I stepped back. Miller and I returned to our table.

"That was exciting," I said.

"You saved his life," Miller said.

"Oh, I just . . . yeah, I kind of did, didn't I?" I smiled. "Hey. I did! Wow!"

My savior buzz didn't last long. Miller looked at his phone. "Shit. Kimmy says she needs me home now." He hit the button. "What's wrong? Is she hurt? Oh, God. Okay. Yeah. I'm on my way." He slid his phone into his pocket and sighed. "Tess poured corn oil on the cat, and it went all over the kitchen floor, and the cat ran upstairs, and Tess chased him, and basically, the house is a wreck and Kimmy can't deal."

"Okay. I'll drive, mister. You chugged that drink."

"Thank you. You don't have to stay, though."

"I love cleaning up corn oil."

He gave me a look and raised an eyebrow. "Well, you just saved a man's life. I guess cleaning up corn oil will be easy compared to that."

Cleaning up corn oil was a lot harder than jamming an EpiPen into someone's leg. A lot less rewarding, too.

"This is quite a mess!" I said cheerfully. "How will you clean it up, Tess?" She was currently diving on the floor and sliding around like a cheerful otter, completely soaked in corn oil. Miller was paying Kimmy, who was more than ready to leave and stink-eyeing Tess. The cat was MIA, the lucky thing.

Apparently, Kimmy had been trying to make brownies, and even without the corn oil, the kitchen was a disaster. The handheld mixer was still on the counter, the beaters dripping chocolate, and eggshells were in the sink. Flour and sugar had spilled on the counter, and every ingredient was out and unwrapped, including a stick of butter that looked like Tess had taken a bite out of it.

But the real mess was, of course, the floor. An entire half gallon of corn oil. According to Kimmy, Tess had poured it on the cat to make him "pretty." There were smears of oil on the walls, on the floor; Kimmy had fallen and bruised her knee and was quite grumpy.

"All right, Tess, let's clean this up," Miller said, rolling up his sleeves. He handed her some paper towels.

"Thank you, Daddy." She smeared them in the oil and put them on her head. Miller sighed.

"Put them in the trash, honey," I said. "Otherwise, we'll slip and fall on the floor, and it will hurt."

"I like hurt," she said happily, rubbing the paper towels on her face.

"In the trash, Tess," Miller said.

She complied.

It was good that he was trying to make her take responsibility for the mess, but this wasn't a job a three-year-old could do. After a few token paper towels, I said, "Great job, Tess. Why don't I finish, and Daddy can give you a bath?"

"Are you sure?" he asked.

"Yeah. No problem," I lied. If I got this cleaned up, and Tess went to bed, maybe Miller and I could . . . I don't know. Sit on the porch and talk. Maybe kiss a little more, because that kiss had been really, really nice.

Thus motivated, I got to work. It immediately became apparent that there weren't enough paper towels in the world to do the trick. I tried sprinkling the floor with salt, but there was only about a quarter cup left. Ditto the baking soda. Too bad it wasn't corn oil they were short on.

Half an hour later, I'd gone through an entire roll of paper towels and yesterday's newspaper and still hadn't made a lot of progress.

"Hi." Tess, dressed in clean pajamas, stood in the doorway, looking deceptively like an angel.

"Hello."

"I help you."

"No, honey, you stay there. I'm almost done, and you're nice and clean." My jeans were soaked from knee to ankle with corn oil.

"I have to find Luigi," Miller said. "He's probably miserable."

"He shiny now," Tess said, sitting down on the living room floor to watch me.

"Tess," Miller said, "we talked about putting things on Luigi. He doesn't like it. It's not nice."

"He like it."

"No, Tess! He doesn't. You have to be gentle with him. He's old." Miller looked at me. "I'm so sorry about this."

"It's really okay," I said. "The toddler years can be really frustrating." *No shit, Sherlock*, said my inner critic. But hey. Validating feelings was one of the things we therapists did best.

Miller gave a little nod. "Tess," he said, "you stay here. Right here. Don't go anywhere else, okay?"

"You can make sure I'm doing a good job, Tess," I said, so she'd have a reason to stay put.

Miller went to find his cat.

"It's fun to make messes, isn't it?" I asked Tess.

"Yes. It fun."

"They can be hard to clean up, though. Maybe next time, you can make a mess in the bathtub or the sink. Or outside."

"No. I make messes here."

I opted not to argue and got back to wiping. The corn oil smeared rather than absorbed. Once I got it all up, I'd have to wash the floor. Maybe I should use kitty litter or something. I could Google how to clean up corn oil, but I didn't want to touch my phone. I glanced at Tess, who was scootching in a circle but still technically obeying her dad.

This kitchen was adorable—true to the arts and crafts nature of the house, with plain white-painted cabinets and soapstone counters. Miller had nice taste. Or Miller and

Ashley did, as the case probably was. There was a picture of them on the fridge, arms around each other, back when Miller's hair was completely black.

I'd forgotten how pretty Ashley was. Tess looked so much like her. They looked so . . . content. So certain of their love. My throat tightened. *I liked you, Ashley. Thanks for being nice to me.*

Then I gathered up another wad of newspaper, turned to throw it out, knelt down and got back to work.

Tess wasn't sitting in the doorway. Shit! Before I could finish the thought, I heard a mechanical whine, and my head was jerked back as my hair was pulled mercilessly tight. "Ow!" I yelled, jerking away. I slipped on the greasy floor, sprawling, hitting my chin. The noise stopped. What the hell? I reached back and felt metal.

"I make you hair pretty," Tess said.

Oh, no. No. No.

The kid had put the beaters in my hair. It was tangled so tightly I had tears in my eyes, and the mixer, which I'd unplugged when I fell, hung heavily. I tried to move it, but my hair was wound right to my scalp.

"You look funny," Tess said, and she began to laugh. Then she slid and fell to her tummy and started licking the floor.

Fuck. "Miller?" I called. "Um . . . we have a problem here!"

He came running.

"Slow down," I said. "The floor's slippery."

"Holy shit."

"Holy shit!" Tess echoed.

"Tess, what did you do? Is that the mixer? Oh, God, Emma, I'm so sorry." He came into the kitchen, sliding on the floor, and helped me up as Tess swam around the floor, flipping onto her back. So much for her bath.

"Here. Let me at least pop out the beaters." I heard a click, and some of the weight was relieved.

"Maybe I can get them out," I said, taking baby steps toward the bathroom. I slipped and grabbed the counter, my foot grazing Tess's leg as she scooted under the chairs.

"No kicking!" she shouted. "No kicking me!"

Yeah, she was a handful, all right.

The bathroom mirror showed me smeared in corn oil, red-faced from the pain of my neck hairs being pulled, and two metal beaters jammed against the base of my skull. My hair was wrapped around every part of the beater that I could see. I touched one, then yelped a little. God, that hurt! The entire back of my head throbbed with pain. This was what happened when you didn't wear a ponytail.

I was going to have to cut them out. Or go to a salon, but it was eight thirty at night already.

"Tess, no!" Miller shouted from the kitchen, and then came a high-pitched scream. "Shit! Oh, honey!"

I went out, my feet still greased with corn oil. Miller held Tess in his arms, and she was screaming in fury—and bleeding from the chin all over Miller's shirt.

"She climbed on the table and jumped and hit her chin on the counter," he said, panic in his voice.

"Let me see," I said, slipping over to them, grabbing onto Miller's shoulder when I started to fall. I could barely hear myself over Tess's screams. She had about a half inch cut on her chin. "It'll need stitches," I said.

And so it was that, with two metal beaters stuck in my hair, requiring me to hunch over the steering wheel to avoid contact with the headrest, wincing every time we went over a bump, I drove Miller and Tess to the Urgent Care Center in Mystic, which, ironically, was just down the street from the pirate restaurant.

Tess screamed the entire fourteen-minute drive, kicking my seat and whipping her corn-oiled hair around as Miller sat in the back with her, trying to press a dishcloth against her chin as she thrashed in her car seat.

I stopped the car. "Meet you inside," I said as Miller

unbuckled his daughter. My ears were ringing; I couldn't imagine how he could still hear with her face against his shoulder. They looked like something out of disaster footage, both of them filthy and bloody.

And then there was me. I pulled the car into a space, got out, and yelped as I caught the damn beater on the car. Cursed, because it hurt like the devil—the whole back of my head was on fire—and went inside.

There were a couple of firefighters in their turnout gear milling around. One did a double take when he looked at me. "Jesus, lady, what happened?" he said. "Oh, hey! You're the woman who gave that guy the EpiPen! Uh . . . date went south from there?" The firemen, accustomed to people's pain, laughed.

"It's like *Fifty Shades of Grey*, kitchen edition," his colleague said, and they guffawed and high-fived.

I would've been irritated, but they were firefighters and saved lives and had twinkly eyes and all that. "Happy to entertain, boys," I said. "And I do mean boys. You see a screaming toddler?"

"They just went in."

"And the guy from the restaurant? How's he?"

"We're not allowed to tell you." He gave me the thumbs-up just the same. So much for HIPAA.

I checked in with the receptionist and was directed through the doors to exam room four. The second the doors opened, I could hear Tess. "You hurt me, Daddy! You hurt me!"

"Honey, you jumped off the table. I didn't hurt you."

"Yes! You did!"

I went in. "Hi, guys."

The doctor was in, and she, too, did a double take when she saw me.

"Are those beaters?"

"Yeah."

"Fun night for you two." She looked at Tess's chin. "Yep, she's gonna need stitches."

"Good luck," Miller said.

The doctor chuckled. "We'd like to give her a little sedation, rather than hold her down. Is that okay with you?"

"Jesus, yes."

"Great. It'll just dope her up a little so she won't fight us. Because we would lose, wouldn't we, honey? You're fierce! Dad, you can stay but only if you're not a fainter."

"Be quiet!" Tess yelled, then resumed sobbing.

Miller kept trying to hold Tess's hand, but each time, she yanked it away and tried to touch her chin. "Honey, don't touch it," he said. "It'll hurt more."

"I hate you," Tess said. "I hate you!"

"That's okay," he said. "I still love you."

My heart broke a little.

The nurse anesthetist got the stuff for an IV and prepped Tess's arm, then injected the drug. Within seconds, Tess relaxed, her eyes glazed. The silence was beautiful.

"Hey." A nurse poked her head in the doorway. "You want help with those beaters?"

"Miller?" I said. "You want me to stay for the stitching?"

"No, no. It's fine." He was petting Tess's tangled, oily hair, and another piece of my heart broke off.

"Thanks," I said to the nurse. "Long story."

"You want me to take a picture of you?"

"No, I do not," I said. "Actually, sure, just one for my daughter."

She took the picture, and I texted Riley. And how is YOUR night going?

OMG! came the immediate response. Is this Tess's work?

It is. They have to cut the beaters out. Also, she cut her chin and we're at urgent care.

Is she okay???

Yep. Needs stitches, though.

Mom, just shave your head. You'll be totally on fleek.

Twenty minutes and half my hair later, the beaters were out. Sophia, the nurse, handed me a mirror, and I flinched.

I had a few thick strands on the right side of my head, almost nothing on the lower half of the back of my skull, erratic lengths on the top, and all of the left side.

"Looks like I stuck my head in a lawn mower," I murmured. "My daughter says I should buzz cut it."

"Think Natalie Portman," Sophia said. "Erykah Badu. Charlize Theron."

"Okay. I'll be totally badass. Maybe I'll get a tattoo while I'm at it."

Sophia smiled. "Can't help you there, but we've got clippers."

I didn't look like Charlize or Erykah when she was done. I looked like a baby bird, featherless and freaky. I texted a picture to Riley, who responded with OMG, you're so beautiful, Mama! and I felt better. If I didn't have hair, I did have the world's kindest child.

When I went into Tess's exam room, she was sitting on Miller's lap, a bandage on her chin, another on the inside of her elbow. She looked groggy.

Miller did a double take. "Uh . . . wow. It looks . . . you're stunning."

"Thank you. That's the only appropriate comment in these circumstances, so really, thank you. How's our little pal here?"

"Who are you?" she said.

"I'm Emma."

"Your hair all gone."

"I know. And you have stitches in your chin."

"I very brave."

"I bet you were." I looked at Miller, who was staring at my head. "I'm totally on fleek, okay? Which means supercool to you old folks. When can we get this girl home?"

"Right now," said the doctor, coming in with a prescription and a sheaf of papers. "She should sleep well tonight. Tylenol for any soreness tomorrow, but don't be surprised if she doesn't complain. Kids are tough." She glanced at me. "Love your hair. Even better than the beaters."

"You think? I wasn't sure."

She grinned. "Have a good night, you two. Take care of your little girl. Bye, Tess! You did great!"

Our little girl. Neither one of us corrected the doctor, who'd obviously assumed I was Tess's mother. Miller was quiet on the drive home. Tess was sleepy in her car seat, and when we got back to his house, he carried her in and brought her upstairs, then returned with a pair of sweatpants and a T-shirt and handed them to me.

"Thanks," I said.

He nodded, went back upstairs, and after a second, I heard the bath running and his deep voice.

Best make myself useful. I Googled "how to clean up corn oil," found that my instinct to use kitty litter had been spot-on, and went down to the cellar to see if I could find some.

"Emma?" Miller called. "Tess is in bed, but I found Luigi and have to wash him. If you want to go, feel free."

"I'm good," I said. "I'll hang out till you're done."

By the time Miller came back down, I'd swept up the kitty litter and mopped the floor once and was starting a second time.

"Emma, please, stop. Don't."

"It's fine. I like to clean."

"It's not fine!" he almost yelled. "Why are you being so . . . *great* about this? My kid is a sociopath, I'm a horrible father, I picked a pirate restaurant for our first date where someone almost died, you started off the night with beautiful hair and now you're bald, we're both covered in blood and corn oil, and Kimmy just texted me to say she forgot to mention that Tess put her own feces in the DVD player. My life is literally shit and blood these days."

He took a shaking breath and looked at the floor.

"Well," I said, "who really watches DVDs anymore?"

"Emma," he began, and I hugged him.

My head felt strange against his shoulder. After a second, he hugged me back, his hand going to my head.

"Does this hurt?" he asked, stroking the stubble. God. I had stubble on my head.

"Nope." The truth was, the back of my scalp was still sore, but I wasn't going to add to this guy's burdens.

"It feels kind of nice."

It did. "You're not a terrible father."

"My only child hates me."

"No, she doesn't. Stop the pity party or I'm not gonna make out with you on the couch."

He pulled back and looked at me. "Oh. Well, then. I'm a great dad. A saint, really."

I smiled, took his hand and led him to the living room. There was only the light from the kitchen shining in, hiding the old scuffs and new oil stains on the wall. It was a beautiful room, a fireplace on one end, built-in shelves and funky windows gracing the space. I sat on the rather battered leather couch, pulling him with me, and waited for him to make a move, suddenly feeling unsure of what to do next.

He looked at me, studying my face. Took my hand.

"I like you, Emma. A lot. There's something about you that . . . I don't know. Lights up a room."

My careful heart swelled. It had been a long, long time since a man had said something so lovely to me. My throat was suddenly tight. I had always been so focused on Riley, on getting through work, school, being a good mom, not screwing up. I never thought of myself as lighting up anything.

I thought I saw his cheeks flush, and he looked at our joined hands. "I'm sorry. Was that a dumb thing to say? I haven't had to figure out how to talk to a woman since sophomore year of high school."

I cleared my throat. "It was a great thing to say. Maybe the nicest thing ever."

He nodded slightly. "Good. Good." He looked at me again. "Guess I should kiss you now."

"Guess you should."

He leaned in, and the kiss was gentle and warm and solid. Just like the man.

An hour later, I walked home, turning down his offer to pay for a cab. I was horny, happy and kind of glowing, really (maybe that was the corn oil). I hadn't felt like this in a long, long time. Jason had always been tainted with the knowledge that he was content to let me do all the hard work of raising our child. The other guys I'd gone out with barely warranted a mention.

But Miller . . . Miller was different.

There was nothing more appealing than a man who loved his child. Especially when that child was as challenging as Tess. The image of him carrying her inside, Tess too exhausted to protest . . . well.

Seemed like I might be a little bit in love.

CHAPTER 31

Genevieve

The day Emma told me she was pregnant had been, until that conversation, a rather wonderful day.

She had graduated from high school two weeks before with a 3.75 GPA and the award for excellence in French. Her peers had voted her "nicest girl," which was irritating; I'd have preferred "most likely to succeed." However, she'd done well, gotten into Smith (I was pleased at the choice of an all-women's college) and would be close enough to come to Sheerwater whenever she wanted.

During her junior and senior years of high school, I had pictured her future often—Emma, more mature, more independent, not linked to that vapid boy, surrounded by intelligent, dynamic young people who would inspire her. How she and I would get along better because, with a little distance, we wouldn't grate on each other as much. Perhaps she'd come to admire me a bit more . . . Perhaps her friends would help her with that. "Genevieve London is your grandmother?" I'd imagine them saying the first week of school. "She's amazing! I read that profile on her in *Vogue*!"

In my fantasy, Emma would get into the best sorority and be as happy in college as I was. She had mentioned spending her junior year in Paris, and I heartily approved. After college, perhaps an MBA or other advanced degree. She would have a job waiting for her as my protégé or, if design and management didn't suit her, in marketing. She was clever, unlike her father.

I was proud of her. Yes, she could've done better in high school. Yes, her attachment to that boy made me want to grind my teeth. But she was leaving for college (and apparently he was, too, though I tended to tune out his mother every time she cornered me at a function). More than anything, I was relieved. Ten years prior, I had been flabbergasted the day Clark dropped her off and told me he "just can't do this anymore." I had been fifty-seven years old, expected to raise a shell-shocked, grieving child I barely knew, putting everything else to the side.

Which I had. I had done it, and she was finally going out into the world to find her potential.

I even remember what I'd been wearing that July day— I'd spoken at a Women in Business luncheon in the city and had worn a sleeveless black jersey dress with a lightweight leather motorcycle jacket and a modern garnet and diamond pendant from David Yurman. Tiffany diamond studs. Black and leopard-print kitten heels from Christian Louboutin. A red clutch of my own design.

I'd even mentioned Emma in my keynote, saying how we must be role models for the younger generation, that my own granddaughter was well on her way to becoming a force to be reckoned with and would be attending Smith College in September. At the end of the speech, the women had given me a standing ovation.

In a word, I was feeling fantastic.

Charles had driven me home, and I was looking forward to a drink and dinner and telling Emma about the speech.

Instead, I found her cowering in the front parlor with Jason. "Gigi," Emma said the second I walked in, "we need to talk to you."

Those six words told me everything. Just like that, the future I'd carefully built for my granddaughter turned to ash. I put down my bag, slipped off my coat and handed it to Donelle, who was acting like a housekeeper for once, and closed the parlor door.

Took my time sitting down in a wing chair. I crossed my legs and, though I could feel my blood pressure rising, kept my voice calm. "Do go on."

Jason went first, ineloquent and fumbling. "Mrs. London, we totally didn't mean for this to happen, but it looks like, uh . . . well, we, uh . . ."

"I'm pregnant," Emma said, and her voice was firm and steady.

I let that sit for a few beats. Turned to Jason and said, "Get out of this house. You are no longer welcome here."

He looked at Emma; she didn't argue.

I'm sure you can imagine the conversation that followed. There was nothing unique about it—a foolish young girl who thought she could raise a child; the older, wiser person crushed with disappointment and betrayal. I pointed out all the opportunities she would throw away. I listed the only two options I saw before her: termination or adoption.

I may have raised my voice to her. I did, I acknowledge that now. I didn't cry. I didn't slap her, though I wanted to.

She was so . . . smug! So steadfast, as if having a baby was special and miraculous (which was true, under the right circumstances) and not idiotic and reprehensible, as it was in this case. She was utterly unflappable, and I hated her for that, because I'd given a decade of my life to her, sheltering her, shaping her, creating a path for her, that dirty little motherless girl who'd stood so forlornly in my foyer ten years before. She had been a wreck, confused and filled with mixed messages from both parents, and I'd undone all that! I'd been clear and firm and strong for ten entire years, once again rising to a situation I never wanted.

She simply sat there, a self-satisfied teenaged Madonna, so complacent and even *happy* because she'd been stupid enough to let an egg get in contact with a sperm. As if she were the first female ever to get pregnant.

I spoke a great deal. I gave her an ultimatum—if she planned to have and keep the baby, I would no longer support her.

"That's fine, Gigi," she said. "I'm not asking you to." She had the audacity to put her hand on her stomach. "I want this baby."

"Fine!" I said. "Have your baby and join the ranks of uneducated teen mothers and see how good you've had it your entire life, which, by the way, has been entirely funded by me."

"I don't want your money."

"You're even more stupid than I thought, in that case." And then I said what I wished I could take back from that moment on, one of the few things I've ever said that gave me shame. "You have no skills for this. No preparation. You will fail, and I wouldn't be at all surprised if you ended up like your mother."

She left the room then, quietly. I didn't see her leave the house later. Indeed, I didn't see her for seventeen more years.

If she had ever called, I would have apologized. Well, perhaps not. But I would have set things right. But with each week, then month, then year that passed, the words were increasingly walled in, festering.

That was my punishment for Clark, I suppose, though being Clark's mother was punishment in itself. I had lost

CHAPTER 32

Emma

The first week of August was thick with humidity and mosquitoes. Though Sheerwater had central air-conditioning, the house felt close and still. Every day, we were promised evening thunderstorms, and every day, the sky stayed white and flat. The flowers drooped by mid-afternoon, and the pool was too warm to be refreshing. Jellyfish had found their way into Long Island Sound, so there was little respite from the heat.

I was kind of loving having a shaved head. It certainly made prep time easier. Genevieve kept giving me the side-eye, murmuring about odd style choices and women who could pull certain looks off, and women who couldn't. She didn't seem too interested in just how I'd come to have a shaved head, but that was my grandmother for you. It was always about how things appeared.

I'd been doing more and more counseling with Rose Hill families. It was the best work I'd done as a therapist yet, and I'd been Googling similar facilities back in Chicagoland.

Four more of my online clients were winding down, scheduling their next appointments for weeks out, rather than days. Three of them seemed to be doing well, and I suspected that Jim, the guy with the fascination for tall women, had found himself a girlfriend. He'd met her for coffee three weeks ago, and while he'd said it was hard to be with a woman who was only five ten, he was generously giving her a chance.

Dirk and Amy, the angry couple who'd been trying to find a way back from Dirk's cheating, decided to get a divorce, and honestly, I thought that was best. Dirk had never seemed truly regretful about his affair, and Amy didn't seem like the forgiving type. She'd already put up a dating profile, then had complained about the "losers" who wanted to go out with her. "I want someone way better than Dirk ever was. A surgeon, maybe. Someone really rich," she'd admitted in a one-on-one session, and all my advice about healing and investing in herself fell on deaf ears.

Riley was not quite dating Rav. She went to his house for dinner once or twice a week, and he spent a lot of time at Sheerwater, dutifully playing board games with the three of us older ladies and my daughter. Even Helga joined in once in a while.

Speaking of romance, I seemed to be dating Miller. Every other night or so, I'd walk over to his house under cover of darkness, breathing in the smell of verbena and petunias from the well-tended gardens of Stoningham, and sit on his porch, maybe have a glass of wine or iced tea. We hadn't managed another proper date (which, given how the first one went, was just fine), but the porch nights were lovely. Sometimes, we held hands, sometimes we kissed, but mostly, we just sat and listened to the crickets and cicadas, the soft laughter from the family next door, and talked about our girls and life.

He mentioned Ashley often, his voice still a little wistful for their old life. I didn't mind. Why would I? It was abso-

lutely lovely to hear a man talk about marriage with a sense
of awe that it had been so happy.

"Do I talk about her too much?" he asked one night as
we sat side by side on his porch.

"No," I said. "It's nice to get to know her."

His voice was husky when he answered a minute later.
"Thank you. She liked you, you know. Said you could do
better than Jason."

"Did she?"

He laughed. "Yeah. Sorry. I shouldn't bad-mouth my
cousin. He's just one of those Peter Pan types."

"So I've learned," I said. "What do you think of him and
Jamilah getting back together?"

"She could do better," he said, and laughed again, a low
and smoky sound that made my lady parts hum. "So could've
you, but at least you got Riley."

Dating like this . . . it was pretty fantastic.

On Friday night, Riley and I sat in the conservatory. The
promised thunderstorms were rumbling over Long Island,
and we were waiting to see if they'd come our way. Helga,
Donelle and Gigi had all gone to bed, and we'd opened the
windows to the conservatory so we could hear and smell
the rain.

The thunder boomed, louder now. "One, two, three . . . ,"
we counted in unison. I didn't know if there was any truth
to the seconds between thunder and lightning indicating
how far off the storm was, but . . .

"My mom and I used to do this," I said. "Not here, obviously, but back in Chicago. Sometimes, she'd get me out of
bed so I wouldn't miss the storm, because I could sleep
through anything."

"She sounds like she was so nice. Pancakes for dinner
and stuff."

"She was great."

"You must miss her. I'd miss you, Mommy. So much."

She tucked her head against my shoulder and rubbed my fuzzy buzz cut with her hand.

"I'm not going anywhere," I said.

Riley was quiet for a minute. "Did you ever think about it? Committing suicide?"

"No. Not once. I swear on your life, Riley. I would never do that."

"Me neither. I swear on your life."

"Good."

"Did you ever worry I got the depression gene?"

"Every mother worries, sweetheart."

"Did I scare you this past year? Being all moody and glum?"

I took her hand from my head and held it, still so soft and innocent, in mine. "You did. Depression crossed my mind, of course. But even if you did have clinical depression, the odds are huge that you'd be just fine. We'd deal with it. We'd make sure you had whatever you needed to get through it."

"Were *you* ever depressed?"

"Sure. Everyone gets depressed. I didn't have what my mom did, though. Hers was a sickness, and she didn't get the right medicine. It was more than twenty years ago, and people didn't know as much as they do now."

The thunder boomed right over us, and we both shrieked a little. Then the rain came in a beautiful clamor, so hard it bounced off the glass dome, nearly deafening and lush. We sat cuddled together and breathed in the rich smell of it.

I was so happy. These were the precious moments I pressed against my heart. Thunderstorm at Sheerwater. Riley's first word. Braiding her hair. Her oral report on Teddy Roosevelt, which had made both me and her teacher cry. Cuddling in bed on summer mornings.

I was so lucky.

"Mom!" Riley said suddenly, jolting up in her seat. "Gigi's out there!" She pointed.

And she was right. A flash of lightning showed Genevieve outside at the edge of the yard, down by the stone wall.

I ran to the door of the conservatory. "Genevieve!" I shouted. "Gigi! What are you doing?"

She put her hands over her ears as the thunder crashed again.

"I'll go get her," I said to Riley. "Get some towels, okay?"

I ran across the yard, the rain slapping into me, drenching me, cold on my shaved head. The grass was slick and wet under my feet, and the air smelled sharp and coppery. "Genevieve!" I yelled, and I could see that she was in her pajamas, soaking wet and crying.

"Gigi, are you okay?" I asked.

"Where am I?" she asked. "I'm lost!"

"I've got you, Gigi. It's me, Emma. Come on inside. You're safe."

Her usually sharp blue eyes were wide and scared, darting from side to side in panic. I put my arm around her and guided her in, and when the thunder cracked again, she huddled against me, feeling thin and small.

When we climbed the steps, she looked at me and did a double take. "Do you have cancer?" she asked.

"No. Just very short hair."

Donelle and Riley were waiting with towels and dry clothes, and Donelle hustled Gigi into the bathroom in the hall. We could hear Donelle murmuring, her tone reassuring, as if she were soothing a child.

"Will she be okay?" Riley asked.

"I'll call her doctor in a few minutes," I said. "You know what I bet she'd like? Some tea. Can you make a pot, sweetie?"

"Sure thing, Mom."

When Gigi came out of the bathroom, she was dry and in clean pajamas, a robe and slippers.

"Doing much better now," Donelle said, pulling a face behind Gigi's back.

"Come have a seat, Genevieve," I said.

She obeyed without comment, still looking unsure of herself. I wrapped a cashmere throw around her shoulders, because the temperature had dropped precipitously.

The thunder was more distant now, and the rain steady and full.

"Here we go," Riley said in a cheery voice. She held a full tea tray—teapot, creamer, sugar bowl, even a plate of cookies. My daughter was so thoughtful. "Nothing like a midnight snack. Can I pour you some, Gigi?"

"I take two sugars and no milk," she said. "Thank you, dear."

"Do you know who this is?" I asked gently, putting my hand on Riley's shoulder.

"Of course. She's . . . she's a darling girl."

Riley glanced at me, then back at Gigi. "You got that right." She poured a cup and stirred in the sugar. "Here you go. Nice and hot."

"I'm sorry if you have cancer," she said to me.

"She doesn't," Riley said. "Remember, Gigi? She just got her hair cut really short. Tess put the beaters in her hair and turned on the mixer."

Genevieve nodded, but it was clear she wasn't following.

Donelle gestured for me to come closer. "You need to call her doctor, Emma," she said. "I got his personal cell number. Here." She thrust her phone in my hand. "I'm not allowed to talk to you about it. Sworn to silence and all that."

Dr. Pinco's line was already ringing. "Hello?" he said.

I walked into the breakfast room so Genevieve wouldn't overhear me. "Hi, Dr. Pinco. It's Emma London, Genevieve's granddaughter. I'm so sorry to call this late."

"No, no, it's fine. I gave her this number for a reason. How is she?"

"Well," I said, "she's confused. We found her out on the lawn just now, and she didn't know where she was. She was really scared. I don't think she remembered how to get in the house."

He made a sympathetic hum. "That's par for the course, I'm afraid."

"She doesn't know who my daughter is, even though we've been here all summer."

"That's pretty normal for patients with vascular dementia."

"She—what? Vascular dementia? What are you talking about? I thought she had cancer. A brain tumor."

Dr. Pinco was quiet for a moment. "Do you have medical power of attorney?"

"No."

"Then I'm afraid I can't discuss this with you. She hasn't given me permission."

"That's not very helpful," I said. "I don't think she knows who I am right now."

"I'm sorry." His voice was kind. "It's my best guess that Genevieve will be more lucid in a little while. I suggest you talk to her then, and see if you can get her permission to talk to me about her situation. You're next of kin, aren't you?"

"Yes. Well . . . my father is, technically, but he's not around."

"Call me tomorrow," he said.

I hung up.

Genevieve didn't have cancer. Or a brain tumor.

She had been lying since she first called me.

In the morning, I got up early, went down to the kitchen and told Helga to take the day off.

"You're not my boss," she said.

"Get out of this house, Helga, or I will throw away everything in this kitchen past its expiration date, and you'll have nothing to cook with."

"Expiration dates are for the weak."

"Have a lovely day. Don't come back before six."

When she was gone, I made oatmeal, added some blueberries and cream, made a cappuccino and put it all on a tray, then carried it upstairs to Gigi's room. Riley was still asleep.

My grandmother had calmed down after her tea last night, but I don't think she'd been altogether clear even when she went to bed. When I'd tucked her in, I called Calista, who gave me the rundown on vascular dementia. Based on what I told her, Calista guessed that Genevieve had had a series of small strokes—TIAs, she called them, which stood for transient ischemic attacks. The TIAs cleared up on their own, but they were often linked with dementia.

"Will it kill her?" I asked.

"It's hard to say. It could lead to a bigger event—a real stroke, so she needs to be getting treatment. But we don't have a grip on dementia yet. There are drugs that will slow it down, but it's a tough one. It depends on what kind of dementia—Alzheimer's, Lewy body, frontotemporal—but in a nutshell, dementia means brain function is deteriorating. It can be slow, or it can be really drastic."

"She's sharp as a tack most of the time."

Calista sighed. "Yeah. But almost without fail, we see a decline in cognitive function. And once it digs in, it tends to pick up speed."

It explained quite a few moments this summer, when I'd thought Genevieve was just lost in her thoughts. Donelle covered for her, but looking back, yep.

Always too proud for her own good.

I knocked on her door and pushed it open. I hadn't been in her room all summer—I'd had no reason to come in here—but, as ever, I was struck by the elegance of Genevieve. The walls were pale gray, the comforter pure white, and over the bed hung a gorgeous modern painting—splashes of riotous color. Maybe a Jackson Pollock.

Genevieve was sitting on her couch, looking out at the Sound, a book opened on her lap. A regular Katharine Hepburn she was, the blue of her couch, the smoky gray of her silk robe. Minuet sat snuggled next to her, bright eyes shining.

"Good morning," I said.

"Hello, Emma. Here to gloat?" So she was back. Minuet wagged in greeting, at least.

"I brought you breakfast."

"You didn't have to do that."

"Well, I wanted to." I sat down in the easy chair across from her. "And I want to talk about last night."

"Yes, I'm very sorry. I must've had a nightmare. Please don't make that face. I know how you love to exaggerate, but I simply had a very vivid dream."

"Or the brain tumor flared up?"

"Perhaps." She stroked Minuet's tiny head.

"Or you have dementia."

Genevieve twitched.

"Please be honest with me, Genevieve. I think I deserve that, and lying is beneath you."

She took a sip of coffee. "Very well. Yes. I've had a few small episodes of . . . forgetfulness. I got lost a time or two. After doing some research, I thought it was a brain tumor."

"But it's not, is it?"

"No." She lifted her chin. "You're right. It's dementia. Vascular dementia. Dr. Pinco suspects I've had a few small strokes as well. I believe that's what happened last night."

"Why didn't you tell me the truth?"

"Oh, Emma," she said, setting down her cup and looking right at me. "Don't you know me at all by now? A brain tumor sounds far more noble and tragic than anything as mundane and humiliating as dementia." She raised an eyebrow at me, and I couldn't help a small smile. It was always about how things looked for her. She was nothing if not consistent.

"So what's your prognosis?" I asked.

She didn't answer for a minute. Toyed with her oatmeal. "I don't want to die without my faculties," she finally said.

"I've seen it happen to a couple of friends, and it's a horrible, humiliating way to die." Her gaze dropped back to Minuet. "We euthanize dogs when their discomfort becomes too great. It's a pity we don't do it with people."

I had a sudden, hard tingling in my feet. "You're hardly a dog, Genevieve."

She looked at me. "Nevertheless, it's not my intention to die in a nursing home, drooling and abandoned."

"Nor would you." The tingling was worse. It was a fire alarm of intuition.

"I plan on taking my own life, Emma."

I was standing before I knew I moved. Minuet barked. "What did you say?" I demanded.

"I'm not going to die in inches. I'll take matters into my own hands and just . . . end things when the time is right."

I was shaking uncontrollably. "No, you won't! You can't! Suicide is selfish! Doesn't that sound familiar? How many times did you say that to me, Genevieve?"

"I was wrong," she said. "It's actually quite generous. I was hoping—"

"For ten years, you told me that my mother was selfish and weak."

"I never said that."

"Oh, yes, you did! You did, Genevieve!"

"I tried to get your mother treatment, Emma."

"How good of you! How incredibly kind! But you still treated me like tainted goods because of her. But now you're all in favor? How dare you!"

"I was hoping you'd help me."

"Are you fucking kidding me?" I yelled. "I'm not going to help you kill yourself! It's against the law! I'm not going to jail for you! Are you insane? Is that why you're leaving Riley all your money? Are you trying to . . . to . . . commit murder for hire or something? You think you can bribe me into killing you? And just what did you have in mind, huh?

I just hold you underwater till you drown? Shoot you in the head?"

She said nothing, and I paced back and forth. "You're . . . you have no right to even discuss this with me, Genevieve. Suicide. My God! There's not enough money in the world to make me even think about it. My *mother* committed suicide, and now you're going to do the same thing? What about Riley? She loves you! You think your money will make up for that?"

She remained silent, not looking at me.

The tingling in my feet was abruptly worse.

"About Riley's inheritance," she said quietly. "There's nothing."

I blinked. "You're seriously leaving all this to my father? He'll spend it in six months."

"I mean, there's nothing to leave anyone."

I snorted. "Right. That Jackson Pollock over there is worthless. This house is a hovel. You're a worldwide brand! You own an apartment in the city, you have an entire closet for your jewelry, that diamond alone that would choke your dog—"

"Take a breath, Emma," she said. "You're getting hysterical. And it's a Karel Appel, not a Pollock."

"Are you actually debating art with me right now?"

Yeah, okay, she had a point, I was yelling, and my face was hot. I took a deep, slow breath and let it out. Repeated the action. "Do go on, Genevieve." My jaw ached, I was clenching it so hard.

She sighed. "It would take all day to explain the nuances."

"Try."

"I am. Please refrain from interrupting, and I'll be more successful, I'm quite sure." She gave me her patented rich-woman ice glare and continued. "One would think that with the amount of money I had at one point in my life, I would be rich forever. That's simply not true. For one, there was your father. Once he'd depleted his trust fund, I subsidized his . . . follies."

"When did he blow through his trust fund? That was millions of dollars."

"Yes, it was, but he managed to spend it nonetheless. That was back when your mother was still alive. Then, once he brought you here, I . . ." She pressed her lips together.

"You what, Genevieve?" I ground out.

"I paid him to stay away from you."

It was my turn to flinch.

My father *sold* me. He sold me. I thought he just never wanted me, but it turned out there was money in it for him.

For some reason, that made it worse. My throat was suddenly tight, and—shit. I wanted my mother. *She* hadn't sold me. She left me, but she'd loved me. I knew that.

My father just took cash.

"I bet he didn't argue," I said.

"No," she answered quietly. "He did not. I would apologize, Emma, but I'm not sorry. He was a wretched father, and husband. He failed your mother, and I didn't want him to fail you."

Not that Gigi had been warm and loving, mind you. My eyes were stinging. "Go on."

"When you left, I cut him off, but he'd required a great deal. I sold Genevieve London Designs, and I made a hefty profit. But then Hope was born, and I was afraid of what would happen to her. So I set up a trust for her, which will keep her well cared for all her life. And I resumed bribing your father to keep his distance."

I had always known my father was a loser. I never thought of him as vile until now.

"I still had money, of course," Genevieve said. "I sold the apartment in Manhattan. I had a share of Genevieve London stock, and I sold that as well."

"So why is there nothing?"

She looked out the window. "I invested it with a brilliant

fund manager. I don't remember his name. Buddy? Bennie? The . . . the pony scheme."

"Ponzi."

"Yes. I'm sure you remember the news. I wasn't the only one. Everyone was fooled."

"I'm surprised you were."

"Well, I was. I was ruined. The new CEO of Genevieve London wanted nothing to do with the actual Genevieve London, and I was too old for anyone else to hire me. Or so I was told. 'We want someone with a fresh point of view,' they said. Or 'You should just relax and enjoy life now, Mrs. London.' Condescending idiots."

"But still, Genevieve. I can't believe you put everything in one investment. You have artwork, antiques, jewelry. You must've had savings."

"I had savings, you're right. But I had to make sure Hope would be cared for, so I endowed Rose Hill so that they could provide for adults as well as children."

I drew in a slow breath. That would've required a lot of money. More than I could imagine.

Genevieve looked out the window. "The rest, your father drained in bits and pieces. Bribes from me, I suppose, to keep him away from Hope. As for the artwork, your grandfather and I made arrangements to donate our collection to the Metropolitan ages ago. All the great families do. And honestly, I don't have that much of value. Less than half a million."

I rolled my eyes. Half a million. Such a pittance. Rich people sucked.

"You still have Sheerwater," I said.

Her eyes grew shiny, but she raised her chin. "No," she said, and my stomach sank. "It's reverse-mortgaged, and so are its contents. My jewelry will be sold on my death. I arranged for Charles, Helga and Donelle to stay on until I pass away, and I get an allowance until my death to continue living at my current standards."

I put my hand over my mouth. *Be a good person, Emma*, I told myself. *Be kind.*

I was tired of being kind.

"So . . . you're broke." I paused. "Does my father know?"

"No. He thinks he'll inherit a fortune."

"So you lied to your only living child and bribed me back here by pretending Riley would get something."

"A bribe you accepted."

"Because I want my child to go to college without being terrified of the debt she'll rack up. You're right. I accepted the bribe so she wouldn't have to do what I did, because I didn't want her to have to eat ramen noodles and generic macaroni and cheese the way I did. But there's nothing for her, am I right? You lied, and you've been lying all along."

She didn't say anything. "If the bank had allowed me to put aside something for her, I would have."

"But they didn't, and you chose not to share that little bit of information."

She looked at her hands. "Correct."

"Worse, though, Genevieve . . . for ten years, you made me feel like I was damaged goods because my mother committed suicide. You even predicted I'd kill *myself* because, in your eyes, having a baby at my age would cause me to spiral into despair. Then you ignored me for seventeen years and lied to me to get me to come back here. Why?"

"To . . . to see you again. To meet Riley."

"How wonderful for you. And now you want me to kill you somehow because getting old is hard. Fuck you." I stood up. "Did it ever occur to you that your feelings are not the only feelings that matter? How could you do this to me? Because you want to keep up appearances? Because you're afraid of not being omnipotent anymore? You summoned us out here, made Riley love you and now you're washing your hands of us. Again."

She stood. "Emma, please understand. I don't want to die wondering who I am. Who you are. I can't lose my dignity when it's been the only thing to get me through this wretched life."

"You lost a son. It was tragic, but if you were wretched, that was your choice. My mother killed herself, my father abandoned me, I had a baby at eighteen, and I've had a *beautiful* life, no matter how inconvenient or hard it's been. You wanted me to give up my baby or have an abortion, but look at her now. Look at the two of us and how much we love each other. And now *you* mean so much to her! How can you decide you'll end it with her in your life! 'Hey, kid, nice knowing you, but I'm a little forgetful, so screw you.'"

"I don't *want* her to know me when I'm sitting in diapers, wondering where my mother is! Let her remember me as I was this summer, when I took her shopping."

"Shopping? Are you kidding me? She doesn't love you because you took her *shopping*, Gigi." I was so mad I could hardly look at her. "I'm going out. Riley's going to Jason's today. Do not speak to her about any of this."

I managed not to slam the door.

CHAPTER 33

Genevieve

So that went badly.

After Emma had stormed off, I went through the motions—shower, hair, clothes, makeup. The routine soothed me. Otherwise, I was a bit numb.

Obviously, there had been no easy way to tell Emma I had indeed lied—misled, really—about any inheritance for Riley. I had never put a number value on it, and I did have one thing for her that, granted, she could sell, but—

Oh, hell. I lied. I knew it.

And of course Emma would be furious about the suicide, but my circumstances were hardly the same as her mother's. My life was ending. April's had just been getting started.

My phone rang, startling me. Mac and Carmen began barking at the sound. I looked at the screen.

Paul Riley

"Hello, Paul," I said, shushing the dogs.

"You want to get coffee or something?" he said.

"I'd love to. Do come over."

"You come here. I'm sick of your mansion."

The man had a gift for irritating me. "And where is *here*, Paul?"

He gave me his address, a little apartment over an antiques shop on Water Street. "I'll be there in half an hour," I said.

It dawned on me that he'd be furious with me, too. I was too tired to care. He'd have to find out one way or the other.

I walked, as the day was beautiful after the rain. But I'd forgotten how old I was. My head ached, and my hearing was going in and out. My ankle hurt; I'd bruised something last night in the rain, and found myself listing to the right.

Chances were, I needed a cane. Which could be very regal, I supposed, but I hoped to be dead before I couldn't walk into town or around Sheerwater's grounds without assistance.

By the time I got to Water Street, I was already weary and needed the restroom. My feet burned with nerve pain, and my head was sweaty under my straw hat. The flight of stairs up to his apartment seemed like an Escher painting. I hauled myself up the stairs slowly, remembering college, the endless energy, my dorm room on the fifth floor. The things I once took for granted, just being able to wake up without pain . . . What I wouldn't give for one more day in that strong, young body!

"You look like hell," Paul said as he opened the door.

"You're such a rude man."

"Come on in. You want coffee or something else?"

His apartment was furnished with secondhand pieces, but he had a small balcony with a glimpse of the Sound. "Water, please. May I use your bathroom?"

"There on the left."

It was tidy, at least. As I washed my hands, I saw that he was right. I did look like hell. I fluffed my hair, but it did little to help.

He'd set two glasses of water and two mugs of coffee on the little table on the deck. "Out here okay?" he asked.

"Lovely."

Oh, it felt good to sit, even in the plastic chairs. For a second, I wondered where I was—it wasn't Sheerwater—but then I was back. I was here with Paul, though I wasn't sure why I'd sought him out. Not because I forgot; just because he was bound to take this badly.

"How are you?" I asked.

"Not bad. You?"

"Not good." I sipped my water, then proceeded to tell him, as concisely as possible, about my situation. Health. Finances. Suicide plan.

He looked at me from under his bushy eyebrows. "Jesus Christ, lady. You got some nerve, talking to me about suicide."

"I know April had a true illness, Paul, and I don't judge her—"

"I'm talking about my *wife*, idiot. You think it was a joy for her to die the way she did? She was in pain for years! Lost a little piece of herself every day. But she found something to smile about every day, too. Every damn day. You've got everything—my girls, your friends, your dogs, that ridiculous house—and you want to cut that short. There my wife was, unable to swallow, talk, move, in pain, and she never gave up."

"Yes. Well, she was quite the saint, wasn't she?"

"No!" he barked. "She was heartbroken and sick and tired. Our daughter killed herself, Genevieve, and we couldn't even take our granddaughter! You know what that does to a person? It hollows out your heart."

"I do know something about grief, Paul."

"Yeah. Sure you do. What I'm saying is, that wasn't the only thing that happened to us. We kept trying. We talked about April, what she'd want for us, and we tried to make her proud of us. You, on the other hand . . . you let your lost boy ruin you. That poor kid's legacy to you is that you were a miserable bitch all your life."

I started to contradict him, then stopped. My throat felt tight, and tears stung behind my eyes. I took a sip of water, then held the coffee mug in my hands. Though it was a beautiful day, I was cold.

"How did you do it, Paul?" I asked, my voice shaking and thin. "You and Joan. How did you bear to stay alive?"

He looked away from me abruptly and stared into the distance. Then, surprisingly, he took my hand. His skin was callused and warm, and I felt a surge of gratitude.

His voice was quiet when he spoke. "We just did. Some days, it felt like we were walking corpses, but we just kept going." He sighed. "Some days are still so damn hard. Feels like it all happened yesterday."

"I felt like I died the day Sheppard went missing," I said, and my tears spilled over. "I wish I had. When Garrison died, I hated him for leaving me. That was so long ago! I can't believe I've lasted all these years alone."

He squeezed my hand. "Maybe you weren't as alone as you thought. You've got that Donelle. And what's-her-name. The ogre in the kitchen."

"Helga."

"You seem to have quite a few friends in this town. And this summer, you have the girls."

"Not anymore. I imagine Emma's going to leave and take Riley with her."

"Can you blame her? You asked her to help you kill yourself, you lied about having money to help Riley through college, you didn't even tell the truth about what's wrong with you."

"No. I can't blame her a bit."

"Getting old and sick . . . it's not easy," he said. "But come on, Genevieve. Why should you be any different? You think you're only worth something when you're flashing cash and pretending you're the queen of America. Maybe you're worth more when you're not doing that stuff. Even if you forget things and need help. Even if you're old. There still could be something good in you."

"Like what?"

"Like the fact that you're loved. I never understood how you could turn away such a gift."

He was talking about Emma.

"I did love her," I said.

"You hid it well."

A seagull landed on the railing of the deck, calm and undisturbed by our presence. It looked at the both of us.

How wonderful to be a seagull! I'd always loved them, so capable in the air and on the water. The way they could glide on the wind, easily adapting to the varying air currents. I never felt they were common at all.

"I'm so tired," I said to the bird. He looked as if he understood.

"Come on inside," Paul answered. "Have a rest." He stood up and offered his hand, and I needed it. My knees ached from the walk, and I felt a bit dizzy.

He brought me to the bedroom, and I slipped off my shoes and lay on my side. He covered me up with a flannel throw, and when he lay down beside me, I wasn't even surprised.

"Don't read anything into this," he said. "I'm still mad about you lying to my granddaughter."

"Our granddaughter," I said. "By all means, simmer away."

He gave a gruff laugh, and put his arm around me, and before I could even process how good it felt, I was asleep.

CHAPTER 34

Emma

went to see Hope after Genevieve finally told me the truth. I didn't have to work at Rose Hill, but I wanted to see my sister.

Emotions sloshed around in my gut like acid—fury, betrayal, hurt.

Sympathy.

No, no. Genevieve didn't deserve that, not yet.

But as I pulled into Rose Hill, I couldn't help feeling a little . . . awe, too.

Genevieve had taken care of Hope forever, and that was huge. My sister would be cared for all her life, and she could stay here, at the only home she'd ever known. Once Genevieve died, my father wouldn't be able to profit off of her the way he had off of me.

She paid my father to stay away from me.

That was either superheroic or utterly shitty. My father hadn't been horrible, after all. He never beat me or yelled at me. My memories of him in the first eight years of my life were . . . fine. I remember him setting up the sprinkler so I could run through the water . . . I remembered piggy-back rides and a fort made out of a cardboard box. I remembered that, after my mom died, he let me stay up watching TV, the two of us wrapped in a blanket. I had loved him.

I could see that nothing in Clark's life had prepared him to be responsible for anyone. He couldn't even take care of himself. I could've forgiven him, maybe, if he'd visited more . . . but Genevieve had bribed him to keep his distance. Maybe he would've gotten to know me and we would've bonded. We could've gotten closer as I grew older. Once the pain of my mother's death faded, maybe he would've stepped up.

The therapist in me asked if there was any evidence to support this scenario.

No. There wasn't. He sold me. Genevieve's money was worth more than his own child. And then he sold the next kid, too. He was too lazy and self-involved to want to care for Hope himself. Her issues were complicated; even the most loving, dedicated, knowledgeable parent would need help, and my father was none of those things. But he had never even tried.

Hope was on a special swing in the back with one of her aides, smiling faintly at the grass as the breeze blew her messy hair.

"Hello, sweetheart," I said, smooching her head. "Hi, Gerry."

"You want some alone time with your sis?" he asked.

"That'd be great. I'll find you when I have to go."

"Alrighty. Miss Hope, I'm leaving you with Emma, okay? See you later, sweet girl."

I sat on the empty swing next to her and reached out for her hand. "How's my darling?" I asked her. "Are you having a good day?" She liked the swing, which looked like a big plastic scoop with straps, specially designed to keep her comfy and safe and unable to fall off.

Hope and I had had really shitty luck with parents. Her

mother had dumped her, our father had dumped us both, and depression had stolen my beautiful mom, its insidious lies telling her I'd be better off without her. But she had loved me. She'd shown that to me every day we had together, and I knew it down to my bone marrow.

Genevieve wasn't depressed, not clinically. The idea that she wanted me to help her take her own life twisted like a knife in my stomach.

Hope made a little cooing sound.

"What's that? You want a song? 'Baby Beluga,' then?"

I obliged, and she stole looks at me, smiling a little. There was something magical about my sister. I don't know how her parents had chosen her name, but it was perfect. She brought out the best in people . . . at least in me. And Genevieve. And Riley, too, though Riley was pretty great all around.

If Genevieve died—and of course she would—I'd always pictured myself taking Hope back to Downers Grove, a happy little fantasy that had nothing to do with reality. She needed extensive care, and I had a daughter, a job and no home of my own. It wouldn't be fair to her—Rose Hill was the better place for her.

But I was her guardian now, even if money was not an issue. Genevieve wasn't long for the world, one way or the other. There was no cure for vascular dementia.

"Hey," came a familiar voice. It was Miller, dressed in jeans and a faded red T-shirt that said *Finlay Construction*. My heart lifted.

"Hi. You working here today?"

"Yep."

I smiled, feeling myself blush. "Miller, this is my sister, Hope. Hope, this is my friend Miller."

She didn't lift her gaze from the grass, but when he knelt down to be at eye level, she smiled a little and brought her hands to her chin, showing she was shy but not entirely displeased.

"It's nice to meet you, Hope," he said. He sat down on the swing to my left. "I'm gonna get a lot of flak for this from my crew," he said.

"Swinging on the job."

"Exactly. With two beautiful girls, no less. How's your day?" he asked. He gave me a crooked smile that went straight to my heart.

"Better now. Kind of shitty this morning."

"Why is that?"

"I found out Genevieve's been lying to me all summer." His eyes widened. "About what?"

"About everything. Her health, her finances, what Riley was going to inherit. Oh, and she wants me to help her commit suicide." I tried to keep my tone light and failed miserably.

"Jesus."

"Yeah. So . . . I'm probably going back home sooner than I thought."

He twisted the swing to look at me. "What do you mean?"

"I think I need to get Riley out of here. Fast."

His face was serious, the earlier smile gone without a trace. "Seems like Riley's pretty good at dealing with people."

"Yeah, well, she's a teenager. And she had a really rough winter. I don't want her getting crushed by someone else she thought she could depend on."

"Genevieve? She loves that kid."

"Oh, okay, Miller, I guess you know my grandmother and daughter better than I do. Tell me what I should do, since you're doling out advice."

He raised an eyebrow at me. "Is this what you shrinks call transference?"

I looked at the ground and let out a sigh. "Yes. Sorry."

"Want me to leave you to sulk?"

"No." I swallowed, got up and started braiding Hope's messy hair. At least it would stay out of her face that way. "I'm sorry."

"It's okay." He leaned back, hands on the ropes, and stared at the sky. "Guess I was hoping you'd stay in Connecticut."

"I have a whole life back in Illinois," I said.

"People move."

Hope made a little sound, and I stopped fussing with her hair and knelt in front of her. "You okay, sweetheart?" I asked.

She didn't answer. She never did, of course. A small lump was rising on her neck—another benign tumor, according to her doctor's report. No need to operate now. They'd watch it and see how it went. She needed oral surgery this fall, since one of the issues she faced with TS was pitting of her teeth.

Shouldn't I be here for that? I loved my sister. She was my responsibility now.

"It took me a long time to build what I have out there," I said, more to myself than to him.

"So what?" Miller said.

"So *what*?" I said, my voice sharp. "Stoningham was never exactly warm and welcoming, Miller. I was always Genevieve's poor little orphan grandchild, proof of her royal goodness. *Your* family dumped me as soon as it was clear I wasn't going to inherit a shitload of money. Courtney and Robert have never even met Riley, Jason won't commit to helping with college, and now Genevieve told me she's flat broke, so I wasted this whole summer, hoping for scraps from her table so my kid wouldn't have to scratch her way through school the way I did. And Riley, the poor kid, loves that gorgon, and that gorgon is about to off herself because she doesn't want to get old like a mere mortal."

Miller stood up. "Okay. Two things." He shoved his hands in his pockets. "One. You haven't wasted the summer. Your daughter is doing great and got to meet her great-grandmother. She made friends here and spent time with her brothers. You got to spend time with your sister. You got a job here. You met a nice guy who likes you a lot."

I gave a begrudging nod.

"Don't just nod at me," he said, and I smiled a little, respecting him for not putting up with my tantrum.

"You're right. I met a nice guy, and I also like him a lot. And his daughter."

"Thank you. And two . . . I'll pay for Riley's college, Emma. The Finlays owe you that much. The company is doing great. If that asshole cousin of mine won't step up, I will."

I could probably love Miller Finlay. I probably already did. "You won't pay for my daughter's school, Miller. But thank you."

"Personally, I'd like it if you stayed. I'm not asking you to marry me since we've been on all of one shitty date, but I'd like Stoningham a lot more if you were in it. And so would your sister. Your daughter could be close to her brothers. You'd be here for the gorgon, because you love her, no matter what you say."

He was right. I always had, and I still did. No matter what she'd done to me after I got pregnant, no matter her harsh words that day and her seventeen years of silence, I loved my grandmother. She'd taken me in when I was alone, and if she wasn't soft and loving, she'd made me . . . strong. Self-sufficient. Independent.

I was a London after all.

"Well?" said Miller. "You gonna admit I'm right?"

"Can you just shut up and stop being wise and calm?"

"It's kind of my thing."

"I like you better when you're desperate and exhausted." I sighed, then smiled. "You're right."

He knelt down in front of me, then looked at Hope. "Is it okay if I kiss your sister?" he asked.

She didn't answer, of course, which he took as a yes.

This kiss was different. In the past, we'd been a little

tentative, me too aware of his widower status, his sleeping child, my temporary status in his life. Those kisses had been nice, for sure.

This kiss was a man making a statement. Warm, hard, deep and perfect, his hands cradling my shorn head.

Hope laughed, and we broke apart. "Way to kill the mood, Hope," Miller said, not looking away from me.

"Can you get away for an hour?" I asked, my voice husky.

"Hell yes."

I scooped Hope out of her swing, took her hand and led her over to the courtyard, where Gerry was scrolling through his phone. "Just about to come get you," he said. "Time for swim class, missy."

"See you tomorrow, Gerry," I said, then kissed my sister's soft cheek. "Love you, angel."

Then I followed Miller to his truck. We didn't talk as we drove, and when he pulled into a motel, I waited as he got us a room. Number 101. My lucky number. At least, it was from now on.

We went inside, and the room was completely unremarkable in every way, except he was here. Miller locked the door, tossed his keys on the table and then took my face in his hands and kissed me, and it was even better than before, hot and hard, tongue and teeth, his hands sliding down my back to cup my ass. I pulled his shirt out of the waistband of his jeans and ran my hands up his ribs, around his back. His skin was sun-warm and smooth, and when I kissed his neck, he tasted like salt and sweat, and my knees wobbled.

Then he pulled my shirt over my head and gently pushed me back on the bed into a patch of sunlight and took off the rest of my clothes.

You forget how it is to be with another person when you've gone for so long without one. How his weight on top of you is so welcome, how the heat of skin against skin feels at once shocking and familiar. How you can feel languid and charged with electricity at the same time, sinking into the mattress and pushing up against him for more contact, your eyes fluttering shut while every nerve ending buzzes and hums. You forget the pleasure of giving pleasure, the smug sense of satisfaction when you find out what the other likes. The sweet shock of connection, the bliss of togetherness.

You forget what it is to rely on someone, to trust someone, to feel so full of happiness just because one person—*your* person—has chosen you.

Miller drove me back to Rose Hill so I could get my car.

"I have a lot to think about," I said.

"You do."

"Thanks for being . . . yourself."

"Look," he said, leaning against my car. "If you need to go back to Chicago, I get that. My own life isn't really under control, so I probably shouldn't be giving anyone advice."

It sounded like a precursor to *this was a mistake*. I nodded, feeling my muscles start to tighten.

"But if you did stay, I'd be really, really happy. Selfishly. Because I'd get to see you more than if I have to fly out to Chicago."

My heart practically jumped out of my chest into his hands. "So . . . you'd come out and visit? We're not just a summer fling?"

"You're the second person I've ever slept with, Emma. I don't do flings."

"You're the second person I've slept with, too."

"We're basically freaks of nature in this day and age."

"That's fine with me." The happy, warm buzzing was back.

"Me too." He smiled, tugging my gooey caramel heart, then kissed my nose, which thrilled me. Yep. I had it bad.

"I have to get back to work," he said.

"Then get out of here."

"I'll call you later."

"Okay." Smiling like a happy dope, I got into my car before I blurted out my love for him and the names of our future pets.

And as I drove away, I decided it was time to pay Jason a visit. I called his house, and Jamilah answered. "Hey, it's Emma!" I said.

"How are you?"

"I'm good. Is Jason there? I was thinking I'd stop by."

"Oh." There was a pause. "Um . . . he's still living with his parents, Emma." She dropped her voice to a whisper. "I filed for divorce."

"Oh! I thought . . . I thought you were getting back together."

"No. I tried, but no."

I paused. "Is it okay if I say something judgmental right now?"

"Go for it."

"You deserve so much better."

She laughed. "I've been thinking that about you since the day we met."

"I'll remind him of your sons' birthdays, too. You know. The way you did for Riley. Your boys are part of our family, too."

Her voice was husky when she spoke. "That Jason. He sure gets the best women, doesn't he?"

"He does. Let's get together this week, okay?"

"Sounds great. Thanks, Emma."

I took the all-too-familiar road to Courtney and Robert's house. It was time for Jason to tell me just how much he was contributing to Riley's college expenses. No more tap dancing around my goodwill.

Their house hadn't changed much. Courtney still had those ugly plaster geese lining the walk. I knocked on the front door, loudly, and a second later, she answered, then jumped back in surprise like I was going to hit her. "Emma! What are you doing here?"

"So nice to see you, too, Courtney."

"What do you want? Jason, I suppose. I hope you're proud of yourself, breaking up him and Jamilah. She was the best thing that ever happened to him."

I leaned past her head. "Jason! I need to talk to you."

"You have no manners," Courtney said.

"Really? This from the woman who has ignored her granddaughter for sixteen years? Who blamed her son's girl-friend for getting pregnant, like I could do that on my own? You're trash, Courtney. No amount of ass kissing and social climbing will ever change that."

Jason appeared in the foyer, chewing something. Right. It was dinnertime. The afternoon at the motel had taken a lot more than an hour. I squished down the pleasure that thought induced and stuck with righteous anger.

"Hey, Em," Jason said. "What's up? You want to grab a drink somewhere?"

"No. I need you to tell me exactly how much you'll give to Riley's college expenses. Now. Miller told me the company's doing really well, so how much, Jason?"

"Robert!" Courtney called. "You need to come here."

"Why do we have to talk about this now?" Jason asked. "I can't predict how well the company—"

"How much, Jason? Can I put you down for half, or would you like to cover it all?"

Robert Finlay appeared in the front hall. "Oh. Hello, Emma." Like we'd seen each other yesterday, not seventeen years ago when he let his wife kick me out of their house for having the audacity to get pregnant by his son.

I ignored him. "How much, Jason?"

"Look," he said. "Jamilah and I are getting a divorce, so things will be tight."

"So you've never saved any money for your daughter's education? You just figured she'd turn eighteen and your child support payments would end, and she'd be on her own for college. Is that it?"

"He's not obliged to pay anything," Courtney said.

"Legally, no. Morally, another story."

Jason's face was getting that look I knew so well, since I'd seen it so many times. The jaw hardening, the eyes going flat. The look that said, *Don't push me.*

All these years, I'd told myself he was a good guy. A good father. A good friend.

He wasn't. He was just . . . nothing. A man who had to be reminded to interact with his daughter.

"I can't commit to a figure," he said. "I'll help if I can."

"But you won't help, will you? In fact, you're the one who's always needed help, haven't you? From your parents, from the family business, from Jamilah. And here you are, living in Mommy and Daddy's basement. How proud you've made everyone, Jason."

I turned and walked down the path to my car. As I got in, I saw Robert scuttling down the path toward me.

"Emma, wait," he said.

"What?"

"Uh . . . well, it's nice to see you again."

"Don't waste my time, Robert. What is it?"

"I'll pay for Riley's college."

"I'm surprised you even know her name."

He sighed. "Yeah. We should've done more. Courtney . . ." He looked off to the house. "I should've done more. I'm sorry."

"Too little, too late."

"Let me pay for her college. We can afford it."

For a second, I imagined it—my daughter living with the knowledge that the grandparents who didn't find her worthy of a single visit had soothed their guilt with a check.

"Take your money, and shove it up your ass, Robert. You're a weak man, and you raised a weak son. And your wife is a heartless, shallow bitch."

"I know," he said. "But please. Let me do this. Riley doesn't have to know where the money came from. It's the right thing to do. We owe her that much." He paused. "We owe her a lot more."

I swallowed. I didn't want his guilt money. I wanted . . . I wanted to do it all myself.

But I couldn't.

If I let Robert pay for college, Riley would know her grandfather cared enough to at least write a check. That he felt remorse. That he was trying to make amends.

Maybe Riley deserved the chance to be forgiving. She'd forgiven Gigi, after all, and maybe Robert deserved the same chance.

"I accept your offer," I said.

"I'd like to meet her. I always wanted to, but . . . yeah. I'm a weak man."

"People can change, Robert." With that, I backed up and drove home, feeling oddly calm.

I would wait on telling Riley about this, of course. But she was no dummy. I had the sneaking suspicion she knew more than I gave her credit for, about Jason, and me. That despite my education and practice, I was pretty damn naive about people.

Not anymore.

When I got to Sheerwater, I went straight to my room and took a long shower in the glorious bathroom, then got dressed in my pajamas—it was seven o'clock, after all. Went downstairs and found Riley, Donelle, Rav and Helga playing cards in the conservatory, the windows open, the fireplace on to counter the chilly breeze.

Gigi and Pop sat in wing chairs by the fire, watching the card players. There was an air of camaraderie between those two, which struck me as both strange and comforting. My only grandparents. The ones who'd stepped up when my parents had failed me.

"Hi, Mom!" Riley said. "How was your day?"

I went over and kissed her head. "It was great," I said. "How about yours?"

"Also great. Want to play? It's poker. Donelle is killing us."

"I warned you," she said.

"Hi, Dr. London," Rav said.

"Hello, dear boy."

Riley snorted.

"I need a moment with Gigi," I said. "Maybe you can deal me in after that."

"You missed dinner," Helga said. "Don't go messing around in my kitchen just because you're late."

I ignored that. "Genevieve? Can I talk to you? Hi, Pop." I kissed his bristly cheek.

"I was wondering when I'd get acknowledged," he grumbled.

Gigi got up, wobbling a bit, and my grandfather reached out a hand. I took her arm, and we went into my grandfather's study, where it was quiet and dark. I turned on a lamp—a Tiffany original, probably—and ushered Gigi into a fat leather chair, then sat across from her.

"I couldn't play cards tonight," she said. "I seem to have forgotten how."

"I'm sorry."

"Are you angry with me?"

"A little. Here's the deal. We're staying. We'll take care of you, Riley and I. Make me your medical proxy, and I'll do right by you. You won't die alone, Gigi."

Her face stayed carved in stone for a second. Then she put her hand over her eyes. "I don't want to die badly, Emma. I don't want to be in diapers, drooling and afraid. Please help me die with some dignity. Some grace."

"I won't help you die. But I will help you live, however long you have left."

"I don't want Riley to see me when I'm senile."

"I understand that. But we don't get to pick how we go, Gigi. And we can't teach her that just because things are hard, you check out. We have to do better than that for her."

She started to cry, and I moved over to her chair and sat next to her.

"Why would you take care of me, Emma? I failed you."

"I won't fail you."

"How can you say that? I was horrible."

"You did your best."

"It wasn't enough."

"Well, lucky for you, I'm not petty." I put my arm around her shoulders. "I love you, Gigi," I said. "It always drove me crazy that I did, but I did, and I do." I hugged her a second, and her hand went to my cheek.

That was all.

It was enough.

CHAPTER 35

Miller

Miller had to work late to make up for the afternoon delight with Emma, which didn't thrill his mother-in-law. He stood in the kitchen, getting a summary of his child's misbehavior, noise volume and destruction and why her hair had a marshmallow half melted into it, all while Tess ran around the kitchen, banging a pot with a candle, naked. David, his father-in-law, was apparently asleep in the living room, which was about par for the course.

"You need to get her potty trained," Judith said.

"We're working on it." In fact, last night, Tess had woken up four times, promised she would go on the potty, then sat there for half an hour each time, staring stonily at him, easily winning the battle of wills.

But nothing was going to crash his good mood today.

Oh, and speaking of that, he should probably say something to his former mother-in-law about dating Emma.

"Tess, let's get your clothes on, honey," he said.

"No! I *not* get my clothes on!" She ran into another part

of the house, and Miller followed. The talk about dating could wait.

Half an hour and some more inner ear damage later, courtesy of his child's screams, Tess was diapered, mostly dressed and strapped into the car seat. "You so mean, Daddy. I hate you."

"It would be easier for us both if you just kept your clothes on."

"I hate clothes. I hate you. I hate Nana. I hate car."

"It's hard, being three. I'm sorry you're upset." It sounded like something Emma would say, and Tess side-eyed him. But she stopped her tirade, and he couldn't help a smile.

When he got home, he let Luigi out so the cat would be safe from Tess's attention, locked the door, set the alarm. Tess watched him, her eyes narrowed.

"You can play or color if you want. Daddy has to make dinner. Or you could help me, if you want."

"I hate dinner."

"Doesn't matter. Everyone has to eat."

She went into the living room, which looked like it should exist in a war-torn country and not peaceful Stoningham. But it was childproofed, and if she dug another chunk of stuffing out of the couch, well, someday he'd get another couch. He put on some music (Bach's cello concertos, hoping they'd soothe the savage toddler) and opened the fridge.

Closed it.

There was a picture of him and Ashley.

What would she think of his dating Emma? They'd talked about their dying the way smug, healthy young adults do. "I'd want you to find someone else," he'd said. "But he can't be better looking than me. Someone like . . . Christopher Walken. So you'd still miss me."

"Christopher Walken is smokin' hot," she'd said. "I'll take it. But if I die first, I'm gonna haunt the hell out of you and your new wife."

That would be okay, Miller thought now. He wouldn't mind a visit from his wife.

"You there, Ash?" he asked softly.

There was no answer.

There was no guilt, either. Just that old familiar feeling of missing her, loving her, liking her. She'd been his best friend. His only friend, really. They'd had couples they spent time with, and she'd had friends, being a woman. It was different for men. They had wives.

Genevieve had become his friend, sort of.

And Emma definitely was. He had that nanosecond impulse to call Ashley and tell her about Emma and share his happiness, tell his wife he didn't feel so alone anymore.

He touched her face in the photo, remembering the freckle to the left of her mouth, her curly, silky hair, the sound of her laugh. He didn't want to be the widower of Ashley James Finlay, but here he was. He'd wished a million times she hadn't died, had begged God to bring her back, cursed his life, wished he'd die, and shook in loneliness and fear at raising a child alone.

But he was doing it. He was getting through.

And he was falling in love with Emma, and the thought didn't hurt. It didn't hurt at all.

Ashley would approve of Emma. Any woman who hadn't so much as shed a tear when she'd had to shave her entire head because of their daughter was someone Ashley would've liked. Had liked, in fact.

"I love you," he said to the picture. "I'll always love you."

Then he put the picture back and took out carrots and chicken breasts and started making dinner.

It wasn't until a good ten minutes later that he realized he hadn't heard any noise from the living room.

"Tess? You doing okay?" he called, washing his hands. He went into the living room. She wasn't there. "Are you hiding, honey? Remember, you have to tell Daddy if you want to play hide-and-seek."

He looked under the couch and behind the curtains.

She wasn't there. "Tess? Where are you?"

No answer.

Shit.

He looked in the den and the dining room, then ran upstairs. She wasn't in her room, or his, or the guest room. Not in the bathroom. Not in the laundry chute, where she'd once hidden, bracing her arms and legs against the sides and scaring the life out of him.

Not in the closets. "Tess! Tess, answer Daddy!"

Nothing.

He ran back down to the kitchen, looked in the pantry, the coat closet, ran down into the cellar, which, the house being old, was dark and smelled like limestone and dirt. "Tess! Answer now!"

She wasn't there.

His panic rose with each stride, and he could hear his voice changing, getting louder, more urgent, unrecognizable.

Then he saw the light blinking by the living room door. Next to the door was an overturned bowl, a big wooden salad bowl that had been a wedding gift. Tess liked to pretend to make soup in it, and it was sturdy enough that she wouldn't break it.

If she stood on it, she'd be tall enough to reach the alarm, which was a four-digit code.

She was an evil genius. He knew that better than anyone.

He bolted onto the porch. "Tess!" he yelled. Shit, the road was right there, and it was summer, and cars went past way too fast. "Tess, answer Daddy!"

He pulled his phone out of his pocket and called 911. "My three-year-old daughter left our house," he said, running down the street. "I can't find her." He managed to give his address. Saw Jim Davies in the front yard. "Have you seen Tess?" he yelled.

Jim shook his head and came running down. "Need help?"

"Yes. I don't know where she is. It's been maybe ten minutes."

"Anyplace you think she'd head?" Jim asked. "A friend's house?"

"No. Nothing I can think of."

"Go around the block. I'll go in this way," he said. "Tess! Hey, Tess, honey, want a cookie?"

Around the block. That was smart. Where the hell were the police? Why was it taking so long?

What if she drowned? Could she have gotten down to the water that fast? What was he saying? She was a fucking cheetah when it came to getting into trouble.

The neighborhood looked strange and full of danger. The bushes, the trees, the houses . . . what if his daughter was inside one of them, being molested or murdered? Or both? Jesus Christ, why did he ever have a child? "Tess!" he called, his voice breaking.

A car passed, and he waved it down. "Be careful!" he barked. "There's a missing toddler. Look out for her."

"Sure thing," the lady said.

God. What if she'd been taken? Like Sheppard London, like the daughter in the Liam Neeson movies, like the thousands of kids who went missing every year and who were never found?

What if, after all he'd been through, his baby was dead right this minute?

He was running, trying to see everything, under every rhododendron, behind every hedge, every car. His thoughts skittered and slid with panic. "Tess, please, honey," he said, and he realized he was crying.

Bebe Leiderman was standing on her porch. "Have you seen Tess?" he asked.

"Your little girl?"

"Yes."

"I'm sorry, no. Want help?"

"Yes." He kept running, his heart pumping too hard. God wouldn't be this cruel, would he?

He turned again, back onto his own street, past the Quinns' place, checking their yard. Past the Oliverases, who were having some kind of family celebration, as they did about four times a month.

"Have you seen Tess?" he yelled. "She ran out of the house."

They came down their walk immediately, Joe, his wife, the three adult daughters, asking him questions, but he couldn't hear anymore; there was ringing in his ears, the roar of blood, his own breath.

Please. Please.

There was his own yard, fenced in so it would be safe; joke was on him—

And there she was, sitting on the front steps, clutching Luigi in her arms, the cat looking beleaguered and limp.

"Hi, Daddy," she said. "I get out."

"Jesus *Christ*, Tess!" he yelled. "Don't you ever, *ever* do that again! Do you hear me?" And then he was holding her, probably too hard, sobbing into her shoulder, bending over because the terror bowed him in half, the noises barking out of him.

Someone was patting his back . . . Joe Oliveras. "Just twenty years off your life, right? Oh, the times I thought my girls would kill me."

"Parenting is not for sissies," came Bebe's voice. A couple of people laughed, because apparently there was a small crowd here with him, because they wanted to help, which was nice, but he couldn't think now. Nothing mattered except that his daughter was safe, alive, and God, he loved her so much, he'd die for her, he'd die without her because the little terror was everything to him. Everything.

The sobs were still wrenching out of him, and he couldn't seem to let go of her.

She was safe. She was safe. She was here, and she was safe. She was alive.

"You squish me, Daddy."

He finally pulled back a little, and she looked at him, frowning. "No crying, Daddy."

"Tess, you can't run away like that." His voice was ragged and hoarse. "What would I do without you?"

She patted his face with her grubby little hands. "No crying, Daddy," she repeated. "You okay now."

CHAPTER 36

Riley

We're moving to Connecticut permanently. I would be lying if I said that made me anything but incredibly happy. I can see my brothers whenever I want, and my dad. And Jamilah and Hope, too.

Mom enrolled me in the public school, and I don't even care that I'll be the new kid my last year. I mean, yeah, walking into school without knowing anyone will be hard, but better that than going back and trying to scrape together some friends since Mikayla, Jenna and Annabeth ditched me.

They did try to be friends again over the summer, on Snapchat and Instagram. Like I couldn't see through that. **You look amazing!!!** when I posted a picture of myself in New York with Gigi, or **legit jealous!** and **looks so pretty there!!!** for one of me and Rav at the July picnic. *He* posted that one. I didn't respond to their comments, but I didn't block them, either. I didn't care enough to make the effort.

I'm gonna miss Rav a lot when he leaves at the end of the summer, even though we're not really a couple. We hold hands sometimes, like at the movies last week. I know there are kids my age who are already having sex and doing things, but that seems far, far away for me. I like the way things are now. We're friends. We take walks and hikes together, and we're still young enough to do stupid things like go out to the farthest tip of Gigi's property and pretend we got stranded on an island. Soon enough, I'll have to figure out dating and romance and sex and stuff, but not for a good long while. College, maybe. I'm in no hurry. Mom says I'm wise beyond my years.

The Talwars live in New Haven for most of the year, which is an hour from here, and Rav will be going to some swanky private day school. Saanvi won't let him go to boarding school. So I do have one friend in Connecticut, and one good friend is better than three shitty friends, that's for sure.

Besides, I'm not completely unknown here. I'm Genevieve London's great-granddaughter, Duncan and Owen's half sister, Jason Finlay's daughter, and Jamilah Rochon's stepdaughter. (She's using her maiden name since she and Dad are getting a divorce, and she's as great as ever. We had lunch the other day, just us two.) I'm Paul Riley's great-granddaughter, and that's hilarious, because Pop knows more people here than Genevieve, I think. Mr. Popularity. He comes to the house almost every day and bickers with Gigi. It's almost flirting. He hasn't said if he'll stay here in Connecticut with us. Obviously, I'm hoping he'll stay.

Mom's going to keep working at Rose Hill, because the guy who left wants to be a stay-at-home dad. She also is going to rent some office space downtown to see other clients. We'll stay with Gigi for the time being. I get to see Hope whenever I want, and I'll be volunteering there when school starts for my senior community service project.

The only sad part is, Gigi's not doing great. After that rainstorm when she didn't know who I was, things seemed to change. She goes to bed earlier and takes more naps, and there are times when I can tell she's trying not to let on that she's in one of her fogs. Donelle and I have this way of talking to her when she's forgetting . . . We ask about old times, because those memories are easier for her to talk about.

At least Gigi is being nicer to Mom. The way she talks to her now has changed, too.

I kind of ran out of ways to look for Great-Uncle Sheppard. The only new thing was when I got those age-progression photos—you send in baby pictures of the person, and pictures of relatives, and get a composite of what the person would look like.

If the photos were right, Sheppard would've looked a lot like my grandfather, Clark. Gigi keeps a few pictures of him around. Mom says he'll come out at Christmas. Big whoop, right? At any rate, I took the doctored photos of Sheppard and did a reverse Google image search on them, hoping the results would pop up with a name or a photo of some sixtysomething-year-old who might've been Sheppard. I was thinking CEO or senator or architect, you know? Because he would've had a lot going for him, being Gigi and my great-grandfather's kid.

The only result that came up was "man smiling." I guess that was better than nothing. If you're going to be categorized as something, *smiling* isn't so bad. But it made me sad, not ever knowing what happened to him, not being able to run into Gigi's room and say, "Look! This might be him!" I knew it had been a long shot, but still. She misses him so much. Almost every day, she tells me I have his eyes. I don't know if that's true or not, but it makes her happy.

It's funny how weird this house and situation seemed when I first got here in June. How stiff and tense things were with Mom and Gigi. Now there aren't any subtle jabs or undercurrents . . . It's all out in the open.

"How is the rent-a-friend business going? Does it pay well?" Gigi asked the other night, full of piss and vinegar, as Pop says.

"Hey, I'm not the bankrupt person sitting at this table," Mom said. "And yes, it pays pretty well. Want to sign up? You could use it."

So we're doing okay. Better than okay.

It feels like home.

CHAPTER 37

Emma

The big stroke happened in early October, when the leaves were changing and the sky was heartbreak blue.

The past two months had been tinted with poignancy, because it was clear Genevieve the Gorgon was fading into Genevieve the little old lady, confused and anxious, still trying to hang on to her pride. She didn't need diapers, but I had to help her in the shower. Donelle's toe, which had more problems than just an infected toenail, had to be amputated at long last, so I was taking care of the both of them.

I did fire Helga. She still lives here at Sheerwater, and still gets paid, but enough was enough. No more gray meat, no more limp green beans, no more ogre in the kitchen. Riley and I had always liked cooking, although now she had a lot of after-school activities and couldn't help that much. And friends. Nice friends, too. Good kids, and of course they were, because my daughter, who was older and wiser herself, had chosen them. They came over a lot, and

Sheerwater was filled with the sound of thumping feet, laughter and music.

Sometimes, Miller would come over when Kimmy could be convinced to babysit. Miller . . . I loved Miller Finlay. I hadn't said it to him yet, but he probably knew just the same. He'd told me about the day Tess ran away, his panic, the realization that he loved her with every molecule no matter how much she shrieked, destroyed the house and kicked him. Which, of course, everyone already knew and had known from the start. Parenting isn't always a peachy-colored glow. Half the time, it's just showing up and doing your best.

Some nights, Beth and Jamilah came over, and Jamilah could get Genevieve talking about women in the corporate world, start-ups and fashion, while Beth and I scrolled through Facebook, looking for a father for her future children.

Genevieve, even when she was with it, was quiet. She'd taken to carrying a picture of Sheppard with her, which broke my heart . . . In it, he stood in Sheerwater's backyard in the spring, his smile huge, his blond hair cut short. He looked so happy.

In the evenings, we'd sit in the conservatory or on the screened-in porch and watch the sunset, the dogs milling about, yacking up grass, always rubbing their butts on the carpet, shedding, ever shedding. I didn't mind. I'd come to love Mac, the poor old guy, and Carmen. Minuet was firmly Genevieve's dog, and Allegra the wheezy pug had taken to Riley. Valkyrie was Helga's dog, having the same personality. Donelle would tap away at her iPad or go to watch TV—I had the feeling that it was too painful for her to see Genevieve's decline.

Pop, on the other hand, had gotten to be quite the fixture at the house. When I asked if he planned to stay in Connecticut, he brushed off the question. "Can't wait to get rid of me?" or "None of your business, little girl." He'd taken to doing some gardening, digging up the dahlia tubers, cutting back the hydrangeas, even though the yard service still came each week.

Most nights, though, it was just Gigi and me. The fact that she was no longer infallible (in her own mind) had made her gentler, and I'd never felt closer to her. Some nights, she'd ask if Garrison would be home soon, or she'd call me Melanie, who was her assistant way back when. She got lost in her closet one day, unable to find her way out, and another day, Donelle found her eating dog kibbles, thinking it was cereal. She forgot how to button things and needed me to cut her food for her.

But she was still Gigi. On her better nights, I'd ask her about her life, her work . . . and Sheppard. For the first time in my life, I got to learn a little bit about my uncle. Sometimes, she'd laugh, recounting his antics, or pride would light up her face as she discussed his talents.

"You must miss him so much," I said.

"It's been almost sixty years," she said, "and I think of him more than any other person." She was quiet a moment. "I never thought I'd die without finding out what happened to him. To see him again . . . or at least to bury him . . ."

"Oh, Gigi," I whispered. "I'm so sorry."

She sniffed, then turned to me, once again the consummate conversationalist. "What about your mother, dear? Do you mourn her still?"

"Yes. I wish she'd met Riley."

"Of course."

"She was a good mom. I know it sounds strange to say that, but she was. She tried so hard to make life fun for me. I never really understood what depression took from her."

"I'm sorry I didn't do more for her," Gigi said. "I knew she was unsteady, but I never thought she'd . . . kill herself."

"And you, Gigi? Do you still wish you could end it?"

She looked at me and raised her chin, and for a moment, she was the Genevieve London of old. "It was a momentary weakness," she said, her tone regal. "Then again, I thought you'd be abandoning me at the end of summer. I didn't think to ask you to stay."

"You never know what you'll get if you ask," I said.

"Ask *me* something," she said. "Whatever you've always wanted to know. Quickly, before my brain melts and I can't answer."

I was surprised by her question. Chances like this didn't come that often with her. Thinking a minute, I took a sip of my wine and petted Mac's enormous head, watching a clot of his fur drift to the floor. Now or never. "Are you proud of me, Gigi?"

She looked at me a long minute, then took a sip of her martini (against doctor's orders, but hey; a person had to have some vices). "You turned out nothing like what I'd hoped," she said.

Super. Should've known. "Thanks."

"You're much, much more, Emma. I'm rather in awe of you." She looked away, a little embarrassed, as the words sank into my heart. "You're the best mother I've ever met."

I got up, went to her chair and knelt in front of it. "That's the nicest thing you've ever said to me."

"I've made you cry, have I?"

"For the best reason."

She patted my head. "Well. Let's not get sloppy, shall we? Be a good girl and make me another drink."

And so I did, my heart as full and happy as it had ever been.

The Thursday before Columbus Day weekend was the kind of day that proved the Northeast was the best part of the country to live in. The leaves were golden and red, the sky utterly clear and blue. The Sound was calm, the air cool, the sun warm. The Talwar family was coming up tomorrow, and we were planning to have dinner here at Sheerwater, so I was going to have to bring my A game to the kitchen and start by cooking dessert tonight. Apple pie, I was thinking. 'Twas the season.

I stopped at an orchard on the way home and picked up some apples that made my car smell like heaven. Riley came into the kitchen as I peeled and sliced, telling me about her AP Gov class and how she'd been assigned to present the arguments for a Supreme Court case decided in 2011. "It's pretty interesting," she said. "This guy was shot, and he told the cops who shot him, but then he died, and originally, the case got thrown out—"

A crash came from upstairs. "Gigi?" I called.

There was no answer.

Riley and I both ran upstairs.

My grandmother was lying on the hallway floor, her mouth opening and closing. Donelle knelt at her side, and the five dogs were barking.

"You better call Dr. Pinco," Donelle said tightly. "It's okay, Gen. We're all here."

"Gigi?" Riley said, her voice sounding young and scared.

"Sweetheart, go get my phone," I told my daughter. "Take the dogs and put them out back." She did, and I knelt beside my grandmother. Her mouth was drooping on one side, and she was flapping one hand. The other lay still. "I've got you, Gigi," I said. "Let's get you to your room. Good thing I'm strong, right?"

She was lighter than I expected, but still, it wasn't easy, carrying her down the hall. Donelle flipped back the covers, and I set Gigi down awkwardly, but not dropping her. Riley ran in, her face white, blue eyes too wide, and thrust the phone at me.

"She's having a stroke," I told her. "Looks like this is bigger than the others." My voice was calm, but my heart thudded sickly against my ribs.

Dr. Pinco and I had talked about this—what to do, what could be done, whether or not to go to the hospital. Gigi was adamantly against going anywhere and had all her wishes written up by her lawyer—do not resuscitate, no heroic measures, pain control only. At the end of August, she'd made me her medical decision maker.

But now that the moment was possibly here, the little girl in me wanted to beg her not to die.

I called the good doctor, and he said he'd be on his way and to make her comfortable in the meantime.

There was a hard lump in my throat. "We're here, Gigi. Dr. Pinco's on his way. Can you smile for me?"

She tried, but the left side of her face didn't move.

"How about talking? Can you say 'Nice to see you'?" I was talking too fast, my voice too chipper.

"Nahsh ee oo," she said.

Shit. "Good! That's great. Okay, just take it easy, Gigi. We'll take care of you."

There were tears in her eyes.

"Shouldn't we call 911?" Riley asked.

"No," Gigi said. "No. No." That, at least, was crystal clear.

"She said no hospital," Donelle reminded me.

Riley was crying. I stood up and walked her over to the window. "Call Pop."

"Is Gigi dying?"

I pressed my lips together. "I don't know. Maybe. It might be her time."

Riley's face scrunched up, and I kissed her forehead. "Call Pop," I said again.

"Hello! It's Jeff Pinco," came a voice from downstairs.

"Up here!" Donelle called. "Hurry, Doc."

He came in the room, doctor's bag in hand. With him was a nurse—Sophia, the same one who'd shaved my head. She nodded at me in recognition. "Let's see how you're doing, Mrs. London," he said. "Out of the room, everyone."

We left, a cluster of worry and teary eyes. Riley called my grandfather, and we all went into the upstairs sitting room, which looked out over the water, to wait.

The view was almost too beautiful for what was happening.

A few minutes later, my grandfather appeared, squeezed my shoulder, kissed Donelle on the cheek and sat next to Riley, tucking her against him.

We waited. And waited. No one said much. Charles came up from the garage and sat with us, crying surreptitiously. Riley texted someone.

After an eternity, Dr. Pinco came in. "It's a stroke," he confirmed. "The nurse is with her now, making her more comfortable."

"Is it ischemic or hemorrhagic?" Donelle asked, and we all looked at her in surprise. "I read the Internet," she added, scowling.

"Ischemic," he said. He glanced at Riley. "There's a blockage in a blood vessel in Mrs. London's brain," he explained. "It's cutting off blood flow, and that's why she's having trouble walking and talking. I gave her a shot that should clear it up, but she won't go to the hospital for a CAT scan, which is what I'd prefer." He looked at me. "You're her medical decision maker. At this point, she's impaired, so the call is yours."

My throat was tight, and my nerves buzzed in fear. I knew she was old, and I knew her wishes, and I didn't want the responsibility.

"Get her to the hospital, Mom," Riley said. "She could get better."

I cleared my throat. "No. She stays here." My eyes filled. "That's what she wants. If this is going to clear up, her odds are better if she's home. And if it doesn't . . . she deserves to die here."

Riley put her head against Pop's shoulder and started to cry softly.

"Good job, honey," Pop said to me. His eyes were shiny, too.

"Yep. Good job. Excuse me." Donelle got up and started out of the room. We heard her start to sob.

"Come on, honey," Pop said to Riley. "Let's go down-stairs and make some sandwiches."

Dr. Pinco said it was a wait-and-see situation. That, yes, it was possible she'd be her old self in a few hours, but with the vascular dementia, chances were higher that this would be the beginning of the end. If she recovered from this stroke, her cognitive functioning would be worse.

I went into her room. She was sleeping, and Minuet was on her bed, having apparently sneaked back in. That was fine. "Good girl," I said to the little dog. She didn't lift her head from Gigi's arm.

Sophia left, and I dragged a chair to the bedside and sat, taking Gigi's hand in mine. "Don't be afraid," I said. "We're taking good care of you."

Riley came in, and Gigi's eyes fluttered open. "Hi, Gigi," she whispered.

My grandmother looked at her. "Shhep," she said. "Shhep . . . ard."

"That's right," I said. "She has the same blue eyes as Sheppard."

"Shheppard."

"It's okay, Gigi. Try to rest. You'll feel better soon."

Her eyes closed again, and after a second, she was snor-ing faintly.

"I have to make a call," I whispered to my daughter. "Can you stay here for a second?"

"Sure. Um, stay close, okay?"

"I'll be in your room." It was closest to Gigi's.

I went in and took a deep breath.

Funny how you can know someone is winding down, and then still feel panic-stricken when you turn the corner and there it is—death. There was no coming back from that.

I didn't want my grandmother to die. I wiped my eyes and pulled out my phone, then saw something on Riley's desk. A large mailing envelope from FutureFoto. I opened it and saw my father.

No. It was Sheppard, or an estimate of what he'd look like. I'd almost forgotten that Riley had started this project. My father's eyes weren't as sky blue as Sheppard's (or Riley's), but wow.

I called the last number I had for him, and to my surprise, it was answered.

"Hello?"

"Clark?"

"Yes? Who is this?"

I took a deep breath. "It's Emma. Your daughter."

There was a pause. "Oh! Hi! How's it going?"

"Genevieve had a stroke. You might want to get to Sheerwater and see her."

"Oh. Uh . . . I don't know if I can."

"Why, Dad? Writing another book?"

"I'm in DC, actually. Uh, research. Hey, Stu, how you doing?" I could hear the unmistakable sounds of a restaurant in the background.

"Yeah, well, your mother is dying," I said.

"And you know this how?"

"Because I've been here all summer. With my child. Hope is doing well, in case you're interested."

"Yeah, yeah! That's great to hear. Good. Well, uh, yeah, I guess I can make it up midweek sometime . . . Don't really see what good it would do, though. If she had a stroke, she's pretty out of it, right?"

For God's sake. Then again, why should I expect him to be different from exactly who he was? He wouldn't come. And did anyone really want him here?

I glanced at the pictures of what my uncle might look like.

"She was talking about changing her will earlier this summer," I said slowly. "Riley and she really hit it off. Riley's my daughter, in case you forgot."

"What? She changed her will?"

I had his undivided attention now. "I'm not sure," I said.

"She did say she had a big surprise for Riley, though." She hadn't. "I'm just so glad we've been here all summer. I forgot how much I love it here."

"Maybe I should come up. Yeah, I can catch the train. I'll get there as soon as I can. Tomorrow by the latest. See you soon."

Mission accomplished.

My grandmother would get to see her son once more.

CHAPTER 38

Clark

When you try to forget something, even when you're good at forgetting things, it becomes seared in your brain.

Clark had only been five when his brother *went away*, and a lot of years had passed since that day. He forgot his wedding anniversary, his daughters' birthdays, forgot the thousands of things Choate and Dartmouth had tried to teach him, forgot dates, names, appointments. He forgot to vote. (But really, what was the point? Sometimes he forgot who was running.) He forgot to check in for flights, forgot luggage, forgot his laptop more than a dozen times.

But he remembered so *fucking* much about That Day. For years, he'd wake up in the middle of the night, terror crushing his heart, almost killing him. Even now, he dreamed about the woods at Birch Lake, the water. The rocks.

That Day had started out as the best day ever. Mama made waffles, and even though she often told him he was chubby, she let him have two. With whipped cream. And strawberries.

Then, "the boys" were doing something together. Daddy wouldn't let Mama know what it was. It was *manly stuff*, and she wouldn't understand. Clark remembered his father winking at them. Sheppard and he looked at each other with glee. A funny feeling happened in his stomach, like on the elevator in New York when they went up so high and fast. Sheppard was sometimes nice to him and sometimes wasn't, but today was going to be a good day, Clark could tell.

Manly stuff. That sounded fun. Just the three of them, too, which was nice, because Clark liked Daddy better than Mama.

So Daddy packed the big car, including the tent, which worried Clark because no one said anything about sleeping away from home. They had the canoe on top of the car, and Clark hated the canoe. It was so tippy.

"Mama?" he said.

"Clark, you're too old to call me that," she said, her voice tighter than when she talked to Sheppard. "Call me Mom or Mother, like Sheppard does."

"Mom?"

"What is it?"

"I want to come home tonight." He didn't want to sleep away. He loved his bed with its heavy quilt and stuffed animals.

"It's camping, dear. It'll be fun."

Sheppard was so happy about camping. He was asking Dad about all kinds of things that Clark didn't know about . . . lines and weights and flies and fish grippers, firewood and owls. Clark tried to join in.

"How big are owls? What's a bass?" he asked. "Why do we need corn?" Only Daddy bothered to answer, which made Clark feel small and stupid.

Daddy patted his butt as he got in the car, ruffled Sheppard's hair. Sheppard got to sit in front. "It's not fair," Clark said, and Dad told him he could sit in front on the way home. They drove out of town, past the ice cream stand. "We'll stop there tomorrow," Dad said. "Maybe even tonight for dessert."

Clark felt better. He loved ice cream.

They drove out to Birch Lake—Mama wasn't allowed to know their secret location, but once they turned down the dirt road, Clark vaguely remembered coming here another time. The road was bumpy and long.

They got to the lake, the only car there. Clark wasn't sure, but maybe it was just their lake and no one else could come. They were on a cove, sheltered from the wind, Dad said. It made it feel like a secret place. Clark played under a pine tree in the sandy soil, making roads with a stick, while Dad and Sheppard set up the tent and put things away.

"You can help, too, you know," Shep said, but Clark pretended not to hear. He opened the cooler. There was soda in there. Good. Mama didn't let him have soda.

"Get in the canoe, Clarkie!" Dad said.

Clark did, reluctantly. Dad helped him in, then got in the back, Shep in the front. They got to paddle; Clark just had to sit there and hold on to the sides.

"Can I have a turn, Shep?" he asked. He wasn't supposed to call him Shep because Mama (Mom) didn't like it. Daddy said it was okay for brothers to have special names for each other. Shep didn't have a special name for him, though.

"Maybe later," Sheppard said. "I can show you where the water's not so deep."

Yes. Shep was going to be nice to him today.

The lake was blue, and the water was warm enough to swim, Dad said. They paddled around for a while. Dad pointed out a blue heron, and Shep saw a turtle, which wasn't fair, because Clark didn't see one. When he leaned over to look, the boat tipped, and Dad yelled, "Sit up straight, Clark!" and he felt bad.

"We don't want you falling in the drink, son," Dad said, and Clark felt his father's big hand on his shoulder, taking away the sting of the yelling.

They went back to shore, and Clark was glad, because he was bored.

"Get into your suits," Dad said.

"In the car?" Clark asked.

"No, dummy," Sheppard said. "Out here. No one's around. No one will see."

So they did change. Clark looked away from his father, not liking him naked, seeing all that hair and other things. The private things. He hoped he would never look like that. Shep was fast and didn't seem to worry that someone would see him naked.

Clark dawdled, not wanting to take off his clothes. "Get moving, son," Dad said, so he had to. It felt funny, the air on his parts, on his butt. He put both feet into the same leg hole; Shep laughed and didn't help him.

That made Clark mad, a little bit. He pulled his leg out and put it in the right hole, then found the suit was on backward, so he had to do it again. He didn't like Daddy and Sheppard seeing him, even if they were his family.

Dad and Sheppard ran right in. Clark was slower, and scared. The bottom of the lake was squishy and dark. He went in up to his shins, then came back out.

"Don't be a baby!" Sheppard said as Clark walked on the shore back and forth. "It's great in here! Come on! You can see the lake shark!"

"There's no lake shark," Dad said. "Sheppard, honestly. Be nice to your brother. Come on, honey. Swim to me. I'm right here."

Clark liked that his dad called him honey. Some dads just said *son* or *fella* or *buddy*. It was nice to hear *honey*. It made him feel . . . safe.

He wanted his father to be proud, so he went in and in and in and then he was swimming, trying to keep his face out of the water, trying to keep his mouth closed. The water was silky and tasted strange, and he hated swimming.

"Nice job!" Dad said, catching him in his arms and pulling him close, and Clark coughed a little and held on tight. His father was warm and strong, and it felt so good to be safe again. Daddy never told him he was too big to be held, like Mama did. Clark *was* big, bigger than all his classmates, heavier than Sheppard, but he wasn't too big for Daddy. To Daddy, he was still a little boy, and that felt so good.

"Dad! Watch me!" Sheppard said, and he ducked underwater and was gone. Dad smiled, but Clark felt fear run through his bones, and he clutched Dad a little tighter, feeling his father's water-slick skin slide against his legs and belly.

Where was Sheppard?

Then Shep's blond head popped up, way, way out in the lake. "Pretty far, huh?" he called, laughing.

"Great job!" Daddy called.

"I can swim underwater, too," Clark said.

"Can you? Let's see, then!"

Daddy let him go, and Clark tried with all his might to get his head underwater, but it wasn't like Sheppard. He couldn't get his body to go under all the way. Still, he got his face in, and that was a lot.

"Good boy! Excellent," Daddy said.

"You have to kick harder," Sheppard said, demonstrating. "You're too floaty."

He tried, but it was more Sheppard showing off than teaching him how to do it right. After a few tries, he paddled to where his feet could touch the slimy bottom. Daddy and Sheppard did all sorts of tricks that Clark wanted so much to do. Shep stood on Dad's shoulders and dived into the lake. Swam between their father's legs. Did a somersault in the water, like a dolphin.

He was better at everything. No wonder Mama liked him best.

Clark looked at his pruney fingers and went back to shore and pretended to shiver, waiting for them to notice. But they didn't. They played for way too long. He tried making roads in the sand again, but it wasn't as fun.

Then, finally, they came in.

"I have to pee," Clark said. His father should've known that.

"Go behind a tree," Sheppard said. "Or in the lake." He laughed, and so did Dad, and it didn't feel good, being left out like this.

"Go ahead, Clark," Dad said. "Behind a tree. Sheppard's right. Right there, buddy. You can see us the whole time."

He *wanted* to go to the bathroom. A *real* bathroom. *His* bathroom, which still had toys in the bathtub, even though Sheppard said they were for babies and he should get rid of them. But then, how would bath time be fun? Floating his boats in the tub, making Elmer Fudd and Bugs Bunny fly through the air and dive into the water . . . he didn't want to get rid of them. Sheppard was too bossy and know-it-all.

He trudged away from the shore, wishing Daddy would come with him.

The truth was, Clark didn't like the woods. Sheppard loved the outside, loved going to the spooky spots at home, out by the water where the pine trees sounded like people whispering scary things. But Clark hated it. Once, Sheppard had told him a story about the Tree People, and how they ate children who wandered off, and kept their teeth for a necklace, and he'd only stopped telling the story when Clark started to cry. Sheppard hugged him then, and said he was sorry, it was just a story, and please don't tell. So Clark didn't. But the scary feeling stayed.

He pulled his bathing suit down. What if there was someone watching? What if someone saw his butt? The pee wouldn't come. His stomach hurt with holding it in, but it wouldn't come.

Then there were footsteps, and the pee shot out in terror without his permission.

It was just Dad. "You doing okay, honey?" he asked.

"I peed on my trunks," Clark said, feeling close to tears.

"We'll just rinse them out," Daddy said. "Here. Step out."

So Clark went naked back to the car, feeling somehow ashamed, and pulled on his other clothes. Sheppard was getting dressed, too, and he was so quick and sure and skinny. It made Clark feel slow and big, but Daddy said he'd be a great football player someday. So there. No one ever said that about Sheppard.

After that, it was a little better. They ate lunch, and even if Sheppard called him Piggy, he ruffled his hair and didn't say it in a mean way. They fished, Daddy putting on the lures and the corn and the worms. Clark caught sunnies, and it was horrible to see them gasping as Daddy took the fish off the hook and let them go. They disappeared into the deep water, flashing before they were gone. Clark hoped they swam far, far away and didn't come back for more worms. Stupid fish.

One fish didn't swim away. It seemed dead. It was floating, white and spooky, in the water. Clark hated it.

Sheppard caught the biggest fish. Of course.

"We'll cook that up for supper," Daddy said. "Let me take a picture of you first. Mother will be so proud. Get in there, Clark, honey. She'll be proud of you, too, with all your sunnies!"

They didn't seem to notice the dead fish.

Sheppard and Daddy went swimming again, but Clark didn't want to get near that dead fish. Besides, he was cold and bored and sleepy. He didn't like being dirty. He had sap on his hand that lake water wouldn't wash off. There was sand in his butt crack. He didn't want to camp. He wanted to go home.

The woods were getting dark, and he wished Daddy and Shep would come out of the lake.

What if there were spies out in the woods? Mama and Daddy had been watching the news one night and Clark heard the TV man talking about spies from far away who hated Americans. What if they were watching him? What if they'd seen him when he was changing? What if the Tree People were real?

"Daddy, I'm scared," he called.

"Don't be a chicken," Sheppard called, and that was that. Clark started to cry. He could cry pretty easily, and before long, he was gulping in sobs.

"What's wrong, honey?" Dad asked, coming out of the water (finally).

"I want to go home! I don't feel good," he sobbed. Daddy picked him up and held him close, but over his shoulder, Clark could see Sheppard's mean face on.

"Don't ruin this, Clark," his father said.

"My tummy hurts," Clark said to his father.

"You think you just have to poop?"

"No. I want to go home."

Dad sighed, so Clark kept crying and hugged Daddy tighter. "It hurts a lot, Daddy," he lied. "Like a sword."

"Okay, sweetheart," he said. "Let's pack up, Sheppard."

"Just bring him home! Let him stay with Mother if he's such a baby. I'll stay here and wait for you, Dad."

"Sheppard. Your brother is sick. I'm not leaving you here in the woods."

"Then we can bring him home and come back," Shep pleaded.

Dad hesitated. "He seems really sick, son," and Clark cried harder to prove it. "We can come back next weekend. No, no, don't talk back. Start packing up." He set Clark in the front seat of the car, and Clark couldn't help a small, triumphant smile.

"He's faking!" Shep said, and his voice was mean.

"Sheppard! Stop it." Dad's voice was sharp. "Clark, can you hang in there while we pack up?"

"I think so." He made sure fat tears still rolled down his cheeks.

"Good boy."

They took down the tent and packed up the fishing stuff, Sheppard cutting him resentful glances. Clark didn't care. He'd take a bath at home with Elmer Fudd and Bugs Bunny. He wouldn't be sandy and dirty and sticky. He'd smell nice and sleep in his bed and be away from the stupid woods.

Dad was tying the canoe to the roof of the car, tugging on the straps.

Where was Sheppard? Was he swimming again? That would be just like him, doing something so Clark would have to wait.

Or maybe he had found something. Sheppard always found neat stuff . . . the robin egg shells, the Indian arrowhead, a five-dollar bill. What if he had found something now? He wouldn't share it, not when he was mad at Clark.

Dad was packing up the picnic stuff now. Without saying anything, Clark slipped out of the car and went to find Sheppard. If he was swimming, he could tattle on him. His brother wasn't in sight, though. Clark climbed around the point of their little cove, and there was Sheppard, standing way up high on an outcropping of rock that looked like it would tumble into the lake at any second. Sheppard was brave, going up there.

"What are you doing?" Clark asked.

"I found something really neat," Sheppard said.

He *knew* it. "What is it?"

"Come up and see for yourself."

Clark climbed up, too, but at the top, the reach was too far. "Help me," he said.

"Help yourself, chicken. Why'd you have to ask to go home? You're not sick. You ruined everything."

"No, I *didn't*. I want to go home. I don't feel good."

"You're a liar."

Clark was slipping. He grabbed the rock and tried to pull himself to the top, but he wasn't quite strong enough, and his foot slipped. Pain shot up his shin. "I'm falling!" he said, and then Sheppard, stupid Sheppard, did grab him and pull him up.

"I'm bleeding," Clark said, looking at his shin.

"It's just a scrape. Don't be a baby. Come on. Look at what I found."

It was a huge feather, dark gray with a small patch of white at the base. "This is from a bald eagle," Sheppard said.

"It is?"

"Yep. See how big it is? Almost as long as your arm. And it cuts in up here, see? That's because it's a raptor." Sheppard knew so much. He read all the time.

"Can I have it?" Clark asked.

"No. It's mine."

"Can we share it?"

Sheppard tipped his head to one side. "You know what? I would've shared it, but you ruined our camp-out because you're a big baby. So no. It's just mine."

"Mommy thinks you're so nice, but you're mean."

"Mommy thinks you're so nice, but you're mean," Sheppard echoed in the baby voice he used when he was mad at Clark.

"Shut up!"

"Ooh, I'm telling," Sheppard said. "Mother says we're never supposed to say that. You're a baby, Clark. You can hardly swim and you're afraid of being eaten by Tree People. You're not sick. You're just poor wittle Clarkie, scaredy-cat of the woods who wants his mama."

Clark shoved him. He was a big boy and strong and would be a good football player someday, and Sheppard was surprisingly light. For a second, Sheppard's arms waved in the air, and he was just . . . gone. There was a thud.

Uh-oh. Clark was going to get in big trouble. He stood

there a minute, waiting for Sheppard to yell at him or call for Dad.

He didn't. There was no noise at all. Not one sound.

Clark felt like he'd been dipped in ice water all of a sudden. Inch by inch, he went to the edge and looked over.

Sheppard was lying on the rock, the eagle feather next to his head.

"Sheppard?" he whispered. His brother didn't answer.

Clark didn't remember getting down to him.

But he did remember that when he got to his brother, Sheppard's eyes were a little bit open but not blinking. Clark nudged him with his foot, hoping Sheppard would jump and say, "Boo! Got you!"

But he didn't. His almost-closed eyes didn't flicker.

Clark remembered the bird that had flown into the window the week before, then fallen to the grass right when they were eating breakfast.

"Poor thing broke its neck," Daddy had said. Its eyes had been the same way.

His breath hitched out of him. He couldn't tell on himself. He was very cold now. Very cold.

Maybe the water would revive Sheppard. Maybe he had fainted, or bumped his head really hard. It was easy to roll him into the water. Clark was a big boy and strong. He would make a great football player.

Sheppard sank, his white skin shining in the water like the belly of the dead sunfish. The water was deep.

Clark waited, but Sheppard didn't come up again.

Then he went back to the car. His shin hurt. The rest of him was somewhere else. He was shivering harder now.

"Where were you?" Daddy said as he came to the car. "Did you go poop?"

Clark shook his head. He couldn't speak.

"Get in the car, honey. You're shaking! We're on our way home, don't worry. Here, put this towel around you. It's dry. Sheppard! Come on, son! Time to go!"

Things went gray after that. He heard his father's voice drift in and out of his head, sometimes loud, sometimes not, getting more and more afraid. When Daddy jumped in the car and beeped the horn, Clark didn't twitch. When he ran up and down the path, Clark just sat there. When Daddy drove like a maniac, as Mama said, down the dirt road to the nearest house, Clark didn't say a word. When the police came, when Mama came, when Daddy finally remembered that Clark was sick and a policeman put him in the car, and more and more people came to the lake, he still never said a word.

At some point, he fell asleep. He woke up in his own bed, but he was still gritty and sticky from the lake. It was morning now. He listened from the top of the stairs.

Sheppard was gone. No one could find him.

Clark knew that he'd get in trouble if he told. Mama would hate him. Even Daddy would hate him.

He padded back to his room and took a bath. He didn't play with Elmer Fudd and Bugs Bunny, and when the bath was over, he took the big scissors from his desk and cut off their heads and put them in the trash.

Later that day, when the police asked where he last saw his brother, he said, "Packing up the car," and added, "with Daddy."

They asked if he'd seen anyone in the woods, and he said he'd been scared, but he hadn't seen anyone. But maybe he had heard someone. He asked if there were Tree People out there who ate children, and meaningful glances were exchanged. "Why do you think there are Tree People?" the policeman asked, and Clark shook his head.

They asked if he knew where Sheppard had gone, and he said no. Then he started to cry, and his crying got out of control so he couldn't breathe, and his mother told the police to stop asking him things. A doctor had to give Clark a shot, and he went right to sleep.

He had nightmares that Sheppard came out of the lake,

accusing and furious, his eyes missing because the fish had eaten them. He woke up screaming. He dreamed that Sheppard was sitting on his bed, smiling, saying it was okay, he'd swum to shore, did Clark want to play?

He knew they were looking in the lake for his brother. He wanted them to find him. He prayed they wouldn't.

As the days passed, and then the weeks, Clark missed his brother so much. Was this really how life was going to be now? Was Sheppard gone forever? Had Clark really done this bad, bad thing? It was so hard not to tell Daddy, because Daddy was still nice to him. Instead, he cried against Daddy's chest, and Daddy cried, too, and told him he was a good boy, and how could Clark say anything then?

Mama didn't seem to be herself anymore. She was here, but not here. People talked a lot about how nice Sheppard was, how perfect, how smart and kind, and eventually, a resentment started to grow in Clark. He remembered how Sheppard showed off that day. How he called him a baby and Piggy and didn't help him on the rock when he was slipping. How he wouldn't share the feather. What if Clark had been the one to fall? He almost had, and . . .

. . . and Sheppard had helped him.

No. Clark could never tell. What everyone said was right. Sheppard was better, and Clark was just . . . leftover.

People told Clark to be brave. They told him he was a good boy, and a good brother. He must miss Sheppard a lot, they said.

As the months trickled past, Clark got tired of how things were now. His parents didn't get happy again. They cried and whispered a lot, and it was always Sheppard they talked about. Everything was about Sheppard, even more than it had been before. Finding Sheppard. Looking for Sheppard. Remembering Sheppard. It was as if Clark had gone away, too, except when his father tried to be nice, and even then, his father was forgetful and sad and not fun anymore.

This was really Sheppard's fault. If Sheppard had been nicer, Clark wouldn't have shoved him. If Sheppard had cared more about his stomachache—and he *had* had a stomachache, sort of—he wouldn't be dead. If Sheppard hadn't told him the story of the Tree People, Clark maybe would've loved camping. Maybe, just maybe, Sheppard deserved that shove. Not to go away forever, but to be shoved. Clark hadn't meant for his brother to disappear. He'd just wanted him to shut up.

When Daddy died and everyone said it was from a broken heart, Clark knew he could never tell, ever, because then he would have killed Dad, too, and Dad was the only one he loved anymore.

Sheppard had become perfect in death, whereas Clark just *was*. His mother started that company, abandoning him almost completely, and before long, he didn't even care. He knew how to get what he wanted. He knew she didn't love him the way she'd loved Sheppard, or Dad. He knew he'd spend the rest of his life in the shadow of his dead brother.

Sheppard's body was never found. Maybe the divers hadn't searched that area. Maybe the muck at the bottom had swallowed him. Maybe there really were Tree People who ate children.

Over the years, he learned to banish that day from his thoughts. He wrapped himself in self-interest, because who else would care about him? He learned to take what he could get and not expect anything else. He taught himself how to have fun—drink, get high, sleep around. He decided he deserved everything he wanted, because Sheppard should've been nicer, and his parents should've cared about their other son more. So he took everything without question, because he deserved it.

Later, when his wife died, when Hope was born, and cracks appeared in that armor, he did what he'd learned to do, been taught to do—pretend it didn't happen. It almost *didn't* happen, really. A childhood accident, no big deal.

CHAPTER 39

Emma

Gigi drank a little water and took a few spoonfuls of soup, but that was it. She kept trying to talk, but her words were incomprehensible. I told her she'd be better tomorrow, but I had no idea if that were true. Dr. Pinco came again late that evening but said outside of brain surgery, there was nothing to be done.

And I wouldn't put Genevieve through brain surgery.

I slept in her bed next to her. Strange, that it was the first time ever. Around two a.m., she woke up and looked at me.

"Mama?" she said, and I almost sobbed.

"I'm right here," I whispered. "Go back to sleep." I smoothed her white hair back as if she were Riley, and she smiled at me and closed her eyes.

Mac slept by the bed; Minuet snuggled between Gigi and me. The other dogs were with Donelle and Riley. Pop stayed overnight, and Miller came by in the morning and hugged me a long minute when I ran downstairs to get breakfast. He'd brought yellow roses, which were Gigi's favorite, and his kindness made me crack a little . . . just the fact that he knew and remembered.

"I'll stay as long as you need me," he said.

"It's okay. I'll call you, though."

"Good." He kissed me and hugged me again, and I tried not to cry.

Gigi mostly slept, and we all gathered in her room, Helga, Charles and Donelle playing cards. Pop came in and held Gigi's hand.

"You'll be all right, old girl," he said, and his eyes were suspiciously shiny.

Around one in the afternoon, she opened her eyes. "Where . . . Sheppard?" she asked.

Riley and I looked at each other.

"You'll see him soon," I said.

"Tell him . . ." She tried to get more words out, then closed her eyes.

Dr. Pinco came. No change. Her heart sounds were faint. "You may want to prepare yourselves," he said. "She's winding down, but she's not in any pain."

Jamilah came by, and Beth, and Calista called twice, confirming what Dr. Pinco said. The hours dragged and sped. Miller came by again, this time with huge flower arrangements from the garden club, Rose Hill, the historical society, Franklin's General Store. I debated getting Hope, then decided against it, then called to ask her pediatrician his thoughts, which were to keep her put.

I called Brooklyn Fuller, Genevieve's attorney, and asked her to draw up some papers.

It was brutal, this waiting, hoping she'd slip away, hoping she'd revive and scold us for messing up her room. There were glasses and half-finished sandwiches and dog hair everywhere. Pop opened a window so she could smell the salt air, and I put another blanket on her bed. For the first time in ages, Donelle tidied the room.

The Talwars came over, bringing a boatload of food, and offered to have Riley come to their house for the night, but Riley wanted to stay. Of course she did.

"I'll come by tomorrow," Saanvi said, hugging me. She kissed Genevieve's forehead and said, "Thank you for making us so welcome in your home, Genevieve." A tear dripped onto my grandmother's forehead, but she didn't stir.

Around six, I told everyone to go have dinner, and I'd stay with Genevieve. Give her some quiet time. The dogs went, except for Mac and Minuet, her favorites.

I lay down beside her and held her hand, straightening her engagement ring.

A quiet knock came at the door, and I looked up to see my father.

He was thicker than he'd been last time I saw him, and his hair was silver, but he was a good-looking man, still.

I jumped off the bed, grabbed his arm and dragged him into the hall. "She's dying," I said without preamble. "She had one wish—to see Sheppard again."

My father rolled his eyes. He wore a cashmere sweater and smelled like cologne, and his nose and cheeks bore the signs of a life of hard drinking. Only the best liquor, of course, and all funded by Genevieve.

"Clark," I hissed, "you have never in your life done something for someone else. That changes right now. If you don't go in there and pretend to be your brother, I'll contest the will, and I have a pretty good feeling that I'll win."

"I'm supposed to be a boy who died more than fifty years ago?"

"Yes." It was amazing how little I felt seeing him. In fact, the only thing I did feel was a fierce sense of protectiveness for Gigi. Mac growled, and I knew exactly how he felt.

"Will you do it?" I asked.

He sighed. "Sure. Whatever. She always loved him best, anyway."

It was good enough. I led my father back into her room, and patted Genevieve's shoulder. "Gigi, wake up. Guess who made it? It's Sheppard. Your son is here."

Her eyes fluttered open. "He's right here, Gigi," I said, pointing to my father. "Sheppard's here." I pushed him in the chair next to her bed.

She struggled to sit up, so I boosted her up on the pillows. She reached for his hand, but she was too weak.

Clark took it. "Hello, Mother," he said.

"Sheppard?"

"Yep. It's me. Sheppard. Your favorite son." His tone dripped with derision, and I wanted to kick him.

"You . . . safe?"

My eyes filled with tears. All these decades, and all she wanted to know was that her boy was safe.

My father's voice changed a little. "Yes. I'm safe. And I'm right here. With you."

"Missed . . . you." Her voice was so weak, her breathing fast and shallow. "Love. Love."

He swallowed. "I missed you, too. I . . . I love you, too, Mother." At least he was playing his part.

Her eyes kept trying to close, but as always, her sheer force of will kept them open. "Tell Clark . . . I . . . sorry. Bad . . . mother."

My father looked at me, then at her, and something in his face fell. "It's okay, Mom."

"Tell Clark . . . sorry."

"We'll tell him, Genevieve," I said, wiping my eyes. "We'll tell him you're sorry."

"Clark is sorry, too, Mom," my father said. "I know he is."

She sank back against the pillows and fell asleep once more.

My father kept holding her hand for a long, long time.

When Riley, Donelle and Pop came up, my father stood. My grandfather made a disgusted sound and looked out the window. If Clark was surprised to see him, he didn't show it. Then again, he might not have recognized his former father-in-law.

"Good to see you, honey," Donelle said, the only one who spoke.

"Hey, Donelle," he said. "Well. I guess I'll stay in a hotel tonight."

"Stay here," I said.

"No, I, uh . . . I'll stay in town. I have a meeting tomorrow, but I can come back in the afternoon, maybe, or Sunday."

I got it. He was leaving again, and he wouldn't be back.

"Come with me, Clark," I said, and we left the room and went downstairs to his father's office. "Before you go, you need to sign this." I pushed the papers Brooklyn had drawn up across the desk.

"What is it?"

"It terminates your parental rights to Hope."

He raised an eyebrow. "Why?"

"I'm her guardian now. I don't want you involved."

He didn't move. "Is she . . . okay?" Something flickered across his face, and for a second, I felt pity for him.

Not everyone was strong. Not everyone rose to the occasion. Not everyone could carry the burdens of life. And weakness was a burden unto itself. Gigi, though imperfect herself, had done me a favor by paying my father to stay away. She'd been strong. Every damn day. And no matter what I'd been through in life, here I was, strong, too, and filled with love for the people around me. Even this pathetic man here.

"Hope is doing really well," I said. "She's happy and safe, and I'll be living in Connecticut now, so I'll take really good care of her."

Still, he hesitated.

"We both know you're not really father material, Dad," I said.

He looked down. "No. I guess I'm not." He leaned forward and signed the papers where Brooklyn had marked.

"Thank you," I said.

He shrugged. "I'm sorry. I did my best."

"You did nothing, Clark," I said. "Let's at least be truthful, shall we?"

"You sound like my mother."

"Thank you. By the way," I added, "there's no inheritance. Genevieve's broke, the house is reverse-mortgaged, as are all its contents."

He closed his eyes. "Shit. I wondered if I was out of the will, but I didn't think the money was all gone."

"It is."

Knowing my father, he'd find someone else to pick up his tabs. He'd marry a wealthy woman and keep living his life.

But once, I'd loved him, even if I didn't really know him. "Take care of yourself." We looked at each other for a long moment. "I mean it, Dad," I added.

"You too." He stepped toward me, and for a second, I thought he would hug me, but he didn't. "I . . . I hope things work out for you."

"They will. You should go now."

He nodded and left the room. A few seconds later, I heard the front door open and close, then the purr of an expensive car engine, and my father was gone.

CHAPTER 40

Genevieve

'm in the backyard of Sheerwater, and the grass is so green. The air smells divine, rich with the scent of lilacs and wisteria. The Sound is brilliant and sparkling, the flag waving cheerfully in the breeze. I'm dressed in a green and blue dress, and it flutters around my legs.

I'm waiting for someone . . . but I don't know who. Something wonderful is going to happen, though. I can feel it.

"Are you ready for your surprise?" Emma says, smiling, and Riley is there, too, looking so lovely. She squeezes my hand.

Then, down by the rock wall, where Garrison and I sit each night, the gate opens of its own volition.

A boy comes running through it, his hair white blond, his arms stretched open, and his eyes . . . his eyes are so blue! He laughs as he runs, runs right toward me, and I drop to my knees as finally, finally, my boy is back. He pulls back and looks at me, his face just as I remembered, and the feeling of him in my arms is everything. Everything.

Then Garrison comes through the gate, so handsome, grinning, striding across the lawn, wearing his linen suit and red tie, and I can tell he was in on the surprise.

"Is this real?" I ask Emma.

"It is, Gigi. It finally is."

Then Garrison has Sheppard and me both in his strong arms, and I can feel us lifting, lifting away, and the sun is so bright and warm, and finally, finally, I am home.

CHAPTER 41

Emma

Genevieve died that night just before midnight, with Riley and me holding her hands, and Donelle crying softly at her side. Mac let out a mournful howl, and Minuet put her head on her paws and sighed.

We covered her in a sky-blue cashmere blanket and fixed her hair, crossed her hands. Then I took my daughter in my arms, and we cried for the loss of our Gigi.

A month after she died, we had the memorial service. It had taken some time, because we wanted to put together a proper tribute . . . and because we wanted Sheppard to be buried with her.

The day after his visit, my father had sent a letter to the Connecticut State Police, detailing what had happened that day, all those years before. My heart actually ached for him, bearing that burden alone for so long. I knew there was no coming back from that kind of accident and subsequent trauma when it happens to a small child who doesn't tell anyone about it. Tragedy and fear had been carved into my father's soul, ruining him.

It explained so much, though.

He was in Europe now. No charges would be pressed, but he said he didn't want to be around. His letter had told the police exactly where he'd pushed Sheppard into the water. Three days later, the bones of my uncle were brought up from under four feet of silt.

An accident. A five-year-old pushed his brother and the brother fell. My poor father. If he had told, what a different life he might have had.

But he hadn't, and here we were. He didn't come for the funeral, and I was glad.

The church was standing room only. The Metropolitan Opera, one of the recipients of Genevieve's generosity over the years, sent a soprano to sing from Verdi's Requiem. Pop was one of the pallbearers, and so was Miller . . . and so was I.

Riley gave the eulogy, and it was beautiful and funny and moving.

The luncheon was held at Sheerwater, and I think the entire population of Stoningham came. Riley and I had till the end of the week to stay, and then Sotheby's would come for the art and some furniture, and the bank would evict us. We'd be moving to one of the condos Miller was renovating in the old prison, living just the two of us for the first time ever, because Pop had decided to go back to Downers Grove . . . but only to sell the house and come back east.

"Why would I live a thousand miles away from my girls?" he'd said.

Miller stayed by my side the whole day, and when the last of the guests had left and Riley had gone to bed, we sat in the conservatory and he rubbed my feet.

"You were a good daughter," he said, and I burst into

tears, because in a way, it was true. Genevieve was my mother. And in her last hours, I had been hers.

On our final night in Sheerwater, Riley and I walked the grounds for the last time. Under the wisteria bower, now just vines for the winter, through the patio and the rose garden, past the pool. We went to the two Adirondack chairs where Gigi and Garrison used to sit, and I left a yellow rose on each seat, and one more for Sheppard. It brought a lump to my throat, thinking of them together at last with their son, lost no more.

I put a bouquet of calla lilies on Ashley's grave—the bank had promised to stipulate that the new owners would have to allow Miller access to that spot forever.

"She'd be glad you and Miller are together," Riley said.

"You think?"

"Sure. Who better? Except you inherit Tess."

"I love Tess."

"Me too. Glad I'll be in college before you guys move in together, though."

"Who said we're moving in together?"

"Oh, Mom. You always need someone to take care of. Of course you'll move in. Probably get married."

I didn't argue. Maybe I would. Not for a while, though. Next year, my baby would be in college, and I didn't want to rush off to try to fill the hole in my life. I loved Tess, and I loved Miller, but there was no need to hurry.

My daughter and I walked hand in hand down to the dock and sat. There was no moon, and the stars shone brilliant and sharp. The wood of the dock creaked gently, and a loon called far away.

"It was nice to live in a mansion," Riley said.

"Sorry you have to move."

She laughed. "It was fun while it lasted. And I have this as a souvenir." She picked up the chain she now wore around her neck. On it was Genevieve's engagement ring, the one thing my grandmother had bargained to keep so that she could leave it to the great-granddaughter she loved.

It was worth an obscene amount of money—probably enough for at least two years of college, maybe more. But I knew my daughter would never sell it. I wouldn't want her to.

"She was great, wasn't she?" Riley said.

"She was. She was strong. She lived through a lot of heartbreak, but she always did what she had to do, and she did it as best she could. And her best was usually pretty great."

Riley was quiet for a moment. "Are you still afraid I'll be like your mom?"

I looked at her sharply.

"Oh, come on," she said. "It's okay if we talk about it."

My wise daughter. I took a slow breath and lay back on the deck. Riley did, too, snuggling her head against my shoulder, that old familiar feeling of my sweet daughter fitting against me. The best feeling in the world.

"My mother was a great woman, too," I said. "She was all love. You get that from her. And the red hair. But you have Genevieve in you, too. Total badass."

"True," Riley said, and I laughed.

"You forgot the best part of me," Riley said.

"What's that?"

"You, Mama."

She didn't even mind when I started to cry. But instead of blurring the stars, my tears made them brighter, shining with such beauty, such generosity, such benevolence, that a person just couldn't ask for more.

life
and
other
inconveniences

KRISTAN HIGGINS

QUESTIONS FOR DISCUSSION

1. Genevieve copes—and teaches her family to cope—by soldiering on despite life's hindrances. Do you think this helps or hurts her family? In what way?

2. Genevieve's treatment of her two sons goes from one extreme to the other. Do you think parents sometimes favor one child over another? Are we blind to our own children's faults? Are we blind to our faults as parents?

3. Why do you think Genevieve has so many dogs?

4. In what ways are Genevieve and Emma similar?

5. How do you think the tragedies and hardships that Emma faces shape her as a person? What about as a parent? How do they shape her for the better?

6. Why do you think Emma agrees to go back to New England when her grandmother asks her? Is it really just for Riley's sake?

7. How does Riley bring Genevieve and Emma together?

8. How are Emma's grandfather Paul and Genevieve able to get over their differences?

9. Parenting is a major theme in the book, especially when it comes to the role of the father: Clark as a father to Emma, Garrison as a father to Clark, and Miller as a father to Tess. How do their experiences affect their parenting of their children?

10. Choice is another major theme in the book: Emma's choices to keep Riley; to move in with Paul, her pop; and to allow Genevieve to meet Riley. How do Emma's choices shape her life? Do you disagree with any of the choices she makes?

11. Why do you think Riley is able to connect with Genevieve in a way that Emma can't?

12. Emma says, "Life tooketh with one hand and gaveth with the other." Several of the characters either go through tragedies or make choices that alter the course of their lives. In what ways does life work out anyway? How do you think their lives would have been different if these events had not occurred?

13. How does Genevieve show that she truly does care for Emma? In what ways does Emma show she truly cares for Genevieve? How do you think they could have shown it better to each other?

14. What do you think makes it possible for Emma to be by Genevieve's side when she dies?

15. Four generations of women are featured in the book: Genevieve, April, Emma and Riley. In what ways are they similar as mothers and as daughters? Why do you think the author chose to create this family dynamic? How does the author use the characters to display the nuances of motherhood and childhood?

Keep reading for an excerpt
from Kristan Higgins's next novel . . .

Always the Last to Know

Available Summer 2020 from Berkley

Sadie

"You're engaged? Oh! Uh . . . huzzah!"

Yes. I had just said *huzzah*.

You know what? I couldn't blame myself. *Another* engagement among the teachers of St. Catherine's Catholic Elementary School in the Bronx. The fifth this year, and yes, I was counting.

I couldn't look away from the diamond blinding me from the finger of Bridget Ennis. The stone was the size of a bumblebee, and my hypnotized eyes followed her hand as she waved it in excitement, telling the rest of us teachers— six women, one man—about how *romantic*, how *unexpected*, how *thrilling* it had been.

I had nothing against Bridget. But it had been raining diamond rings lately, and despite my having had bubbly hopes on my own last birthday, the fourth finger of my left hand remained buck naked.

Bridget was talking about save-the-date magnets and paper quality and color schemes and flower arrangements and the seventy-nine dresses she was already torn between. Bridget was an only child from wealthy parents. This did not bode well for me, her sort-of friend. *Please don't ask me to be a bridesmaid. Please. Please. I am way too old for this shit.*

"My daddy said whatever I want, and I want it to be perfect, you know?" Bridget looked at me, and I felt the cold trickle of dread. "Sadie, obviously I want you as a bridesmaid." Her pure green eyes filled with happy tears.

Oh, the fuckery of it all.

"Of course!" I said. "Thank you! What an honor!" My cheek began to twitch as I smiled.

"And you, Nina! And you, Vanessa! And of course, Jay's three sisters and my gals from Kappa Kappa Gamma. And my cousin, because she's like a sister to me. Do you like violet? Or cornflower? Off the shoulder, I was thinking, but I think *my* dress might be off the shoulder and . . ." I stopped listening as she began speaking in tongues intelligible only to those addicted to *Say Yes to the Dress*.

"You don't have to say yes, idiot," came a low voice next to me. Carter Demming, my best friend at St. Catherine's.

"She's sweet," I murmured back.

"Oh, please. Let her sorority sisters be her bridesmaids. Show some dignity for your age."

"I'm thirty-two."

"Your most fertile years are behind you."

"Thanks, Carter."

"Miss Frost? I need you for a second," Carter said loudly. "Mazel tov, sweetheart," he added as Bridget brushed away more glittering tears.

We left Bridget's cheery classroom and went to the now-empty teachers' lounge, where we teachers discussed which kids we hated most and how to ruin their young lives (not really). Carter posted the occasional Legalize Marijuana sticker somewhere, just to torment our principal, the venerable and terrifying Sister Mary.

I was the art teacher here. No, I could not support myself on a teacher's salary at a Catholic school in New York City, but more on that later. I loved teaching, though it hadn't exactly been my dream. Just about every kid loved art. If I didn't have the same stature as the "regular" teachers, I made up for it by being adored.

"So you're thinking about marriage and why you're still single," said Carter, pulling out a chair and straddling it.

"Yep." I sat down, too, the normal way, like a human and not a cowboy.

"So propose already."

"What?"

"Propose marriage to your perfect boyfriend."

"Meh."

"Why should men have to do all the work? Do you know how hard it is to buy the perfect ring, pick the perfect moment and place, say the perfect words and still have it be a fucking surprise? It's very hard."

"You would know." Carter had been married several times, twice to women, once to a man.

"Listen to your uncle Carter. Some men need a shove toward the altar, honey. Shove him. Do you really want to go out into the Tinder world again?"

"Jesus, no."

"Your window is closing. Match and eharmony worked fifteen years ago, but now they're filled with criminals. As you well know."

"He was a minor felon, and it wasn't exactly listed in his profile. But yes, I see your point."

Alexander (not a felon) and I *had* been dating for a couple of years. We had a marriage-worthy relationship by any measure. Maybe it was the distance factor—he was a traveling yacht salesman (someone had to do it)—so we weren't bothered by the slings and arrows of daily life together. He was constant—we saw each other almost every weekend. He brought me presents from his travels—a silk scarf

printed with palmetto leaves from the Florida Keys, or
honey from Savannah. He'd met my parents, charmed my
mother (not an easy task), chatted with my father and wasn't
in awe of my older sister, which was definitely a point in his
favor. Alex had great stories about his clients, some of them
celebrities, others just fabulously wealthy. He was, er . . .
tidy, a quality that shouldn't be undersold.

Why he was dating me, I wasn't a hundred percent sure.
"You have no idea how hard it is to find a nice girl," he said
once, so I guess it was that.

But I wasn't really a girl anymore, not like Bridget. Already past my prime fertility years, according to Uncle
Carter, who did tend to know everything.

"Hello?" he said, scratching his wrist. "Sadie. You're in
vapor lock. Make a move."

Another fair point. "Yeah," I said. "Sure. I could do it.
We're seeing each other tonight."

"See? Written in the stars." He winked at me. "Now, I
have to go wash the grime from these little motherfuckers
off me because I have a date."

"I don't want to know."

"Josh Foreman," he said, referring to the security guard
who worked at St. Cath's.

"Please stop."

"His hands are so soft. That smile. Plus, he screams like
a wildcat in bed."

"And . . . scene." I brought my hands together, indicating
cut. Carter grinned and left the teachers' lounge.

More evidence of Alexander's plans to marry me someday flashed through my head. Once he'd said, "Margaret's
a nice name for a girl, don't you think? I wouldn't mind a
daughter named Margaret." Another: "We should look at
property on the Maine coast for a summer place. It's so
beautiful up there. And Portland has a great art scene."

Maybe it *was* time for me to take action. It was just that
when I pictured being married, it was never to Alexander.

The vision of a black-haired, dark-eyed boy standing in the gusty breeze came to mind. My own version of Jon Snow, clad in Carhartt instead of wolfskin.

But Noah and I had tried. Tried and failed, more than once, and that was a long time ago.

Bridget's bumblebee ring flashed in my mind. Call me shallow, but I wanted a big diamond, too. My materialism ended there. (Or not . . . was it too soon to picture buying a brownstone in the Village? Alexander was loaded, after all. As for a wedding, we could elope. No color schemes or Pinterest boards necessary.)

He was due in around four, depending on traffic. Where was a romantic place in New York in January? It was freakishly mild today—thanks, global warming!—so maybe I could go to Chelsea Market and buy some nice cheese and wine. We could watch the sunset from the High Line and I'd just say it: "*I love you. Marry me and make me the happiest woman on earth.*" And the tourists and hipsters who frequented the area would applaud and take pictures and we'd probably go viral.

I imagined calling my dad tonight. He'd be *so* happy.

Yes. I'd propose tonight, and enter the next phase of my life, where I was sure Alexander and I would be very, very content.

As luck would have it, the temperature took a plunge, as weather in the Northeast is cruel and fickle. What had been sixty-two was the low forties by the time Alexander met me in front of the Standard, an odd-looking hotel that straddled the High Line. "God, it's freezing," he said as the wind blew through us. "I found a parking spot on Tenth, but I didn't know it would be this cold."

"Oh, it's not so bad!" I said. I had a plan, and I was sticking to it. "Just brisk! The sunset will be gorgeous." Or it wouldn't. There was a thick bank of clouds on the horizon, the kind that swallow up the sun. Only one other couple seemed to be around, the other folks hurrying to wherever New Yorkers hurry.

"Christ. I didn't dress for this," Alexander said. Neither had I—pretty black knit dress, hair in a ponytail (now being undone by the wind), the necklace he'd given me for Christmas and a cute red leather jacket that did nothing to keep me warm. Should've worn pants. And a parka.

"Well, come on," I said. "We don't have to stay too long. It'll be fun."

He followed me down the sidewalk, past clumps of grass and dead flower bushes. Come spring, this most elegant of New York's parks would be filled with color and life, but as it was, it was a little, uh, barren.

Shit. Well, I'd make it quick. "Sunset's in ten minutes," I said.

"I'll be dead by then."

"I'll revive your cold, hard corpse. Or at least give it a really strong attempt, then go into the Standard and drown my sorrows at the bar."

He laughed, and my heart swelled a bit. He really was a good, kind person. Great husband material. Never too demanding, always cheerful . . . the opposite of Noah, which was probably no coincidence. I glanced at the other couple. Would they film us when I got down on one knee? Also, *should* I get down on one knee? These were my only black tights.

"I cannot *believe* you're saying this!" Ah. The other couple was fighting. Not a great sign.

Alexander sighed. "Are we about done, babe? I'm starving."

"I bought cheese." I pulled the block out of my bag. Shit. We'd have to bite right into it, since I didn't have a knife.

"Hon. It's forty degrees out here. Maybe thirty-five. It's supposed to snow tonight."

"It's not so bad. See? That other couple's brave. Plus, we're Yankees. This is practically summer."

He glanced at the other couple. "They have winter coats on."

They did, those down coats with patches that announced them as explorers of Antarctica. The woman crossed her arms. "Are you shitting me, Dallas?" she practically yelled.

"I never said I wanted to be exclusive! That was all in your head!" the unfortunately named Dallas answered.

"How many women have you been seeing, you cheating bastard? Belinda? Are you seeing that whore again?"

"She's not a whore!"

"So that's a yes! Jesus! We're done, asshole. If I have an STD, I will slit your throat and burn your apartment to the ground."

She stomped past us, cutting us a look.

The cheater skulked past us, arms folded, head down against the wind.

"Okay, so that was fun," Alexander said. "They do have the right idea about leaving, though. What do you say, babe? Shall we go? Grab a drink somewhere with heat?"

Do or die. "Right. Okay." Shit. We were sitting. I scrambled to my feet. "Um, can you stand up for a second?"

"About time. Do you want to go out for dinner?" The cold wind whipped his blond hair, and his ears were bright red.

"Just one thing first." I looked into his eyes, which were watering a little from the wind. Just then, the sun slipped behind a bank of clouds that had come out of nowhere. So much for fiery skies burnishing the moment.

It didn't matter. I loved him. He was rock solid, this guy, and we . . . we had such a good thing going. Before I changed my mind, I knelt down. Felt my tights catch on the rough surface of the walkway.

"You all right?" he asked.

"Alexander Mitchum, will you marry me and make me the happiest man—shit, I mean *woman*—alive?" The wind gusted again, blowing my hair into my face.

"Uh . . . what are you doing, Sadie?" His face was incredulous.

"I . . . I'm proposing." My heart felt like the sun, abruptly swallowed in clouds. *Do not make me go back on those dating websites, Alexander Mitchum.*

"I'm the one who's supposed to propose."

"Okay! Sure. Go for it." Thank *God.*

He laughed a little. "Well, babe . . . I'm not ready. There are things I need to have in place. A ring, for one."

"We can get one later. Cartier is open till seven. Probably. Not that I checked."

He laughed. "Well, I'd like to surprise you. When the time comes."

"I'm down on one knee here, Alexander."

"Get up, then! This is crazy." He pulled me to my feet. I felt my tights tear. "You nut. It's the man's job to propose."

Sexist, really. "It seemed like a good idea. I mean, we've been together two years. We're the right age." I forced a smile.

"What is the right age, really? Is there an age that's wrong?" he asked, but he kissed my forehead. "I'll do it when the time is right. Okay?"

Well, didn't I feel stupid. "Okay."

"I want the moment to be when we're not freezing our asses off in the dark. Don't worry. It'll be perfect."

My heart felt weird. Happy weird, or disappointed weird? "I mean, now that we're talking about it . . . you could just . . . ask."

"No. I want it to be really romantic. Not on a night so cold my balls are retracting."

"Got it."

In case there was any doubt that my plan sucked, those dark gray clouds opened and a cold rain started to fall.

"I'm gonna pass out if I don't eat soon. Want to grab something, then go back to my place and fool around so we can salvage this night?"

"Sure."

Feeling like a dolt, I followed him to the stairs that led to street level.

Alexander's phone chimed. He studied it, then looked up. "Shit, babe," he said. "I have to go up to Boston. That idiot Patriots player is pitching a fit over a painting of himself that was supposed to be hung on the ceiling over his bed, and the designer put it on the wall instead. What time is it? Damn. I'll have to drive up tonight." He looked at me. "Want to come? We could grab some fast food on the road and stay overnight. A suite at the Mandarin with some spa time tomorrow, maybe?"

That was the thing about Alexander. He was so thoughtful. But my feeling of ineptitude lingered.

"I think I'll just go home. I have a painting due Sunday."

"Gotcha." We stood there awkwardly. "Want me to drive you home?"

"Subway's faster," I said.

"Okay."

"Well. Drive safely."

"I will. Talk to you, babe." He kissed me quickly and strode off.

It really was cold. I started walking toward Eighth Avenue to catch the subway. Soon, I'd be home. Maybe I'd take a shower to warm up. Order Thai food and work on that blue-and-white "like van Gogh except not as a swirly" painting I'd been commissioned to do. Bitter sigh, followed by the reminder to be grateful that I had these gigs at all and wasn't living in a paper bag.

Just then, my phone rang. My sister, Juliet, who almost never called me. "Hi!" I said. "How are you?"

"Listen, Sadie," she said, her voice strange, and instinctively, I stopped walking, my free hand covering my ear so I could hear her better. "Dad had a stroke. He's in surgery at UConn, and it's pretty bad. Get here as soon as you can."